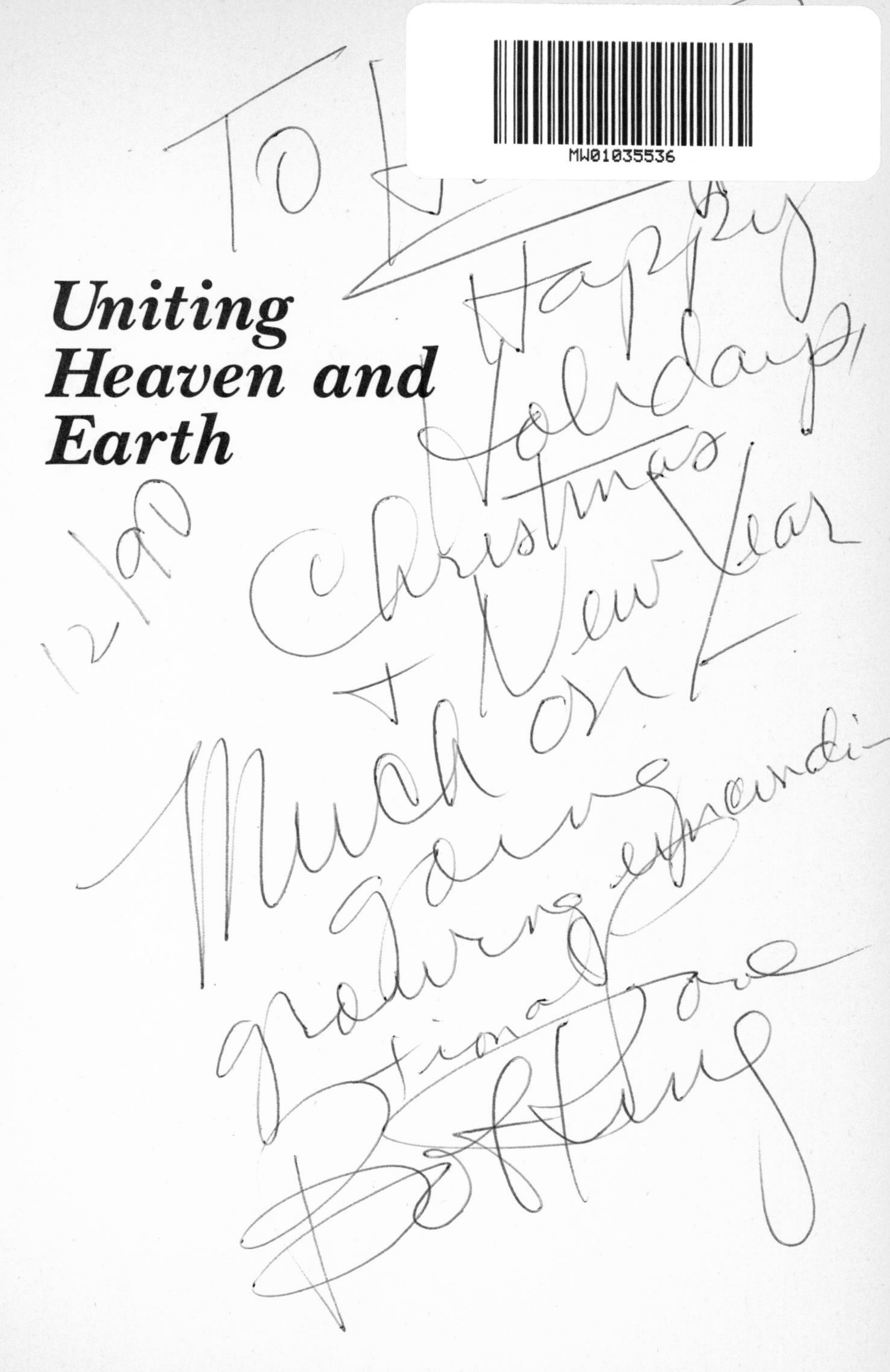

Uniting Heaven and Earth

Also by Sukie Colegrave:

By Way of Pain: A Passage into Self

Uniting Heaven and Earth

Sukie Colegrave

Foreword by Robert Bly

JEREMY P. TARCHER, INC.
Los Angeles

Library of Congress Cataloging in Publication Data

Colegrave, Sukie, 1948-
[Spirit of the valley]
Uniting heaven and earth / by Sukie Colegrave: foreword by Robert Bly.
p. cm.
Reprint. Originally published: The spirit of the valley. London: Virago, 1979.
Bibliography.
Includes index.
1. Androgyny (Psychology) 2. Yin-Yang. I. Title.
[BF692.2.C64 1989]
155.3'3—dc19 88-34413
ISBN 0-87477-505-1 CIP

Jeremy P. Tarcher, Inc.
9110 Sunset Blvd.
Los Angeles, CA 90069

Distributed by St. Martin's Press, New York

Manufactured in the United States of America
10 9 8 7 6 5 4 3 2 1

First Edition

To my parents and my twin brother
for intimations of androgyny

Contents

Acknowledgments

An acknowledgment at the beginning of this book is entirely inadequate to express my gratitude to Charles Curwen. His comments and criticism have supported me from the origin of the study as an inchoate idea to its present form. I also want to thank David Black, Susanne Chowdhury, John Graham, Margli Matthews, Betty Roszak, Signe Schaefer, Thomas Weihs and my mother, Esmé Colegrave for reading and criticising the manuscript, and Ann Pennock and Maggie Sutherland for their help with the typing. I would like to apologise to my daughter Laura for the days and weeks when the problems of thinking and writing intruded too much on my relationship with her. Finally I want to thank my editor at Virago, Ursula Owen, for her helpful comments.

The Story in Three Stages

Sukie Colegrave tells, with the help of ancient Chinese images and philosophies, the one story we all love. I'll make up a narrative, to give an idea of what this story is like.

Once we lived in the mouth of the cow. We were the hay and the cow, and the stomach, and the ears. We enjoyed the mouth cavern, and the saliva and the great grainy tongue, for we were the tongue, and the tongue rang in the bell of the mouth, and we too were the sound of the bell, and the clapper and the bell and the sound were all one, and had no names. And that was lovely and we wanted it to go on forever, but it didn't.

The cow started to lick a rock—and all of a sudden—it took about eighty thousand years—a woman appeared. The rock became a woman, and when the cow licked a flint nearby, the flint became a man. And the man was determined not to be eaten by the cow, so he—that is, the man and woman together, now both out of the cow's mouth—developed language. The first thing they did was to create two words, one for human beings and one for cow's mouth, so they would not forget the difference. Then for a hundred and ninety thousand years (a time which is just now ending) they thought of nothing but differences: the difference between leaf and root, between black and white, between man and woman, between post and hole, between tongue and book, between sound and silence, between going right and going wrong. During this time silence didn't say much, and we remembered the fragrant noisy silence of the cow's mouth as a Golden Age.

But an odd thing happened: because the man and woman had invented a word for night, and one for day, they began to experience night and experience day in a different way than they had inside the cow's mouth. (Night and day were fused or confused inside the cow's mouth.) Night led them to experience the moon, and day led them to experience the sun; the word "darkness" led them to experience the smaller darkness on the underside of every leaf, and "the sun" led them to experience the small light on the tip of the lance, and so eventually they became at home on the earth; they established a residencia en la tierra. They were free of the Great Unity, which was too high up anyway, and their feet felt firmly placed on the earth.

Once they felt firmly at home on earth, they began to long for the third thing that was neither light nor dark. It is strange: the same power, language, that leads us to divide human being and cow's mouth leads us to this longing.

The danger that language will trap us in opposites, of right and wrong, man and woman, is tremendous, but language when loved and entered contains also the healing of opposites. The poet Friedrich Hölderlin said "Where the danger is greatest, there the saving power grows most intense."

Historically the first stage involves matriarchies, the second patriarchies. The author finds the third part of the story especially beautiful, and she tells it with elegance, and a certain gay daring. Her feet go swiftly here, and with assurance; perhaps because she not only depends on Western stories, but brings us also the tales scattered through Chinese history, poetry, and speculative books. It's possible the Chinese arrived at the third part of the story two thousand years or so before us, a mere sliver to time, a feather—and she tells the third part with metaphors from their ancient sages, Lao Tzu, Zhou Dunyi, and Li Ji, as well as our recent sages, Freud, Jung, and Rudolf Steiner.

How can we imagine a state in which we each have some of night, and some of day? "Li Ji (Li Chih) a Ming philosopher, maintained that the intuitive mentality associated with the female was complementary to the rational mentality of the male, and he insisted that the difference between the sexes was only one of degree, that each possessed both types of intelligence, and should be allowed and encouraged to develop both." As a comparison and complementary idea Sukie Colegrave restates Rudolf Steiner's belief in multiple interior bodies. He declares that if the outer physical body is male, the interior body is feminine. If the physical body-husk is female, the interior body is masculine. That is a beautiful metaphor, and I think it is not fanciful, but a metaphor in truth. One can also say that in the third part of the story we have arrived at the *soul.* (It isn't clear if people living in the cow's mouth have a soul or not.) And the "human soul is simultaneously male and female." (Steiner).

If society, and each person separately, passes from the matriarchy stage to the patriarchy stage, and to a third stage, just now becoming, there are two turning points. I'd like to quote here a few of the author's comments on those two turning points.

> The first awakening to the masculine and feminine polarity can be traced back to the Oedipus crisis, but only much later does the individual realize this polarity and internalise it in his or her own psyche. Our frail egos succumb over and over again to the temptation to return to the secure embrace of the Great Mother consciousness in which the polarities are fused. Sometimes these regressions are cases of *il faut reculer pour mieux sauter,* but often they are primarily neurotic attempts to escape the pain of ego-development. The final development of a strong ego does not usually happen before 21, but even thereafter we are rarely immune to the attraction of the old consciousness. While our bodies appear to evolve relatively peacefully from one stage to another, each step forward in consciousness requires Herculean efforts of will.

I like the emphasis on struggle and failure. We have all experienced seminars in which the leader on Sunday afternoon, after having resolved all opposites in some blissful formula, retires with the participants to the hot tub, and we sense the frail ego has succumbed to the "secure embrace of the Great Mother." California to the contrary, if we just "follow the flow" things may not necessarily turn out well at all. As Rilke said in a poem written two years before he died: "Being carried along is not enough."

Sukie Colegrave states that in the matriarchy there was no need for relationship.

> The Great Mother rules over a pre-polarized consciousness, a time or stage of psychological development when everything appears to be embraced in one undifferentiated unity. Under Her there is no need for relationship, as the masculine consciousness has not yet split human awareness into subject and object, mother and child, or male and female.

This is a startling speculation. "But with the birth of the masculine consciusness this ancient way of seeing is overthrown by the introduction of an "I" and "Thou" experience. . . ."

She praises the appearance of the masculine principle in her own life with a kind of passion. It is clear that the appearance of the masculine principle gave her for the first time a sense that she had a life, a life to be created and lived, and a soul to be exercised and developed. "For the masculine principle does not only help us to differentiate the world in which we live, to discriminate between the different aspects of nature, to classify and order, it also leads us to an experience of our essential individuality."

She also makes a firm distinction between "matriarchal consciousness" and "feminine consciousness." It is possible that a woman, if she is suspicious of the masculine principle, may accept too little of it when she enters the second stage, or be unwilling to give up the Old Unity. If a woman does this, she remains matriarchal, and does not grow into feminine consciousness. If a man overvalues the female, he may make the same mistake in the second stage; he may accept too much of the matriarchal and give up too much of the masculine. "A similar psychological stagnation and imbalance can result from an excessive reliance by the conscious mind on the feminine principle. It drags consciousness into a mystical ocean of sameness, a bog in which all differences are submerged, all identities lost."

She turns to recent brain research for other metaphors on this first "turn." The male fetus in the womb is female, and completely so at first. Massive revision takes place. Later the male fights against the female not because he dislikes the female, or wishes to oppress her, but because his very existence as a being in the body requires resistence to female hormones. If a man is too open in early years to female pressure, he may become an early androgyne, rather than a late or alchemical androgyne. She suggests that a woman needs to be cautious also in her adoption of the male thought-sword.

If the second stage of the story can be described as a stage in which human beings distinguished between the feminine mode of thinking and the male mode of thinking (which were confused in the matriarchy), then it is essential, Colegrave says, that these two modes be carefully, lovingly, scrupulously distinguished, and lived. The third stage then could be described as these two souls, the feminine and the masculine, talking to each other.

> In whichever way the individual is inbalanced, whether she or he is too masculine or too feminine, the psyche will suffer. An excessive reliance on the feminine soul blinds the person to outer things, people, and feelings, thereby depleting his or her inner resources, while too great a dependence on the masculine soul results in psychological aridity, isolation and meaninglessness. Either way leads, eventually, to diminishing contact between the two souls.

She recounts at this point the teaching of *The Secret of the Golden Flower,* which says that if the two souls, the masculine and the feminine, do not talk to each other, they become separated and the separation leads to death. In Chinese terms, if the "po" soul and the "hun" soul do not join inside, they both go down to death.

If they talk to each other well, or join, the psyche achieves a new life, and becomes spontaneously productive. She quotes Philo of Alexander who said, "The congress of men for the procreation of children makes virgins women. But when God begins to associate with the soul, He brings it to pass that she who was formerly woman becomes virgin again." So for a woman we could describe the three stages as a progression from the Self-Sufficiency of the Great Mother to Woman to the Completeness of the Virgin. In the *Gospel of Thomas,* Jesus, speaking to both sexes, said, "And when you make the inner as the outer, and the outer as the inner, and the upper as the lower, and when you make male and female into a single one, so that the male shall not be male and female (shall not) be female, then shall you enter (the Kingdom)."

Such statements make sense to many of us only after we have made a circuitous route through thought not generally accessible in our Christian culture, through strange seas of Chinese or alchemical thought; and it is the gift of this book to invite us on that route.

Robert Bly, 1981

Chronology of Principal Legendary and Historical Periods in Chinese History

2853 BC. (*legendary date*) PERIOD OF THE THREE SOVEREIGNS:
Fu Xi/Nu Gua, Shen-nong, Yen Di

2697–2597 BC. (*legendary date*) THE FIVE EMPERORS:
Huang Di, Chuan Xun, Kun, Yao, Shun

2183–1766 BC.? XIA DYNASTY

1766?–1027 BC. SHANG DYNASTY

1027– 221 BC. ZHOU (CHOU) DYNASTY

} *ancient feudalism*

481–221 BC. WARRING STATES PERIOD

221–206 BC. QIN (CH'IN) DYNASTY:
the first united Chinese empire

206 BC.–AD. 220 HAN DYNASTY:
Confucianism established as the state orthodoxy

AD. 220–589 SIX DYNASTIES:
a period of political disunity during which Buddhism and Daoism flourished

589–618 SUI DYNASTY:
reunification of the empire

618–907 TANG (T'ANG) DYNASTY

907–960 period of the TEN KINGDOMS AND THE FIVE DYNASTIES

960–1279 SONG(SUNG) DYNASTY:
Neo Confucianism. Apogee of Chinese painting. Footbinding introduced.

1279–1368 YUAN DYNASTY:
Mongol rule

1368–1644 MING DYNASTY:
Neo-Confucian restoration

1644–1912 QING (CH'ING) DYNASTY:
Manchu rule

1912–1949 WARLORD PERIOD:
Japanese invasion. Civil war between the Chinese Communists and the Guomindang

1949– CHINESE PEOPLE'S REPUBLIC

Introduction

'What a man thinks, that he becomes.'

Upanishad

'What we observe is not nature itself but nature exposed to our method of questioning.'

Heisenberg

My earliest memory is of sitting in a double pram opposite my twin brother. Both hoods were up protecting us from the rain which tapped on the canvas above our heads. Outside was the cold, wet country lane. Inside we were secure in the warm darkness of our private world. I looked across at the person with whom I shared every day and night, with whom I had even shared the months in my mother's womb, and suddenly, out of this moment of complete security and belonging, arose a feeling of utter aloneness. In this instant I met my own individuality for the first time. Although I was only two years old and still intimately bound to my brother, I was now also separate, independent and isolated.

For much of the following twenty-five years I struggled with the disturbing implications of this experience. I knew I was separate and different from my brother, and from everyone else. I knew also that the sense of wholeness and identity which I had experienced first with him and later in other relationships was just as vital a part of myself as my experience of otherness, but was constantly dismayed by the sense of suffocation, the lack of freedom, which this feeling invariably provoked in me. I began to despair. It seemed I had to accept that the paradise of early infancy could never be recovered, not even in a different form, and that I must choose between independence and relationship. At this point I sought help from a Jungian psychotherapist. During the following years I began to understand the two impulses in a way which finally made it possible to experience both together. I learnt to recognise separateness and belonging as a polarity, to know that I was neither an isolated individual nor an undifferentiated aspect of the cosmos, but that I was, instead, simultaneously unique and universal, that the one implied the other. I learnt to recognise that this polarity, which hitherto I had primarily experienced in relation to other people and the outside world, had its correspondence in my own psyche expressing itself through my thoughts and feelings.

The experience of Jungian therapy together with my interest in the work of Rudolf Steiner helped me to see this polarity of belonging and separateness as the expression of the masculine and feminine principles which are present at all the different levels and stages of creation. This insight coincided with my study of Chinese culture which, perhaps more than any other, recognises the importance of the harmony of two sexual principles within each individual for health and understanding. In four different ways – from Jungian psychology, Anthroposophy, Chinese philosophy and my personal experience – I was introduced to the idea of a masculine and feminine polarity within the human psyche. This coincided with the re-emergence of the women's liberation movement in the late sixties and early seventies.

Initially this movement was primarily concerned with abolishing sexual discrimination in political, social and economic life, and ensuring the provision of services which would allow women to take advantage of equality of opportunity. In theory these aims are now widely accepted, and although much more still needs to be done to guarantee the translation of principle into practice, as well as to help all women to acknowledge and respect themselves as equal members of society, both processes are now already under way. So it seems an appropriate moment to question more deeply the impulses beneath the call for sexual equality, in order that both women and men may acquire greater conscious understanding and insight into the enigmatic problem of sex and gender.

This book reflects the coincidence of my own personal development with the outer events of the women's liberation movement. It attempts to contribute to the discussion of the meaning and nature of sexuality and its relation to the individual and humanity by exploring the hypothesis that the true nature of the human being is androgyny – a synthesis of the masculine and feminine principles in the psyche – but that few have realised this potential because just as the body is more male or female so consciousness, too, is imbalanced. It suggests, however, that such psychological one-sidedness is not a necessary or an absolute factor of human existence but, on the contrary, an essential though transitory stage in the history of humanity's awareness of itself and of the world. It attempts to show that a process of evolution in consciousness can be observed comparable to the patterns of biological development, and that this can be understood as the evolution of the masculine and feminine principles from an undifferentiated unity towards greater differentiation in preparation for their eventual synthesis and harmony in androgyny.

Such an idea could obviously be examined in a variety of ways and from within many different cultural and historical contexts. I have chosen to explore it through Chinese culture primarily because the recognition of the feminine and masculine principles – Yin and Yang – as the primal polarity in the individual and the cosmos remained central to Chinese consciousness from its earliest expression in myth, legend and verse over three thousand years ago, until the early decades of this century. Even today, in the Chinese People's Republic, the conception of Yin and Yang as polar energies plays a vital part in the theory and practice of Chinese medicine.[1]

Moreover there is another reason for selecting Chinese culture as the arena within which to explore the idea of androgyny, one which, while not directly relevant to the argument of the book, is, I think, pertinent to the situation in the second half of the twentieth century. We seem to be caught between two impulses, the one leading us towards a greater experience of our own separateness, our independence from all group identities, whether of family, race, culture or nation and another awakening in us a new and vastly wider group identity, a sense of universality. For these two impulses to develop creatively without leading either to egotism or to a general blurring of all differences, I think it is necessary, hand in hand with the search for increased self knowledge, to hasten the bridge building between different cultures so that the world view of each may become more intelligible to the others, so that understanding of the particular grows in tandem with understanding of the whole. In this book I have attempted to contribute to this by focusing on the conceptions of a cultural tradition very alien to that of mainstream western thought, and referring to western thinkers when they can elucidate, clarify or expand Chinese ideas.

In the notorious Monkey Trial of 1925 John Thomas Scopes was convicted for teaching Darwin's theory of evolution in Tennessee.[2] Now, 50 years later, Darwin's central principles of biological change are widely accepted. The idea of an evolutionary principle in human consciousness, however, remains considerably less acceptable. This may partly be because consciousness itself is such a difficult concept to define, one which has been used in many different contexts with as many different meanings. I use it to describe the way we think, feel and experience 'reality', how and with what faculties we look at ourselves and at the world. In this sense, consciousness can be compared with a pair of spectacles with many lenses, each offering a different view of the world. The evolution of consciousness is the process whereby simple lenses are gradually replaced by more sophisticated ones, revealing an increasingly detailed picture of humanity and the cosmos, its various parts as well as the relations between them.

In a fundamental sense the argument in this book arises from subjective experience. This may disquiet those seeking 'proof' and 'objectivity' according to the customary definitions of these words, but I believe it is vital for the development of human understanding that fresh questions and theories be continually asked and explored, for only by increasing our repertoire of questions is it possible to improve our answers. New questions depend, at some stage, on the imagination. Much of what is imagined may subsequently prove to be wrong, but this is a necessary risk if knowledge is to grow.

The theories in this book begin as hypotheses, and even after they have been examined, expounded and supported by a variety of evidence, they remain hypothetical. Their empirical confirmation can only come to people who have worked with them and experienced their validity both in themselves and in others. This alone may give some grounds for their being considered objective and of general value. But for this to happen the reader must be willing to co-operate with the book in such a way that a purely intellectual grasp of its contents is complemented by an intuitive and imaginative response. The ideas demand, for their full understanding, to be inwardly explored in the light of each person's own experience and half-forgotten memories. I do not think that we can become conscious of anything which at one level we do not already know, and which we are not, in some way, prepared for and willing to recognise. It was out of this conviction that the present study was conceived and written.

I have chosen androgyny to describe the synthesis of the feminine and masculine principles in consciousness, the way of seeing that is neither Yin nor Yang but embraces both. This word which derives from the Greek 'andro' meaning male and 'gyne', female, has been criticised by some people for its dualistic connotations and also for giving pre-eminence to the male gender. In the course of this book it will, I hope, become clear that no dualism or value statement about the feminine and masculine is intended by my use of the word. It may help those who are troubled by this second point to remember that the substantive 'androgyne' has an adjectival form 'gyandrous', in which the halves of the compound are reversed.[3]

Throughout the book I have adopted the Pinyin system of romanisation of Chinese characters. This has the disadvantage of being less familiar to most western readers than the older Wade-Giles system, but since it has been officially adopted by China, it will eventually become universal; it has the advantage of being phonetically more accurate. I have added the more familiar form in brackets, following the first inclusion of each Chinese name and concept.

A glossary is included at the end of the book to help those readers who are unfamiliar with Chinese history and philosophy. I decided to include some of the necessary information in this form, so as not to encumber the text with too many digressions.

CHAPTER ONE

The Golden Age

I am not often awake before dawn, but some time ago I had to catch a five o'clock boat in Greece. Walking along the beach to the jetty, I looked across the bay to the mountains blocking the sky from the sea. Very soon the sun would climb over their bare contours, beckoning women to their washing, and signalling the time for the early morning bus to cough into motion. But for a moment I was standing in a space before the beginning of the world. The light was not strong enough to awaken the colours of the day, nor weak enough to give the certainty of night; everything, everywhere, was grey and still, shapes without substance. Nothing to feel, nothing to see and nothing to hear—an infinite neutrality. Rationally, I knew it was merely the beginning of another day, that its strangeness was no more than its unfamiliarity, but another part of me marvelled at this eternal nothingness. Then, as the sun's rays appeared and divided the world into light and shadow, I was offered intimations of what the ancient Chinese meant when they described the beginning of the world as the Great Nothingness, the Mysterious Sameness, the Chaos, or the Great Ultimate, and expressed it with the symbol of *wu ji* (wu chi), the empty circle:

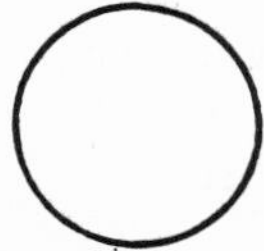

This great Nothing, the source of everything, the Chinese called the Dao (Tao), and their philosophy and literature are replete with eulogies to it. One of the most beautiful is in the *Dao de Jing* (*Tao Te Ching*) a Daoist classic reputedly written by the sixth century sage, Laozi (Lao Tzu) but, more likely a compilation of a later date:

> Before the Heaven and Earth existed
> There was something nebulous:
> Silent, isolated,
> Standing alone, changing not,
> Eternally revolving without fail,
> Worthy to be the Mother of All Things.
> I do not know its name
> And address it as Tao.
> If forced to give it a name, I shall call it 'Great'.
> Being great implies reaching out in space,
> Reaching out in space implies far-reaching,
> Far-reaching implies reversion to the original point.[1]

Dao is sometimes translated as 'God', but the Christian conception of the Supreme Being as static and transcendent is misleading. The ancient Chinese experienced no need for a God outside the world to create and direct its course. The cosmos, in their view, was an organic unity which spontaneously, out of itself, evolved the manifest and unmanifest worlds. This indescribable source, without beginning or end, but which ordains all beginnings and all ends, is better rendered in English by the ambiguous word 'Way': it is the Way of creation as well as the Way which precedes creation. Nothing is inferior or external to it, for all that exists is merely a more ordered expression of what was at the Beginning.

The concept of Dao is one of the oldest and certainly the most fundamental in all Chinese thought, from its emergence out of prehistoric myths up until the twentieth century. The character for Dao 道, composed of a foot 辶 and a head 首, suggests the idea of walking and thinking, of knowing the correct path and following it. In combining the idea of 'foot' and 'head' it symbolises personal wholeness (from head to foot), and since the 'head' was often equated with 'Heaven' and the 'foot' with 'Earth', it also suggests cosmic wholeness. The Dao is the primal principle of the universe and the way to achieve a personal realisation of it.

This concept received different emphases from the different schools of Chinese thought, but the various interpretations complement, rather than contradict each other. For as Xunzi (Hsün Tzu), the philosopher of the third century BC pointed out, different views only represent single aspects of the Dao, its essence is constant and includes all changes: 'It cannot be grasped by a single corner. Those with perverted knowledge who see only a single aspect of the Tao will not be able to comprehend its totality.'[2] Zhuangzi (Chuang Tzu), a Daoist, who possibly lived during the third or fourth century BC, emphasises the all-embracing nature of the Dao in the following characteristically direct dialogue:

Tung Kuo Tzu asked Chuang Tzu, saying, 'What you call Tao – where is it?'
'There is nowhere,' replied Chuang Tzu, 'where it is not.'
'Tell me one place at any rate where it is,' said Tung Kuo Tzu.
'It is in the ant,' replied Chuang Tzu.
'Why go so low down?' asked Tung Kuo Tzu.
'It is in a tare,' said Chuang Tzu.
'Still lower,' objected Tung Kuo Tzu.
'It is in a potsherd,' said Chuang Tzu.
'Worse still!' cried Tung Kuo Tzu.
'It is in ordure,' said Chuang Tzu. And Tung Kuo Tzu made no reply.[3]

The Dao 'knows nothing and is capable of nothing yet; there is nothing which it does not know, nothing of which it is incapable.'[4] Because it is the source of everything it is indefinable. After it has begun to manifest itself we can observe its forms, but in its primal state the Dao moves and rests beyond the confines of human language:

Formerly the sages reduced heaven and earth to a system by means of the Yin and Yang. But if all that has shape was born from the Shapeless, from what were heaven and earth born? I answer: there was a Primal Simplicity, there was a Primal Commencement, there were Primal Beginnings, there was a Primal Material. The Primal Simplicity preceded the appearance of the breath. The Primal Commencement was the beginning of the breath. The Primal Beginnings were the breath beginning to assume shape. The Primal Material was the breath when it began to assume substance. Breath, shape and substance were complete, but things were not yet separated from each other; hence the name 'Confusion'. 'Confusion' means that the myriad things were confounded and not yet separated from each other.[5]

Chaos, Confusion, the One – these are some of the nebulous names selected to lead the mind beyond the confines of either-or categories and ways of thinking, and to help it to experience the common origin of all things. The Way, in the beginning, is undifferentiated, hence Chaotic, and even after it begins to manifest itself in the myriad forms of creation, it never relinquishes its essential unity. Words and definitions are only suitable for describing the differentiated world, since their function is to distinguish between things. They are unsuitable for communicating the unity which lies behind the differences. In this realm, silence is as important as an accurate use of language in the phenomenal world. The ancient Chinese knew that to speak about the Dao was to betray one's ignorance of it: 'One who knows does not speak', wrote Laozi, and 'one who speaks does not know.'[6]

> The way that can be told
> Is not the constant way;
> The name that can be named
> Is not the constant name.
> The nameless was the beginning of heaven and earth;[7]

But if the ultimate cannot be expressed in words how can we trust those who have used words to describe it? Bo Ju-i (Po Chü-i), a famous poet of the ninth century AD, posed this question:

> Those who speak do not know
> Those who know do not speak
> This is what we were told by Lao Tzu.
> Should we believe that he himself was the one who knew;
> How could it then be that he wrote no less than five thousand words?[8]

Two centuries later Bo Ju-i received an answer from Wuzi Fa yan (Wu tzu Fa-yen). 'I make an embroidery of ducks and drakes and let you examine and admire them. As for the golden needle, I cannot pass it on to you.'[9] The Dao itself cannot be communicated. In the end every person has to find its meaning and nature alone in the depths of their own psyche, but in the beginning the experience of others who have struggled in search of it is invaluable. Herein lies the importance of the *Dao de Jing* and other writings. They teach that it is impossible to grasp the Dao directly, but that it must be looked for in the patterns and forms which it creates, in the clattering of the typewriter keys, the dripping of the kitchen tap, and in the April wind shaking the new leaves. In the world around us, in all its shapes, in its beauty and its ugliness, we can find the Way. But not only there, for the Dao is also within us. Humanity is not separate from nature, but an integral part of it, emerging from the same originally undifferentiated beginning, and developing according to similar laws. This is as true for human consciousness as it is for the physical body. Just as the evolution of the world is a process of increasing differentiation and sophistication from an amorphous, chaotic and unknowable origin, so, too, is the evolution of human consciousness. It has its beginning in a chaos, reflecting the primal chaos which preceded creation.

In their creation stories, the ancient Chinese did not distinguish between the personal and the universal because they were describing a world before the arrival of self-consciousness, a world in which cosmos and psyche were still inextricably one. Freud wrote that 'originally the ego includes everything, later it separates off an external world from itself. Our present ego-feeling is therefore only a shrunken residue of a far more inclusive – indeed all-embracing feeling which corresponded to a more intimate bond between the ego and the world about it.'[10] Erich Neumann, a Jungian psychologist, discussed this stage of human history in his study of the origins of consciousness: 'Not only is the psyche open to the world, it is identical with and undifferentiated from the world; it knows itself as world and in the world and experiences its own becoming as a world becoming, its own images as the starry heavens, and its own contents as the world-creating gods.'[11]

Until the beginnings of individual consciousness, there is no way to differentiate between the emergence of the world and the emergence of the human psyche. The one is identical with the other. They are locked in a unity which the ancient Chinese expressed with the *Wu ji* symbol, and which modern analytical psychologists designate as the uroboric stage of human development. The Uroboros, the image of the snake biting its own tail, comes from ancient Egypt where it was described as that which 'slays, weds and impregnates itself . . . man and woman, begetting and conceiving, devouring and giving birth, active and passive, above and below at once.'[12]

The Uroboros represents the collective unconscious, the abyss or chaos in which all life begins. It expresses simultaneously the infancy of the child and the infancy of humanity, a stage before the birth of the masculine and feminine principles, of Yin and Yang. Within it, female and male still rest together in incestuous embrace.

Since both the Uroboros and the *Wu ji* express a pre-conscious stage, it is not easy to acquire a feeling for their meaning, but it is not impossible. I remember one such moment when I was alone in a room holding a three-day-old baby. At first I was entirely preoccupied with thoughts about whether he was comfortable. These were followed by a rapid survey of my feelings towards babies in general, of memories of my own daughter as a baby, and thoughts about myself as a mother. But after some moments I put aside these these random feelings and ideas to make space for the baby whose warmth was beginning to creep through my jersey. I looked at the loose folds of skin under his chin, and the long thin fingers and toes. I felt his powdered skin and smelt the smell of new-born babies, and, almost imperceptibly, I realised there was no longer a woman holding a baby; the two had merged into one. My 'I' had expanded into a 'We' which included the baby, and also, in a mysterious way, the whole world.

In those brief moments when I had relinquished my separate identity, the definitions and categories of the world disappeared, leaving in their place a feeling of enormous peace and strength. In an important sense experiences like this are not comparable to the pre-conscious paradise of the early Daoists, precisely because they *are* conscious. But a surrender of individual consciousness and an imaginative identification with the world of the newly born may activate memories of a primal state before the birth of human awareness. The Daoists made frequent use of the new-born baby analogy when writing about the strength and virtue of identification with the Dao:

> One who possesses virtue in abundance is comparable to a new-born babe:
> Poisonous insects will not sting it;
> Ferocious animals will not pounce on it;
> Predatory birds will not swoop down on it.
> Its bones are weak and its sinews supple yet its hold is firm.
> It does not know of the union of male and female yet its male member will stir:
> This is because its virility is at its height.[13]

Interpreted literally, this passage is clearly absurd; appalling things can happen to new-born babies. But in another sense, it is true that they are protected, not from disease or accident, but from the struggles and pain of being individuals. They have a strength which comes from being unconsciously contained by and at one with the whole world instead of being separate members of it. For a few hours or days after their birth they can live without the pain of consciousness; breathing, eating and existing completely spontaneously. This is their attraction, their haunting quality. It is not that they are free from physical stress, but simply that their awareness has not yet caught up with what is going on in their bodies, and they live still in some paradisal Golden Age. Those who have experienced this with a young baby, or in other ways, however briefly, will not find it difficult to understand the nostalgia of the early Daoists as they looked back to the dawn of humanity and longed for its pre-conscious peace. The world they describe, as the following three passages from the *Zhuangzi* illustrate, is a world without death, disease, unnatural laws, morality or immorality, a world in which everything happens instinctively in harmony with everything else, free from discord and free from fear:

> In the Golden Age, good men were not appreciated; ability was not conspicuous. Rulers were mere beacons, while the people were free as the wild deer. They were upright without being conscious of duty to

their neighbours. They loved one another without being conscious of charity. They were true without being conscious of loyalty. They were honest without being conscious of good faith. They acted freely in all things without recognising obligations to anyone. Thus their deeds left no trace; their affairs were not handed down to posterity.[14]

And so in the days when natural instincts prevailed, men moved quietly and gazed steadily. At that time there were no roads over mountains, nor boats, nor bridges over water. All things were produced, each for its own proper sphere. Birds and beasts multiplied; trees and shrubs grew up. The former might be led by the hand; you could climb up and peep into the raven's nest. For then man dwelt with birds and beasts, and all creation was one. There were no distinctions of good and bad men. Being all equally without knowledge, their virtue could not go astray. Being all equally without evil desires, they were in a state of natural integrity, the perfection of human existence.[15]

Primeval man enjoyed perfect tranquillity throughout life. In his day, the Positive and Negative principles [Yang and Yin] were peacefully united; spiritual beings gave no trouble; the four seasons followed in due order; nothing suffered any injury; death was unknown; men had knowledge, but no occasion to use it. This may be called perfection of unity . . . At that period, nothing was ever made so; but everything was so.[16]

Whether such an earthly paradise ever existed is not easy to discover. Its extreme antiquity, together with the absence of all artificial products and written records, make it inaccessible to the conventional tools of archaeologists and historians. Along with a host of other theories and speculations about our primordial origins it must await the development of more sophisticated methods of scientific research. But these Paradise tales do not have to be kept in cold storage for such a time. For the study of the evolution of human consciousness, they have a value beyond that of socio-economic and political fact or fiction.

The Chinese stories attribute the peace and instinctive harmony of the Golden Age to the innocence of its inhabitants. The people had no knowledge of good and evil, of duties and obligations, or even of life and death. It was a 'state of natural integrity' in which primitive humanity enjoyed 'perfect tranquillity throughout life'. Furthermore it was an age when the Yin and Yang were still peacefully united, an age with no consciousness of sexual differences. These descriptions of Chinese paradise are strikingly similar to the Judaeo-Christian story of the Garden of Eden in which Adam and Eve lived at peace for as long as they obeyed the Lord's injunction not to eat or touch the fruit of the Tree of Knowledge of good and evil which stood in the centre of the Garden. But when one day the serpent explained to Eve why God had forbidden them to eat of this fruit, saying 'God doth know that in the day ye eat thereof, then your eyes shall be opened, and ye shall be as gods, knowing good and evil',[17] the desire for wisdom proved irresistible. She ate the fruit and persuaded Adam also to accompany her into the new world of consciousness. Until that moment both had been naked and knew not their nakedness, but now they recognised it and hastily covered themselves. In eating the fruit they rent apart their pre-conscious identity with the supreme principle. They lost their instinctive communication with God and gained freedom of choice and the possibility of understanding. They fell from innocence and instinctive perfection into consciousness and a world of good and evil.

Such wisdom is costly. Tranquillity and spontaneous order were possible in Paradise precisely because there was no consciousness. With its emergence humanity severed itself, a little, from the cosmos and began the slow, difficult and painful struggle towards self-consciousness and understanding. Eve's act of defiance has been condemned for introducing evil and discord into the world, but she also introduced the possibility of freedom. The birth of consciousness is humanity's damnation and its triumph.

Christians have tended to condemn Eve while extolling the advantages of her action. The ancient Chinese were divided on the subject; there were those who valued the birth of consciousness and those who, like some of the early Daoists, scorned the benefits of knowledge and focused instead on recapturing the bliss of the Golden Age. Parts of the *Dao de Jing* perhaps belong to this second school of thought. They seem to negate consciousness as a precondition of the discovery of the Dao. Laozi says:

> In the pursuit of learning, one knows more every day; in the pursuit of the way one does less every day. One does less and less until one does nothing at all, and when one does nothing at all there is nothing that is undone.[18]

And in another passage, the sage says:

> Block the openings;
> Shut the doors.
> Blunt the sharpness;
> Untangle the knots;
> Soften the glare;
> Let your wheels move only along old ruts.
> This is known as the mysterious sameness.
> Hence you cannot get close to it, nor can you keep it at arm's length;
> You cannot bestow benefit on it, nor can you do it harm; you cannot ennoble it, nor can you debase it.[19]

Other Daoist passages are more realistic. They acknowledge that the search for the Dao cannot be undertaken through the denial of consciousness but only through its unfolding and refinement. But perhaps it was the Confucians who understood most clearly that human consciousness is not only responsible for our expulsion from identity with the Dao but is also, paradoxically, the only way to a new paradise. They realised that the human mind is not separate from the creative principle but a microcosmic reflection of it. The great Neo-Confucian philosopher, Zhu Xi (Chu Hsi) attempts to clarify this conception with the image of moonlight:

> The relationship between the Great Ultimate in the universe and the Great Ultimate in each individual thing is not one of whole and part, but one similar to moonlight shining on objects. Each object has its own moonlight but this moonlight is moonlight as a whole.[20]

According to Zhu Xi, all things, cosmic and individual, including human consciousness, are created through the interaction of Yin and Yang, the primal polarity which evolved from the Dao. Nothing can come into existence, neither stone nor plant, neither animal nor human awareness, without the workings of these two cosmic principles:

> The principle of the mind is the Great Ultimate. The activity and tranquillity of the mind are the Yin and Yang. Mind alone has no opposite. Question: Is consciousness what it is because of the intelligence of the mind or is it because of the activity of material force? [Qi - energy or life force. This was the term used to denote Yin and Yang.]
> Answer: Not material force alone. [Before material force

existed] there was already the principle of consciousness. But principle at this stage does not give rise to consciousness. Only when it comes into union with material force is consciousness possible. Take, for example, the flame of this candle. It is because it has received this rich fat that there is so much light.
Question: Is that which emanates from the mind material force?
Answer: No, that is simply consciousness.
Question: Mind is consciousness and the nature is principle. How do the mind and principle pervade each other and become one?
Answer: They need not move to pervade each other. From the very start they pervade each other.[21]

Zhu Xi explains that consciousness existed in principle from the beginning, but that, in common with the rest of creation, it could not come into being without the interaction of Yin and Yang, the primal polarity. While the movements of these two principles, he states, are the precondition for human consciousness of the Dao, they are also responsible for obscuring the nature of the Supreme principle; the Yin-Yang polarity which creates consciousness also restricts consciousness. It is only when Yin and Yang are in perfect harmony that the Dao can be truly reflected, and since this is an extremely difficult state to achieve, most things and most human beings are to a greater or lesser extent imbalanced and hence ignorant. Zhu Xi compares human nature to a precious pearl lying in water:

In the case of a sage the water is pure and clean so the pearl shines in all its loveliness. With most men the water is turbid and muddy so that the pearl can hardly be seen or its quality perceived.[22]

Now as the Great Ultimate begins its activity, the two material forces (Yin and Yang, passive and active cosmic forces) assume physical form, and as they assume physical form, the myriad transformations of things are produced. Both man and things have their origin here. This is where they are similar. But the two material forces and the Five Agents,[23] in their fusion and intermingling, and in their interaction and mutual influence, produce innumerable changes and inequalities. This is where they are different.[24]

It is only when yin and yang are harmonized . . . that a man has the qualities of the Mean and correctness and becomes a Sage.[25]

Without the dynamic interaction of Yin and Yang, there can be no creation and no consciousness. The sexual polarity is fundamental not only to physical procreation but also to the procreation of things and ideas. This connection between the feminine and masculine principles and physical and conceptual creativity is not unique to ancient Chinese thought. English, also, contains an implicit acknowledgement of the link in the word 'conceive'; we conceive children and we conceive ideas. Only the separation and subsequent meeting of these two primordial principles can generate the necessary energy for creation and consciousness, and only their harmony can bring about a conscious understanding of the Dao, the discovery in freedom of the original pre-conscious wholeness and immortality. The relationship between Yin-Yang and the Way is symbolised by the famous Yin-Yang circle which expresses the two principles as polar manifestations of the Dao:

The task of all who wish to discover consciously the Golden Age which was once theirs as a pre-conscious gift, is to realise the feminine and masculine principle within their own psyche and to allow their harmony to unfold. But if it is true that consciousness depends on the interaction of Yin and Yang, then, it might be asked, how is it possible to harmonise these two principles without negating consciousness? Such a question can only arise from a misunderstanding of the concept of 'harmony'. It does not imply a general blurring of differences a merging of two into one in which both natures are sacrificed. (This might be a correct interpretation of what is advocated in parts of the *Dao de Jing*, but it is certainly not what Zhu Xi had in mind.) On the contrary, harmony means the combination of the different parts so as to produce an aesthetically satisfying whole, not the negation of the separate parts to create a soup of sameness. The harmony between the feminine and masculine principles, advocated by Zhu

Xi as the path to wisdom, is one which recognises their separate natures as the precondition of their relationship and synthesis. What this means and how it develops in human consciousness is the central subject of this study.

The Golden Age was not harmonious in the sense in which I have just defined the term. It was chaotic. In it the Yin and the Yang were still undifferentiated. The progress from chaos to order is the pattern of the evolution of consciousness. Described in these terms it seems unequivocally beneficial, but creation, whether of consciousness or of the phenomenal world, depends on death. Differentiation is born out of the sacrifice of the undifferentiated unity. The idea of creation as the dying of the whole primordial human being, of God or the divine principle, is common to many different mythologies. There is the old Germanic myth of Ymir:

From the flesh of Ymir the world was formed,
From his blood the billows of the sea,
The hills from his bones, the trees from his hair,
The sphere of heaven from his skull.

Out of his brows the blithe powers made
Midgarth for sons of men,
And out of his brains were the angry clouds
All shaped about the sky.[26]

Chinese tradition has a similar tale in the popular story of Pan Gu (P'an Ku). Born from the original Yin-Yang polarity, this primordial giant grew ten feet each day for eighteen thousand years, pushing the heavens away from the earth. When he died the various parts of his body were transformed into the world. His breath became the wind and the clouds, his voice the thunder and his sweat the rain. His left eye became the sun and his right eye the moon. From his body issued the great mountains. His blood and bodily fluids became the rivers and the seas, and his nervous and venous systems became the layers of the earth. The fields were the transformation of his flesh and the stars and planets developed from the hairs of his head. Metals and stones were the products of his teeth and bones. His semen became the pearls and his bone marrow turned into jade. The human race developed from the fleas of his body.

This cosmic sacrifice is usually regarded with an approval

which glosses over its cost. But the early Daoists were, as we have noted, less favourably disposed to creation. The following story from the *Zhuangzi* expresses the event in considerably less glowing terms. Two beings, Heedless and Hasty, often met in the middle space of Chaos-Unconscious. Chaos-Unconscious was always very friendly towards them. Heedless and Hasty now wondered how they could reward the kindness of Chaos-Unconscious. They said that all human beings had seven orifices, so that they could see, hear, and eat and breathe, but he had nothing of the kind, so they would try and make them for him. Every day they drilled a hole into Chaos-Unconscious, and on the seventh day he was dead.[27]

The murder of Chaos-Unconscious, or pre-consciousness, is the price of the freedom to think, to understand and to experience oneself as an independent individual. The creation stories, the symbols and the paradise tales of the ancient Chinese are more than simply nostalgic echoes of a Golden Age, epitaphs to a bygone time. They are also reminders of the flower of human psychological unfolding. The dismemberment of Pan Gu, the death of Chaos-Unconscious are the preconditions of consciousness, for understanding depends at certain moments on fragmentation and differentiation. But the evolution of consciousness leads eventually to psychic integrity, to the making whole, the healing of the divided self. The struggle towards the realisation of a conscious harmony of Yin and Yang, the search for androgyny, can be seen as a way of redeeming an ancient debt. In describing our past, the myths of the Golden Age indicate our future. But they also underline the inescapable fact that all birth entails death, all transformation, dying. This is as true for the evolution of consciousness as it is for the physical world.

The struggle for androgyny is a voyage of exploration and discovery no less daring than the courageous journeys of the fifteenth century Chinese explorer, Zheng He (Cheng Ho),[28] or those of Vasco da Gama, Magellan and Columbus. It demands that we meet and experience the masculine and feminine principles. This chapter has described their origin, indicated their role in the development of human consciousness and suggested that they have to be clearly differentiated before they can unfold their synthesis within the individual psyche. The following four chapters will explore the evolution and nature of these two primal principles in Chinese consciousness.

CHAPTER TWO

The Virgin Birth of Yin and Yang

In the beginning there was as yet no moral nor social order. Men knew their mothers only, not their fathers. When hungry, they searched for food: when satisfied, they threw away the remnants. They devoured their food, hide and hair, drank the blood, and clad themselves in skins and rushes. Then came Fu Hsi and looked upward and contemplated the images in the heavens, and looked downward and contemplated the occurrences on earth. He united man and wife, regulated the five stages of change, and laid down the laws of humanity. He devised the eight trigrams, in order to gain mastery over the world.[1]

The Chinese attribute the beginnings of civilisation to men. It is the legendary male emperors of the third and fourth millenia BC, Fu Xi (Fu Hsi), Shen Nong (Shen Nung) and Huang Di (Huang Ti), who are revered for bestowing the benefits of settled agriculture, medicine, philosophy, laws and social institutions on the Chinese people. Western culture has also often assumed that the time when 'men knew their mothers only' is synonymous with barbarism, but recent archaeological discoveries have seriously challenged this masculine assumption. It now seems possible that civilisation was not originally conceived of as the gift of a God or Gods but of a Great Goddess, and that while the societies over which She ruled were probably structured very differently from the later patriarchal cultures, the assumption that the differences between the two are those which distinguish civilisation from barbarism is rapidly losing its credibility.

Some striking support for this new view comes from the archaeological work of James Mellaart in the ancient sites of Anatolia. In his book *Çatal Hüyük* he describes the society which flourished there in the seventh millenium BC 'There had been no wars for a thousand years. There was an ordered pattern of society. There were no human or animal sacrifices. Vegetarianism prevailed, for domestic animals were kept for milk and wool – not for meat. There is no evidence of violent deaths . . . Above all, the supreme deity in all the temples was a goddess.'[2]

Merlin Stone corroborates: 'More recent discoveries suggest that the experience of Anatolia was not a cultural aberration but the norm. There is now sufficient evidence from other archaeological sites to suggest that much of the near and Middle East, as well as parts of Europe, Asia and America, once lay under the domination of the Great Goddess.'[3]

The suggestion that patriarchy (the authority of men) has not always characterised human society but may, instead, have been preceded by a time of matriarchy was argued by J. J. Bachofen in the nineteenth century, and Robert Briffault in his three volume study *The Mothers* early this century. Their pioneering works are frequently cited in more recent discussions of the subject (for example, Elizabeth Gould Davis, *The First Sex* and Evelyn Reed, *The Evolution of Woman*). Briffault attempted to show that the socialising element in human history has been the operation of the maternal instincts for the gestation, bearing, nurturing and education of children. The real social bonds he said, developed from the woman's natural biological dominance over the community she protected and cared for. Her authority was 'organic', based on a natural reverence for her powers and a free consent to her dominance, not one in which women established and maintained control over men as men have done to women under patriarchy. This 'organic' matriarchal society ended, according to Briffault, when men, who are individualistic and aggressive, revolted against it by establishing economic domination and usurping some of the power of the mothers.

The principal foundation of Briffault's arguments and others who have attempted to prove the existence of matriarchal societies,[4] is the socialising effect of the maternal instinct. However, this instinct has also been used to argue precisely the opposite case. Simone de Beauvoir (*The Second Sex*) and Shulamith Firestone (*Dialectic of Sex*), for example, both deny the existence of matriarchal societies and point to women's maternal function as the root cause of her oppression. Thus the debate about the existence or not of matriarchal orders continues to throw up interesting questions and ideas but, so far, no conclusive answers or resolutions.

My intention is not to enter directly the debate by any discussion of the case for the existence of a Chinese matriarchy, because this would be an almost impossible task with the present paucity of evidence. Early this century Briffault admitted that 'China is perhaps of all countries the one where the patriarchal principles are most strongly emphasised and where the subjugation of women and their complete effacement in every sphere of life is most absolute. It is also the country where indications of any former matriarchal state of society are, it is generally considered, most completely lacking.'[5] My purpose, instead, is to suggest that a reading of the earliest tradition of Chinese mythology and literature points to a radically different *consciousness* from the one which provided the foundation of the Chinese Empire. Following the Jungian psychologist, Erich Neumann, I have labelled this Chinese consciousness 'matriarchal' since, as will be seen, its salient symbols are those associated with the Mother.[6] In his essay *On the Moon and Matriarchal Consciousness*, Neumann wrote:

> Matriarchy and patriarchy are psychic stages which are characterised by different developments of the conscious and unconscious, and especially by different attitudes of the one toward the other. Matriarchy not only signifies the dominance of the Great Mother archetype, but, in a general way, a total psychic situation in which the unconscious (and the feminine) are dominant, and consciousness (and the masculine) have not yet reached self reliance and independence. ('Masculine' and 'feminine' are here symbolic magnitudes, not to be identified with the 'man' or the 'woman' as carriers of specific sexual characteristics.) In this sense, a psychological stage, a religion, a neurosis and also a stage in the development of consciousness can be called 'matriarchal', and patriarchal does not mean the sociological

> rule of men, but the dominance of the masculine consciousness which succeeds in separating the systems of consciousness and unconsciousness, and which is relatively firmly established in a position opposite to, and independent of, the unconscious. For this reason, modern woman must also go through all those developments which lead to the formation of the patriarchal consciousness which is now typical of, and taken for granted in, the Western conscious situation, being dominant in patriarchal culture.[7]

This chapter will explore the matriarchal consciousness in China and its gradual takeover by the patriarchy, as a preparation for understanding the emergence of the feminine and masculine principles in thought, and the advantages and disadvantages of this for human understanding and experience. Revolutions in consciousness cannot be dated in the same way as social, political and economic revolutions, for they occur at different times among different individuals and sections of society, so that older forms frequently co-exist and even continue to challenge later ones long after these have emerged. In the discussion which follows, therefore, the emphasis lies primarily on the contrast and dynamics of change between two stages of consciousness – matriarchy and patriarchy – rather than on any particular period of history. Myths, legends, archaeological discoveries and literature are brought together from widely different periods of Chinese history and pre-history to present a portrait of the matriarchal experience and perception of the cosmos. Although certain important correspondences between consciousness and political structure become apparent, the chronology here and throughout the book is primarily psychological rather than sociological.

The starting point for this exploration of matriarchal consciousness lies not so much in archaeology as in psychology, but, as Esther Harding explains in her study of the Goddess myths, it is exceedingly difficult to recapture the significance which a god or a religious symbol held for a people of a bygone time:

> For a symbol is the concretization of an actual living spirit or feeling which is yet not completely known or realized. So long as the spirit is living everyone senses its meaning and its power, although none of them could define it exactly . . . Only when the cult of the god was already declining did certain writers feel it to be necessary to preserve

in 'texts' a value which was in danger of being entirely lost.

Consequently our knowledge of the Great Mother is somewhat scanty . . . As far as written information is concerned, there are occasional references and allusions in the literature of the periods in which the Moon Mother flourished. Certain passages also occur in the writings of a later period which give a philosophical or metaphysical explanation of the older religion . . . In addition there have come down to us a few ritual hymns and prayers addressed to the Mother . . . and a multitude of sacred objects and pictures whose meaning looked at with the eyes of the rational intellect can only be dimly discerned. If, however, we regard them as symbols, referring to psychological, instead of historic facts, their inner meaning often flashes out in unmistakable clarity.[8]

The fragmentary relics – the myths, symbols and images – of Great Mother cultures may be entirely inadequate as evidence or clues to the existence and nature of pre-patriarchal socio-economic structures, but they can be most revealing about the psychological state, or stage of consciousness which inspired them. Such an interpretation assumes, as its starting point, that we fashion our gods and goddesses in our own likeness, that how we see and understand the world depends, to a significant extent, on the nature of our own consciousness.

This is not a new idea. Subatomic physics has, for example, recognised for some time the indivisibility of question and answer, subject and object in scientific exploration. Heisenberg concluded that so-called 'objective' descriptions of reality reveal no more of the 'truth' than the questions which prompted them. In other words, our scientific knowledge is rigidly circumscribed by the limits of our own consciousness, our models of the universe are mirror images of our own minds. Fritjof Capra writes in *The Tao of Physics*:

The crucial feature of atomic physics is that the human observer is not only necessary to observe the properties of an object, but is necessary even to define these properties. In atomic physics, we cannot talk about the properties of an object as such. They are only meaningful in the context of the object's interaction with the observer. In the words of Heisenberg, 'What we observe is not nature itself, but nature exposed to our method of questioning.' The observer decides how he is going to set up the measurement and this arrangement will determine, to some extent, the properties of the observed object. If the experimental arrangement is modified the properties of the observed object will change in turn.[9]

Without becoming subatomic physicists we can all observe, at a simpler level, the workings of this interdependence between subject and object, question and answer, in the drawings and stories of young children. Their early figures are often composed of a smaller circle on top of a larger one with an arm sticking out each side of the head and legs pointing down in parallel lines from the body. The absence of neck, ears, hands, fingers and toes, as well as the even more surprising fact that the arms come out of the head rather than the body, is usually put down to technical incompetence. A more plausible explanation might be that the young children's drawings are primarily portraits of their consciousness, not of the 'outside' world. This would also seem likely to be true of children's stories. The feelings, patterns or events which they describe appear to be carbon copies of their own feelings and experiences. The picture of the world which emerges is, in many ways, a picture of their own psyche. As adults, operating from within very different levels of consciousness, it is easy to feel patronising towards these childish pictures of monsters and fairies but, for obvious reasons, we are often not much more capable than the child of perceiving the limitations of our own descriptions of reality. The world we describe and see may appear to us more rational and more real than that of the child, but it is possible that our mechanistic description of the universe is no more accurate a representation than the childish world of angels and goblins.

Once we accept the notion of a universe in which question and answer, description and consciousness, cannot be separated, the possibility of reaching any understanding of truth seems to recede with alarming rapidity into a never-never land. But fortunately, the implications of this monistic model of the universe may not be as bleak as they at first appear. If it is true that the answers we receive depend on the questions we ask, then it follows that the way to increase our collection of answers is to expand our repertoire of questions, and this can only be done by acquiring familiarity with as many different levels of consciousness as we can, and tolerating, at least in the short term, the apparent contradictions and paradoxes which these different ways of seeing will create. Whether this path towards knowledge is ultimately a finite or an infinite one, remains, at the moment, unanswerable, but it is clear that it leads away from alternative, single vision models of the universe, each struggling for exclusive credibility, towards a multi-dimensional perspective. To embrace it is to depart from that conventional pattern of human thinking which has been characterised, particularly in the West, by a series of philosophical explanations of reality, each claiming a monopoly of the truth. Such one-sidedness, or narrow-mindedness, may often be of inestimable value for the emergence and development of a particular perspective. But at a certain moment, different for each person, it is necessary to begin to experience the visions of the world, which lie behind the different descriptions, as complementary rather than fundamentally antithetical. When this happens, ancient forms of consciousness begin to acquire an importance and meaning beyond the purely historical. They tell us about our past, but they can also begin to tell us about our future. The Great Mother consciousness is no exception for, as Laozi recognised, She lies at the beginning and at the end of human development:

> The world had a beginning
> And this beginning could be the mother of the world.
> When you know the mother
> Go on to know the child.
> After you have known the child
> Go back to holding fast to the mother,
> And to the end of your days you will not meet with danger.[10]

But getting to know the Mother is a difficult undertaking. Patriarchal consciousness has done a masterly (sic) job of obscuring and deleting references to the Great Goddess, and nowhere more so than in China. The Confucian bureaucrats subjected the ancient Chinese classics to centuries of rigorous editing and commentaries. They dismissed all ancient myths and legends which did not directly support their world view as either meaningless or misguided. Only isolated fragments, probably from widely different historical periods and often inextricably confused with popular folktales, have survived this dual process of neglect and censorship. Evidence of a prepatriarchal consciousness in China is, therefore, slight and inconclusive. However, when these fragments are explored alongside the far richer mythological and philosophical remains of other ancient civilisations, it seems likely that China too was at one time dominated by a matriarchal consciousness.

But such a conclusion or even hypotheses cannot be arrived at through exclusively intellectual analysis or quantitative evidence; the exploration of all levels of consciousness demands the use of the feelings as well as the intellect, intuition as well as logic. If myths are to yield their secrets they must be approached unashamedly with the complete faculties, not merely with one part of the person. Marie Louise von Franz stresses this point in her study of creation myths:

> In psychology we need the feeling function which considers the feeling tone of an archetypal image as well as its logical connections with other images. . . . We are scientific when we use it, and we are not scientific if we do not use it, because without feeling we start swimming intellectually, calling everything everything, for due to the nature of the archetypal contents of the unconscious, we cannot approach them with only the thinking function.[11]

Furthermore, to understand different ways of seeing and experiencing the world, the different stages of consciousness expressed through myths and symbols, it is necessary, at some point, to discover these ways within oneself. For just as we can know a fact without comprehending it, so while it is possible to acknowledge the reality of certain feelings and ideas, it is not possible truly to know and understand them until we have made a personal relationship to them by discovering them within our own psyche.

The images of a Great Goddess which appear from time to time in the mythology and literature of ancient China tell of a divine being who ruled over life and death, creation and destruction. She appears in various guises, as the mountain of the dawn that brought forth the antelope form of the sun, as hawk, eagle, or human, or as the egg containing the sun god. The five holy mountains of China appear originally to have been connected with this Great Goddess whose sons became the gods of the four quarters.[12] As the origin of all creation, inorganic, organic, animal and human, She is symbolised by the gigantic peach tree, which, according to the Chinese, grew in Paradise among the Kun-lun mountains in Tibet where it supported the universe. Its fruit took three thousand years to ripen and it was surrounded by a beautiful garden, cared for by the fairy, Xi Wang Mu, (Hsi Wang Mu) Queen of Immortals, Royal Mother of the West. Earliest traditions describe Xi Wang Mu as the Mother Goddess, who lived together with Her sister and Her attendants, who included the Blue Stork, the White Tiger, the Stag and the gigantic Tortoise. The Chinese Goddess was similarly associated with time in Her manifestation as the celestial year tree, beneath whose branches gather the beasts of the months, each ruling over a two-hour watch. The association between the Great Goddess and a primordial tree is not unique to China. In Egyptian art of the XVIII dynasty She is symbolised as the sycamore or date palm that confers nourishment on souls.[13] Hathor, whom the Greeks later called Aphrodite, is sometimes represented as the tree Goddess and revered as the mother of the sun; at other times She is associated with Nut, the Goddess of the sky, who was also considered to be mistress of the beasts of the zodiac.

In Crete during the Minoan period (roughly 2900–1350 BC) and possibly during the preceding Neolithic times (5000–3000 BC), religion was dominated by a Great Goddess who was closely associated with the vegetation cycle. The relation between the waxing and waning of the seasons and the natural world as a whole was symbolised by the young God, who died and was resurrected each year, and his consort/mother, the Great Goddess, who is sometimes represented as carrying him in her arms, appears in many guises – as Mountain Mother, Mistress of the animals, Tree, Snake, Dove and Poppy Goddess. Sometimes She appears as a warrior with a sword or shield and, at other times, as a Sea Goddess travelling in her ship.[14] Her worship clearly expresses the intimate relations between the human and natural worlds which characterise the matriarchal consciousness.

It may seem bewildering that the Goddess appears in so many different forms and that her jurisdiction stretches indiscriminately over the whole universe, but this confusion is a valuable indication of Her nature. She is the universal principle who gives birth to all things, protects them in life and calls them to Her in death. She is the vessel which contains and generates the cosmos, the Dao, or unifying principle, which guards, guides and permeates the infant consciousness of humanity. The distinctions of our 'either-or' consciousness are not relevant to the Great Mother, for in Her these polarities are still undifferentiated. Neumann comments on this phenomenon in his study of the Great Mother archetype:

> In the early situation of human culture, the group psyche was dominant. A relation of *participation mystique* prevailed between the individual and his group, and between the group and its environment, particularly the world of plants and animals . . . almost everywhere the original group experienced itself as descended from an animal or a plant with which it stood in a relation of kinship. What makes this phenomenon possible was that the differences between man, animal, plant and the inorganic world were not perceived as in modern consciousness.[15]

The concept of *participation mystique* was first formulated by Levy-Bruhl after observing how 'primitive' men seem to be psychologically identified, or 'continuous', with 'external' objects, so that they experience the objects as filled with power. Jung extended the use of this concept to explain a stage of consciousness in the psyche of 'civilised' people, which because it has no experience of subject-object boundaries, identifies with the suffering and celebrations of nature and the 'external' world. The Great Mother rules over this level of consciousness. Historically it is a level of awareness which precedes the emergence of polarity in human thought. There is no better illustration of this than the enigmatic sexuality of the Great Mother.

Morphologically the Goddess is usually personified as female and yet, quite clearly, She is also male, or, at least, contains the seeds of an undeveloped masculine principle. In Chinese mythology She is Yin-Yang before their separation into Yin and Yang. This is expressed in the figure of Nu Gua (Nu Kua), a divine being, who, according to earliest tradition, brought civilisation and order to China after the devastation caused by the Great Flood. In later texts She is described as the wife and sister of Fu Xi and still later Her name is erased altogether, so that Fu Xi, alone, can assume the credit for the beginnings of Chinese civilisation. The fate of Nu Gua reflects the fate of the maternal principle. In the beginning She reigned supreme without need of an external husband. Then She shared her kingdom with Her son-lover, and finally She was entirely replaced by Her own offspring. According to tradition it was only with the ascendancy to the throne of Fu Xi that marriage, as the sacred union of male and female, was introduced, which suggests that prior to the rule of the masculine principle there was no need for it. The explanation for the relatively late appearance of the institution of marriage as an image in mythology appears to be related to the bisexuality of the Great Mother. As long as both the masculine and feminine principles are united in one being, or undifferentiated in human consciousness, there can be no relationship between them. The separation of the male and female, as Plato recognised in *The Symposium*, is a precondition of human love.[16]

The bisexuality of the Goddess is stressed in the myths and literature of many different cultures. In *The Golden Ass* by Apuleius, the Goddess describes Herself:

> I am Nature, the universal Mother, mistress of all elements, primordial child of time, sovereign of all things spiritual, queen of the dead, queen also of the immortals, the single manifestation of all gods and goddesses that are. My nod governs the shining heights of Heaven, the wholesome sea breezes, the lamentable silences of the world below. Though I am worshipped in many aspects, known by countless names, and propitiated with all manner of different rites, yet the whole round earth venerates me.[17]

In Egypt She was called Isis, 'Mother of all, being of both male and female nature'.[18] In Babylonia She was Ishter, goddess of the Moon and addressed as 'O my God and my Goddess'. The Greek moon goddess, Artemis, was also considered to be both male and female. Plutarch says of Her: 'They call the moon the Mother of the Cosmical Universe having both male and female nature.'[19] In the *Dao de Jing* the Great Mother is described as ruling over heaven and earth. She is referred to as Tai Yi (T'ai I), the Great One, who represents the universe before its differentiation:

> The spirit of the valley never dies.
> This is called the mysterious female.
> The gateway of the mysterious female
> Is called the root of heaven and earth.

Dimly visible, it seems as if it were there,
Yet use will never drain it.[20]

There is a thing confusedly formed,
Born before heaven and earth.
Silent and void
It stands alone and does not change,
Going round and does not weary.
It is capable of being the mother of the world.[21]

Since the Great Mother is worshipped as the mother of polarity or that which transcends polarity, She rules over both heaven and earth, the two cosmic forces widely associated with the masculine and feminine principles. (No Chinese myths survive associating the Goddess with the Moon. Chinese moon stories largely date from the Han dynasty, or after, when the moon is associated with the feminine Yin principle, and presided over by the Moon goddess Heng E (Heng O).)

Another testament to the bisexuality of the Great Mother is Her frequent association with virginity and parthenogenesis. Virgin births play a prominent part in early Chinese legends and mythology: Huang Di, the Yellow Emperor, was conceived miraculously by his mother from a flash of lightning which entered her from the constellation of the Great Bear. She was pregnant for 25 months before giving birth to Huang Di, who spoke as soon as he was born. *The Book of Songs* contains another story of parthenogenetic reproduction:

She who in the beginning gave birth to the people,
This was Chiang Yüan.
How did she give birth to the people?
Well she sacrificed and prayed
That she might no longer be childless.
She trod on the big toe of God's footprint,
Was accepted and got what she desired.
Then in reverence, then in awe
She gave birth, she nurtured;
And this was Hou Chi.

Indeed, she had fulfilled her months,
And her first-born came like a lamb
With no bursting or rending,
With no hurt or harm.

To make manifest His magic power
God on high gave her ease.
So blessed were her sacrifice and prayer
That easily she bore her child.[22]

The popular Chinese story of Yuanshi Tian wang (Yuan-Shih T'ien-wang), an old man who preached from the mountain tops in antiquity tells of another virgin birth associated with the Great Mother. One day Jin Hung (Chin Hung), God of Tai Shan (T'ai Shan) (one of the five sacred mountains) asked Yuanshi Tian wang where he lived: 'Who so wishes to know where I dwell must rise to impenetrable heights,' he answered. Two genii, Chin Jingzi (Ch'in Ching-tzu) and Huan Lao descended on Tai Shan summit and said to Jin Hung: 'If you wish to know the origin of Yuan-Shih, you must pass beyond the confines of Heaven and Earth, because he lives beyond the limits of the worlds. You must ascend and ascend until you reach the sphere of nothingness and of being, in the plains of the luminous shadows.' They did this and they saw Xuan xuan Shangren (Hsuan-hsuan Shang-jen) surrounded by a bright light. He told them the history of Yuan-Shih and told them to spread it:

When P'an Ku had completed his work in the Primitive Chaos, his spirit left its mortal envelope and found itself tossed about in empty space and without any fixed support. 'I must,' it said, 'get reborn in visible form; until I can go through a new birth I shall remain empty and unsettled.' His soul, carried on the wings of the wind, reached Ru-yu T'ai. There it saw a saintly lady named T'ai Yuan, forty years of age, still a virgin, and living alone on Mount Ts'uo. Air and variegated clouds were the sole nourishment of her vital spirits, an hermaphrodite at once both the active and passive principles, she daily scaled the highest peak of the mountain to gather there the flowery quintessence of the sun and moon. P'an Ku, captivated by her virgin purity, took advantage of a moment when she was breathing to enter her mouth in the form of a ray of light. She was *enceinte* for twelve years, at the end of which period the fruit of her womb came out through her spinal column. From its first moment the child could walk and speak, and its body was surrounded by a five-coloured cloud. The newly born took the name of Yuan-Shih T'ien-wang, and his mother was known as 'Tai-Shih Shang-mu, the Holy Mother of the First cause.[23]

This myth is probably of relatively late origin, but it is nevertheless interesting that it summarises the salient characteristics of the Great Mother: Jin Hung is told that the answer to his question can only be found by going beyond the confines of Heaven and Earth, beyond, in other words, all polarities, to a woman who is an hermaphrodite, a virgin and also a mother.

The riddle of virginity has long perplexed the Christian Church and been skilfully used to justify the oppression and denigration of both women and sex throughout the centuries.[24] But a preoccupation with virginity is not specific to Christianity. It is a central motif in many of the great mythologies; Isis and Ishtar were both virgins, and like the Chinese Goddess, they were also mothers. A solution to this riddle is offered in a study of *The Virgin Archetype* by the Jungian psychologist, John Layard. He suggests that virginity does not mean chaste in the conventional usage of this word as meaning one who abstains from sex, but, on the contrary, suggests one who is psychologically so complete, so whole, that she has no need for fructification by an external male because she contains within her both sexual principles. She is thus spontaneously productive in the same way as a virgin forest or virgin land.[25] A virgin birth is therefore an expression of the instinctive union of the Yin and the Yang, the feminine and masculine principles. It suggests the highest level of psychological development, as Philo of Alexander explains when he says: 'The congress of men for the procreation of children makes virgins women. But when God begins to associate with the soul, He brings it to pass that she who was formerly woman becomes virgin again.'[26] The Great Mother is virgin because she reigns before the differentiation of the sexual principles; the marriage between male and female which characterises human history, takes place in Her internally rather than externally.

Our thinking is so imbued with the models of a dualistic, fragmentary conception of the world that, while we can intellectually grasp the images of the Great Mother, it is difficult to appreciate their meaning for people living under Her dominion. The matriarchal consciousness is a diffuse, undifferentiated and all-embracing vision of the world which it knows from within rather than from without, subjectively rather than objectively. It experiences the essential unity of the cosmos, and knows humanity as integral rather than separate from the whole. To this consciousness life and death are part of one continuous process controlled by Mother Earth. It is She who imbues the seeds with life and She who receives them into Her embrace in death. In pre-Zhou China (before 1200 BC), since fertility was believed to be due to the spirit of the earth, the dead were covered thickly with brushwood and placed in the open country without burial mound or grove of trees.[27] Each person was fed back to the earth, thereby enabling the creation of new life. According to the *Yi Jing* (*I Ching*) these ancient burial customs were barbaric and the 'holy men' of a later time ended their practice by introducing the custom of inner and outer coffins. In this way the dead ceased to merge with the earth but, in principle, retained their separate identity. This was considered a sign of civilisation, a mark of respect to humanity. But to a consciousness which feels and sees the unity of all creation there is nothing intrinsically disrespectful in giving the human physical body no greater protection after death than nature accords to animals and birds. Elaborate burial and mummification rituals only have a place after the birth of a consciousness which experiences the differences between humanity and nature or between the individual and others.

> To the primitive tribesman, the individual life matters very little, either to the man himself or to the group, for the value of *being* is vested in the group alone. *It* is the individual, the operative and effective being whose life is of paramount importance. The individual man is merged in the group. He does not make any important decisions for himself. The council of leaders decides everything – when to sow the seed, when to go to hunt, how to interpret big or important dreams, which are frequently taken as applying to the tribe as a whole. Consequently the individual has hardly any personal responsibility; his consciousness is practically identical with that of the group. Each man, in himself, is nothing, a mere integer, but he is also, or feels himself to be, a carrier of the tribal consciousness and importance, and this gives him a sense of dignity. This situation is illustrated in the ancient Hebrew idea of man's relation to God. For Jehovah was primarily interested in the tribe, not in the individual. It was what the chosen people did that mattered, while the individual man counted for very little.[28]

Individual thought and feelings do not belong to the matriarchal consciousness, for it experiences the world as a whole rather than as a sum of individuals. This is illustrated in the famous Da Tong (Ta t'ung) passage from the *Li Ji* (*Li Chi*), the *Book of Rites* (a compilation of the second century BC of a miscellany of earlier materials), which describes the workings of the ancient consciousness in political and social life.

The practice of the Great Way, the illustrious men of the Three Dynasties – these I shall never know in person. And yet they inspire my ambition! When the Great Way was practised, the world was shared by all alike. The worthy and the able were promoted to office and men practiced good faith and lived in affection. Therefore they did not regard as parents only their own parents, or as sons only their own sons. The aged found a fitting close to their lives; the robust their proper employment; the young were provided with an upbringing and the widow and widower, the orphaned and the sick, with proper care. Men had their tasks and women their hearths. They hated to see goods lying about in waste, yet they did not hoard them for themselves; they disliked the thought that their energies were not fully used, yet they used them not for private ends. Therefore all evil plotting was prevented and thieves and rebels did not arise, so that people could leave their outer gates unbolted. This was the age of Grand Unity.

Now the Great Way has become hid and the world is the possession of private families. Each regards as parents only his own parents, as sons only his own sons; goods and labour are employed for selfish ends. Hereditary offices and titles are granted by ritual law while walls and moats must provide security. Ritual and righteousness are used to regulate the relationship between ruler and subject, to insure affection between father and son, peace between brothers, and harmony between husband and wife, to set up social institutions, organize farms and villages, honor the brave and wise, and bring merit to the individual. Therefore intrigue and plotting come about and men take up arms.[29]

Although the *Li Ji* identifies the time of Grand Unity with the reign of the first three male emperors, it is clear that what is being eulogised is a consciousness and society radically different from later patriarchal practice. Whether or not the glowing descriptions are exaggerated by nostalgia, and whether or not they correspond to a social and political reality, it seems likely that there was once a time when people were communally rather than individually motivated, a time before the birth of ego-consciousness, which reflected itself in the absence of desires, and even in the absence of personal names and the personal ancestors which played such a vital role in Imperial China.

The peace of the age of Grand Unity is attributed to the absence of ego-consciousness. As long as people remain asleep to their individuality there is nothing to divide their will from either the instinctive will of the community or from nature. Huai Nanzi (Huai Nan tzu) who died in 122 BC wrote:

> The world was a unity without division into classes nor separation into orders . . . : the unaffectedness and homeliness of the natural heart had not, as yet, been corrupted· the spirit of the age was a unity and all creation was in great affluence. Hence, if a man with the knowledge of 'I' appeared, the world had no use for him.[30]

Some of the archaeological discoveries made by the Chinese in the last twenty-five years seem to support the statements of the philosophers that an ancient pre-patriarchal society once flourished free from warfare, class or sexual oppression. They also suggest that the Mother was the focal point of the culture. An 8,000-year-old village excavated near Xian in 1953 is considered by some modern Chinese archaeologists to have been organised as a primitive matriarchal commune, prior to the appearance of patriarchy, private property and class distinctions. It was constructed around the house of the Great Ancestress. The women's graves contain more funerary objects – pottery, bracelets, bone hairpins, whistles, etc – than the men's, and children, apart from young babies, were all buried with the women. Another site suggests that the 'Mother' enjoyed the most prominent position in the community: in the burial grounds she occupies the central place surrounded by her family.[31]

While, as I have mentioned, our knowledge of ancient China is still too scant to make any conclusive statements about the existence or not of a matriarchal society, vestiges of matriarchal consciousness probably lingered on into the ninth and tenth centuries BC. According to one sinologist:

> it seems reasonable enough to admit that in Shang and early Chou times, the mother, the clan ancestress, the tribal genetrix, had a great role in cult and belief. Above all, the female shaman – medium, dancer and exorcist – whose body was the actual but temporary repository of the spirits, and whose soul could be sent on frightful or

lovely journeys into the hidden worlds of sky and earth, was a common and important figure in the cultural life of north China in the Bronze Age.[32]

* * *

What, then, was this ancient way of experiencing the world reflected in its reverence for the Mother? Ontologically its meaning will be explored in greater detail in chapter six. We can acquire intimations of it in observing the way young children relate to animals and nature. They do not stand outside the world and study it, but, like ancient humanity, are intimately identified with it. Many children quite unsentimentally shiver as a tree is cut down or when they come across a dead bird lying on the road. As adults with our more highly developed ego-consciousness, it is often difficult to offer other than fraudulent words of comfort. It requires a major leap in imagination to enter once again the consciousness which distinguishes so little between 'external' and 'internal' events, and which considers animals and plants as important as human beings. But one sinologist has succeeded, to a remarkable extent in doing precisely this. Marcel Granet made an exhaustive study of the oldest extant work of Chinese literature, the *Book of Songs*. He suggests that these sung poems span a period of time during which a more communal, spontaneous and instinctive way of life was gradually supplanted by a hierarchical and feudal structure. As a sociological document his conclusions remain tenuous and speculative, but as a portrait of the contrast between two stages of consciousness – matriarchy and patriarchy – his study is an inspired and illuminating work.

Granet describes an ancient time when people lived at peace in small communities with little or no social life for much of the year. A strict sexual division of labour was enforced, but one entirely devoid of value judgements. During the summer women gathered mulberry leaves and looked after the silk worms while men worked in the fields. Throughout the hard cold winters both sexes retired indoors and the men applied themselves to the necessary repair work while the women worked full time making thread and weaving cloth. Their carefully structured lives left little space for contact between the sexes, but, twice a year, in Spring and

Autumn, at those times when the work patterns changed in correspondence with the change of seasons, two great festivals were celebrated. These community gatherings functioned as institutions of social control and it was during them that the contacts between the communities were regularised through marriage. In the Spring Festival boys and girls would come together in the 'holy' places where water and mountains met, and amidst the singing and dancing competitions they would gather flowers and cross the river to meet one another in a spontaneous expression of song. Surrounded and embraced by a world coming to life after the winter sleep, the two sexes attracted each other and fell in love. They betrothed themselves, wandered off from the general assembly, and 'as the water birds fly away in pairs to hide in the islets in the river, as the woodland birds in couples take refuge in the depths of the forest, so these young people withdrew to the low grassy meadows or beneath the great trees and tall ferns on the hills and there came together'.[33] Later in the year, following the fruitful consummation of their passion, the young people celebrated their marriage during the Autumn festival.

Psychologically these songs echo the feelings and consciousness of a pre-patriarchal age. Things happen according to highly structured and pre-determined laws, but they are natural not artificial laws. Nature, not man or woman, is the authority. Instinct, not conscious knowledge, the guide. Biologically the difference between the sexes was clearly perceived and society was structured on the basis of this difference, but there is no indication that sexual polarity had, as yet, reflected itself in human consciousness. On the contrary, the songs suggest that while men and women led different lives in accordance with their different biologies, they shared one general consciousness which focused on the unity and equality of creation. Nowhere is this better illustrated than in the love songs. Here the dominant emotion appears to be relief at finding wholeness through sexual contact with the opposite sex: 'Thus the alternating attraction between the sexes consists in a feeling of loss and bereavement, of regret for the incompleteness of their nature.'[34] In the songs all lovers seem to be alike and all express their feelings in the same way.

Not a single picture suggests a particular individual . . . The themes of meeting, betrothal, quarrels and separations are common to all and all men and women react to them in the same way. No heart feels any individual emotion, no case is peculiar, no one loves or suffers in a fashion all of his own. All individuality is absent and there is no attempt at any individuality of expression.[35]

The need of the lovers is to heal the wound of their biological incompleteness, to find a unity with the other corresponding to the unity of the world around them.

In the Autumn Festival the emphasis on finding and maintaining an identity with the world around receives more explicit emphasis. 'From all that is known of this thanksgiving Festival it is evident that it made obvious the unity of the All, the world of matter and the world of men, and that consciousness of this unity was the result of setting over against each other things arranged according to their opposites.'

Polarities were valued for the unity they implied rather than for the differences they revealed. The sacrifices at this festival were experienced as a means of repaying nature's gifts, a necessary compensation for human consumption and destruction of the natural world. They restored balance and harmony to the universe and thus acted as a ritual affirmation of the living bond between the human and non-human worlds. Furthermore, 'sacrifice was offered to everything and everything was used in sacrifice; all were bound to serve as offerings and all shared in the offerings, the members of the human group were divided into two groups, just as the things in nature were divided into two categories.'[36] This consciousness recognised no distinction between the sacred and the profane but felt and saw everything as 'holy', or possessed of numinous qualities. Everyone experienced this in sex and honoured it with sacrifice, but a few special individuals were selected to develop a greater awareness and insight into the oneness of nature. These were the Shamanesses, or Wu.

The evidence of Shamanic practices in China dates largely from the time of their repression (beginning as early as the eighteenth century BC.). But it is possible to piece together a rough picture of the nature of Shamanic initiation from the comparative studies by Mircea Eliade of these ancient techniques of ecstasy, as well as from the nature of its condemnation by the patriarchs of Imperial China. Its earliest practice seems to have been almost entirely the preserve of women who learnt to so identify with the natural world that they could spontaneously communicate with the birds and animals, understand their language, sing their songs, and sometimes even assume their forms. The Wu were trained to discover the source from which all life springs by merging with it so that they could direct its flow and understand its manifestations.[37] They had to become instruments capable of expressing the unity of nature. It is not surprising, therefore, that in many primitive cultures Shamen were considered to be androgynous and honoured specifically for the greater power and insights this gave them.[38] Among the Ngadju-Dayak of Borneo, for example, there was a special class of Shaman called *basirs* (meaning incapable of procreation). They were hermaphrodites who dressed and acted like women and were considered to be the intermediaries between heaven and earth since they united in their person the masculine heaven and the feminine earth. In pre-Zhou China the Wu held important positions; they were revered as healers and priestesses and consulted for their insights into the future.

But genuine Shamanism declined with the rise of patriarchal consciousness. There is evidence as early as the eighteenth century BC. that the Wu's drunken revelries were not favoured by the rulers.[39] At the same time, it seems Shamanism gradually degenerated into 'possession' and the proportion of female to male Shamans declined. Finally, in the early centuries of Confucian rule during the Han dynasty Shamanism became the focus of intense repression. Although some Wu of both sexes were given official employment they were classified with the very lowest class of officials. In the eyes of the Confucian bureaucrats persecution was, of course, entirely justified; Shamanism, which included the use of alcohol and the practice of certain sexual techniques in the pursuit of initiation, must have appeared not only grossly immoral and debauched, but also to constitute a considerable threat to the new sober and puritanical consciousness of the patriarchs.

Shamanic initiation was designed to develop insight into the oneness of the natural world symbolised by the Great Mother. With the emergence of a new and more independent consciousness, it is not surprising to discover a change in the values associated with the Mother and with the Earth. Images of Her as the all-nourishing, all-protecting, instinctive benefactress were gradually replaced by those of an all-devouring monster of the West who swallows the sun and is responsible not for life but for death. She became the symbol of all that threatens the development of consciousness, the force which seeks to fetter human progress. As Great Mother of the West, She is portrayed as a fearful creature, with a human face, tiger's teeth and a leopard's tail, who dwells in a cave in the mountain with her hair flowing round Her, ruling over plague and pestilence. Or She is represented as the Old Woman of the Waters responsible for the Great Flood which drowned the world, enveloping it in chaos. A parallel development can be observed in Assyro-Babylonian mythology: Tiamat, the feminine personification of the sea, which gave birth to the world, becomes, at a certain moment, the image of blind primitive chaos 'against which the intelligent and organising Gods struggle'.[40] Hindu mythology also contains ambivalent descriptions of the Goddess: Kali, the divine mother, is represented as eternal womanhood, cherishing mother of the world, but She is also the Terrible Spider Woman, the all-devouring maw of the abyss.

The demise of the positive aspect of the Great Goddess is considerably easier to chart than it is to explain. The manifestations of evolution, both biological and psychological, can be explored and described, but the principle itself can only, it seems, be assumed or intuited. The process which leads to the overthrow of the matriarchal consciousness appears to have its origin in the Fall, the first impulse for knowledge which shattered the Golden Age of the pre-conscious. Under the Great Mother, humanity was ruled and protected by an instinctive wisdom in which higher consciousness was achieved through ecstasy rather than analysis, drunken intuition rather than sober insight. The matriarchal consciousness experienced the interdependence of all creation, the correspondence of human and natural rhythms. Its overthrow brought the beginnings of egoism, private feelings, discord, loneliness and war, but it also brought the possibility for ego-consciousness, independence and free choice. In no sense, however, was the patriarchal revolution itself a free or conscious decision. Indeed, it appears that although evolution may bring greater consciousness and therefore greater freedom, our subjection to it, as a principle of change, is entirely unfree. There is a certain relentlessness with which we are dragged, crying or laughing, through our stages of development from birth to death, a certain tyranny from which we have no escape other than into neurosis or suicide. It seems that Peter Pan dreams are unrealisable in life. Sickness, appears to be the only alternative to following the laws of change and development. This can be observed in the decadence which rapidly overcomes so-called 'primitive' people when their cultures are protected from change and turned into anthropological zoos. For some obscure reason we cannot opt out of psychological development and stand still. The overthrow of matriarchal consciousness is part of this relentless process. Like Zhuangzi we may regret its passing but we cannot preserve it:

> By and by virtue[41] declined. Sui Jen and Fu Hsi ruled the empire. There was still natural adaptation, but the unity was gone. A further decline in virtue. Shên Nung and Huang Ti ruled the empire. There was peace, but the natural adaptation was gone. Again virtue declined. Yao and Shun ruled the empire. Systems of government and moral reform were introduced. Man's original integrity was scattered. Goodness led him astray from Tao; his actions imperilled his virtue. Then he discarded natural instinct and took up with the intellectual.[42]

Implicit in Zhuangzi's catalogue of disasters lie the characteristics of the new consciousness. Instead of unity and natural integrity, politics, classes and conscious moral codes arose; instead of natural adaptation and natural instinct there developed the desire and the capacity for analysis and understanding and instead of a spontaneous unity the seeds of independence and autonomy germinated.

The struggle to overthrow the matriarchal consciousness assumes a variety of forms in mythology, but they share an essential characteristic; they describe the battle to vanquish the old consciousness as a battle to bring order and differentiation into the world, to transform the bisexual Mother into the male and the female. This act of separation is the task of the masculine principle, the son of the Great Mother who rejects Her protection and finally usurps Her authority.[43] In Chinese mythology the battle can be traced in the evolution of dragon symbolism.

Originally the dragon or serpent was associated with the power of the Goddess; as late as the Han dynasty a stone relief was made depicting Xi Wang mu with a snake entwined around Her. She is described in myths and legends as the Dragon Mother who gave birth to the sun god of the east. But gradually She is robbed of Her control over the sun and deprived of the power of the dragon, which becomes the most powerful symbol of the Yang principle. The Emperor, in Confucian China, ruled from the Dragon throne, the supreme emblem of patriarchal authority. Elsewhere the association of dragons and serpents with the Great Goddess is well documented; the famous snake Goddess of Minoan Crete is a familiar example of what was, clearly, a widespread phenomenon. With the differentiation of the bisexual Great Mother into separate male and female principles, the dragon leaves the embrace of the Goddess and becomes the symbol of the newly independent masculine principle. This struggle by the masculine to slaughter the Great Mother is expressed in the Chinese myth of Shenyi (Shen I), whose piercing arrow destroys the power of the Goddess, transforming her into a tame female companion to rule over the moon complementing his own rule over the sun.

One day ten suns appeared in the sky, storms uprooted trees, floods overspread the country. A serpent, 1,000 feet long, devoured human beings, and wild boars of enormous size did great damage in the eastern part of the kingdom. (The East is the domain of the masculine principle in Chinese mythology.) Yao ordered Shenyi to slay the devils and monsters who were causing this damage and gave him 300 men to help him. Shenyi found the storms were caused by Fei Lien, the Spirit of the Wind, who blew them out of a sack. Fei Lien sued for mercy and swore friendship to Shenyi and the storms ceased and Fei Lien killed the Giant Serpent and wild boars (a common symbol of the Great Mother). Another day Shenyi went to a swollen river and shot an arrow into it. The water returned to its source. In the flood he saw a man clothed in white, riding a white horse and accompanied by a dozen attendants. He shot him in the left eye. A young woman was with him, Heng E (Heng O), young sister of Ho Po, the spirit of the waters. Shenyi shot an arrow into her hair. She thanked him for sparing her life and agreed to be his wife. Shenyi, also known as the chief mathematician of all works in wood, had previously been given the secrets of immortality. One day his wife, Heng E, found the pill of immortality by climbing a ladder up to the roof where her husband had hidden it. Swallowing it she fled from Shenyi's wrath into the air. He followed her but a blast of wind struck him to the ground. When Heng E reached the moon, she vomited the covering of the pill which changed into a rabbit, as white as the purest jade. Heng E was popularly believed to be the ancester of the Yin or the feminine principle, rescued from the Chaos of the floods by the sharp arrows of Shenyi. According to tradition, when she went to the moon, Shenyi was given the Palace of the Sun by the God of the Immortals and thus Yin and Yang took up their respective places on the Moon and Sun. On the fifteenth day of each month Shenyi was believed to visit Heng E, causing a conjunction of the two principles. But Heng E was definitely inferior to Shenyi, for it was his daring, his piercing arrow, which rescued her and brought order to the world. So the masculine and feminine polarity entered Chinese consciousness linked to a value judgement which will remain until such time as the importance of the feminine principle, as distinct from the maternal-feminine principle, is recognised.[44]

Whereas the matriarchal consciousness experiences the world in terms of complementarity and unity, the masculine consciousness focuses on differences and hierarchy. The cost of the new way of seeing to women and to the feminine is readily apparent in the *Book of Songs*. Compare, for example, the following two songs:

I

On the moor is the creeping grass,
And how heavily is it loaded with dew!
There was a beautiful man,
Lovely, with clear eyes and fine forehead!
We met together accidentally,
And so my desire was satisfied.

On the moor is the creeping grass,
Heavily covered with dew.
There was a beautiful man,
Lovely, with clear eyes and fine forehead!
We met together accidentally,
And he and I were happy together.[45]

II

Sons shall be born to him:
They will be put to sleep on couches;
They will be clothed in robes;
They will have sceptres to play with;
Their cry will be loud.
They will be [hereafter] resplendent with red knee-covers,
The [future] king, the princes of the land.

Daughters shall be born to him:
They will be put to sleep on the ground;
They will be clothed with wrappers;
They will have tiles to play with.
It will be theirs neither to do wrong nor to do good.
Only about the spirits and the food will they have to think,
And to cause no sorrow to their parents.[46]

These songs chart the rise of hierarchy and masculine supremacy in China. Women, for the first time, were considered impure and isolated in their homes. According to Marcel Granet, sexual rites disappeared from public and religious ceremonies and the significance of community marriages declined, to be replaced by a new focus on elite marriages. 'As all the hallowed powers once set free in the festivals now seemed to be concentrated in the virtue of the lord, so now marriage of the chief appeared to have as much influence on national life as the general celebration of marriage once possessed.'[47] Double standards and the oppression and exploitation of women became the norm, as well as sexual puritanism. Women were regarded as the incarnation of all that was evil, decadent and impure.

A wise man builds up the wall [of a city],
But a wise woman overthrows it.
Admirable may be the wise woman,
But she is [no better than] an owl.
A woman with a long tongue.
Is [like] a stepping-stone to disorder.
[Disorder] does not come down from heaven;
It is produced by the woman.
Those from whom come no lessons, no instruction,
Are women and eunuchs![48]

It is women as the representatives of the Great Mother consciousness, not the feminine, which are the objects of abuse in these songs. This is a crucial distinction. The matriarchal embraces both the masculine and feminine principles in an undifferentiated unity. Her overthrow is the precondition of the separation and development of the two principles in human consciousness. Without Her slaughter the further development of understanding would have been paralysed, for in the incestuous embrace of the Great Mother, humanity would have remained an unwitting prisoner of nature's ways, never her conscious collaborator. Before the slaying of the Mother there may have been greater peace, greater equality between the sexes and greater harmony between people and nature, but there was little freedom of choice, little understanding, little control and little individuality. There may have been no oppression of one sex by the other but there was also no real possibility of relationship. There may have been an instinctive obedience to the ways of nature, to the Dao, but there could have been no conscious knowledge of human and natural laws. For relationship with nature, either external nature or nature of the psyche, as well as relationship between individuals depends on a sense of otherness, an ability to recognise separateness as well as unity. Jungian analyst Ann Belford Ulanov explains the importance of psychological separation for relationship by emphasising the distinction between 'relationship' and 'relatedness'. She writes:

> The psychic urge for relatedness does not have the same meaning as *relationship*. Relatedness means being connected to, in the middle of, involved with, part of; relationship refers to a consciously developed and worked upon relation to the 'other' that needs both distance and differentiation as well as closeness and sharing. Relatedness describes an unconscious drive that operates upon and within a person . . . Relationship presupposes conscious intention.[49]

The creation of the separation necessary for relationship is the work of the masculine principle. So when we are tempted to look nostalgically backwards to the security and peace of the matriarchal consciousness in reaction to the aggression, inequality and oppression of what followed, it is well to remember the disadvantages as well as the advantages of Her rule.

The Great Mother as the dominant consciousness in Chinese culture was overthrown in the interests of freedom and understanding, but this does not mean that Her interest and value is exclusively historical. Her rule and overthrow is recapitulated, as we shall see, in the psychological development of each child. Every individual has had a personal experience of the patriarchal revolution and this 'memory' is of vital significance for the future development of consciousness. The birth of a masculine and feminine way of seeing and understanding the world does not in the end deny the insights of the matriarchal consciousness but, on the contrary, by expanding, deepening and clarifying them, prepares for a later stage of development in which both principles can meet in a psychological marriage leading the individual back to the harmony of the Great Mother and knowing it consciously and freely for the first time.

CHAPTER THREE

The Theory of Yin and Yang

The story of human consciousness begins with humanity's fall from innocence, from a pre-conscious identity with the whole universe. Its early history is presided over by the image of the Great Mother who contains all things and people in her embrace. Slowly the impulse towards independence acquires the necessary strength and momentum to challenge and overthrow the old consciousness and introduce a polarised vision of the world. Mythology represents this battle as the struggle of the male against the female, or the son against the mother, but the association of consciousness with either the male or female begs certain questions about the nature of 'masculinity' and 'femininity'. We need to know what these concepts describe. The researches of anthropologists suggest that the links between sex and gender are considerably more tenuous than was once assumed; the cultural definitions of gender are too diverse to permit a genitally determined definition of masculinity and femininity.

Gender is increasingly acknowledged to be as much a product of culture as of biology.[1] This awareness has performed the valuable function of freeing people, to some extent, from traditional role stereotypes. Women and men are less obliged to perceive and experience themselves, and to model their behaviour according to traditional definitions of 'male' and 'female'. While the old prejudices about a 'woman's work' and 'place' still intrude into discussions of gender and sexuality, and still linger unrecognised and unquestioned in the ideas and emotions of many people, there is increasing theoretical and practical support available to those who choose to challenge the idea that their biology prevents them from developing and experiencing both 'masculine' and 'feminine' psychological and behavioural traits. However, the desire to be free from the restrictive sexual role stereotyping can become as much an inhibition to the development of individuality as what preceded it, particularly when this desire takes the form of rejecting difference in the pursuit of sameness, or undifferentiated oneness. Psychological 'unisex' may have the laudable objective of recognising people first as individuals and only second as sexually differentiated, but it can have the less salutary consequence of denying the existence of the masculine and feminine principles as a crucial polarity in body and psyche. The growth of self knowledge depends, I think, not on restricting discussions of sexuality to cultural patterns or to the arena of chromosomes and hormones, but in exploring the sexual principles at every level of human nature. A premature pursuit of 'unisex' risks taking a short cut to the wrong destination.

The meaning and nature of sexuality, of masculine and feminine as nouns as well as adjectives, remains central to an understanding of the individual. The difficulty lies in finding a framework within which to explore the question. Here is the attraction of Yin-Yang theory. It regards biology as merely one expression of a primordial sexual polarity which lies at the foundation of all existence, cosmic and human, biological and psychological, organic and inorganic. Hence it offers a more productive way of understanding 'masculinity' and 'femininity' and their relation to individual development, as well as providing a framework within which to examine the relationship between sexuality and consciousness. In this chapter the salient characteristics of the theory will be described as a prelude to exploring the influence of Yin and Yang in human thought. A later chapter will look at the implications of this theory for the relationship between biology and psychology.

The history of Yin-Yang theory begins in the obscurity of legend and gradually unfolds during three or four thousand years until its full flowering in the minds of the Neo-Confucian philosophers of the Song (Sung) dynasty (AD. 960–1279). At no point were all the implications and dimensions of meaning of this cosmology tied together into one coherent system of thought, so the following discussion draws, inevitably, from widely different sources and historical periods.[2] It will present a composite portrait of Yin-Yang theory which, as I see it, lies at the basis of much of Chinese thought through the centuries, without always being made explicit. The theory is given different emphases and interpretations by the different schools of Chinese philosophy but I consider that these complement rather than contradict each other, and that the basic conceptions are sufficiently common and fundamental for Yin-Yang theory to be regarded as a central characteristic of Chinese attempts to decipher the riddles of human and cosmic nature. It could be argued that my presentation and interpretations are private fantasies which ignore the very significant differences between the various schools of Chinese philosophy, and project on to certain obscure and ancient texts a theory which they do not contain or, if they do, means something quite different from what I suggest. In support of such an argument the critic can point to my use of texts like the *Yi Jing* (*I Ching*) and the *Dao de Jing*, and argue that these are too old, too complicated and too overlaid with subsequent commentaries, to be interpreted with any degree of confidence. I agree that the ancient texts are extraordinarily obscure and need to be approached with considerable care, but I do not consider this means they should not be approached for fear of the approach being wrong – merely that all interpretations must remain tentative and hypothetical. As I stressed in the introduction, the purpose of this book is not to prove but to stimulate in others new questions, insights and ideas.

Another major difficulty confronting anyone who chooses to explore Yin-Yang in Chinese thought is the different ways this concept is used. At times its function is purely symbolic; it expresses a conception of the cosmos and its manifestations and processes as founded on a primal polarity which generates sub-polarities, all of which reflect in some way the parent principles. An extension of this idea was that all opposites, physical, psychological and spiritual, are either Yin or Yang. This led to the confusing situation in which something could be labelled Yin in one context and Yang in another. For instance, a man could be

Yang in relation to a woman, but Yin in relation to another man if the second man's Yang tendencies were more pronounced than the first man's. This has resulted in much uncertainty and obscurity regarding the two principles. Some people even doubt that they have any value beyond that of symbolising polarities. I do not consider this the case; but to understand the meaning of Yin and Yang it is necessary to separate them from their associations, and explore their fundamental nature as two primal polar principles.

The idea of a primal polarity can be traced to the concepts of 'above' and 'below' found in the earliest sections of the *Yi Jing* parts of the *Book of History*, the *Book of Songs* and on the oracle bones.[3] The Shang people (1751–1112 BC.) were the first to emphasise the polarity of heaven and earth; the earth was not regarded as a base material body in contrast to a spiritual heaven, but, on the contrary, was revered as a numinous power complementary to that of heaven. The oldest ideogram meaning earth shows a tumulus, a sacred spot, on which sacrifices were offered.[4] It was associated with the feminine and valued as more important than its polar opposite, the masculine sky. Later, this scale of values was reversed. A parallel reversal occurred in the qualities attributed to the male and female. The animal symbolism of the early texts indicates that the female was originally associated with change and transformation; later these qualities were considered masculine. Early conceptions of Yin-Yang, the polarity which was to embrace all other polarities and become the central feminine-masculine conception, underwent a similar change in values; the assumption which dominates Confucian thinking, that Yang is superior to Yin was preceded by a time when Yin was unequivocally valued more highly than Yang.

The extreme simplicity of Yin-Yang theory is reminiscent of the saying in *I Corinthians*: 1:18 that 'God hath chosen the foolish things of the world to confound the wise'. While it is the pivotal theory in traditional Chinese thought, so that no aspect of Chinese civilisation, philosophy, government, art, medicine, architecture, personal relationships, sex or ethics has escaped its influence, its salient points can be summarised quite briefly. It teaches that everything is the product of two forces, principles or archetypes, Yin and Yang, whose interaction generates the Five Elements, the wu xing (wu-hsing) (metal, wood, water, fire and earth), which, in various combinations, constitute the foundation of the cosmos in all its forms. Yin and Yang are the polar manifestations of the Supreme Ultimate, the Dao, which by definition, defies description. The process of generation is conceived of as cyclical, an endless beginning and ending, in which everything is constantly changing into its polar opposite. This is Yin-Yang theory in brief. For a clearer understanding of it and the concept of change it implies it is necessary to turn to the *Yi Jing (Book of Changes)*.

The origins and early history of the *Yi Jing* remain uncertain. Fong Yulan, an eminent historian of Chinese philosophy, maintains that it was originally a book of divination, and his opinion is shared by a number of other sinologists, but Helmut Wilhelm argues that it is impossible to know whether its function was originally philosophical or divinatory. Chinese tradition asserts that the linear complexes *ba gua* (pa kua), the eight trigrams, which constitute the foundation of the Yi Jing were first conceived by Fu Xi (Fu Hsi) (2853 BC.), to whom they were revealed by a dragon horse which came up out of the Yellow River with the curious symbols traced on its back. This legendary emperor copied them down and thus acquired the first explanations of the cosmos.[5] Following his reign the eight trigrams underwent extensive and repeated revisions until the time of King Wen (1231–1135 BC.), father of the founder of the Zhou (Chou) dynasty (1150–249 BC.), who is credited with the composition of the *Book of Changes* as we know it. In 1144 BC. King Wen was imprisoned by the Zhou for attempting to introduce social and political reforms, and in prison he began his work on the *Book*. He arranged it into the present order and added the *Duan* texts (the judgements), and it was at this point that the first two hexagrams, *Qian* (Ch'ien) and *Kun* (K'un), were reversed, giving the masculine principle, *Qian*, predominance for the first time over the feminine one, *Kun*.[6]

In the oldest parts of the book the primal polarity is referred to as the Yielding and the Firm, and expressed by a divided and undivided line. It is associated with earth and heaven, female and male, dark and light. In the course of time the polar opposites became known as Yin and Yang, and are first referred to by these names in the fifth chapter of the *Da Zhuan* (*Ta Chuan*), *The*

Great Treatise: 'The light and the dark are the two primal powers, designated hitherto in the text as firm and yielding, or as day and night.'[7] One of the central qualities of this primal polarity is the Change it generates. 'Change' is conceived of as the movements of the Dao and is intended to convey the idea of cyclical development which lies at the centre of human and cosmic existence. As H. Wilhelm explained, the opposite of Change is not standstill, but perversion – a movement contrary to the natural law of development, the growth of what ought to decrease, the downfall of what ought to rule. The principle of Change expresses the essential unity of all things and of the world, since in its course it moves cyclically, introducing what has been under-emphasised in the preceding stage, just as the day introduces the night and summer makes way for winter.[8] The years pass in a process of cycles, the smaller contained within the larger. However, since Change contains an evolutionary as well as a cyclical dimension, each cycle is not the same as the preceding one, nor each year identical with the old year. The evolutionary aspect receives most prominence in some of the Neo-Confucian writings, in particular from Shao Yong (Shao Yung), 1011–1077 BC., who stated that 'everything follows the evolutionary order of the Great Ultimate'.[9] But this aspect of Change, as a principle of development, is also integral to the *Yi Jing* with its conception of the emergence of the myriad from the one, the complex from the simple and wisdom from ignorance.[10]

For those accustomed to regarding unilinear and cyclical direction as irreconcilable, it is difficult to understand how these two concepts could co-exist in one principle. The image of a circle can be helpful in this respect. It is not possible to draw a circle without moving forward, yet the moving forward eventually leads back to the starting point. The beginning of the circle is from one perspective the same as the end, but from another, the two are clearly distinguished by the journey in between. (The image of a spiral conveys this idea better but it was not one the Chinese used). This, according to the *Yi Jing*, is the journey from chaos to order. Western sinologists have tended to focus on the cyclical aspect of the Chinese concept of Change in contrast to their own unilinear conception of history, but the idea of Change, as it is expressed in the *Yi Jing* and developed by the Neo-Confucians, clearly contains both. The *Yi Jing* views civilisation as a systematic and progressive development from simple, undifferentiated beginnings towards a complex structure, and the development of the individual as following a parallel course from ignorance to wisdom, from unconsciousness to consciousness, from unwitting identity with the Dao to knowing the Dao. The momentum for both developments is provided by the interaction of the Yin and Yang. These ideas are also expressed in the *Zhuangzi*:

In the great beginning, there was non-being. It had neither being nor name. The One originates from it: it has oneness but not yet physical form. When things obtain it and come into existence, that is called virtue (which gives them their individual character). That which is formless is divided [into Yin and Yang], and from the very beginning going on without interruption is called destiny (ming, fate). Through movement and rest it produces all things. When things are produced in accordance with the principle (li) of life, there is physical form. When the physical form embodies and preserves the spirit so that all activities follow their own specific principles, that is nature. By cultivating one's nature one will return to virtue. When virtue is perfect, one will be one with the beginning. Being one with the beginning, one becomes vacuous (hsu, receptive to all), and being vacuous one becomes great. One will then be united with the sound and breath of things. When one is united with the sound and breath of things, one is then united with the universe. This unity is intimate and seems to be stupid and foolish. This is called profound and secret virtue, this is complete harmony.[11]

All things comes from the originative process of Nature and return to the originative process of Nature.[12]

The task of the sage, or aspiring sage, is to understand the way in which Change operates, to understand, for example, in what order things occur, and to learn to recognise their moments of germination, maturity and decay. Psychological and political peace depends on this understanding, since it alone can ensure that people act in conformity with the natural patterns of development, and assist, rather than obstruct, their process. As the final hexagram of the *Yi Jing*, the *Weiji* (Wei Chi) (Before Completion) suggests: 'The conditions are difficult. The task is great and full of responsibility. It is nothing less than that of leading the world out of confusion back to order.'[13] The hexagram is composed of the interaction of Yin and Yang lines. It expresses the idea that 'completion' depends on establishing the right relationship between Yin and Yang. Its image is fire over water. Fire flows upward and water flows downward, but harmony depends on creating a relation of complementarity rather than of opposition between the two.

> When fire which by nature flames upward, is above, and water which flows downward, is below, their effects take opposite directions and remain unrelated. If we wish to achieve an effect we must first investigate the nature of the forces in question and ascertain their proper place. If we can bring these forces to bear in the right place, they will have the desired effect, and completion will be achieved. But in order to handle external forces properly, we must above all arrive at the correct standpoint ourself, for only from this vantage can we work correctly.[14]

It is a fundamental postulate of the *Yi Jing* that inner development is a precondition of healthy action in the outside world, not only because we are acting out of confusion until we have harmonised the Yin and the Yang principles within our psyches, but also because of the relation of correspondence which exists between the individual and the universe. The human being, in Chinese thought, is conceived of as an organic part of the cosmos so that her or his thoughts and actions never take place in isolation from the universe but always leave their mark on that world, just as its workings reflect themselves in each individual psyche. As long as we remain ignorant of the principles of Change we shall remain the victims of its processes. The struggle towards wisdom is at the same time the struggle towards freedom. In our ignorance of Change we remain its puppets, but with knowledge we can become the puppeteers.

One of the first steps towards becoming co-creators is learning to understand the relationship between Yin and Yang. As the polar manifestations of the Dao, they are immanent in all things and can never be separated, since the one will always contain the seed of its opposite. A diagram of the eleventh century philosopher Zhou Dunyi (Chou Tun-i) expresses their relationship to each other, to the Dao and to the 'ten thousand things' of creation.

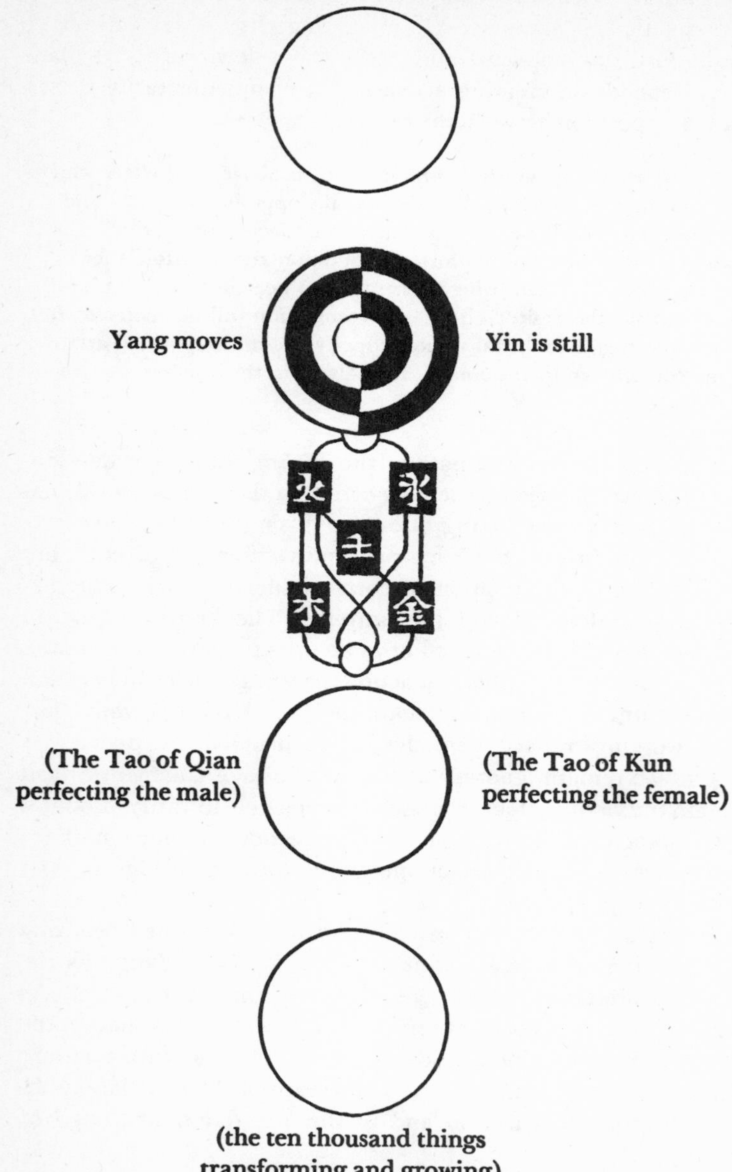
Yang moves
Yin is still
火
水
土
木
金
(The Tao of Qian
perfecting the male)
(The Tao of Kun
perfecting the female)
(the ten thousand things
transforming and growing)

Zhou Dunyi's exposition of his diagram is as follows:

> The true (principle) of that which has no Pole, and the essences of the Two (Forces) and the Five (Elements), unite (react) with one another in marvellous ways and consolidations (ning) ensue. The Tao of the heavens perfects maleness and the Tao of the earth perfects femaleness. The Two Chhi (of maleness and femaleness), reacting with and influencing each other (chiao kan), change and bring the myriad things into being. Generation follows generation, and there is no end to their changes and transformations.[15]

This diagram underlines the essential relativity of Yin and Yang. The one cannot exist without the other any more than there can be day without night or silence without sound. As the *Dao De Jing* says:

> When Everyone recognises beauty as beautiful,
> There is already ugliness;
> When everyone recognises goodness as good,
> There is already evil;
> 'To be' and 'not to be' arise mutually.
> Difficult and easy are mutually realised;
> Long and short are mutually contrasted,
> High and low are mutually posited;
> Before and after are in mutual sequence.[16]

There is an interesting parallel between the *Dao de Jing* and Heraclitus who lived in Greece in about 500 BC. His paradoxes are strikingly similar to those of the ancient Chinese Daoists: 'God is day and night, winter and summer, war and peace, satiety and want.' And 'It is one and the same thing to be living or dead, awake or asleep, young or old. The former aspect in each case becomes the latter, and the latter again the former by sudden unexpected reversal.'[17]

To establish the right relation between Yin and Yang demands more than an understanding of their relativity or of the principle of Change they generate. It is essential also to understand the nature of the two principles. This is not satisfactorily provided by Chinese philosophy, much of which offers schematic explanations which are not really explanations at all, but because they have considerable internal symmetry and poetic beauty, they tend to hinder the pursuit of more complete explanations. Joseph

Needham, whose insights into Chinese science and civilisation are as valuable as they are famous writes that: 'the *Book of Changes* was almost from the start a mischievous handicap' to the development of scientific thought in China. It was 'a system for pigeon-holing *novelty* and then doing nothing more about it. Its universal symbolism constituted a stupendous *filing-system*.'[18] Without the *Yi Jing* it is possible that the Chinese might have hastened their steps towards the industrial revolution; however, the twentieth century, with its highly specialised information, might have been deprived of a framework within which to integrate its insights. The *Yi Jing can* provide the necessary framework, but only if its intuitive insights are examined alongside the discoveries of modern science and psychology. The possibility of doing this is only just beginning, but already modern physics and analytical psychology have contributed much to providing the poetry of the *Yi Jing* with a more coherent dimension, and thereby elucidating the nature and meaning of Yin and Yang.

The generic name for the two principles in Chinese is *Qi* (*Ch'i*). Sinologists have had considerable difficulty in translating this concept into English because they have largely been prisoners of a dualistic conception of the world which divides reality inexorably into matter and spirit, form and space. Within this point of view, the classical Newtonian vision of matter as a concrete phenomenon which forms the building blocks of the manifest world, there is no room for a concept which describes both matter and space. But this is precisely the domain of *Qi*, as Zhang Zai (Chang Tsai), AD. 1020–1077, points out: 'If material force [Qi] integrates, its visibility becomes effective and physical form appears. If material force does not integrate, its visibility is not effective and there is no physical form.'[19] In some circumstances *Qi* becomes form and in others it remains space. This conception of the relativity of 'matter' and space receives some clarification from Fritjof Capra's description of modern physics:

> The high-energy scattering experiments of the past decades have shown us the dynamic and ever-changing nature of the particle world in the most striking way. Matter has appeared in these experiments as completely mutable. All particles can be transmuted into other particles; they can be created from energy and can vanish into energy. In this world, classical concepts like 'elementary particle', 'material

substance' or 'isolated object', have lost their meaning; the whole universe appears as a dynamic web of inseparable energy patterns.[10]

He goes on:

The distinction between matter and empty space finally had to be abandoned when it became evident that virtual particles can come into being spontaneously out of the void, and vanish again into the void . . . the vacuum is far from empty. On the contrary, it contains an unlimited number of particles which come into being and vanish without end.[21]

Modern physics sees matter and energy as part of a single continuum known as the quantum field. The concept of *Qi* appears to be an intuitive recognition of this reality long before there were the scientific instruments with which to observe it. It is the equivalent of the modern quantum field, which is in the constant process of creating and disintegrating matter. But what accounts for the very different forms which the interactions of Yin and Yang produce? As was indicated in chapter one, the Chinese explain that the 'myriad things' result from the different proportions of Yin and Yang in each thing. Zhu Xi said that only the two principles interacting in perfect harmony could reflect the Dao, but all people and things are disharmonious. We are like mirrors in the centres of which are one or two spots of light while all around is black: only a small portion of the Dao can be reflected. This accounts for the one-sidedness of phenomena, including that of human consciousness:

Of phenomena in general, it may be said that if the endowment is great in one direction, it is at the expense of some corresponding defect in another direction, as when tender-hearted men are lacking in the judicial faculty while men in whom the judicial faculty is prominent tend to be tyrannical.[22]

The concept of imbalance plays a prominent role in Jungian psychology, which sees the development of the Self, our true individuality, as dependent on the realisation of all aspects of our nature, in particular the masculine and feminine archetypes. The Self, or psychological wholeness, however, is extremely difficult to realise and it is one of the tasks of the analyst to help us towards a recognition of the underdeveloped aspects of our psyche.

Wisdom and health, according to both Jung and the Neo-Confucians, lies in rectifying the imbalance. Zhu Xi explains that such rectification is possible for humans because the greater degree of balance between Yin and Yang in their natures, compared to animals, allows them the possibility for understanding.

In their earliest forms the characters for Yin and Yang were not the same as they are today.

> They lacked the classifier now common to both meaning mountain 'slope'. [Instead of 陰 陽 they were written 侌 昜]. Originally Yin had only the character for 'cloud' and thus meant 'the overshadowing', the 'dark'. In addition, the idea of life-giving water as a dispenser of nourishment is implicit in the image. The character for Yang shows a yak-tail, or a pennant fluttering in the sun. Thus something 'gleaming in the light', something bright, was meant. The power of command that raises this banner as the symbol of superiority in rank is also contained in this picture, and this added meaning was not lost later.[23]

The classifier meaning 'mountain slope' was added to Yin and Yang at a later date, which gave them the meaning of the dark and light sides of the valley. At this point their relativity became explicit, and they expressed the idea of polarity as constituting the fundamental nature of the world.

The structure of the hexagrams in the *Yi Jing*, which are formed from the combining of the eight trigrams with each other, express the conception of all situations created out of the interaction of Yin and Yang. The sixty-four symbols are built up out of different combinations of the Yin and Yang lines, but the first two, *Qian* and *Kun* are composed exclusively from six Yang and six Yin lines respectively. It is these which reveal most about the different natures of the two principles:

Qian	Kun
䷀	䷁

Qian is usually translated as the Creative and *Kun* as the Receptive, but these translations reveal more about the values of

Confucian thinking than about the essential meaning of Yin and Yang. This is a general problem in seeking to understand the masculine and feminine principles; their essence is frequently obscured by the variety of symbols with which they are associated. It is necessary to distinguish their fundamental qualities from the values attached to the two principles during different historical periods and stages of consciousness, 'Creativity' is an unsatisfactory translation of *Qian* because it is only in certain circumstances that creativity is a monopoly of the masculine. At other times it is the feminine which is creative, and more often both, as in much artistic and cerebral work.[24] However, at the time the *Yi Jing* was being formed by the commentaries of Confucian scholars the masculine principle was, indeed, the creative force, in that it was responsible for the overthrow of the old matriarchal consciousness and the introduction of a new polarised conception of the cosmos. Its association with creativity, and in other contexts with the sun, is testimony to its role as the purveyor of new insights,[25] but for an understanding of the qualities it represents we must look behind the value judgements.

According to the commentaries on the *Qian* hexagram, the masculine is an active, strong force whose energy is unrestricted by any fixed conditions in space and is, therefore, conceived of as motion. Its action is to lend form to the archetypal ideas which exist before creation. In this function it is associated with the rain: 'The clouds pass and the rain does its work, and all individual beings flow into their forms.'[26] The masculine is the principle which leads through its powers of conservation to the 'continuous actualization and differentiation of form'.[27] Its course alters and shapes all things until each attains its true, specific nature. To live in accordance with *Qian* is to bring peace and security to the world through one's activity in creating order. It brings the possibility of seeing with 'great clarity causes and effects'.[28] As the principle of leadership, of order, of differentiation, of individuality, of motion in time and of cause and effect, *Qian* is the polar opposite of *Kun*.

The feminine is the principle of relatedness. It nourishes and embraces all things, giving them uncritical protection and support. 'Embracing all things it becomes bright and shines forth. Its essential characteristic is glad acceptance.'[29] *Kun* is the principle of the earth in that it receives the seeds from *Qian* and brings them to birth. 'While the success of the Creative [Qian] lies in the fact that individual beings receive their specific forms, the success of the Receptive [Kun] causes them to thrive and unfold.'[30] In its devotion it carries all things good and evil without exception. It is the principle of calmness, of reserve, of yielding and of moderation. The movement of *Kun* is an opening out in space in contrast to the idea of direction implicit in *Qian*. 'In the resting, closed state, it embraces all things as though in a vast womb.'[31] It has no need of purpose; everything becomes, through it, spontaneously what it should rightly be. Its characteristics are gentle and accommodating. It is the principle of devotion and the force which gathers things and people together rather than dividing them. One of its symbols is water, the element which creates uniformity and equality, which covers and embraces all things in its still, dark depths.

A comparison of the structures of the two hexagrams further elucidates the difference between them. According to one commentator there are two types of compositional structure in the *Yi Jing*. The first clearly suggests a musical pattern of theme and variations, the chosen theme persisting through the six stages of the hexagram; the other lacks any recurrent leitmotiv, being structured in a mosaic rather than an evolutionary pattern.[32] *Qian* belongs to the first category and *Kun* to the second. Each line of the masculine hexagram contains the seeds of the situation expressed in the following line, whereas the lines of *Kun* do not follow each other in order but instead, fit together as a whole, each revealing a different aspect of the feminine principle. So *Qian* expresses the idea of development in time while *Kun* suggest an acausal spatial principle.

It is now possible to construct a list of the essential qualities of the two principles:

Yin	*Yang*	*Yin*	*Yang*
relationship	individualisation	nourisher	fertiliser
space	time	unity	polarity
community	hierarchy/order	acausal	causal
not judging	judging	spontaneous	planned
purposeless	purpose	oneness	differentiation

This is a highly abstract list. If it is to serve its purpose as an introduction to the respective natures of the feminine and masculine principles, it is necessary to explore their workings at a less abstract level. This will be done in the following chapters which examine the different visions of the world produced by the predominance of each principle in human consciousness. But first it is interesting to supplement the Chinese definitions of the two principles with two other views on this polarity, both of which originated in twentieth-century Switzerland and both of which strikingly endorse the ancient Chinese intuitions. The first comes from Carl Jung; the second from Rudolf Steiner.

Jung's approach to psychology was predominantly empirical. He observed that all human beings have a contrasexual element within their psyches; men, a feminine 'anima' and women, a masculine 'animus'. The principles of the anima and the animus he called Eros and Logos. Eros, the archetype of psychic relatedness, is responsible for joining, involvement and a reaching out from one person to another, or from one aspect of our psyches to another. Logos, in contrast, is the principle of objective interest, the principle of discrimination, judgement, insight and non-personal truth. But implicit in Jung's work is also the notion of the anima and animus as archetypes which cannot be attributed to or located exclusively within the psyche of either sex, but are common to both men and women.[33]

The 'archetype', in Jungian psychology, has caused considerable definitional problems, but one way of beginning to understand its meaning is through the analogy with the instincts. In *The Structure and Dynamics of the Psyche* Jung writes: 'Just as the instincts compel man to a specifically human mode of existence, so the archetypes force his ways of perception and apprehension into specifically human patterns.'[34] Elsewhere Jung explains that archetypes 'direct all fantasy activity into its appointed paths and in this way produce, in the fantasy images of children's dreams as well as in the delusions of schizophrenia, astonishing mythological parallels such as can also be found, though in a lesser degree, in the dreams of normal persons and neurotics. It is not, therefore, a question of inherited *ideas* but of inherited *possibilities* of ideas.'[35]

The anima and animus constitute a polarity in all human

beings, but they are rarely brought into harmonious relationship with each other; usually one is emphasised to the detriment of the second. This accounts for the psychological imbalance which most of us have, and for which we unconsciously compensate by our attractions and dependencies on people or ideologies which represent the undeveloped aspect of our own psyches. Psychological maturity depends, according to Jung, on finding a relationship between these two principles within ourselves. This is the sacred marriage which forms the central motif of many religions and philosophies, and which is the highest mark of psychological development. It cannot take place before the complete differentiation of the masculine and feminine from each other.

Rudolf Steiner's insights developed in a very different way from Jung's. The eldest of three children of a village station master in Austria, Steiner was born in 1861, only a few years after the publication of Darwin's *The Origin of Species*, and was educated in science at an Austrian Secondary School and at the Technical University of Vienna. According to his own account, he was, already by the age of eight, aware of certain realities that differed from those of the material world, phenomena which were as clear to his vision as the things of everyday life, but which were not accessible to touch or physical contact. When he tried to speak about this world, his words met with incredulity, so he chose to remain silent about his knowledge for much of the first part of his life. During his early years he was very preoccupied with the question of the relation between the two realities, the one which most people acknowledged and the other which he alone seemed to see. He became convinced that the discovery of truth depended on developing higher forms of consciousness, which he considered a possibility for certain people at their present stage of evolution and for humanity as a whole, at a future stage. During the first part of his life Steiner worked on the development of his own consciousness, checking and re-checking his insights until, finally, at the beginning of this century he felt ready to begin to publicise his conceptions.

He began the Anthroposophical society, whose name was intended to suggest that wisdom may be found in the knowledge of the human being and its relation to the universe, and furthermore that whereas, in the past, the divine wisdom was imparted to human beings, now the individual must reach towards this wisdom through his or her own efforts at self knowledge. He offered guidance as to how this may be achieved in his book *Knowledge of the Higher Worlds.*

The 'higher worlds', Steiner explains, are not spatially separate regions. They completely interpenetrate the 'lower ones'.

> What divides them is that each world has a more limited and controlled level of consciousness than the world above it. The lower consciousness is unable to experience the life of the higher worlds and is even unaware of their existence, although it is interpenetrated by them. But if the beings of a lower world can raise their consciousness to a higher level, then that higher world becomes manifest to them, and they can be said to have passed to a higher world, although they have not moved in space.[36]

Steiner emphasises that while the attainment of higher levels of consciousness is a normal process which characterises human evolution in the long term, it is, nevertheless, an extraordinarily difficult task for any individual today, and demands a very special moral preparation. The searcher must develop complete humility, a sense of reverence towards the whole world, an inner tranquillity, a realisation of the supreme importance of the inner life of thought and meditation, and an increasing control over the faculties of thinking, feeling and willing. For every one step that is taken towards higher knowledge, he wrote, three steps must be taken towards self-perfection.[37]

Steiner's description of the masculine and feminine principles corroborates and elucidates both those of the *Yi Jing* and of analytical psychology. He identified the masculine as the principle of differentiation, the individualising principles in contrast to the maternal principle of resemblance. 'Forces that bring about resemblances are inherent in the female principle, while all that reduces it, that creates differences, lies within the male principle.'[38] The masculine individualises, specialises and separates, while the feminine tends to generalisation. Steiner is here specifically describing the influence of the two principles on the formation of the physical body, but in another of his lectures he states that the soul, too, is simultaneously male and female, carrying both natures within itself. Precisely what he meant by the bisexuality of the soul is not very clear, but in a series of lectures on the *Study of Man* he describes a polarity working within all psyches which, while nowhere identified with the masculine and feminine principles, contains such marked similarities to his other descriptions of the two, that it may well be a description of them from a different viewpoint. He calls it the polarity of sympathy and antipathy. Sympathy is the force which involves us in the world and with other people, whether by love or hate or anything in between. Antipathy separates us from the world, creating the possibility for memory, perception and cognition. In animals, Steiner says, the forces of sympathy are much stronger than that of antipathy. So if human beings had no more antipathy for their environment than the animal, they should be much more intimately connected to nature than they are.

> The animal has much more sympathy with his environment, and has therefore grown together with it much more, and hence is much more dependent on climate, seasons, etc, than the human being is. It is because man has much more antipathy to his environment than the animal that he is a personality. We have our separate consciousness of personality because the antipathy which lies below the threshold of consciousness enables us to separate ourselves from our environment.[39]

From Steiner's comments, antipathy seems to be a different description of the principle which emerged during the Great Mother stage of consciousness, bringing about an increasing separation of humanity from its environment and a corresponding development of individual consciousness. Antipathy permits the losing which is a precondition of new finding, or the differentiation which is a prerequisite of a new relationship and unity. The formulation of Yin-Yang theory could not have taken place without this birth of the masculine principle and the polarity in consciousness it created.

But while the rudiments of a conception of the world based on the polarity of Yin and Yang began to emerge as long ago as the second millennium BC., its insights were never wholly reflected in a single school of Chinese philosophy. Most schools, even to a large extent the remarkable philosophical synthesis of Zhu Xi, emphasised, in their interpretations of human and cosmic nature, one principle to the detriment of the other. The Confucians tended to focus on the process of polarisation inherent in a polar conception of reality, while the later Daoists and *Chan* (Ch'an) or Zen Buddhists concentrated on the unity which underlies polarity. The one-sidedness had its advantages; it helped to allay the constant danger in Chinese thought of harmony being pursued before the achievement of a sufficient differentiation of the masculine and feminine poles. It is even arguable that it did not go far enough; a sense of the unity of all creation tended to outweigh, in Confucian as well as in Daoist philosophy, an appreciation of difference. The consequence was a kind of suffocating interdependence, comparable at a personal level to the simplistic interpretation of marriage as being the creation of one body on four legs rather than the free relationship of two individuals. But the seeds of a truly polar conception of the world, one which gives equal weight to the differences and the unity, were present in Yin-Yang theory. Before exploring the two poles in Chinese thought, the main points of the theory may be briefly re-stated.

Yin-Yang theory, which receives some affirmation and elucidation from modern physics and analytical psychology, argues that there are two cosmic principles, the masculine and the feminine, inherent in all phenomena and responsible, by their interactions, for the emergence and dissolution of all things. Sexuality is, therefore, a cosmic or archetypal phenomenon, which expresses itself, in different forms, in all creation, from the level of the inorganic through to the level of human consciousness. Since Yin and Yang are responsible for both the manifest and non-manifest worlds, they describe a world in which mind and body, space and form, constitute different expressions of one continuum, rather than irreconcilable opposites. Since, also, they are the polar manifestations of the Dao, the principle lying behind all creation, the pursuit of physical and mental health, as well as wisdom, depends on the attainment of a harmonious relationship between the two principles. Human nature can only reveal itself in its essential wholeness when Yin and Yang are brought into conscious communion with each other. The precondition of this is their differentiation from an undifferentiated Dao. Human consciousness has the possibility of finding wholeness if it learns to recognise the principle of development inherent in the Changes of Yin and Yang. This involves a gradual evolution, moving cyclically from chaos to order, from undifferentiation to differentiation. It is a development in which the Dao is divided into Yin and Yang by the active, separating energy of Yang, which, in turn, calls forth its polar opposite, the feminine principle. The dialectical relationship of the two principles leads to their increasing polarisation, but not, if the laws of Change are allowed to follow their course, to their irreconcilable alienation.

CHAPTER FOUR

The Masculine Consciousness

The birth and development of the masculine principle in consciousness revolutionises humanity's experience of itself and of the world. Instead of participating instinctively in the rhythms of nature, being contained and regulated by her laws, a consciousness emerges, which assumes that people, not nature, should be primarily responsible for structuring human life. It seeks to differentiate itself from the old pre-conscious identity with the cosmos and replace the previous acceptance of control by unknown natural forces and law with the ambition to tame and order nature through understanding her. Such a consciousness searches for independence, autonomy and freedom. It pursues these aims through the development of a number of characteristics and skills which, in different ways, all express the central differentiating impulse of the masculine, or Yang, principle.

The urge to separate from nature's hegemony and become the arbiter of one's own destiny is a relatively new phenomenon in human history. It seems unlikely that it became dominant in any culture much earlier than four thousand BC. and in a time-scale of human development which reaches back millions of years, six thousand years ago is strikingly recent. It remains basically a mystery why individuals, followed by groups of people, in certain societies began to experience themselves and their relation to the world differently; but there are sufficient indications from various parts of the world that this indeed happened.[1] A radical change in human consciousness began which was to have important implications for the future evolution of humanity. One way of exploring its nature is to examine the thinking and values of its promoters in one of the cultures which experienced this revolution – Chinese society. The two schools of traditional Chinese thought which most clearly reflect the new masculine consciousness are Legalism and Confucianism.

The Chinese Communists have consistently declared themselves the enemies of Confucianism. They condemn the package of theories and superstitions which provided, they argue, the main ideological foundation for the extreme oppression and exploitation suffered by Chinese men, apart from members of the ruling élite, and by Chinese women of all social classes. They credit themselves with having provided a much more humane alternative to Confucian rule. But their attitude towards Legalism, the traditional enemy of the Confucianists, is more ambivalent; while acknowledging the élitism and exploitation integral to this school of thought, they have attempted to clear away the abuse heaped on it by generations of Confucian scholars and to re-assess its fundamental contribution to the Chinese people. Their studies express an admiration for the Legalists' attack on ancient superstitions and archaic thinking patterns, and praise them for introducing a new rationalism into Chinese political thought and for advocating a greater independence for humanity from the whims and dictates of the gods, the exchange of nature's rule for human rule. Furthermore they honour the Legalists for their success in establishing the first united Chinese empire.[2] But behind this guarded praise there may be another reason for the Communists' recognition of Legalism's contribution to China; in certain significant ways, the Communists, Legalists and Confucianists all share a common approach to humanity and the world.

Their definitions of good government are clearly different. The Legalists favoured a tightly structured system founded on a strict body of laws which were enforced by rewards and punishments designed to keep all sections of society firmly in their place. The Confucians maintained that good government depended on rule by those who had made the most progress in the development of their moral and reflective minds, and the Communists believe that since government should serve the interests of the working people – 'the masses' – by providing the most favourable circumstances in which they can improve their material conditions, political power should be given to those who have demonstrated themselves most capable of understanding and promoting these interests. In political theory, therefore, the differences between the three schools are obviously fundamental. In the evolution of human consciousness, however, there is a sense in which all three are expressions of the masculine principle. Each advocates the need for control and order, and argues that these depend on a prior differentiation and analysis of the differences between the human and natural worlds, and between people themselves. They praise activity over passivity and discrimination and reason over intuition and imagination, and all three value a hierarchical and critical rather than an impartial, accepting and yielding approach to humanity and nature.

Legalism represented an extreme development of the authoritarian ideas of the Confucian philosopher, Xunzi (Hsün tzu) who lived in the third century BC. The brainchild of Han Feizi (Han Fei-tzu), Shang Yang and Li Si (Li Ssu), it provided the foundations for the unification of China under the Qin (Ch'in) in 221 BC., and for an empire which was to last, though not without breaks, for more than two thousand years. A central administration was set up and China divided into thirty-six commanderies which were themselves subdivided into prefectures. A system of private landholding, with equal, impersonal laws and taxation which had been developed first in the old Qin state before it achieved dominance, was extended throughout the empire. The hereditary aristocracy of China (about 120,000 families) was collected together at the capital to separate it from the roots of its power, weights and measures were unified, coinage and, to facilitate transport, even the axle lengths of wagons standardised. Li Si, chief administrator of the Qin, standardised Chinese characters, the style of Chinese composition acquired a form which scarcely changed during the subsequent two thousand years, and in 213 BC., he completed his rigorous pursuit of uniformity with the infamous Burning of the Books, designed to eradicate all heterodox literature and thought. The only texts spared the flames were utilitarian ones on medicine, agriculture and the divinatory *Book of Changes*. Within a remarkably short time China was transformed from a collection of warring states into a unified empire. But the dynasty which had achieved this was shortlived; after only 15 years the first empire collapsed, overthrown by the oppressed and exploited peasantry. Its fall marked the end of the first and only experiment in exclusively Legalist rule.

Central to Legalism was the idea that man rather than nature, conscious control rather than the instincts, the present rather than the past and hierarchy rather than equality should provide the basis of the social, political and economic order. It argued that since there is no evidence of any essential morality in human nature, a rigorous system of laws, backed by an equally rigorous system of rewards and punishments was the safest, most disciplined and therefore most rational way of ensuring political stability, protecting humanity from the ravages of nature and from the unreliability of its own feelings. The Legalists were unequivocally opposed to all expressions of the instincts. Sex, therefore, became the target of a series of strict edicts and regulations. When Qin Shi Huangdi (Ch'in Shih Huang Ti) unified China greater sexual freedom between men and women still existed in border and coastal regions.[3] The Qin dynasty did their utmost to wipe out all 'impurities' and to regularise sexual practices. Adultery, for example, was severely punished. A stone inscription of the time reads:

> If a widow with a son remarries, she is faithless and unchaste. The sexes are strictly separated, licence is forbidden, and men and women are pure and honest. If a man commits adultery, it is no crime to kill him; thus men must observe the proper rules of conduct. If a woman elopes with her lover, her son may disown her; thus women become chaste and good.[4]

The Legalists stressed the value of measurement, classification and clear organisation, and maintained that laws and regulations should take precedence, at all times, over sensitivity or consideration for the circumstances of a particular person or situation. This was sometimes taken to extremes, as the following anecdote from the Han Feizi, a third century BC. text, indicates:

> Once in the past Marquis Chao of Han got drunk and fell asleep. The keeper of the royal hat, seeing that the Marquis was cold, laid a robe over him. When the Marquis awoke, he was pleased and asked his attendants, 'Who covered me with a robe?' 'The keeper of the hat,' they replied.
>
> The Marquis, thereupon, punished both the keeper of the royal hat and the keeper of the royal robe. He punished the keeper of the robe for failing to do his duty, and the keeper of the hat for overstepping his office. It was not that he did not dislike the cold but he considered the trespass of one official upon the duties of another to be a greater danger than the cold.[5]

While this story highlights the potential inflexibility of Legalism, it is important not to underrate the contribution of order, clarity of thought and powers of discrimination and differentiation for a people still powerfully influenced by the undifferentiating, holistic power of the Great Mother consciousness.

Although the Qin state collapsed, the spirit of Legalism constituted an integral part of the ideology of most subsequent dynasties including its successor. Founded by a peasant rebel leader Liu Bang in 206 BC., the Han dynasty marked the emergence of Confucianism as a state orthodoxy, a position which it retained, apart from some significant interludes, for much of the following two thousand years until the abolition of the examination system in 1905, which heralded the collapse of the Qing (Ch'ing) dynasty, and the end of the imperial system. In 175 BC. the Confucian Classics were carved on stone, and in 124 BC. Emperor Wu Di established the first imperial university designed to train bureaucrats in the new orthodoxy.[6] During the following centuries, notably from the eighth century onwards, the proportion of officials who gained their posts through examinations gradually came to exceed those who won them through purchase or nepotism. This did not mean that the link between wealth and office was entirely severed, because education was always expensive, so that those with large landholdings or official positions, and usually both, were in the most favourable position to finance the education of their sons or clansmen. It did mean however, that the empire was increasingly run by an elite trained to see and interpret the world through Confucian lenses. A passport to the ruling class became conditional on proficiency in the new masculine consciousness.

Confucianism as the state orthodoxy was a composite ideology, an amalgam of Legalist beliefs in hierarchy and firm control through absolute laws, with the ideas of Confucius, his disciple Mencius and the Neo-Confucians of the Song (Sung) dynasty, tenth to eleventh centuries AD. (See glossary). That such a synthesis of Legalism and Confucian thought was possible was due less to the complementary nature of the ideas of the two schools than to the similarity of the consciousness behind them.

Rationalism is the dominant note in Confucianism. The neo-Confucian philosopher, Cheng Yi (Ch'eng I), AD. 1033–1107 wrote: 'All things in the world can be understood in the light of reason. Each entity works according to its principle or the order of nature. In each, therefore, there is reason.'[7] Confucius himself reserved some of his severest rebukes for irrational behaviour: 'There are two things,' he said, 'I do not understand; women, and the common people. And I fail for the same reason to understand them: if you are stand-offish with them they resent it, and if you are familiar with them they take advantage of it.'[8]

Dislike and oppression of women and the feminine became one of the foundations of the Confucian state. A famous poem by the third century AD. poet Fu Xuan (Fu Hsuan) reads:

> How sad it is to be a woman,
> Nothing on earth is held so cheap.
> Boys stand leaning at the door
> Like Gods fallen out of heaven.
> Their hearts brave the Four Oceans.
> The wind and dust of a thousand miles.
> No one is glad when a girl is born:
> By her the family sets no store.

The history of the Chinese empire from the third century BC. Qin dynasty to the Qing (AD. 1644–1911) and particularly from the Song dynasty (AD. 960–1279) onwards, is in part the story of the gradual deterioration in the position of women. Sometime during the tenth or eleventh centuries, coinciding with the growing urbanisation of Chinese society, foot-binding was introduced along with an increase in concubinage (secondary wives), and the strengthening of the social rules against the remarriage of widows among the ruling class. The power of the masculine, and the authority of men over women continued largely unchallenged during the following centuries. In late Ming (seventeenth century) and Qing law if a woman was found guilty of a crime she was placed in the custody of her husband and not imprisoned.[9] The *Nu-jie* (Nü-Chieh) (Woman's Precepts) written by the woman Ban Zhao (Pan Chao) in the first century AD. became the basic text for the education of women. It taught them to be gentle and sedate, constant and quiet, chaste and orderly, to be careful in their conduct, and to adhere to the rules in all their actions, and since it considered women inferior to men, it taught them to serve and revere the male and cultivate an attitude of humility towards them.

To the Confucians the world was an entirely rational phenomenon and they argued that since the supreme principle, the Dao, was reason, and since each person reflected the Dao, humans can all, by virtue of their reflective and rational minds, understand the secrets of the universe. 'For a man to give full realization to his heart is for him to understand his own nature, and a man who knows his own nature will know heaven.'[10] But the decision to comprehend one's own nature was not a free choice; on the contrary, the Confucians considered it a social duty. Everyone, they believed, should develop his reflective mind not only so that he can create order and tranquillity in the midst of the conflicting claims on his passions and emotions, but also so that he will be able to put the world in order. The Confucian 'gentleman', (the *chün tzu*), could not be a recluse quietly pondering the secrets of the universe in some leafy retreat. He had to involve himself actively in public life. There could be no fulfilment for him in isolation from his fellow men, for what defined his humanity was his moral sense, his inborn sense of mission to make the Dao prevail in the world. The desire for social or political responsibility was seen as a natural corollary to a mature and healthy psyche. To be true to himself the Confucian gentleman had to devote some part of his life to helping and guiding others.

Reason, in Confucian usage, implied the capacity to understand an intelligible world; it was by no means an exclusively cerebral exercise. Confucianists considered the rational mind essentially a moral mind involving the feelings as well as the thoughts. By thinking, the mind distinguishes between different aspects of the psyche as well as between different situations and people in the outside world. By feeling, it distinguishes between right and wrong and experiences the emotions appropriate to the circumstances. They believed it was the development of this mind which distinguished humans from animals. According to Mencius: 'whoever is devoid of the heart of compassion is not human, whoever is devoid of the heart of shame is not human, whoever is devoid of the heart of courtesy and modesty is not human, and whoever is devoid of the heart of right and wrong is not human.'[11] To understand in this sense it is necessary to evaluate as well as to discriminate. Without the capacity for evaluation, Mencius warns, we may make the error of 'caring for one finger to the detriment of the shoulders':

> A man loves all parts of his person without discrimination. As he loves them all without discrimination, he nurtures them all without discrimination. If there is not one foot or one inch of his skin that he does not love, then there is not one foot or one inch that he does not nurture. Is there any other way of telling whether what a man does is good or bad than by the choice he makes? The parts of a person differ in value and importance. Never harm the parts of greater importance for the sake of those of smaller importance, or the more valuable for the sake of the less valuable. He who nurtures the parts of smaller importance is a small man; he who nurtures the parts of greater importance is a great man. Now consider a gardener. If he tends the common trees while neglecting the valuable ones, then he is a bad gardener. A man who takes care of one finger to the detriment of his shoulder and back without realising his mistake is a muddled man. A man who cares only about food and drink is despised by others because he takes care of the parts of smaller importance to the detriment of the parts of greater importance. If a man who cares about food and drink can do so without neglecting any other part of his person, then his mouth and belly are much more than just a foot or an inch of skin.[12]

The emphasis on discrimination in Confucian thought extended into every sphere of life. Mencius said: 'It is the nature of things to be unequal . . . If you equalize them all, you will throw the world into confusion.'[13] This led to a concept of graded love and duty.

Between father and son Confucians maintained there should be affection, between ruler and minister there should be righteousness, between husband and wife attention to their separate functions, between old and young order, and between friends faithfulness. The Confucians believed that every relationship had its appropriate feelings and strongly condemned the suggestion of the fifth century BC. philosopher, Mozi (Mo-tzu) that the interests of the world could best be served if everyone would love every other person as much as he or she loved himself.

The moral feelings so important to Confucianism must not be confused with the passions. While these come and go, leaving chaos in their wake, genuine moral feelings arise from the centre of our nature and, like correct thinking, guide and clarify rather than mislead and confuse. They can imbue our actions with confidence, direction, dignity and freedom. But it is not always simple to distinguish between these pure feelings and subjective emotions. To do so demands a high degree of self-knowledge and this, Confucianism teaches, is the pre-requisite of all wise thinking and action:

> If others do not respond to your love with love, look into your own benevolence; if others fail to respond to your attempts to govern them with order, look into your own wisdom. If others do not return your courtesy, look into your own respect. In other words, look into yourself whenever you fail to achieve your purpose.[14]

And again:

> 'Benevolence is like archery: an archer makes sure his stance is correct before letting fly the arrow, and if he fails to hit the mark, he does not hold it against his victor. He simply seeks the cause within himself.'[15]

The *Yi Jing* teaches a similar lesson. It suggests that the way out of seemingly impossible situations lies in self-examination: 'While the inferior man seeks to put the blame on other persons, bewailing his fate, the superior man seeks the error within himself.'[16] Only by freeing ourselves from control by vested interests and unconscious compulsions can we discover the kernel of our being that can see, think and feel clearly, know not only what needs to be done but also how and when to do it. This is the mind.

Its realisation within the individual is the Confucian goal, the hallmark of the sage.

The masculine approach to knowledge through discrimination, analysis, and evaluation depends for its effectiveness on precise and meaningful concepts. An arbitrary language, or one used carelessly, obstructs such a path of understanding. Confucius was deeply concerned with this matter. He considered that while words contain genuine meanings which reflect certain absolute truths in the universe, most people have lost contact with these truths and so use language to suit their own convenience. This led, he felt, to lax thinking, erroneous judgments, confused actions and finally to the wrong people acquiring access to political power. He argued that the rectification of names was the pre-requisite of good government, for until people can rediscover the true meaning of such concepts as 'benevolence', 'humanity' or 'righteousness' it will remain impossible to understand, develop and practise these virtues. In a conversation with his disciple Zi Lu (Tzu-lu) he explains what he means:

> Tzu-lu said, 'The ruler of Wei is waiting for you to serve in his administration. What will be your first measure?' Confucius said, 'It will certainly concern the rectification of names.' Tzu-lu said, 'Is that so? You are wide of the mark. Why should there be such a rectification?' Confucius said, 'You! How uncultivated you are! With regard to what he does not know, the superior man should maintain an attitude of reserve. If names are not rectified, then language will not be in accord with truth. If language is not in accord with truth, then things cannot be accomplished, if things cannot be accomplished, then ceremonies and music will not flourish. If ceremonies and music do not flourish, then punishment will not be just. If punishments are not just, then people will not know how to move hand or foot. Therefore the superior man will give only names that can be described in speech and say only what can be carried out in practice. With regard to his speech, the superior man does not take it lightly. That is all.'[17]

The masculine consciousness, in the form in which it developed in traditional China, offered, to the élite, a liberation from the previous instinctive and emotional bondage to nature. It provided them with a way of understanding the cosmos instead of being enslaved by it, of directing and planning their own lives instead of being the unwitting participants in nature's designs, and of discovering their own individuality and inner freedom instead of being compelled by the collective impulses of the group. Through the masculine, men acquired a hitherto unknown possibility of creating their own society according to their own conceptions of order and justice.

In practice, of course, the potential of this new consciousness was only realised by a small minority. Even for most of the ruling class Confucianism was probably more important as a means of securing wealth and status than as a way of psychological and intellectual liberation. These people parrotted its principles but missed its message. For the millions of Chinese peasants, and for women of all classes, the influence of the masculine consciousness was unequivocally negative. Confucianism was fundamentally hierarchical and anti-feminine. Confucius' disparaging observations on women and the 'common people' quoted above set the tone for two thousand years. His disciple, Mencius was quite explicit about the relationship between the rulers and the ruled; 'There are those who use their minds and there are those who use their muscles,' he wrote. 'The former rule; the latter are ruled.'[18] The virtue of the rulers is 'like wind; the virtue of the common people is like grass. Let the wind sweep over the grass and the grass is sure to bend.'[19] Most of the time the grass complied with the demands made on it by the wind, the manual workers submitted silently to their task of feeding the landlords and bureaucrats, but not always. At intervals throughout the history of the empire, parts, or all, of China were convulsed in rebellion. When this happened the rebels, not surprisingly, rarely looked to the ideology of their exploiters for inspiration but turned instead to the ancient Mother consciousness for the emotional ammunition with which to attack the abuses of the hierarchical, male-dominated Confucian system.

The importance of supernatural omens, faith healing, collective sexual orgies, ritual drunkenness, Shamanistic ecstasies and other expressions of the matriarchal consciousness are most apparent in the rebellions of the early part of the empire. The Yellow Turbans and Five Pecks of Rice revolts in AD. 184, both of which claimed descent from Xi Wang Mu (Royal Mother of the West), and the rebellions against the Sui dynasty in AD. 613 are notable examples. In later centuries the appeal of the old consciousness with its emphasis on intuition and ecstatic identification with nature, rather than sober understanding and organisation, diminished; but it never entirely disappeared, as is illustrated by the extraordinary success of the White Lotus secret society which provided the foundation for the major White Lotus rebellion of 1795. This important secret society whose roots probably reach back to the fourth century AD., revered the 'eternal venerable mother without birth,' the Virgin Mother honoured by the matriarchal consciousness as the source and Protectress of all creation.[20]

It was not only in peasant rebellions that the Great Mother consciousness resurfaced into public life to challenge the growing power of the masculine. There were also intellectuals and poets who turned to drink, to sexual orgies and to shamanism to rediscover and celebrate the oneness of humanity and nature. The strongest sentiments in much of their writing are an anti-intellectualism, nostalgia for psychological identity with nature, for anonymity, reverence for the instinct as opposed to the thoughts, longing for spontaneity, and love for the natural as distinct from the human world, for country rather than urban life. The following three poems suggest some of the flavour of their ideas:

On Returning to Live in my Own Home in the Country by Tao Qian (T'ao Ch'ien) AD. 376–427, translated by Andrew Boyd

From my youth I was never made for common life
My nature was ever to love the hills and mountains.
By mischance I fell into the dusty world
And, being gone, stayed there for thirteen years.
A captive bird longs for the woods of old,
The fish in the pond dreams of its native river.
So I have returned to till this southern wild,
To a simple life in my own fields and garden.
Two acres of land surround my home,
My thatched cottage has eight or nine bays,
Willow and elm shade the courtyard,
Peach and plum spread in front of the hall.
Dim, dim in the distance lies the village,
Faintly, faintly you see the smoke of its chimneys.

A dog barks deep in the long lane,
The cock crows on the top of a mulberry tree.
There is no dust and no confusion here,
In these empty rooms, but ample space and to spare.
So long have I lived inside a cage!
Now at last I can turn again to Nature.[21]

Question and Answer Among the Mountains by Li Bo (Li Po), AD. 701–762, anonymous translation

Asked why I lodge in the green mountain
I smile, and in my heart's ease I do not answer.
The flowing stream carries the peach-blossom far away.
It is another world – not of men.[22]

The Fisherman: to Magpie Bridge, anonymous author and translator

A rod in the moonlit breeze,
A grass cape in the misty rain;
My home is west of the fisherman's jetty.
Even selling fish I shun the city gate;
How could I venture still deeper into the dusty world of cares?
When the tide rises I slip the mooring;
At high tide I take the oars;
As the ebb-tide falls I return home singing.
Some mistake me for a recluse like Yan Guang;*
But I am only a nameless fisherman.[23]

(* Yan Guang (Yen Kuang) was a fellow student of the first emperor of the later Han dynasty, Guang Wu (Kuang-wu) AD. 25–57. On his accession, Yan Guang changed his name and became a recluse, steadfastly refusing the Emperor's offers of appointment.)

The contrast between the poetry of the eighth century AD. poet Li Bo, (Li Po) and that of his close friend, Du Fu, (Tu Fu) offers an illuminating insight onto the differences between the matriarchal and patriarchal consciousness. Li Bo was a Daoist wine lover who, according to an apocryphal story, drowned when he reached for the reflection of moon in drunken ecstasy while boating. Almost all Li Bo's poems are 'to some extent dream-poems; many of his longer ones spirit-journeys, for which he had precedents in ancient poems related to the trances of mediums in early Chinese religious dances.'[24] Du Fu's life and verse is quite different. While

Li Bo's recurring symbol is the reflected light of the moon at night, Du Fu's is the phoenix, the Fire Bird. While Li Bo retired from public life to enjoy his dreams, Du Fu's life as a minor official and poetry show, among other things, his public responsibility, his concern with developing a conscious selflessness and his love of heroes. Many of his poems are inspired by the public events of his time, and he, himself, scarcely distinguished his poetic from his political ambitions.

The appeal of the Great Mother consciousness never totally died in traditional China. Her spirit attracted many of those who rejected or were excluded from the advantages of the masculine consciousness and the urban-based system of government it inspired. But the archaic matriarchal consciousness is inappropriate for the creation of political, social and economic institutions. A precondition of their formation is the recognition that humans, by virtue of their capacity to discriminate, think and organise, can free themselves to some degree from an instinctive subservience to nature and thereby acquire a certain independence. No political system can be established by those who still experience themselves and others as inseparably bound to nature. Peasant rebels in traditional China never entirely resolved this dilemma. While they often inspired their followers with memories of an ancient, more communal way of life, free from the inequalities, exploitation and authoritarian practice of the Confucian elites, when they came to create their own organisations they were unable to separate the new consciousness from the system which it had influenced, and formulate an alternative political theory. They focused their attacks on what they considered to be the abuses of the Confucian system rather than on the system itself. As a result the effect of peasant rebellions in China, until the nineteenth century, was largely beneficial rather than destructive to the status quo; they provided the excuse for a thorough spring-cleaning of the system, sometimes through a change of dynasty, and thereby acted as the agents of reform rather than revolution. This situation did not alter fundamentally until the Communist revolution in the twentieth century.

The Chinese Communists offered an entirely new system of government in place of the old rule either by Confucian bureaucrats or local warlords. They turned upside down, or abolished, many of the traditional values and practices; manual work, for example, became respectable and ancestor worship unrespectable; co-operative, communal and state ownership of land and property replaced private holdings and landlord-tenant relationships; a marriage law introduced qualified freedom of marriage and divorce; women were liberated from the power of fathers, husbands and sons and acquired, in principle, equal rights in all things; child marriage, foot-binding, and infanticide were prohibited, and education as well as the right to participate in the political process ceased to be the privilege of the elite and became the fundamental right of every individual.

The social, economic, political and ideological differences between traditional and contemporary China are immense, yet in their praise for analytical thinking, reason, discrimination, evaluation, individual responsibility, personal initiative, self-reliance, and control of rather than subservience to nature, the spirits of Confucianism and Chinese communism are similar. But whereas under the old order the advantages and disadvantages of the masculine consciousness were largely confined to members of the ruling elite, under the present system they are being rapidly extended to the whole people. Nowhere, ironically, is this more apparent than in the Communist definition of women's liberation. The central slogan of the movement has always been 'anything a man can do a woman can do'. Women are encouraged to excel in traditionally male jobs in industry, agriculture, medicine, teaching, science and engineering. They are expected to take an active part in decision-making and, like men, are taught from an early age to devote their energies to developing the rational, organising and discriminating sides of their natures at the expense of their more intuitive, imaginative, receptive, maternal and passive qualities. In practice women have not yet achieved full equality with men; they are still to be found doing many of the lower-paid jobs, or identical jobs for lower wages, and they are rarely found in the higher echelons of power. Moreover, women are still expected to take the major responsibility for children and domestic work alongside their other jobs. Nevertheless it is quite clear that for the first time in their history, Chinese women have begun to experience some of the independence, self-respect and personal responsibility which are an expression of the differentiating impulse of the masculine in consciousness.

The Chinese Communist party has given everyone the right to a secure livelihood by allowing the masculine principle unchallenged supremacy in all forms of social, political and economic life. But this has been executed within very rigid controls designed and protected by the Party. While the Chinese people are encouraged to become self-reliant, to use their own initiative, to accept responsibility for their own relationships and personal lives, to control rather than be controlled by nature, and to understand rather than passively accept what happens to them, the power to decide how society should be structured, to assess the priorities, to formulate the laws and, in every sense, to exercise the ultimate authority, rests firmly in the hands of the Communist party and its representatives at the head of the social and political institutions which rule the country. Contemporary China is therefore a transitional stage in the development of the masculine consciousness from its position in the Confucian order as the acknowledged privilege only of the elite, to its realisation by every individual. The implications of this final stage for the society may be as revolutionary as the earlier overthrow of the traditional order or the ancient patriarchal revolution, for when every individual fully experiences the masculine principle, he or she discovers a personal centre of authority and analyses, organises, controls and creates his or her own life according to this inner source of knowledge rather than according to the dictates of an external group, institution or ideology. For the masculine principle does not only help us to differentiate the world in which we live, to discriminate between the different aspects of nature, to classify and order, it also leads us to an experience of our essential individuality. It gives us the certainty that we stand utterly alone in this world, unsupported by institutions, personal relationships and ideologies, or by identities of race, sex and class. It brings the extraordinary and often alarming knowledge that we can look to no one and no thing other than ourselves for directions and answers. To discover and live with such a consciousness is to stand entirely naked in the world, able only to say that 'I am I' and to know that this is not an impoverishment of our nature, but that in as much as it reveals to us the inner essence of our being, it is the portal to freedom and the beginning of self-knowledge.

Such a peak of self-realisation, hinted at by Confucianism though rarely attained by Confucianists, implies a concept of individuality distinct from the notions of eccentricity and anti-social or freakish behaviour often associated with this concept. The individual becomes someone who is no longer possessed or controlled by 'external' things – people, institutions, ideas or subjective passions – but one who has discovered the centre of being is his or her own authority. Such a level of self-knowledge and individuality reveals that loyalty to the self does not encourage isolation from humanity and from nature, or the pursuit of self-interest at the expense of others, but on the contrary, it suggests that the destiny of each person is intimately involved with the destiny of the world, that love of self is love of others and service to self, service to others. Jung wrote:

> Again and again I note that the individuation process is confused with the coming of the ego into consciousness and the ego is in consequence identified with the self, which naturally produces a hopeless conceptual muddle. Individuation is then nothing but ego-centredness and auto-eroticism. But the self comprises infinitely more than a mere ego, as the symbolism has shown from of old. It is as much one's self, and all other selves, as the ego. Individuation does not shut one out from the world but gathers the world to oneself.[25]

But a recognition of this interdependence of the individual and the world cannot arise until the insights of the masculine meet with the insights of the feminine. When this happens the lonely 'I' becomes something much more: without losing its uniqueness the human being acquires intimations of a sense in which he or she is both separate and, at the same time, a reflection of a much larger 'I' which embraces not only all humanity but all creation.

An awareness of the feminine consciousness is valuable to all stages of the development of the masculine. But at the beginning its importance is likely to be less significant, for here the urgent need is to differentiate from the Great Mother consciousness and acquire independence and autonomy. To stress the polar principle at this moment might well encourage its confusion with the undifferentiated bisexual Mother. But once sufficient independence from the old consciousness has been achieved, societies, just as much as individuals, need the complementary influence of the feminine if they are to avoid the human cruelty, oppression, ecological destruction, and psychological impoverishment which can result from the urge to dominate nature and repress the instincts. If and when the Chinese begin to feel that it is time to pay a little more attention to the neglected areas of their group and individual psyches they will not have to turn to other cultures for their understanding. They will be able to look back instead into their own history and rediscover the feminine principle as it lived in the consciousness of some of their greatest poets and writers.

CHAPTER FIVE

The Feminine Consciousness

Jung was the first of the modern psychologists to understand the feminine as an archetype inherent in the psyches of both women and men. Freud and some of his followers, like Erik Erikson, relied primarily on the physical body for their clues to the feminine psychology, while others, like Karen Horney and Margaret Mead asserted the primacy of sociological factors in the formation of 'femininity'.[1] Jung denied that 'feminine' and 'masculine' are only psychic reflections of either biological or cultural phenomena, and argued that they are psychic principles present in both sexes. He considered that the feminine is not confined to females, nor the masculine to males, but that all individuals have the potential for self-realisation which involves the recognition and development of both sexual principles within the psyche.[2]

Recent years have witnessed a growing acknowledgement of Jung's insights; a number of studies of the feminine have appeared, prompted in part by the recognition that many of the psychological, political and social problems of our time can be directly attributed to misunderstanding, denigration and neglect of this principle.[3] However, our understanding of the feminine in consciousness remains in its infancy. Jung, as we saw in chapter three, described it as the principle of relatedness in contrast to the masculine principle which he associated with discrimination, judgment and relation to non-personal truth.[4] Jungian psychologists, like E. Neumann, Esther Harding, A. B. Ulanov and I. de Castillejo, offer further insights into the feminine principle, its components and manifestations at different stages of psychological development. But they do not offer a comprehensive portrait of the feminine consciousness. They do not answer the question of what it means to experience and see the world through the eyes of the feminine, as distinct from the matriarchal and patriarchal consciousness.

The elusiveness of the feminine is only partly a reflection of its nature; primarily it is an expression of its neglect. The attempt to explore and re-evaluate it as a way of seeing is beset with difficulties. Confusions abound and this situation will probably continue to a greater or lesser extent until more people have realised this principle within themselves. Premature attempts to define the feminine could inhibit rather than assist its understanding. This chapter will indicate a few of the difficulties attending its study and suggest, through the context of traditional Chinese culture, some of the ways the feminine expresses itself in consciousness.

One common misunderstanding about the feminine is the idea that it is synonymous with the unconscious, that it constitutes everything which has been disparaged, repressed or neglected by the dominant analytical, rational and discriminating masculine consciousness. This has encouraged in some a reverence for all kinds of impulsive behaviour in the name of the feminine and a tendency to respect unconscious rather than conscious actions. But the feminine is no more intrinsically unconscious than the masculine. Both have their origin there, but both are equally capable of conscious understanding and expression, and both depend on these for their maturity and value. To respect the unconscious in the sense of acknowledging the existence of psychic dimensions of which the individual has no conscious knowledge, and of developing sensitivity towards them is essential for the attainment of self-knowledge. Furthermore in a masculine-dominated culture, and at a certain stage of psychological development, many of these unrealised aspects of the psyche are likely to be feminine ones. But to identify the unconscious with the feminine itself is to limit the feminine to a stage of impulsive and chaotic expression and, thereby, to perpetuate its elusiveness and obscurity. Only by gradually bringing it to a greater consciousness is it possible to develop a freer relationship to the feminine: while it remains unrealised it will continue to influence our thoughts and feelings in ways beyond our knowledge, comprehension and control.

A second obstacle to understanding the feminine principle is the polarisation of thinking and feeling along sexual lines that has occurred under patriarchy. Joseph Campbell writes that it is a characteristic of the masculine to divide the world into pairs of opposites, one of which is preferred to the other. This, he says, is a 'solar mythic' view, since all shadows flee from the sun. In the 'lunar mythic' view, which is the more naturally feminine one, dark and light interact in the one sphere – the interplay of opposites creates wholeness.[5] The masculine consciousness encourages analytical, rational and organisational skills in men at the expense of all other forms of thinking and feeling. Masculine *feelings* such as assertiveness, self confidence, and all those which reflect independence and self-control and those which promote discrimination and moral values are respected or tolerated but it is masculine *thinking* which consistently receives the loudest accolades. In women the reverse is true: instead of being encouraged to be thinkers, women have been taught, by patriarchy, to develop the maternal aspect of their feeling nature at the expense of the rest of their psyche.

The consequence of this is the conventional association of women with the feelings and men with the mind. The women's movement has challenged these traditional role stereotypes. Increasing numbers of women and men are angry at the psychological and political repression engendered by a consciousness which regards a certain type of thinking as a male prerogative, rewarding it with wealth and power and relegates to women the role of procreation, domestic and sexual service. But some sections of the women's movement are in danger of strengthening the consciousness it purports to attack. Instead of urging a new and wider definition of thinking and feeling to include both the masculine and feminine principles uninhibited by a value system which regards thinking as superior to feeling, or masculine thinking as superior to feminine thinking, they have largely restricted their demands to securing equal rights for both sexes to develop the masculine thinking and feeling sides of their natures, and to freeing women from the obligations of motherhood. Their actions are thus not very different from those of the peasant rebel who overthrows his landlord, expropriates the estate and then assumes in his place the title and role of landlord. Obviously, there is a certain liberation to be derived from this action but to the extent that it still perpetuates the master-slave situation the freedom is limited. Women may win a more respected place in society but the strength of the consciousness which exalts masculine thinking over feminine thinking, and all thinking over feeling, will remain intact.

The only effective challenge to the hegemony of the masculine in consciousness is one which confronts not only the relative power positions of men and women, but also the relative power positions of thinking and feeling and their gender associations which provide the foundation of these positions. It is necessary to recognise that thinking and feeling are neither intrinsically feminine nor masculine; but that in both as well as in the physical body of the human being, there is a polarity of the two principles, and that health and psychological maturity of the individual depend on the realisation of both poles at each level. As one Jungian, Ulanov, describes it:

> The feminine is half of human wholeness, an essential part of it, without which wholeness is impossible. Wholeness means both poles, both modes, and wholeness is not simply identification and fusion but polarity and union. We need both poles to understand either one because each is involved in the development and completion of the other. These complementary poles mean maleness and femaleness, not as directly characterising men or women but as sets of qualities which describe the two sexes symbolically.[6]

Ulanov explains that masculinity and feminity must be seen 'as two modalities of separating the ego out of the original unconscious matrix, of giving oneself to the world and others, and of making the world for oneself'. Masculine and feminine elements exist only in relation to each other and complement rather than fight each other. Feminine and masculine, then, are archetypal principles of the human psyche whose polarity and complementarity are to be found in the interaction of both sexes and in the interaction within a single person of the ego with the anima or animus. In becoming whole the individual must grow into a conscious relationship to the masculine-feminine polarity within.

The workings of the masculine and feminine principles in the body as well as in feeling and thinking have received certain acknowledgement from some psychologists, philosophers and sexologists, but the polarising tendency of the masculine, a negative expression of its influence in consciousness, often prevents us from recognising and developing both principles. Our eagerness to discover one answer to the question 'Who are we?' to label it as right and all others wrong, has encouraged the development of one principle at the expense of the other. The present debate about the female orgasm is an excellent example of the dangers inherent in the 'either-or' approach. In the last few years a number of books have argued that the clitoral orgasm is the fundamental female sexual response, and that the most efficient way to achieve it is through direct clitoral stimulation. Any other form of sexual excitement is, they imply, inferior. We may tolerate or even welcome vaginal stimulation, but if so we are probably deriving our pleasure more from pleasing our partners, from being 'good', passive females, than from our natural sexuality. Implicit sometimes in this approach to sexuality is the assumption that the most important aspect of making love is deriving the maximum personal pleasure irrespective of one's lover's likes and dislikes. The idea and feeling that sex can be a loving exchange, an erotic relationship between two people in which body and mind act together, and that giving sexual pleasure may be as pleasurable and satisfying as taking, is often confused with ideas of self-abasement and servility. Obviously in a culture which regards men as the takers and leaders and women as the givers and followers, the association of giving and yielding with oppression is likely, and in the process of challenging such cultural assumptions it is clearly necessary for women to acquire greater confidence in defining their likes and dislikes to themselves, to each other and to men. However it is also necessary, at a certain point, to recognise that striving towards clitoral or penile orgasm is not the whole story. Sex can also involve receiving and giving physical and emotional caresses, and, ultimately, meeting the wholeness of the other person with the wholeness of oneself. The implications of the arguments of the 'clitoral school' are just as alarming as Freud's contention that the mature feminine response is vaginal, not clitoral. In the space of fifty years both views have been expressed with equal ferocity, and two generations of women have been encouraged to feel insecure about an important part of their bodies. The early generation learnt to repress their clitoral feelings, the later to master the clitoral orgasm and neglect the vagina. The result has been much confusion, misery and dependence on an authority other than personal thoughts and experiences for both sexes.

However, this dramatic swing of the sexual pendulum also has its advantages. It is considerably easier now than before for women to recognise that the advocates of both the vaginal and the clitoral schools have some right on their sides. Furthermore, the uncertainty in people's minds which the debate between the two has encouraged is beginning to have the beneficial effect of forcing women to look to themselves for the answers instead of relying on the 'ones who know'. This can lead to the liberating conclusion that female sexuality is not clitoral or vaginal, but both. Through the clitoris women can experience their masculine, active, focused, goal-oriented sexuality, and through the vagina their yielding, waiting, rhythmical all-embracing and pervasive sexual response. In becoming alive to both the masculine and the feminine principle working through their bodies, the sexual lives of women can become richer and more balanced, their sexual response freer and more flexible. To discover both the yielding and the active aspects of the body is to be capable of experiencing a wider variety of sexual experience, to be able to demand less from relationships and to enjoy them more.

A similar one-sidedness is apparent in thinking, whether publicly in philosophy or privately in individual thought patterns. Alan Watts in *The Book on the Taboo Against Knowing Who You Are* argued that all philosophical disputes can be reduced to an argument between those who are 'tough-minded, rigorous, and precise, and like to stress differences and divisions between things', and those 'tender-minded romanticists who like wide generalisations and grand syntheses, and stress the underlying unities. The first group, he says, prefers the idea of particles to waves and discontinuity to continuity as the ultimate constituents of matter, while the second prefers the concept waves.[7] This polarity in consciousness leads to diametrically opposed political philosophies. Those influenced by the masculine favour structuring society according to hierarchies kept in place by rigorous control and discipline, while adherents of the feminine approach advocate the way of passive impartiality. They trust in the underlying unity and harmony of all creation and the spontaneous capacity of people to know what is right for themselves. A story in the *Zhuangzi* indicates how little the feminine consciousness can find to praise in the masculine way of political rule.

> One day Poh Loh appeared, saying, 'I understand the management of horses.' So he branded them, and clipped them, and pared their hoofs, and put halters on them, tying them up by the head and shackling them by the feet, and disposing them in stables, with the result that two or three in every ten died. Then he kept them hungry and thirsty, trotting them and galloping them, grooming, and trimming, with the misery of the tasselled bridle before and the fear of the knotted whip behind, until more than half of them were dead . . . Those who govern the empire make the same mistake.[8]

The masculine political philosophy, in this case Confucianism, argues for the necessity of grooming, trimming and putting a halter on society. The feminine argues that this kills nature's ability to reveal its own way and people's abilities to become sensitive to their own psyches.

The feminine way of government is through service and stillness, through allowing the Dao to manifest and following it. This is clearly expressed in certain passages in the *Dao de Jing*, in which the imagery is taken from observations of nature's way. For instance:

> The reason why the River and the Sea are able to be king of the
> hundred valleys is that they excel in taking the lower position.
> Hence they are able to be king of the hundred valleys.
> Therefore, desiring to rule over the people,
> One must in one's words humble oneself before them;
> And, desiring to lead the people,
> One must, in one's person, follow behind them.
> Therefore the sage takes his place over the people
> Yet is no burden; takes his place ahead of the people
> Yet causes no obstruction. That is why the empire
> supports him joyfully and never tires of doing so.

> It is because he does not contend that no one
> in the empire is in a position to contend with him.[9]

Each consciousness examines the world through different lenses and therefore sees different worlds. Since we are still very far from having discovered which is right, or even whether either, unaccompanied by the insights of the other, can be correct, it would seem more prudent not to restrict our vision and understanding of ourselves and the world by adopting either consciousness at the expense of the other, but, instead, develop both so as to create a richer, more composite picture.

There is another important disadvantage in relying exclusively on either the masculine or feminine consciousness: it can inhibit the development of that consciousness itself. Neither principle can realise its full potential without continual reference to its opposite. This expresses itself psychologically in a number of ways. 'If a man fails to develop his relation to . . . [the] female element in himself, he suffers at least a partial diminution of being and at worst, a serious mental illness.'[10] The same is true of women. A person excessively controlled by the masculine discriminating principle may feel, at a certain point, that life has lost its meaning. He or she may oscillate violently between arrogance and despair, experiencing a growing alienation from other people and from the self, as the masculine continues to differentiate unaided by the complementary influence of the feminine to experience and reveal the connections and relationships. Such a person becomes psychologically marooned, incapable of building bridges either to the neglected areas of the psyche or to other people and nature. Psychological growth becomes impossible because new insights, feelings and ideas are prevented from entering consciousness by the rigid, divisive influence of the masculine. The psyche stagnates. Aridity, meaninglessness and a total lack of any sense of direction ensue. At such a point only the feminine attributes of listening, yielding, accepting, waiting and trusting, and the capacity of surrender to the outside world as well as to the inner promptings of the unconscious, can re-vitalise the psyche. The feminine alone can nourish the lonely dried-up ego and create the necessary relationships to inner and outer nature as well as to other people which can restore meaning and purpose to life.

A similar psychological stagnation and imbalance can result

from and excessive reliance by the conscious mind on the feminine principle. It drags consciousness into a mystical ocean of sameness, a bog in which all differences are submerged, all identities lost. The person becomes an intellectual and emotional cripple, without the capacity or will to act and think as an individual and at the mercy of every outside demand or influence. An awakening of the masculine principle is necessary to give the person a sense of self, of independence, and the ability to discriminate, essential for understanding. And as with the masculine, by relying too heavily on the feminine we eventually lose it. It can only live and develop in consciousness by being continually explored and developed in relation to its opposite; otherwise it is not the feminine which expresses itself in the psyche, but an undifferentiated chaos. We need the masculine to be able to focus and understand the different feminine qualities.

Instinctively we may express some aspects of the feminine, but to know her nature and, more importantly, to learn to recognise the appropriate moments to allow her expression, we must have already acquired a good relationship to the masculine in consciousness. To understand the feminine at every level of our nature, and thereby to have a free rather than obsessive or compulsive relationship to her, depends on continual reference to her opposite. 'Over-awareness of diffuse feminine values may paralyse us and make action impossible, in the outer world. On the other hand a too-focused consciousness may render the wisdom from the feminine layer of our psyche, invisible, and burn it up with too bright a flame.'[11] It seems that the feminine in consciousness is dependent, for its realisation and maturity, on a prior development of the masculine. The conventional saying that the masculine leads and the feminine follows which, in its indentification with gender has caused considerable oppression to both sexes, acquires in the specific sense of the relation between the two principles, new and important value.

A notable example of the dangers inherent in the search for the feminine unassisted by the masculine skills of analysis and discrimination is the identification of the matriarchal consciousness with the feminine. The discovery of the feminine depends, first of all, on the capacity to distinguish her from the matriarchal experience. The Great Mother rules over a pre-polarised consciousness, a time or stage of psychological development when everything appears to be embraced in one undifferentiated unity. Under Her there is no need for relationship, as the masculine consciousness has not yet split human awareness into subject and object, mother and child, or male and female. The Great Mother consciousness does not know individual identities, but experiences everything as part of the whole: She focuses not on the separate parts but on the unity which underlies them. But with the birth of the masculine consciousness this ancient way of seeing is overthrown by the introduction of an 'I' and 'Thou' experience. Through this, individuals gradually become conscious of a distance between their conscious and unconscious minds, between the inner and outer worlds and between humanity and nature. This initial separation has two important consequences for the development of human consciousness: internally, it generates the capacity to say 'I' to oneself and 'You' to others, which is an expression of self-consciousness; externally, it leads to an emphasis on exploring the world in terms of differences rather than unities. This is a psychological precondition of the creation of social, political and economic structures. The emergence of a feminine consciousness whose salient characteristics are those of recognising and helping to create relationships, of being receptive and recognising harmony, depends on a prior differentiation by the masculine principle of human awareness; we cannot receive, integrate and harmonise before discovering the separate parts both in the outside world and within our own psyches.

The distinction between the old matriarchal consciousness and the new feminine one can perhaps be clarified through the analogy of the mother and infant. As long as the young child knows no distinction between itself and its mother, but identifies with her, *is* her, it is controlled by the matriarchal consciousness. But the mother can recognise the distinction between herself and the infant. She protects, nourishes and embraces the child with her love, and although she may receive occasional glimpses of the child's consciousness, moments in which her world and that of the child fuse, she is usually conscious of her own separation from the infant she holds. In her mothering she expresses the maternal aspect of the feminine principle, not the matriarchal consciousness.

A one-sided development of either the masculine or feminine principle has another significant consequence for our psychological and intellectual health: it encourages the phenomenon termed 'projection'. This is the process by which we unconsciously project onto other people, things or ideologies, those aspects of ourselves which we have not yet acknowledged, developed, and owned ourselves. The most familiar example of this is the obsession which usually accompanies being 'in love'. A person whose feminine side is unrealised will often 'fall in love' with the feminine which she or he 'sees' in another person, and similarly with the masculine. The experience of being 'in love' is one of powerful dependency. As long as the projection appears to fit its object nothing awakens the person to the reality of the projection. But sooner or later the lover usually becomes aware of certain discrepancies between her or his desires and the person chosen to satisfy them. Resentment, disappointment, anger and rejection rapidly follow, and often the relationship disintegrates. This is a bleak moment, but it is also a potential turning point, offering an opportunity to understand ourselves and, sometimes, to remake the relationship on a freer basis. The difficulties and pain involved in doing this may prove too strong a deterrent, in which case we may react with a rebound relationship, thus clambering back on to the same old merry-go-round of projection and disappointment. But if we can explore our own psyches we may discover within ourselves those qualities we fell in love with by way of our lover. As this happens we begin to see other people a little more clearly. We are freed from some of our needs to make others what we want them to be, and can begin to love them more for what they are.

Though necessary projection not only obscures and undermines personal relationships, it also distorts our vision of other things. Political allegiances, for example, may be prompted by a projection, and neither the fanatical adherent nor the cases she or he claims to support can benefit from this. Ideological projections work in the same way as personal projections in relationships. Just as a woman whose masculine principle is more highly developed may be attracted to the feminine element in other men and women, and be drawn by this attraction into emotional relationships, so people can be unconsciously attracted to ideologies which they feel emphasise those qualities unrealised or less realised in themselves. Some of the emotional support for aspects of Chinese ideology in the 1960s may be seen as an example of this process of projection. Images of a communal, selfless socialism with an emphasis on a holistic approach to ecology and social organisation, in which every person was seen less as an isolated struggling individual than as servant of the whole community, exercised a magnetic hold over many western people suffering from serious neglect of their feminine psyches. They saw in China all that is whole and humane. But this projection blinds them to the other aspects of Chinese socialism which are somewhat less humane and certainly less harmonious. Chinese policy, as was mentioned in chapter four, is primarily intent on promoting the masculine approach to social, political and economic life. It is eager to further the development in the Chinese people of their capabilities for discrimination, organisation and, at least, limited personal responsibility, and to encourage them to control their own instinctive and unconscious nature as well as to control the outer natural environment. To see the Chinese concern with ecology, for example, as a reflection of the reverence for the links between the human and natural worlds and an understanding of the ultimate oneness of the universe is a gross misunderstanding. The Chinese policy on ecology, where it exists, derives from their realisation that pollution eventually boomerangs on human society. The consequences of ecological concern may be similar in the short term whatever the motives behind them. But from the perspective of the development of human consciousness, the decision to protect the environment because this will make it more productive, a more efficient servant of human needs, is quite different from the decision to take care of it out of an appreciation of the profound interdependence between human and natural worlds.

At this point in Chinese history it may be right for the masculine consciousness to be dominant, but judging whether this is so will be difficult for observers and sinologists caught up in some form of projection. For projections blind us to the real nature of the 'other', whether this be another person or a political system. They impel us to see and value in others what we need in ourselves. The unconscious starting point for political or personal commitment born from projection is the assumption that 'what is right for me is right for the other', or, alternatively, 'what is wrong for me is wrong for the other'. Negative projections often work in the same way; we dislike in others what we dislike or fear in ourselves.

Projections impede our judgments and imperil our relationships, and yet they determine many, if not most, of our emotions. As people begin to recognise this, their first reaction is frequently to lose confidence in their feelings, to turn away from them, relying instead on their thoughts. But a purely intellectual, abstract and quantifiable approach to life does not get us very far. Logic can throw up a number of ideas, possible solutions and courses of action, all of which appear eminently rational and sensible. But logic cannot always provide the explanations and directions. These demand an awareness and respect for the feelings, a capacity to listen, trust and act on them as well as the thoughts. Our culture places a considerable premium on thinking, but it offers little guidance for the education of feelings. This we are left to do alone.

The first step is often to withdraw the projections so that it is possible to feel another person or situation unencumbered by personal likes and dislikes. This requires a rigorous appraisal of all feelings to determine their origin; the capacity, for example, to ask such questions as whether we are loving the other person or only an unrealised aspect of ourselves. The first time this is consciously undertaken it can feel as though the feelings are being deliberately exterminated, but usually the reverse is true. Instead of impoverishing the feelings, the withdrawal of a projection makes space for new feelings, hitherto obscured by the strength and urgency of our own sympathies and antipathies. Once we have ceased to be obsessively 'in love', and have created a distance between ourselves and the other person by beginning to disentangle what we want to see from what there is to see, we can begin to love that person freely with a love which benefits and enriches her or his life as well as our own, a love which demands nothing and expects nothing in return.

But if this new freedom is to last, the mere withdrawal of projections is not sufficient; we also have to satisfy the needs which prompted them — if the projection was an aspect of the masculine, the capacity to analyse, for example, then the person must develop this capacity in her or himself. Though this requires effort and time, there need be little confusion about what it is that is being learnt. But if the need is to develop an understanding of the feminine principle, things are not so simple. While our culture is replete with opportunities to train the masculine side of our natures, it notably lacks equivalent opportunities to develop the feminine. Apart from the maternal aspect, most people are somewhat confused about the nature of the feminine principle. Clues sometimes exist in the projection itself, but more often these only indicate a general direction or area, the precise nature and location of which remain obscure. The seriousness of the prevailing ignorance and neglect of the feminine is beginning to receive the acknowledgement it deserves, and the second half of the twentieth century may prove to be an important turning point in the understanding of the feminine principle. But if this is to happen it is necessary to acquire a much clearer understanding of the feminine. It is helpful to look to those who have already searched, and so it is to some of these people, living and writing in traditional China, that I now turn for intimations of the feminine. Ultimately, each person has to rely on him or herself to transform these intimations into something more personal and more coherent.

There is an old Chinese story called 'The Rainmaker' which evokes the spirit of the feminine consciousness. It concerns a remote Chinese village stricken with drought. The harvest is in danger and the people face starvation. The villagers pray and sacrifice, but no rain falls. Eventually, in desperation, they send far afield for a rainmaker. When the little old man arrives they ask him what he needs to perform his magic. 'Nothing,' he replies 'except a quiet room where I may be alone.' He lives quietly there for two days and on the third day it rains.

The magic of the Rainmaker is his capacity to *allow* things to happen rather than to cause them. The villagers had been frantically trying to *make* the rain come; the Rainmaker simply created space for the rain to fall. Because he willed nothing and asked nothing, he exerted a very different influence from the deliberate, organising impulse of the masculine, and revealed by his example that not everything can be forced, some things have just to be allowed to happen. These things we cannot order or control; for them we have simply to wait, and to allow them the possibility of being. Allowing things to happen, including in one's own soul, allowing them to work and develop by themselves in their own way, rather than organising and manipulating, was a central concept in Daoism, and later in Zen Buddhism. It was expressed through the character 自 然 'by itself so', sometimes translated as spontaneity. Another concept used to express this idea was *Wu Wei* which roughly means 'not imposing, not doing anything contrary to nature'. This is the way of non-interference and acceptance which has been praised by poets throughout the centuries. Jung, too, laid special emphasis on it. A woman once talked to him about some of her problems and ended by asking him, 'What do I do about all this?' 'Just wait,' he answered 'and whatever you have to do will come to you.' In a few years it did.[12]

Jung understood that people can only go a certain distance towards actively resolving their problems. A moment may come when action is useless, or even destructive, and the best thing is to do nothing, to wait. During such a time it is important to recognise that passivity is an act of faith, not an expression of despair. Trust is central to the feminine consciousness. Its lack is what propels individuals into premature decisions, urges them to interfere with and inhibit other people and situations which need time and space to develop in their own way.

But to trust in the right things happening at the right moment is not easy for those trained to believe that the directive consciousness should always be in control, and to fear the yielding, receptive way of the feminine. Trust involves a capacity to recognise that there is a sense in which we do not decide and choose things, a sense in which life lives us just as much as we live life. It is the capacity to surrender the individual ego to a meaning and direction which may not, at first, be intelligible, which we have not consciously chosen, and over which we appear to have very little control.

Waiting, trusting, yielding and allowing are the preconditions of being able to receive, which is another characteristic of the feminine. The ancient Daoists placed a high value on this capacity, and they recognised that receptivity is impossible while the mind is choked with ideas, and the feelings disturbed by emotions. It is necessary to learn how to listen, to be supple, weak and unobtrusive. The Chan, or Zen Buddhists also selected the principle of still receptivity as their central message. Chinese civilisation was at least two thousand years old when Buddhism first arrived in the first century AD. At the root of this Indian philosophy lies the realisation of the total elusiveness of the world. To grasp it, measure it or hold on to it is to miss it. For to Buddhists the world is a constantly transforming unity in which nothing is separate from the whole. Suffering arises from defying the nature of the universe by trying to do the impossible – holding and grasping. This includes desires, since to desire something depends on having defined something to be desired, and since definitions depend on otherness, desires belong to a fragmented world. Nirvanà is the way of life and the state of mind which ensues when the clutching has ceased and wholeness is experienced. It cannot be attained because there is no thing to be attained. Thus Buddhism, in its purest form, is a philosophy of attentive being with no aims and no desires. Nirvana is complete identification with the world. This idea is expressed in the Chinese character for *Chan* (Zen). It is composed of two parts, one meaning 'singleness' and the other the 'universe', hence together it means 'becoming one with the universe.'[13]

The origin of Zen Buddhism is unclear. It was probably the creation of Daoists and Confucianists. According to its own traditions, an Indian monk, Bodhidharma, arrived in China in AD. 520 and proceeded to the court of Emperor Wu of Liang, a patron of Buddhism. This monk is considered the first patriarch of Zen Buddhism. However Zen's history only begins to be documented with the sixth patriarch – Hui-neng (AD. 637–713). For the following 200 years (during the Tang dynasty) it flourished, and Zen monasteries became leading centres of Chinese scholarship.

Hui-neng taught that the truth is what comes to those who yield: it is a gift which cannot be grasped, given or defined, but one which is present in each moment, which *is* each moment. If we pursue it, it will elude our grasp, but if we can surrender completely to the moment we may experience the 'Way'. 'Letting go' became the way of the Zen practitioner. It meant allowing the thoughts which come into the mind and obscure it to disappear, not by repressing them, but by letting go of them. Lin ji (Lin-chi), a Chinese master, advised adepts to follow a life in which everything is done quite simply at the right time: 'When it is time to get dressed, put on your clothes. When you must walk, then walk, when you must sit, then sit.'[14]

> Just be ordinary and nothing special. Relieve your bowels, pass water, put on your clothes, eat your food. When you are tired, go and lie down. Ignorant people may laugh . . . but the wise will understand . . . As you go from place to place, if you regard each one as your home, they will all be genuine, for when circumstances come you must not try and change them.[15]

Lin ji taught adepts to let go of all attachments and concepts so that they could begin to taste without savouring, to hear without judging the sound, to touch without pressing, to carry without holding on, and, finally, to love without possessing.

Surrender to the world, receive it in your stillness. This is the advice of the Daoists and the Zen Buddhists. Interestingly it is also the lesson Thomas Henry Huxley (1825–1895), the agnostic advocate of Darwin's concept of evolution, draws from science: 'Science seems to me to teach, in the highest and strongest manner, the great truth which is embodied in the Christian conception of entire surrender to the will of God. Sit down before fact as a little child, be prepared to give up every preconceived notion, follow humbly wherever and to whatever abysses Nature leads, or you shall learn nothing.' Joseph Needham comments on this that 'any ancient Daoist philosopher could have said it, and no Confucian would ever have understood.'[16] Obviously science demands more than simply the capacity to surrender; among other things, one must also be able to analyse the information received. But a pre-condition of new insights is to open and humble the self towards the world, to let go of preconceived opinions and 'established facts' so as to make space to see, feel and think new things.

The surrender of the ancient Daoists was a form of silent contemplation, not a contemplation which makes use of a subject-object relationship to the world, but a way of being and observing in which there is no duality of seer and seen. The Chinese word for this is *Guan* (kuan). *Guan* brings understanding through a reflective identification which involves feelings as much as thinking. *Guan* reveals the quality of things not revealed through quantifiable analyses. It is complete clarity and presence of mind – an active passivity. Intellectual knowledge and understanding take us only part of the way towards deciphering the mysteries of the universe. The philosopher and mathematician Alfred North Whitehead (1861–1947) wrote: 'When you understand all about the sun and all about the atmosphere and all about the rotation of the earth, you may still miss the radiance of the sunset.'[17] The masculine consciousness registers information, analyses and classifies it. The feminine, on the contrary, conceives an idea, walks round it, loving participates in it, letting it grow quietly from within until it is ready to be born into the world. As Ulanov wrote: 'The quality of the feminine ego activity is to accept a conception, to carry knowledge, to assimilate it, and to allow it to ripen. It is a way of submitting to a process, which is seen as simply happening and is not to be forced or achieved by an effort of the will.'[18] Such a way of knowing and understanding cannot be tested and proved in the conventional sense. It can scarcely be communicated verbally. But without it we are likely to miss the radiance of the sunset, and finish up instead with not much more than a catalogue of facts.

The feminine consciousness has been described by Irene Claremont de Castillejo as diffused, in contrast to the masculine 'focused' consciousness. Castillejo writes:

> Focused consciousness has emerged over thousands of years from unconscious, and is still emerging. All our education is an attempt to produce and sharpen it in order to give us power to look at things and analyse them into component parts, in order to give us the capacity to formulate ideas, and the capacity to change, invent, create. It is this focused consciousness which we are all using in the everyday world all of the time. Without it there would have been no culture and no scientific discoveries.

But there is another form of consciousness, 'a diffuse awareness of the wholeness of nature where everything is linked with everything else and [people] feel themselves to be part of an individual whole . . . here lies the wisdom of the artists, and the words and parables of prophets, spoken obliquely so that only those who have ears to hear can hear and the less mature will not be shattered.'[19]

The feminine is a bridging influence. It bridges the conscious and the unconscious minds, and the individual and external worlds. In this capacity it acts as an agent of psychological change and transformation. Without it we ossify. With it we grow and develop through constantly meeting new feelings, new ideas and new situations which demand our recognition and comprehension.

The positive emotional effects of transformation are feelings of being caught up in a creative process, feelings of excitement, zest, vitality, or of being inspired and called out of oneself by something of compelling, life-giving value. The positive quality of the transformative side of the feminine may be expressed by an opening to new insights, or a changing of the shape and texture of one's life or relationships.[20]

Whereas the masculine consciousness promotes a subject-object awareness the feminine encourages an experience of unity between subject and object. A carpenter in the *Zhuangzi* explains how he achieves this kind of consciousness:

Ch'ing, the chief carpenter, was carving wood into a stand for hanging musical instruments. When finished, the work appeared to those who saw it as though of supernatural execution. And the prince of Lu asked him, saying, 'What mystery is there in your art?' 'No mystery, your highness,' replied Ch'ing; 'and yet there is something. When I am about to make such a stand, I guard against any dimunition of my vital power. I first reduce my mind to absolute quiescence. Three days in this condition, and I become oblivious of any reward to be gained. Five days, and I become oblivious of any fame to be acquired. Seven days and I become unconscious of my four limbs and my physical frame. Then, with no thought of the Court present to my mind, my skill becomes concentrated, and all disturbing elements from without are gone. I enter some mountain forest. I search for a suitable tree. It contains the form required, which is afterwards elaborated. I see the stand in my mind's eye, and then set to work. Otherwise, there is nothing. I bring my own natural capacity into relation with that of the wood.[21]

By infusing his spirit with that of the tree, the woodcarver avoids forcing his idea on the wood, and succeeds in allowing the stand to evolve out of the nature of the wood itself. A similar approach to art can be seen in the work of some Western artists, in particular in the sculptures of Auguste Rodin. His figures do not appear to have been imposed on the marble or stone, but seem instead to have evolved out of the mutual desires of artists and material.

The feminine consciousness was vital too for the development and definition of Chinese landscape painting. Where the matriarchal consciousness experiences undifferentiated unity, the feminine sees the connections between the parts, the harmonies that underlie their polarities. (The distinction between harmony and sameness is first explained in the *Zuo Zhuan* (Tso Chuan), a political history dating from between the late fourth and second century BC.: 'Harmony is like soup. There being water, heat, sour, flavouring and pickles, salt and peaches, with a bright fire of wood, the cook harmonising all the ingredients in the cooking of the fish and flesh . . . if water be used to help out water, who could eat it.'[22] The Chinese term for landscape painting, *Shan Shui*, expresses the essence of the art: *Shan* means 'mountain' and *Shui* water. Together they symbolise the harmony of Yang and Yin, the nature of the Dao. Thus the purpose of painting was to depict the rhythm and oneness of nature in all its changing manifestations. This was sought through careful composition; opposites such as growth and decay, space and form, far and near, dark and light, etc., are 'harmonised', not through cerebral calculations, but spontaneously as a result of the long process of self-development which was the pre-condition of painting. This was designed to teach the painter to still the mind so that in the inner tranquillity of his or her nature the Dao could live in its entirety. 'In stilling the heart an individual can become one with the elements of nature, the great creative forces of the *Tao*. This becoming one is the true meaning of wholeness. In painting, this goal is translated into the aim of the painter to identify himself with the object depicted, that is, to relate that in himself with that in all things which shared the Oneness of the *Tao*'.[23] The painter has to find the Dao within as a precondition of being able to depict the Dao without. Painting is thus an entirely natural process unhindered by personal interpretation or egoism of any kind. It is a form of worship of the Dao. 'The anonymity of the ritual act is, in effect, oneness with the *Tao*. And painting is not self-expression but an expression of the harmony of *Tao*.'[24] Wu

Zhen (Wu Chen), a fourteenth century AD. painter, described his experience of painting: 'When I begin to paint, I do not know what I am painting; I entirely forget that it is myself who holds the brush.'[25]

A similar transcendence of the subject-object polarity permeates much of Daoist verse. The eleventh century poet, Cheng He (Ch'eng Ho), celebrated his capacity to immerse himself entirely in the present:

> Heaven and Earth and I live together, and all things and I are one.
> Near the middle of the day, when clouds are thin and the breeze is light, I stroll along the river, passing the willows and the blooming trees.
> People of the day do not understand my joy;
> They will say that I am loafing like an idle young man.[26]

The ability to transcend subject-object orientation and see the world as a whole is an important message of the *Zhuangzi*:

> Point at any one of the many parts of a horse, and that is not a horse, although there is the horse before you. It is the combination of all which makes the horse. Similarly a mountain is high because of its individual drops. And he is a just man who regards all parts from the point of view of the whole.[27]

Zhuangzi frequently stresses the folly of mistaking the trees for the wood. He argues that to focus on any particular point of a thing, or stage in life, is to miss the reality of the whole. The story about his reactions to his wife's death illustrate how he himself put this consciousness into practice:

> When Chuang Tzŭ's wife died, Hui Tzŭ went to condole. He found the widower sitting on the ground, singing, with his legs spread out at a right angle, and beating time on a bowl. 'To live with your wife,' exclaimed Hui Tzŭ, 'and to see your eldest son grow up to be a man, and then not to shed a tear over her corpse – this would be bad enough. But to drum on a bowl, and sing; surely this is going too far.'
>
> 'Not at all,' replied Chuang Tzŭ. 'When she died, I could not help being affected by her death. Soon, however, I remembered that she had already existed in a previous state before birth, without form, or even substance; that while in that unconditioned condition, substance was added to spirit; that this substance then assumed form; and that the next stage was birth: and now, by virtue of a further change, she

> is dead, passing from one phase to another like the sequence of spring, summer, autumn and winter. And while she is thus lying asleep in Eternity, for me to go about weeping and wailing would be to proclaim myself ignorant of these natural laws. Therefore I refrain.[28]

The integrative vision of Zhuangzi enabled him to recognise the relativity of all phenomena. He saw that nothing is absolutely great or small, good or bad, because things exist only in relation to each other and to the whole. 'To know the universe is but a tare-seed, and that the tip of a hair is a mountain' was in his mind the hallmark of wisdom. This is another aspect of the feminine consciousness. It experiences the world as a constantly changing phenomenon comparable to the sea, which continually throws up new waves of all sizes and shapes and then swallows them back into herself. Nothing has an absolute unchanging existence because everything is in a state of flux, separating, forming and re-uniting. Confucius, who died in 479 BC. wrote: 'Everything flows on and on like this river, without pause, day and night' (*Analects* IX; 16).

This idea of existence as continuous change is also central to Zen Buddhism, which sees life as a constant process of re-birth from moment to moment. The feminine consciousness experiences the world as continually waxing and waning, ebbing and flowing, uninterrupted change and transformation. Such an outlook is fundamental to the *Yi Jing* which sees all states and moments as in the process of change. Things are not separate from each other but integral aspects of a changing whole. The hexagrams do not represent things or situations as such but their tendencies in movement; they indicate their past and suggest their future.

The feminine consciousness does not deny the existence of the differentiated world; on the contrary, it could not exist without this differentiation. But it does assert that the separation between things is not the only reality, that there is another way of seeing, one which perceives the unity beneath the differences, and focuses on the relationships between things rather than on their separate identities. Instead of seeing the body as that which separates us from the world, the feminine consciousness sees it as that through which we are joined to the world. To understand things, a tree for example, we need the masculine consciousness to help us focus on the constituent parts of the tree, its trunk, branches, roots and leaves, to see everything which distinguishes the tree both from ourselves and from the rest of nature, and we need the feminine to reveal the inner qualities of the tree, its strength, its life force, and to understand the relationship between its parts, how its branches stretch out, gradually tapering off into leaves, until they intermingle and finally disappear into the air. Explored through the feminine consciousness, the tree ceases to appear as something separate both from ourselves and from the universe and becomes an expression of general principles at work throughout the human and natural worlds. Through the feminine consciousness it is possible to discover and experience the tree in ourselves and ourselves in the tree.

The way of the feminine is beautifully illustrated by the famous story of the butcher in the *Zhuangzi.* One day the king praised his carver, Ding (Ting) for the lightness of his touch, the speed of his actions and the certainty and beauty of his strokes. 'Wonderful,' said the king. 'I could never have believed that the art of carving could reach such a point as this.' 'I am a lover of Tao,' replied Ding, putting away his knife, 'and have succeeded in applying it to the art of carving. When I first began to carve I fixed my gaze on the animal in front of me. After three years I no longer saw it as a whole bull, but as a thing already divided into parts. Nowadays I no longer see it with the eye; I merely apprehend it with the soul. My sense-organs are in abeyance, but my soul still works. Unerringly my knife follows the natural markings, slips into the natural cleavages, finds its way into the natural cavities. And so by conforming my work to the structure with which I am dealing, I have arrived at a point at which my knife never touches even the smallest ligament or tendon, let alone the main gristle . . .'[29]

Before Ding had mastered the art of carving without cutting, he had to go through the stage of seeing the bull first as a whole animal, separate from himself, and then as a thing already divided into parts. He had to develop the masculine capacity to differentiate before he could discover the feminine ability to transcend the subject-object perspective, and apprehend the bull with his soul. Ding's path is the path of all who wish to develop the feminine. There is no value in listening, waiting and nourishing the 'way' in nature or in people, if we cannot distinguish one 'way' from another. We cannot help ourselves to discover a harmonious social and economic life while we do not understand and appreciate the differences between people and between the different sections and interests of society. Reason, analysis and differentiation are pre-conditions of harmony.

The Zen masters went part of the way towards understanding and practising this. Their teaching placed considerable emphasis on learning to distinguish between one thing and another as a prerequisite of discovering its 'intentionless intention' and its harmonious relationship to the whole. This attitude is particularly apparent in the Zen approach to gardening.

> The Zen gardener has no mind to impose his intention upon natural forms, but is careful rather to follow the 'intentionless intention' of the forms themselves, even though this involves the utmost care and skill. In fact the gardener never ceases to prune, clip, weed and train his plants, but he does so in the spirit of being part of the garden himself rather than a directing agent standing outside. He is not interfering with nature because he *is* nature, and he cultivates as if not cultivating. Thus the garden is at once highly artificial and extremely natural.[30]

But the Zen gardener's development of the masculine principle is selective. He ignores the advantages of an individual consciousness and concentrates more on intuition than on rational thought. He develops, it seems, the masculine consciousness, assimilates some of its insights and then rejects it in favour of the feminine identification with the world, thereby remaining a prisoner of an imbalanced consciousness. It is difficult to know whether Zen adepts in the centre of the Chinese empire, could have become less one-sided, but we can ask the question of ourselves. To answer it demands an understanding of the relation between the development of general and individual consciousness, as well as the relation between body and mind. These questions form the basis of the next two chapters.

CHAPTER SIX

The Yin and Yang of the Individual

Yu Hsiung said:

> Turning without end
> Heaven and earth shift secretly.
> Who is aware of it?

So the thing which is shrinking there is swelling here, the thing which is maturing here is decaying there. Shrinking and swelling, maturing and decaying, it is being born at the same time that it is dying. The interval between the coming and the going is imperceptible; who is aware of it? Whatever a thing may be, its energy is not suddenly spent, its form does not suddenly decay; we are aware neither of it when it reaches maturity nor of when it begins to decay. It is the same with a man's progress from birth to old age; his looks, knowledge and bearing differ from one day to the next, his skin and nails and hair are growing at the same time as they are falling away. They do not stop as they were in childhood without changing. But we cannot be aware of the intervals; we must wait for their fruition before we know.[1]

Yang and Yin move rhythmically through our lives, the waxing of one implies the waning of the other. Nothing is static, only our ignorance makes it seem so. 'Turning without end Heaven and earth shift secretly.' But 'Who is aware of it?' The task of the Chinese physician was to acquire this awareness.

Chinese medicine owes many of its central principles to the

Yellow Emperor's Classic of Internal Medicine (the *Classic*), (*Huangdi Nei Jing Su Wen*). According to Chinese tradition the Yellow Emperor reigned from 2852–2205 BC., the third in the 647-year-period of the Five Rulers. He is said to have been miraculously conceived by his mother Fu Bao (Fu Pao) and was revered as the inventor of wheeled vehicles, armour, ships, pottery and many other useful appliances. The close of his reign was glorified by the appearance of the phoenix and the *Qi Lin* (Ch'i lin), the auspicious unicorn sometimes referred to as an hermaphrodite. Whether or not the Yellow Emperor existed and was the author of the *Classic* remains unknown. The present day edition of this remarkable book owes its form to the famous commentator of the Tang dynasty (AD. 618–907), Wang Bing (Wang Ping). However Ilza Veith, who translated the text, concludes her discussion of its origin by stating that it is 'fair to assume that a great part of the text existed during the Han dynasty (206 BC.–AD. 220) and that much of it is of considerably older origin, possibly handed down by oral tradition from China's earliest history'.[2]

The *Classic* presents Chinese medicines as inseparable from its philosophy of the interdependence of the individual and the cosmos, and this idea remained fundamental to Chinese medical theory and practice. The cosmology of the *Nei Jing* reflects the earliest conceptions of the Dao as the unifying principle of the universe, and it describes the task of the physician as understanding the harmony between heaven and earth and to express this harmony in all things so as to ensure that the patterns of human life correspond to the patterns of nature. His or her task was thus primarily to keep people well. To prescribe medicaments and other forms of therapy was a secondary responsibility.

The Yellow Emperor's Classic cf Internal Medicine states that while humanity is divided into males and females, each sex is composed of both the masculine and feminine principles. 'As a male, man belongs to Yang: as a female, man belongs to Yin. Yet both, male and female, are products of two primary elements, hence both qualities are contained in both sexes.'[3] The human being can be understood in three parts, upper, lower and middle, each of which expresses the Yin as well as the Yang. The surface of the body is Yang and the interior Yin, and the pulse is both Yin and Yang. The organs also are classified according to the two principles: the five viscera – heart, liver, spleen, lungs and kidneys – being Yin, and credited with the passive capacity for storing, but not elimination. The gall bladder, stomach, lower intestines and 'three burnings spaces' (described as the sewage system of the body but not located) are active and Yang. The traditional medical view was that the individual organs are closely linked as regards function. The modern Chinese view recognises that

> where bodily energy is concerned, they are like the links in a chain; thus the liver is linked to the lungs, the lungs to the large intestine, the large intestine to the stomach, the stomach to the spleen, the spleen to the heart, the heart to the small intestine, the small intestine to the urinary bladder, the urinary bladder to the kidneys, the kidneys to the circulation, the circulation to the 'triple warmer', the latter to the gall bladder and the gall bladder to the liver, thus completing the cycle.[4]

According to this arrangement the Yin and Yang organs belong together in pairs; liver and lungs, for example, are Yin while the large intestine and stomach are Yang. 'Perfect harmony between the two primordial elements meant health, disharmony or undue preponderance of one element brought disease and death.'[5] The two elements – Yin and Yang – were called the Dao. They were considered the basis of the entire universe, the principle of everything in creation.[6] The Chinese physician learnt to detect the fluctuations of Yin and Yang and to remedy the disequilibrium between them, considered to be responsible for ill health.

This Yin-Yang approach to the human body is the foundation of acupuncture. Discussed in considerable detail in the *Classic* and amplified in subsequent centuries, the theory of acupuncture teaches that numerous widely separated points on the surface of the body affect the functioning of one and the same organ, and that all points affecting one organ are interconnected. The interconnections were given the name of *Jing* (Ching), or Meridians. The *Classic* identifies twelve main ones, and two more were added later. This discovery of the link between the surface of the skin and the internal organs derived from the Chinese understanding of the Yin-Yang relationship between the interior of the body and the surface.[7]

The Meridians, themselves, are also divided into Yin and Yang categories; those flowing along the inside of each arm and leg are

Yin, while those running along the outside of the limbs are Yang. The Yin Meridians belong to the Yin organs and the Yang Meridians to the Yang organs. The Yin-Yang energy of the Meridians is known as *Qi* (ch'i). Its obstruction causes an imbalance of Yin and Yang in the body which expresses itself in ill-health; recovery depends on correcting the imbalance. The influence of Yin was compared to water; it is the life-preserving force, responsible for storing vital strength, controlling digestion and ensuring peace and harmony within the body. Yang was likened to fire; it propels the organs into action, ensures the separation of the body from the outside world and protects it from external influences.

The different forms of Chinese therapy which evolved through the centuries – acupuncture, moxibustion, respiratory therapy, remedial massage, physiotherapy, herbal medicines and *Tai Ji Quan* (T'ai Ch'i Ch'uan) – share the common aim of restoring to the body a harmonious relationship between Yin and Yang. *The Yellow Emperor's Classic* was thus the starting point for a long history of medical theory and practice. It presents a developmental view of the individual and identifies the major phases in the lives of men and women. The female life is structured in seven-year periods:

> When a girl is seven years of age, the emanations of the kidneys become abundant, she begins to change her teeth and her hair grows longer. When she reaches her fourteenth year she begins to menstruate and is able to become pregnant and the movement in the great thoroughfare pulse is strong . . .
>
> When the girl reaches the age of twenty-one years the emanations of the kidneys are regular . . . and she is fully grown . .
>
> When the woman reaches the age of twenty-eight, her muscles and bones are strong, her hair has reached its full length and her body is flourishing and fertile.
>
> When the woman reaches the age of thirty-five, the pulse indicating [the region of] the 'sunlight' deteriorates, her face begins to wrinkle and her hair begins to fall. When she reaches the age of forty-two, the pulse of the three [regions of] Yang deteriorates . .
>
> When she reaches the age of forty-nine she can no longer become pregnant and the circulation of the great thoroughfare pulse is decreased. Her menstruation is exhausted . . . her body deteriorates and she is no longer able to bear children.[8]

The male's life is ordered in eight-year periods:

> When a boy is eight years old the emanations of his testes (kidneys) are fully developed; his hair grows longer and he begins to change his teeth. When he is sixteen years of age the emanations of his testicles become abundant and he begins to secrete semen. He has an abundance of semen which he seeks to dispel; and if at this point the male and female element unite in harmony, a child can be conceived.
>
> At the age of twenty-four the emanations of his testicles are regular . . . At thirty-two his muscles and bones are flourishing . . .
>
> At the age of forty the emanations of his testicles become smaller, he begins to lose his hair and his teeth begin to decay. At forty-eight his masculine vigor is reduced or exhausted; wrinkles appear on his face and the hair on his temples turns white. At fifty-six the force of his liver deteriorates . . . his secretion of semen is exhausted, his vitality diminished, his testicles deteriorate, and his physical strength reaches its end. At sixty-four he loses his teeth and his hair.[9]

The ancient Chinese recognised the second half of life, for both sexes, as a time of declining sexual powers; the body pays for the vigour of the first 35 years with the physical deterioration of the subsequent decades. Thus a balance is brought about in the life of each person. In women an excess of Yin energy inevitably calls forth its demise with the cessation of menstruation and the loss of the ability to conceive children. In men the excess of Yang in youth implies the diminishing sexual secretions and potency characteristic of the second half of life. As they move towards death the bodies of both men and women become increasingly less sexually differentiated and assume a form which, in some respects, can be compared to that of the infant.

These insights into the relationship of Yin-Yang to the individual, which constitute the central rationale behind much of ancient and modern Chinese medicine, derived from intuition or inspiration and were tested by empirical observation. They were never proven or understood according to the modern scientific sense of these words. This was true and remains true of much of Chinese medicine. It is practised because it works, not because its principles are fully comprehended. The Meridians, for example, have yet to be identified with known physiological process or anatomical structures, but there can be little doubt about the value of a theory of the body which can produce such startling results in practice as effective anaesthesia in open-heart surgery. Despite the research now being done into acupuncture its workings remain a mystery. But in some other areas of medicine, such as the role of the masculine and feminine principles in the human body, modern science is beginning to come up with some explanations which, while still very far from being complete answers, make a considerable contribution to our understanding of the intuitions of the ancient Chinese sages.

Roughly twenty years ago western biologists recognised that for the first five or six weeks of intra-uterine life, while each cell contains the possibility of becoming either male or female, all mammalian embryos are morphologically female rather than hermaphrodic or neutral. Genetically our sex is established at conception; the female ovum, containing an X-determining chromosome meets either an X or a Y male sperm. An XX conjunction creates a genetic female and an XY a genetic male. But the influence of the chromosome does not make itself felt until the fifth or sixth week of embryonic life. During the first weeks all embryos are females. 'If the fetal gonads are removed before differentiation occurs the embryo will develop into a normal female, lacking only ovaries, regardless of the genetic sex.'[10]

At about five weeks the genetic male activates the development of testes and the secretions of male hormones – androgens – the principal one being testosterone. From this point it is the hormones, not the chromosomes, which are responsible for further sexual differentiation. Testosterone suppresses the growth of the ovaries and subsequently induces the internal and external male genital tract. Between the twelfth and sixteenth week the male structures are fully established. If the genetic sex is female, the germ cells arrive at the ovaries during the seventh week and stimulate the production of two female hormones, oestrogen and progesterone. But at this point there is a crucial difference between male and female development: oestrogen is not necessary for the continued feminisation of the reproductive tract. 'Female differentiation results from the innate, genetically determined female morphology of all mammalian embryos.'[11]

Female development pursues a direct path, with the reproductive organs not subjected to any 'hormonal differentiating transformation'. 'Fetal and maternal oestrogens merely enhance, and this later, slowly and to a relatively moderate degree, the already unfolding female morphology.'[12] Female growth is therefore autonomous. Male development, on the contrary requires extremely large quantities of androgens throughout foetal life to overcome its innate female anatomy and the effects of the circulating maternal oestrogens. Unless this happens, the embryo, even if it has an XY (male) chromosomal nature, will continue its autonomous development into a morphological female. It is therefore only the male embryo which differentiates itself from the early stage of embryonic life by initiating an active struggle against the powerful and 'natural' tendency to become female. Hence male development can be seen as an ongoing struggle for independence from the influence of the feminine. One of the consequences of this is that after differentiation is completed, male embryos continue to manifest a high resistance to experimentally injected oestrogens, 'requiring large amounts before feminising affects appear.' The reverse is true of females whose female anatomy is genetically set, not hormonally determined; in them small amounts of androgen can have strong masculinising affects. 'All mammalian females tested – embryos, infants and adults – are appreciatively more reactive to androgen than the males are to oestrogen.'[13]

After birth the male and female hormones continue to play a significant role in the development of both sexes. In their somatic organisation the gonads – the ovaries and testes – retain a greater or lesser amount of the opposite sex tissue which remains functional throughout life. The sex hormones affect every part of the body with the possible exception of the cortex. They influence behaviour, feelings and bodily shape in a variety of ways; the castrati singers of the Baroque and Classical European periods, as well as the eunuchs of Imperial China are well known examples of their effects. Changes in the hormonal patterns of individuals are made possible by the fact that our bodies, irrespective of genetic sex, are all to some extent bisexual. This is discussed by June Singer in her study *Androgyny*:

> If there is no evidence for a *structural bisexuality* in the embryo, the question arises as to the source of our concept of bisexuality as a basis for behavioral attitudes. While maleness and femaleness are genetically determined, masculinity and feminity are subject to

hormonal modification. There is a continuous production of both estrogens and androgens by both sexes, although with a preponderance of one or the other. The particular mix in each individual seems to be related to the particular place on the continuum which ranges from the extreme of powerful muscular masculinity on one side to the most delicate version of femininity on the other. In comparison with other animals, however, the genetic code for humans calls for a certain proportion of each hormone, with the result that males and females are not very different. In other species the imbalance is so great that males and females seem hardly to belong to the same species.

Given this information, it appears that there may be, after all, some biological basis for bisexuality, or for the variations in the sexual proclivities of individual men and women. If the balance of male and female hormones affects the masculine/feminine balance from one species to another, it seems reasonable to assume that lesser variations within species would produce individuals who would vary correspondingly from the sexual norms. Thus we might expect to find in men a range of 'masculinity', some tending to be more and some to be less 'masculine' by reason of their hormonal distribution, with women also exhibiting the effects of their hormonal distribution in similar ways. And we would also expect to find some individuals in whom the balance between androgens and estrogens would be such as to predispose an individual to make an easier peace with his or her contrasexual element.[14]

A look at human sexuality reveals considerable variations in the hormonal balance of the individual. Each person enjoys a slightly different position in the sexual spectrum. Moreover, whatever their particular position between the extremes of masculinity and femininity, both men and women are also subject to the changing influence of the sex hormones throughout their lives. Men produce androgens fairly constantly while women release female hormones cyclically. Post-natally the production of androgens in boys decreases slightly, but then it continues to rise gradually until puberty when there is a massive increase in the secretion of androgens. As the ancient Chinese understood, this is the time when the 'emanations of the boys testicles become abundant'. It is followed, around the age of 18, by the high point of testosterone production which declines gradually thereafter until death, with a rapid reduction occurring between the ages of 40 and 55. It is during these years that the man may experience the equivalent of the female menopause: before his mid-life crisis, the male liver carefully monitors the oestrogen supply and rids the body of any excess, but afterwards the liver becomes less efficient, so that from middle age a man's oestrogen production increases moderately, while his production of male hormones, which have been declining slowly since the late teens, drops off.

Female development follows a slightly different path, but the overall pattern is similar to that of the man. Female hormone production increases with puberty. After the cessation of the menstrual cycle the woman's oestrogen production declines to low levels and although her male hormone level does not rise in the same ratio to her female hormones as the female to male ratio in men, nevertheless, the decline in her oestrogen level does create a parallel situation between the sexes during the second half of life, particularly when we remember the greater sensitivity of women to the male hormone. Both men and women, therefore, move in later life towards a state of relatively less sexual differentiation than either has known since before puberty. The decline of male hormones in men, and female hormones in women, is responsible for the familiar observation that each sex acquires some of the physical characteristics of its opposite: men may develop a more rounded and softer physique with slightly swollen breasts, while women's skin coarsens, their voices lower and they begin to grow facial hair.

In the course of our lives, it seems we are all given the chance to experience intimations of some biological characteristics of the opposite sex. Whether we avail ourselves of this opportunity by welcoming and becoming more conscious of this depends on our freedom from sex-role stereotyping. Without such freedom, these biological changes can be sufficiently alarming to send women to hair-removing clinics and hormone therapy specialists in a desperate attempt to regain their 'normal' femininity and conform to the norm which society prescribes. The ratio of masculine and feminine hormones in the body undergoes significant changes throughout our lives: periods of high masculinity or femininity are preceded and succeeded by years of much less marked sexual differentiation. Our biological nature is not static but subject to continual changes. To accept these may involve embarrassment, but it considerably enriches our understanding and experience of our bodies. The balance between Yin and Yang in each person does not conform to a concept of 'normality', for the variations are considerable. But this does not mean that there are not general patterns of change which can be discerned. As the early Chinese sages recognised and modern medicine is beginning to discover, certain changes in hormonal balance are in a general sense common to all people. These changes are not exclusively biological; they can also be observed in psychological development.

Biology and psychology have long been regarded by western medical practice as separate disciplines. In the interests of specialised understanding this is clearly advantageous; precise and detailed knowledge depends, at certain stages, on compartmentalisation. But it is just as important, at other moments, to explore the relationship between the different disciplines or compartments of information, to build the fragmentary expertise into a more complete picture. Understanding of the individual depends in the end on this. The twentieth century has witnessed notable progress in this direction: the effect of environmental and cultural factors on biological and psychological health has received considerable attention. Less attention however has been paid to exploring the relationship between body and mind. European and American thinking remains largely trapped in the traditional mind-body split; we train doctors of the mind *or* doctors of the body, choose physical *or* mental therapies, specialise in physical *or* spiritual skills and practise physical *or* spiritual exercises. Few people have openly challenged this approach to medicine and health. The minority who have done so are more often motivated by the desire to expand their own expertise by acquiring knowledge of two disciplines and practising them separately, than by the recognition that although at one level body and mind are distinct, they remain nevertheless different expressions of the one body-mind totality that is each one of us. Those who have, in their studies and practice, crossed the disciplinary frontiers so that they may treat the whole person are often forced to work outside the established systems. It is often very difficult for a general practitioner to find the time and gain the experience to observe and treat the minds of his patients in conjunction with their bodies, or a psychotherapist to work with physical remedies alongside psychological ones.

But this may be beginning to change. More people are recognising that we do not live out of two separate systems but that whatever happens to us is likely to affect both the mind and the body. In an interesting article, 'Psyche and Soma' Jungian analyst Michael Fordham, writes that the Self is a state of wholeness which includes soma and psyche, and he suggests that we need a way of looking at body and psyche that unites them, 'that reveals them as two ways of looking at the same thing.'[15] There are an increasing number of people who acknowledge that consciousness can influence physical heat just as much as the body can influence consciousness, and that the relationship between the two is more one of mutual interaction and correspondence than determinism by either part. There has been work done, for example, on how a school curriculum can, over the years, effect the physical development of children as well as their minds, and it has been discovered that food allergies can be responsible for a number of different mental disturbances. (I use mind to include psyche and spirit.) Our diet, it seems, is not only vital for physical health, but also has a formative influence on intellectual and emotional development. These are only two examples of many.

Understanding of the subtleties of the mind-body relationship, however, remains in its infancy. Nevertheless, there are discoveries which establish the close relationship between the two, and this is particularly apparent in the area of sex hormones. Sex change operations provide evidence of the dramatic changes that can occur, not only in the body but also in the thoughts and feelings of the patient, following alterations in the hormonal balance. It can, of course, be argued that these changes are due to cultural adaptation. This may be partly true, but it would seem unlikely that massive injections of either masculine or feminine hormones would leave the mind and feelings untouched. The testimony of these who have undergone sex change operations endorses this suggestion. A friend of mine who underwent an intensive course of female hormone therapy for cancer of the prostate gland said that apart from a general softening of his body and swelling of his breasts, his experience and sensitivity to nature and to other people developed to an unprecedented degree. In his case wishful thinking, or cultural role-stereotyping, are clearly insufficient explanations for the changes in his awareness of the world and himself. Less dramatic examples of the relationship between body and mind are more widely available. Many women, for instance, experience pre-menstrual irritability and tension and marked changes in their state of mind during pregnancy and the menopause which cannot be entirely attributed to psychological or cultural factors.

Interesting suggestions about the body-psyche relationship are made in *The Wise Wound*, a book by Penelope Shuttle and Peter Redgrove on menstruation. The authors argue that the menstrual cycle profoundly links the body and mind in such a way that the physical tension before menstruation corresponds to a psychological tension, and the menstrual flow of blood corresponds to a flow of creativity, which they consider the psychological potential of menstruation – the creation of a psychic rather than a physical child. They suggest that the menstrual rhythms, the waxing and waning, have their correspondence in the feminine consciousness of the rhythmical nature of life. Furthermore they argue that the menstrual cycle reflects, physically and psychologically, the two poles – the feminine and the masculine within the female. In support of this argument they refer to M. J. Sherfey's book: *The Nature and Evolution of Female Sexuality* which states that before the period there is a marked build-up of clitoral tension, and during menstruation itself, both progesterone and oestrogen levels decline sharply, but androgen (the masculine hormone) continues to circulate.[16] They argue that the ascendance in the influence of the masculine in the body during menstruation corresponds to a psychological rhythm: at ovulation the woman unconsciously wishes to receive and to accept, but around or after menstruation she is more concerned with building and developing her own psyche.[17] The authors stress that the body-psyche relationship is a two-way process; a woman's emotions can be affected by the biological cycle, and her cycle can be influenced by her emotional and sexual experience.

Further confirmation of the interdependence of body and psyche is offered by biofeedback. This is the name of a procedure that helps people to tune into their bodies and, eventually, control them, thereby awakening in them a new appreciation and sensitivity to the relation between body and mind, giving them the possibility of becoming their own healers and minimising their need for drugs. As a technique it focuses on the mind being in control, so that there is always the possibility that, in the wrong hands, biofeedback could become another way of manipulating the body, rather than a method of becoming more sensitive and respectful to the body-mind unity. However, in its proof of the subtle interdependence of body and mind, it has already made important contributions to the growth of a new mind-body science of the human being, one which points to the extraordinary and largely unrecognised capacities of the mind to lead and transform the body.

Experiments with rhesus monkeys throw further light on the mind-body relationship. When the male monkeys are deprived of contact with other monkeys and then allowed to mix with them for brief periods, they threaten other animals much more frequently than do females. Females reared in isolation show a similar tendency to passivity.[18] Hormones clearly influence the behaviour of these monkeys, to some extent independently of environmental and learning facts. It is easy to disregard animal-human analogies for the excellent reason that they overlook the fact that our humanity lies not in what identifies us with animals but what distinguishes us from them – in our capacity for conscious reflection, control and understanding as opposed to a purely instinctive and species collective response to life. But I am using the analogy not to argue a case for biological determinism but merely to suggest that hormones can autonomously influence behaviour and feelings.

Other experiments with rhesus monkeys suggest the same conclusion in reverse, namely that the experience and behaviour of a monkey can affect its hormone levels:

> When a rhesus monkey is number one in the hierarchy of a primate colony, his testosterone level measures higher than that of any of the other monkeys. One might conclude that testosterone is the take-charge hormone and that the one who has the most gets to the top. But take this primate who is at the top of the pyramid and put him in a colony where he is unknown, where he has to re-establish himself and his hormone level plummets. It all depends on his sense of security.

> A testosterone level is not something that an individual 'has', regardless of the social situation: it is an open system . . . Two more studies . . . show how very susceptible this system can be. After an animal is defeated in fight, his hormone level drops and remains low. But put the low-status male in a cage with a female he can dominate and with whom he can have an active sex life, and up soars his hormone level . . .[19]

It must be remembered that the female body is more sensitive to male hormones than the male body to female hormones. The development of the feminine characteristics in men is therefore likely to be less marked. Research on the mind-body relationship, however, is still extraordinarily inadequate. In the case of sex hormones, it is only now that the techniques in chemistry are being developed to measure sex steroids in human blood with any degree of accuracy. Discussions about the interdependence of our psychic and physical natures must remain, for some time to come, largely speculative. But it does seem possible that our bodies are considerably more sensitive to our thoughts and feelings, and our consciousness considerably more sensitive to our bodies, than most people have been accustomed to accept or believe.

The ideas of a correspondence between body and mind was integral to ancient Chinese philosophy. The sages understood the body as a single organism, the Dao in microcosm, which acquires form, life and consciousness through the interactions of Yin and Yang, the polar manifestations of the Dao. The *Classic* assumes an interdependence of body and mind, and even lists the precise relationship between the different organs and the 'spiritual resources'. It states that the liver controls the soul, the heart the spirit, the spleen the ideas, the lungs the mind or instinctive spirit, and the kidneys the will.[20] Spirit and Matter were never separated, 'and for them the world was a continuum passing from the void at one end to the grossest matter at the other; hence "soul" never took up this antithetical character in relation to matter . . .'[21] Joseph Needham comments that Chinese thought 'did not suffer . . . from the typical schizophrenia of Europe, the inability to get away from the mechanistic materialism on the one hand, and from the theological spiritualism on the other.'[22] Shao Yong (Shao Yung), for example, a Neo-Confucian of the eleventh century AD., wrote that 'without physical substance, the nature (of man and things) cannot be complete. Without nature, physical substance cannot be produced.'[23] The totality of the human being, he believed was body-mind, not two separate systems. (It is important to remember that by 'physical substance' the Chinese did not necessarily mean tangible substance. More often they were referring to the life force principle *Qi*, which evolved from the immaterial Dao and which, in certain circumstance, generated form.)

Since health for the Chinese depended on a harmonious relationship between Yin and Yang, it also implied the need for a harmonious relationship between the physical and the spiritual (or nature as it was sometimes called). For here, as well as in the body and the consciousness, Yin and Yang were involved. The two principles were understood to complement each other in such a way that when the physical substance was predominantly Yang, the nature would be Yin and the other way round. In life the natural tendency was for the two to separate, a process which led, eventually, to death, but this decline was not regarded as inevitable. 'Knowledge of the Tao and of the workings of Yin and Yang was considered even strong enough to counteract the effect of old age.'[24] According to Qi Bo, the Yellow Emperor's wise physician, human beings have the freedom to go 'beyond the natural limits':

> If one has the ability to know the seven injuries and the eight advantages, the two principles can be brought into harmony. If one does not know how to use this knowledge then his span of life will be limited by early decay. At the age of forty the Yin element within the body is reduced to one half of its natural capacity and man's usual behaviour deteriorates. At the age of fifty the body grows heavy and the ears no longer hear well nor is the vision of the eyes clear any longer. At the age of sixty the life-producing force of Yin declines and impotence sets in. The nine orifices no longer benefit each other. The orifices below become insubstantial and vacant while those above remain substantial and real, and the ability to weep is totally exhausted.
>
> Yet it is said: Those who have the true wisdom remain strong while those who have no knowledge and wisdom grow old and feeble. Therefore the people should share this wisdom and their names will become famous. Those who are wise inquire and search together, while those who are ignorant and stupid inquire and search apart

from each other. Those who are stupid and ignorant do not exert themselves enough in the Right Way, while those who are wise search beyond the natural limits.

Those who search beyond the natural limits will retain good hearing and clear vision, their bodies will remain light and strong, and although they grow old in years they will remain able-bodied and flourishing; and those who are able-bodied can govern to great advantage.[25]

(By 'natural limits' it is important to understand 'ordinary patterns'. Qi Bo is not suggesting defying nature but understanding it.)

Understanding the way of nature leads to the transformation of the mind and the body. Through the development of consciousness it is possible, according to the ancient Chinese, to acquire and retain health, and become thereby the co-creators, the collaborators rather than the puppets of nature. Learning, according to Confucianism, was the way to transform the imbalanced and hence imperfect nature so that it may become a perfect mirror of the Dao. Such learning involves, among other things, investigating and understanding the body and the mind, discovering and developing their potential.

The ancient Chinese recognised that human life moves through definite stages in its journey from birth to death. Apart from the physical changes already mentioned, they also noted changes in the human being's relationship to the Dao. The Daoists, for instance, regarded infancy as the perfect moment, since during this time the young child is still identified with the Dao. They considered growing up as the gradual departure from this original paradise, a moving away from perfection towards confusion and imbalance, before once again returning towards the Dao in old age and, finally, in death. The *Liezi* (*Lieh Tzu*) says:

From his birth to his end, man passes through four great changes; infancy, youth, old age, death. In infancy his energies are concentrated and his inclinations at one – the ultimate of harmony. Other things do not harm him, nothing can add to the virtue in him. In youth, the energies in his blood are in turmoil and overwhelm him, desires and cares rise up and fill him. . . . When he is old, desires and cares weaken, his body is about to rest. Nothing contends to get ahead of him, and although he has not reached the perfection of infancy,

compared with his youth there is a great difference for the better.
When he dies, he goes to his rest, rises again to his zenith.[26]

The Chinese respect for the unity of body and mind tended to inhibit the development of a separate discipline of psychology, and also of an understanding of the ways of Yin and Yang in human consciousness. Nevertheless an acknowledgement of the essential androgyny of each individual is implicit in much of Chinese thought. Certain thinkers were even explicit on the subject. Li Ji (Li Chih) a Ming philosopher, for instance, maintained that the intuitive mentality associated with the female was complementary to the rational mentality of the male, and he insisted that the difference between the sexes was only one of degree, that each possessed both types of intelligence, and should be allowed and encouraged to develop both.[27] But in the end the holistic approach to knowledge deprived the Chinese of the advantages of specialised understanding, and for a more detailed picture of the masculine and feminine principles in individual psychic development we must look to Western psychologists.

It was Freud's observations which laid the foundations for some of Jung's later insights. He recognised that in the human soul we can see reflections of the great sexual antithesis, and that here, as in the body, no individual is limited to the modes of reaction of a single sex, 'but always finds some room for those of the opposite one'.[28] Rudolf Steiner, a contemporary of Freud also saw the human being as both masculine and feminine and described this bisexuality in a number of ways. He said that the human physical body is complemented by an etheric body (or life body) and that when the physical is masculine the etheric is feminine, and vice versa. He also stressed that the human soul is simultaneously male and female.[29] According to Steiner the proto-human being was not originally sexually differentiated into male and female but was 'undifferentiated female' or 'male-female'. Its characteristics were the feminine ones of creating resemblance, oneness with the universe and receptivity. But at a certain moment in the earth's history the possibility for sexual differentiation arose: 'From the original dual sex-nature the tendency had continued in the female to produce similarity in the descendants; in the male the influence worked differently, it tended to call forth variety, individualisation, and with the flowing of the male force into the female dissimilarity was increasingly created. Thus it was through the male influence that the power of developing individuality came about.'

Steiner explains that the sexually undifferentiated human ancestor had an entirely different consciousness from the later, sexually differentiated humans:

> If you had asked one of [them] . . . about his experiences, he would have described them as identical with those of his earliest ancestors; everything lived on through the generations. The gradual rise of consciousness that only extends from birth to death came about by the individualising of the human race, and at the same time arose the possibility of birth and death as we know them today. Previously while the body dried up and new ones emerged, consciousness was preserved through the consciousness of the group-soul, so that really a kind of immortality existed.[30]

Later on in the same lecture Steiner emphasises the different functions of the two principles: 'We see in our humanity the feminine to be the principle which still preserves the old conditions of folk and race, and the masculine that which continually breaks through these conditions, splits them up and so individualises mankind.'[31] In other words individuality depends on the development of the masculine principle. This idea has since been explored in greater detail by the Jungian school of analytical psychology.

Jung, who we have noted, formulated the idea of the animus and the anima as the contrasexual archtypes inherent in the psyche of the female and the male, recognised that each person has the possibility of developing and experiencing both principles. The role of the masculine and feminine principles in the evolution of human consciousness has been explored in great depth by Jungian analyst, Erich Neumann. In his study *The Child*, he charts in considerable detail the early stages of this story: 'In the embryónic phase, the mother's body is the world in which the child lives, not yet endowed with a controlling and perceiving consciousness and not yet ego-centred; moreover, the totality-regulation of the child's organism, which we designate by the symbol of the body-Self, is, as it were, overlaid by the mother's Self.'[32] He continues:

With the birth of the body the child's bond with its mother is in part severed, but the significance of the second embryonic phase specific to man is precisely that after birth the child remains in a sense partially captive to its primal, embryonic relationship to its mother. It has not yet become itself. The child becomes fully itself only in the course of this primal relationship, which process is normally completed only after the first year of life.[33]

Neumann explains that during the pre-ego stage characteristic of earliest childhood the polarised experience of the world with its subject-object dichotomy is not yet developed. The child is still, to a significant degree, at one with its mother, who herself is not experienced as distinct from the world; no differentiation between 'I' and 'Thou', or Self and cosmos, has yet occurred. These first two stages are timeless moments of 'participation mystique' an oceanic existence in the round, the golden age of the ancient Chinese.

Gradually this anonymous identity of child and mother is exchanged for a new stage in which the unity becomes personalised as the Great Mother who protects, nourishes, embraces and contains the child: 'The functions that were previously performed by the anonymous formless world in which the still undelineated child "floated" – the functions of containing, nourishing, warming and protecting – are now humanised'.[34] These first two stages are dominated by the matriarchal consciousness, which Neumann characterises as a bisexual experience. The Mother, he explains, in the unitary reality of the uroboric phase, is both active and passive, begetter and conceiver; the child experiences its other as a bisexual primeval being, and through her develops his or her own masculine and feminine modes of reactions: 'Up to this point the opposites are so mingled that just as one can speak of a uroboric Great Mother one can speak of uroboric behaviour in the child. Boy and girl react both in a feminine, passive-receptive manner, and in an active masculine manner, and it is just as natural for a girl child to behave in a masculine way toward her mother as for a boy to react in a passive-feminine way . . .'[35] In his study of *The Origins and History of Consciousness*, Neumann makes the same point with greater emphasis:

Man's original hermaphroditic disposition is still largely conserved in the child. Without the disturbing influences from outside which foster the visible manifestation of sexual differences at an early date, children would just be children; and actively masculine features are in fact as common and effective in girls as are passively feminine ones in boys. It is only cultural influences whose differentiating tendencies govern the child's early upbringing that lead to an identification of the ego with the monosexual tendencies of the personality and to the suppression, or repression, of one's congenital contrasexuality.[36]

Regardless of the child's genetic sex, therefore, the early years are dominated by the Great Mother, in relation to whom the child assumes an essentially passive-receptive attitude, even though he or she will probably express both masculine and feminine modes of behaviour within this overall context. But this changes with the emergence of the ego. Then, for the first time, the child begins to experience the world in terms of polarities. She or he may continue to develop both principles in her behaviour, but in relation to the mother she will become aware of increasing tension as she sets out on the arduous and painful struggle to discover and define her own separateness and individuality. For both sexes this instinctive striving towards independence has a masculine tone. It is formed in opposition to the all-embracing and protecting Mother, and can only attain its goal at the cost of overthrowing the primal identity with Her.

This early psychological crisis – the struggle for ego development and consciousness – has been examined from many different vantage points. Here I am concerned with those of Freudian and Jungian psychology and that of Rudolf Steiner. All three have explored it through the Oedipus myth, and the insights of each complement rather than contradict those of the other two.

Freud recognised the moment when a child has to give up its instinctive longing for an incestuous relationship with the mother as a major crisis. Small boys are compelled to relinquish their mother as a love object when they become aware of their physical inadequacy compared to their father, or the idea of the father, while small girls have to come to terms with their physical inability ever to fully satisfy their mother sexually. These realisations cannot occur for either sex until they have begun to see themselves as different from both parents. The successful resolution of the Oedipus crisis is the discovery of a sexual identity; boys sublimate their desire for their mother into the effort to become men, and girls adjust to their femininity by replacing their mother with their father as the object of their love. The implications of this crisis, as observed by Freud, are different for the two sexes and have cultural as well as other importance: the sublimation demanded of the boy is much greater than that asked of the girl. Boys have to abandon completely their incestuous desires for their mother in order to become men, while girls have simply to exchange their identification with the mother for an imitation of her. In a patriarchal culture it is likely that the Oedipus crisis will be accompanied by considerable – 'penis envy' – on the part of the girls as they recognise, for the first time the inferior status of women in society. In other cultures, where the inequality between the sexes is less pronounced – or where it is reversed, with women assuming the dominant role as in the Tchambuli tribe studied by Margaret Mead[37] – 'penis envy' in its cultural sense is likely to cause fewer problems for girls. But the psychological importance of 'penis envy' remains, whatever the cultural environment. The Oedipus crisis switches the emphasis from the mother to the father; boys learn to become fathers and girls to be worthy objects of their love. Boys, therefore, at this stage have an advantage over girls; their separation from the mother can be swifter and more radical.

Certain Jungians have criticised the Freudian interpretation of the Oedipus story for being too personal. In *The Origins and History of Consciousness*, Neumann identifies the myth as belonging to a realm of universal archetypes working throughout the history of consciousness and recapitulated in the life of each individual. He suggests that it is not the father who is the castrator feared by all boys if they should continue in their desires for the mother, but that the real castrator is the bisexual matriarchal consciousness. It is Her all-embracing magnetic power which can engulf and eventually stifle the emerging ego. After being nurtured and protected by the mother-consciousness, every child reaches a moment when he or she feels the need to begin to stand alone and discover a sense of 'I'. At this time the Great Mother and Her personification, the real mother, become experienced as a threat to the child's developing sense of individuality and independence. The struggle of the child is depicted in Jungian psychology as the battle of the masculine principle against the

Mother, or the slaying of the dragon. This was the struggle of Oedipus, and his failure is a warning to those who wish to follow him. He did what every child longs to do; he committed incest with his mother through the only possible means, slaying the obstacle between him and his loved one – his father. Neumann explains that the parricide must be understood symbolically; it was not his biological father that Oedipus slew but the masculine principle. Only by killing the masculine in his own psyche could he return to the old consciousness of the Mother, only by killing the principle of differentiation could he find again the unity he sought. But Oedipus paid heavily for his regression. A consciousness appropriate and helpful at one stage of development causes sickness at another. This was the sin of Oedipus; he sought the mother when he needed the father and it cost him his sight. It was not physical blindness he suffered but spiritual blindness, the loss of individual consciousness. The Oedipus myth stands as a warning to all who look nostalgically to the comfort and security of the pre-individual state.

From the Freudian and Jungian accounts, it seems that the Oedipus crisis initiates the beginning of life as an individual as opposed to as an indivisible part of a whole or a group. It marks the time when we begin to learn to distinguish between the male and the female, the masculine and the feminine, and as a psychological stage of development, it corresponds with the later sexual differentiation of the physical body. Both physically and psychologically the individual is increasingly encouraged to understand the world and her or himself by dividing the unity into polarity. A considerable danger during this stage is that the experience of polarity leads to polarisation. If this happens the creative tension between the two poles, both within the individual and in the 'outside' world, is replaced by antagonism and extremism in which neither pole is able or wishes to understand the other. Rigid sex-role stereotyping during this phase of development can encourage this, and the hostility between young boys and girls which is too often a feature of primary school education may be partly due to the refusal by our society to allow all children to freely express both poles of their nature.

Furthermore, if girls and boys are expected to ignore the contrasexual principle in their bodies and psyches, a one-sidedness may develop which could severely inhibit the full realisation of both principles within the individual later. When the balance of male and female, which varies in each person, is forced by sex-role stereotyping to conform to a cultural norm of male and female behaviour, individuals are presented with two possibilities: either they restrict and impoverish the development of their psyches by moulding themselves to the cultural definition of male and female gender, or they develop their full potential and become 'abnormal'. When the stereotypes are also associated with value judgements it is impossible for the relationship between the sexes not to be distorted by oppression and exploitation. For in a master-servant situation neither sex is free to recognise and develop his or her contrasexual characteristics without fear of abuse. While, therefore, it is essential during the first half of life to learn to recognise and experience the different natures of the masculine and the feminine, it is not only unnecessary but may even be harmful to identify exclusively with one and ignore the other.

Freud and Neumann approached the Oedipus myth from different perspectives and arrived at different interpretations. Freud was primarily concerned with sexual identities in the narrow sense of the word, and Neumann with the development of consciousness and its relation to the masculine and feminine archetypes. But the two interpretations agree on a fundamental point – that the Oedipus crisis is a time of separation from the mother, whether she is understood as the personal mother, or mother substitute, or the impersonal bisexual Mother archetype. Both recognise the Oedipus crisis as the force propelling the child toward self-consciousness and individuality, and for both it initiates a period in life when the world demands to be experienced and explored through polarity in thought and feeling rather than through the old undifferentiated consciousness. The insights of these two schools of thought offer much to explain the early phases of psychological development and the general character and direction of human consciousness during the first half of life. A spiritual dimension of meaning in the Oedipus myth, however, is provided by the writings of Rudolf Steiner.

Steiner explains that the history of humanity can be interpreted, at one level, as the struggle of the feminine and masculine principles. Both within the individual and within society a battle has raged, since early times, according to him, between the female force which brings about similarity and binds individuals to others and to nations through blood ties, and the male force which promotes all that is individual and unique in the human being.[38] The task of each person is to harmonise the two principles – the masculine and the feminine – and thereby acquire wisdom. But, said Steiner, this was not possible before the Christian era; ancient initiates could only achieve their wisdom, he explains, by sacrificing their individual consciousness. In their ascent towards spiritual knowledge they 'killed' the paternal principle, the father, and married the 'mother'. It was impossible for them to retain a sense or experience of their own individuality at the same time as understanding the truths of the universe. Only by becoming at one with the cosmos could they 'know' the cosmos. But gradually this ancient ability to intuit spiritual knowledge by rising beyond the individual self faded; fewer and fewer people succeeded in receiving wisdom in this way, and as the ancient path to understanding declined, egoism, strife and confusion arose. The instinctive connections binding people to each other and to the environment disintegrated in the face of the growing power of the masculine principle, and a new path to knowledge and understanding had to evolve.

Steiner places the Oedipus myth in this context. He said that Oedipus attempted to discover knowledge through the maternal consciousness at a time when it had ceased to be appropriate. He paid for his error by the loss of sight and by bringing disaster to his country. The new way towards knowledge, Steiner explains, was foreshadowed by Christ whose life was an expression of the masculine individualising principle and the feminine principle of oneness. Christ 'was to represent to humanity the great pattern of a being who has established within himself harmony and concord between his Ego and the maternal principle.'[39] His androgyny made possible the individual consciousness of universal truths. With Christ, wisdom ceased to be something impersonal and general and became individual and universal. No longer did human beings have to lose personal consciousness to find the way; henceforth it became possible to find the Way through consciousness.

The Oedipus crisis marks the beginning of the growth of individual consciousness promoted by the influence of the masculine principle. It challenges the old bisexual oneness which characterises the child's experience of containment within the mother/world during the early years and propels the child toward the discovery of him or herself and an experience of the different natures of the masculine and feminine. The struggle between the collective and individual consciousness, between the maternal and the masculine continues until puberty, and can recur after this. During the early years children discover and assert their individuality in relation to the external world, which they explore by seeing it as something to some extent separate from themselves. After puberty a new exploration adds itself to the earlier one; the exploring of the self prompted by such questions as 'Who am I?' Like the examination of the outer world, the inner one, too, needs to be differentiated. During the first half of life these two processes continue alongside each other and the original unity of experience is increasingly broken down into different parts by the influence of the masculine principle.

However sensitive a particular culture may be to the balance of masculinity and femininity in each person, it remains likely that boys and girls will experience the power of the masculine to different degrees. In accordance with their predominantly male or female bodies they will develop one sexual principle in their consciousness more than the other. The feminine impulse towards relationships, sensitivity and openness to others, towards receptivity and intuition would be more likely to be marked in girls, while the masculine impulse towards assertiveness, authority, analysis and reason is more pronounced in boys. Whatever the cultural situation, girls have certain difficulties during the first stage of life not shared by boys; they are torn between the demands for independence and individuality and the urges of their feminine psyches beckoning them towards experiences of belonging. For boys there are difficulties of a different kind; the conjunction of the masculine tone of this stage of life with the masculine part of their psyche may divorce them too radically from the world and from their own unconscious instincts and feelings, cramping their experience of themselves.

The development of consciousness during the first half of life corresponds to the development of the physical body. Both parts of our nature begin in an undifferentiated unity from which the masculine later emerges bringing about differentiation. Physically this expresses itself in sexual identity and psychologically in the growth of a sense of self. To find ourselves, it seems, we have first to sacrifice a part of ourselves. We have to focus on the differences rather than on the relationships. The first half of life may, therefore, be a relatively easier time for boys than for girls. But during the second half of life the situation reverses, and women, provided they have not entirely repressed and neglected their masculine nature, may find this stage considerably easier to take full advantage of than men. For in the second half of life it is the feminine, not the masculine, which initiates the way forward in the development of human consciousness.

Some of Jung's most interesting contributions to psychology come from his studies of this second half of life – the years from the late thirties and early forties. He observed that the middle years of life present the individual with a crisis, demanding a radical change of direction; certain traits tend to re-emerge from a period of dormancy stretching back to childhood, dominant interests weaken and others push for recognition, cherished beliefs and principles cease to carry the conviction they used to, and a new purpose and direction in life is called for. Often, it appears to me, these changes arise out of a period of acute depression, loneliness, fear or an unparalleled sense of emptiness and despair. The energy and meaning which carried a person through the first half of life, propelling him or her into jobs and relationships, vanishes, leaving nothing to fill the vacuum. The person feels abandoned, left with nothing but a deteriorating body and mind.

Reading and listening to accounts of people who are going through, or who have already confronted this crisis it seems as though the first half of life can be compared to a mountain, up which each person is driven. Half-way through life the person reaches the summit of the mountain and, looking down the other side for the first time, sees nothing but death waiting hungrily at the bottom. There are no further summits to conquer, no alternative route down the mountain which might bypass the abyss. Not only is the future meaningless, but it also invalidates the past. The early struggle up the mountain appears a complete waste of effort, useless pain. There is nothing to do but to stumble willingly or unwillingly towards death. Time becomes finite and the struggles of youth insignificant and childish compared to this final certainty. What is the point of searching for new understanding, formulating and achieving new ambitions when everything must end so ignominiously in death?

We can, of course, pretend it is not happening, blinker ourselves from the future and immerse ourselves in the present. But while the capacity to live each day, and each moment of each day, completely is an invaluable companion to the acceptance of death and consideration for the future, a blind clinging to the present, motivated by nothing other than a desire to stop the clock, leads only to increased pain and neurosis. Living in the present can bring a healthy acceptance of the ephemeral nature of life; the attempt to remain on the top of the mountain brings only ill health. The temptations to do this are, however, considerable, for the view from the top is often bleak. Kate Millet offers her description of it in her book *Sita*:

> I felt old, it is how I feel all the time now. I turned forty last summer and it scared me. Since being here I am obsessed with death. Not the imminent death of my suicidal time, not a death you steel yourself to impose, but the 'natural' and inevitable death that begins when the sense of age begins. If I was forty I was no longer young: when you are no longer young you are old. Old age is only the tedious and debilitating prelude to death, being dead while still being minimally alive.[40]

Hers is one description of the view from the mountain. Jung offers another. His description of the journey down does not lead to a different destination but it does suggest that this destination can be approached with a different state of mind and different feelings, and thereby become a journey towards much greater understanding than was possible during the personal, goal-oriented struggles of the first half of life, a journey which can transform the prelude to death into years of unparalleled wisdom and joy.

Jung tells a story about an Indian warrior chief to indicate the flavour of these later years. In the middle of his life a spirit appeared to this chief telling him that from now on he must sit among the women and children, wear women's clothes, and eat the food of women. The chief obeyed the dream and apparently suffered no loss of prestige. Jung comments that this vision was a true expression of the 'psychic revolution of life's noon, of the beginning of life's decline. Man's values, and even his body,' he writes, 'do tend to change into their opposite . . .'

> The worst of it all is that intelligent and cultivated people live their lives without even knowing the possibility of such transformations. Wholly unprepared, they embark upon the second half of life. Or are there perhaps colleges for forty-year-olds which prepare them for their coming life and its demands as the ordinary colleges introduce our young people to a knowledge of the world? No, thoroughly unprepared we take the step into the afternoon of life; worse still we take this step with the false assumption that our truths and ideals will serve us as hitherto. But we cannot live the afternoon of life according to the programme of life's morning; for what was great in the morning will be little at evening, and what in the morning was true will at evening have become a lie.[41]

Our bodies undergo a change during the second part of life and our consciousness, too, develops in a new direction. One seventy-year-old woman expressed the situation succinctly when she said 'women turn into men inside' at menopause.[42] But whereas the changes in our bodies happen without our volition or control, the same is less true of our psychological development. Unless we can fully understand and accept the direction in which we need to move we risk turning our bodies into our enemies. To benefit from, and enjoy, the process of growing towards death, we have to understand it and not just regard it as a postscript to a useful or unuseful, happy or unhappy life. We need to learn to accept that there are many different stages in life, each with its own different needs and tasks, advantages and disadvantages, and that these stages can only be fully experienced when they are acknowledged and understood for what they offer in themselves rather than for what they follow or what may follow them.

The first half of life, led by the masculine, is a time of differentiation, during which we understand ourselves and the world by taking it to pieces. The second half is characterised by the feminine tendency to make whole, to see and experience the connections between things, to replace separateness with harmony. Neumann describes this time as one of growing stability and wholeness at the expense of the necessary tension and differentiation of the first half of life, a time when each person regains his or her original hermaphroditism.

Everyone, it seems, has the potential for becoming conscious of both masculine and feminine aspects of their psyche and realising that their truest nature is neither male nor female but androgyny. The strength and courage needed to discover this Self are considerable, but the second half of life provides the natural inducements to take up the challenge for it is a time when the body becomes less markedly one-sided, as well as a time when outer achievements often cease to have the lure they once had. The search for androgyny will be different for each person since the neglected and repressed aspects of the psyche vary in everyone. But whether it is the feminine or the masculine, or whether it is aspects of both which demand recognition and development, the consciousness of the second half of life must be guided by the feminine, for the task is one of gathering together rather than dividing. Women, therefore, can have the advantage over men at this time, but only if they have been able to develop their masculine natures sufficiently in the preceding years. When this has not happened, they may become so obsessed in the later years with the expression of the masculine principle that they will find it difficult, perhaps impossible, to take advantage of the intimations of androgyny which the last decades of life can offer. An excessive masculinity in a man's early life may have similar consequences: instead of being able consciously to create a relationship between the two principles and discover the self that is neither male nor female but both, he will become a servant to the psychological need to experience the feminine side of his nature.

The androgynous consciousness of the second half of life is only a possibility, not an inevitability. Whether we search for it or not is a free choice, for whereas during the first half of life we seem to be compelled in certain directions with an energy present from birth, in the second half we have to generate our own energy and choose our own directions unless we wish to be the helpless victims of rapidly declining bodies. It is as though the body carries the consciousness until the middle thirties and, thereafter, the consciousness has to support the body. The first half of life leads us, the second offers us a choice; we can be dragged down the mountain by our bodies or we can carry our bodies down the mountain in the direction of androgyny.

Those who select the second alternative experience the progress towards death as a return to their beginning, a return to the original bisexual wholeness, and a knowing of it for the first time. To go this way demands the capacity to experience the inner and outer worlds with a consciousness which allows the interplay of Yin and Yang, and is dominated by neither. Such a stage of psychological development may seem utopian; imbalance and one-sidedness have been the human condition for thousands, probably millions of years. Furthermore, they are not entirely negative; there are certain advantages to one-sidedness which have already been mentioned, like conscious independence, specialised knowledge, analysis, rational thought etc, all of which depend at some stage of their development on the predominance of the masculine over the feminine. But whereas one-sidedness and imbalance are appropriate during the first half of life, they can be the cause of considerable anguish and difficulties during the second. This chapter has suggested that the search for an androgynous consciousness brings new understanding and excitement to these later years in place of emptiness and despair, and that such a search is not a fantasy but one whose nature and meaning is hinted at in the fundamental patterns of biological and psychological development. However, old age is relatively new in the history of humanity; most people died, and many still do, long before they can take advantage of the second half of life. So what evidence is there to suggest that humanity is capable of beginning to realise this potential? A few exceptional people may be prepared, and this has probably always been so. What about the rest of us? To begin to answer this question it is necessary to explore the relationship between individual development and the development of humanity as a whole.

CHAPTER SEVEN

Microcosm and Macrocosm

To see a world in a grain of sand
And eternity in an hour.
William Blake

In the beginning was the Dao, said the Chinese. The Dao became Yin and Yang, and from these two principles emerged the ten thousand things. This version of creation assumes that nothing exists outside or separate from the Dao, and that everything, however small, in some sense reflects it; as the cell of the body implies the whole so every part of creation implies the cosmos. The 'ten thousand things' are not isolated entities spinning around in empty space; but spirit and matter, mineral and plant, animal and human are all manifestations of the Dao, the one, indivisible and immanent principle of creation. To understand any part demands an understanding of the whole.

The Chinese organic conception of the cosmos involved a view of the human being as a microcosmic image of the macrocosm. This idea is implicit in the cosmology of the earliest texts. Later writings were more explicit on the subject; as intuitive statements were replaced by philosophical enquiries, the microcosmic-macrocosmic theory received conscious attention and affirmation.

The Chinese *Book of History*, the *Shu Jing* (*Shu Ching*), consisting of sayings ascribed to the legendary sage kings, Yao and

Shun of the third millenium BC., contains an early mention of the human and cosmic correspondence: 'Heaven,' it says, 'hears and sees as our people hear and see.'[1] The *Book of Rites*, the *Li Ji* (*Li Chi*) a compilation of the second century BC., describes the human being as 'the product of the attributes of Heaven and Earth, by the interaction of the dual forces of nature, the union of the animal, *gui*, and the intelligent, *shen*, souls, and the finest matter of the five elements.'[2] The idea of a human being as a miniature heaven and earth is also fundamental to the *Yi Jing*, which likens heaven to the head and earth to the belly. Macro-micro correspondences constitute a constant theme in many of the hexagrams and their commentaries. For example, hexagram 22 is *Bi* (*Pi*) Grace. Richard Wilhelm's commentary reads:

> In the upper trigram of the mountain, the strong line takes the lead, so that here again the strong element must be regarded as the decisive factor. In nature we see in the sky the strong light of the sun; the life of the world depends on it. But this strong, essential thing is changed and given pleasing variety by the moon and the stars. In human affairs, aesthetic form comes into being when traditions exist that, strong and abiding like mountains, are made pleasing by a lucid beauty.[3]

Since the *Yi Jing* assumes a correspondence between the way of heaven and earth and the way of humanity, it teaches that the task of the sage is to understand the Dao so as to create a conscious harmony between humanity and the cosmos. Self-knowledge, it asserts, is the way to such understanding. According to the Confucian philosopher Mencius (322–289 BC.): 'For a man to give full realization to his heart is for him to understand his own nature, and a man who knows his own nature will know Heaven.'[4] And again: 'All the ten thousand things are there in me. There is no greater joy than to find, on self-examination, that I am true to myself.'[5] Zhu Xi's philosophy expresses the relationship between macrocosm and microcosm most succinctly. He argued that 'all the individual principles of things are contained in the universal principle, and each individual thing contains in its entirety the principles of everything else.'[6]

It was not until the Han Confucian philosopher, Dong Zhong shu (Tung Chung-shu), who probably lived between 179–104 BC., that the microcosmic-macrocosmic theory received detailed attention. In place of the old unspoken assumptions, Dong offered detailed explanations and complicated systems of correspondence about the relationship of the individual to the cosmos.

> Man has 360 joints, which match the number of Heaven (the round number of days in a year). His body with its bones and flesh matches the thickness of the earth. He has ears and eyes above, with their keen sense of hearing and seeing, which resemble the sun and moon. His body has its orifices and veins, which resemble rivers and valleys. His heart has feelings of sorrow, joy, pleasure, and anger, which are analogous to the spiritual feelings (of Heaven).[7]

He also wrote: 'The breathing of his nostrils and mouth resembles the wind. The penetrating knowledge of his mind resembles the spiritual intelligence [of Heaven] . . . . the portion of the body below the waist corresponds to the earth . . . The agreement of heaven and earth and the correspondence between Yin and Yang are ever found complete in the human body . . .'[8]

Dong Zhong shu explained that the Yin and Yang of heaven influence the Yin and Yang of the individual; when Heaven's Yin arises, the Yin of the human being responds: 'The principle is the same. He who understands this, when he wishes to bring forth rain, will activate the Yin of man in order to arouse the Yin of the universe.'[9] The interaction of microcosm and macrocosm is, therefore, a two-way affair; it is not only Heaven which initiates, for the human being can also initiate and influence once she or he has grasped the principles governing the universe.

However, in the writings of Dong Zhong shu it is possible to detect the beginnings of a sclerotic tendency in Chinese thought which was to accelerate in subsequent centuries, threatening to reduce the ancient intuitive insights to little more than mechanical formulae which inhibited rather than promoted understanding. The writings of the earliest classics, originating in pre-historical dream-like consciousness, appeal to the imagination and intuition for verification. They are not accessible to the intellect. But with the emergence of the masculine analytical consciousness, the ancient apprehension of the Dao, once the privilege of a handful of sages, ceased to satisfy the growing number of people eager to use their analytical and intellectual faculties to decipher the way of the world. In this process the insights of the old sages were often diminished to make them accessible to the exponents of the new consciousness; symbols were reduced to literal explanations in which much of their original meaning was lost. This was the cost of the relative popularisation of the ancient wisdom, the development of individual understanding, and, also, the passing of the old matriarchal consciousness in which people collectively and instinctively accepted and structured their lives according to the correspondence between human and cosmic rhythms.

The spread of a teaching is too often achieved by an impoverishment of its meaning. The sacred may be popularised by cheapening its demands. China was no exception. The popularisation of insights depends, for its success, on a two-way process; the insights themselves need to be understood and presented as clearly as language permits, but the listeners also must prepare themselves to receive and recognise the knowledge. To bring a teaching down to the lowest common denominator of understanding is to diminish the teaching and to demean the individual. This unfortunately, is what tended to happen from about the third century BC. As the intuitive understanding of the cosmos declined and as no new sages were born, convenient diagrams and simplistic explanations came to be confused with the truth.

But the passing of the sages and the loss of the ancient matriarchal consciousness was not wholly detrimental to the development of understanding. It also offered the possibility of acquiring a more conscious and individual understanding of the cosmos to those willing to accept the difficulties of such a search. In China it was the Neo-Confucians of the Song dynasty (AD. 960–1279)) who pioneered this path. Not content merely to mouth the wisdom of the past, they attempted to develop a philosophy appropriate to the masculine consciousness of their time. But their achievements were limited by their temptation to regard as explanations what often amounted to little more than restatements of the assertions contained in the classics. Shao Yong (Shao Yung), for example, who lived from AD. 1011–1077, wrote:

> Man occupies the most honoured position in the scheme of things because he combines in him the principles of all the species . . . The

> nature of all things is complete in the human species. The spirit of man is the same as the spirit of Heaven and Earth . . . Spirit is nowhere and yet everywhere. The perfect man can penetrate the minds of others because he is based on the One . . .[10]
>
> The Way is in all events, whether great or little. They conform to the Way when they are contented with their state of being.[11]

Zhu Xi, probably the greatest of the Neo-Confucians, also devoted considerable attention to this problem. 'The Way,' he said, 'is identical with the nature of man and things, and the nature is identical with the Way. They are one and the same . . .'[12] Neither of these statements add fundamentally to what had been said by Confucius and his disciple Mencius over one thousand years earlier. However, the spirit of the Neo-Confucian writings is strikingly different from the early philosophers, and in this, possibly more than in the content, lies its value for the evolution of human understanding. It heralds a new respect for the potential of each individual to discover for himself, through investigation, the ways of the world. The theory of the individual as a miniature cosmos, as it developed through the centuries, provided the foundations for a political, economic and social system which acknowledged the intimate relationship between the 'ten thousand things', and for an approach to life which considered humanity as responsible for ensuring that the relationship is a harmonious one. For while every part reflects the whole, humans alone, by virtue of their minds, have the possibility of understanding. Neo-Confucianism was no different from its predecessors in its promotion of a highly exploitative and oppressive order based on the assumption that those who work with their hands should support those who work with their minds. However this did not, in any way, invalidate their fundamental conviction that every person, regardless of social origin, has the potential for self, and cosmic knowledge.

The Chinese conception of the relation of the parts of creation to the whole can be expressed diagramatically:

DAO

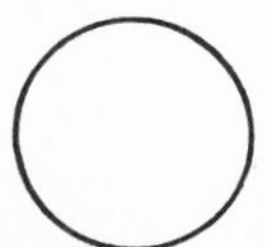

YIN-YANG

EIGHT TRIGRAMS

The nothing, or indefinable everything, generates its polarity, Yin and Yang, from whose interaction evolve the five elements, and, thence, all things. In pouring itself out into the world and acquiring different forms, the Dao does not lose its essential unity; every part remains interdependent with the whole. From this cosmology evolved a complicated system of correspondence:

Emotion	Anger	Joy	Sorrow	Fear	Compassion
Fluid	Tears	Perspiration	Mucus	Saliva	—
Tissues	Ligaments	Arteries	Skin & Hair	Bones	Muscles
Orifices	Eyes	Ears	Mouth	Genitals	Nose
Viscera	Liver	Heart	Lungs	Kidneys	Spleen
Flavour	Sour	Bitter	Tart	Salty	Sweet
Climate	Wind	Heat	Dryness	Cold	Humidity
Colour	Green	Red	White	Black	Yellow
Planets	Jupiter	Mars	Venus	Mercury	Saturn
Elements	Wood	Fire	Metal	Water	Earth
Time	Morning	Noon	Evening	Night	—
Season	Spring	Summer	Autumn	Winter	—
Direction	East	South	West	North	Centre

Such a system was necessary only because the ancient, spontaneous knowledge of the interdependence of all things had faded. Its existence reflects in a small way the need for conscious rather than instinctive knowledge. Previously, as Qi Bo (Ch'i Po), the Yellow Emperor's physician, explains there were people who lived in conformity with the Dao with no need of written laws or numerically based systems.

There was temperance in eating and drinking. Their hours of rising and retiring were regular and not disorderly and wild. By these means the ancients kept their bodies united with their souls, so as to fulfill their allotted span completely, measuring unto a hundred years before they passed away.

Nowadays people are not like this; they use wine as beverage and they adopt recklessness as usual behaviour. They enter the chamber (ot love) in an intoxicated condition; their passions exhaust their vital forces; their cravings dissipate their true (essence); they do not know how to find contentment within themselves; they are not skilled in the control of their spirits. They devote all their attention to the amusements of their minds, thus cutting themselves off from the joys of long (life).[13]

Qi Bo and the *Yi Jing* both accept that humanity cannot recover the ancient instinctive consciousness, when people naturally did what was right. Instead they suggest that the way forward must be through self-knowledge and a conscious understanding of the nature of things and their relation to each other. It demands an individual thinking mind as well as an intuitive and receptive one. Without the interplay of these polar ways, they imply, harmony between body and mind, spirit and matter, individual and humanity, or the human and natural worlds cannot arise.

The later Chinese did not forget or ignore these early teachings. Their culture was, at least in theory, inspired by a reverence for the wisdom of the past. But in practice the names of the Sages and their insights were more often adopted to justify the authoritarian system of Imperial China than to promote deeper understanding of their wisdom. Confucianism, based on the sayings of Confucius and Mencius, but significantly moulded by the Han (206 BC–AD. 220) and Song (AD. 960–1279) thinkers, dominated Chinese government for much of the period from the third century BC. to 1905. It focused more on maintaining hierarchal relationships between different sections of society than on encouraging members of the elite to develop their own wisdom. It maintained that the state was the patriarchal family writ large with the emperor as the father and ruler of the people. The bureaucrats, to whom the government of the empire was delegated, largely qualified for their posts by proving their proficiency as Confucian scholars, through the rigorous examination system, success in which depended on a high degree of rote learning. There was little space for personal interpretation in Confucian education just as there was little space within the society as a whole for the pursuit of understanding and self-knowledge if this involved questioning or challenging the definitions of wisdom as laid down by the Neo-Confucians, in particular by Zhu Xi. Uniformity of thought was regarded as a vital pre-requisite of stable government; new thinking the first dangerous step towards disobedience, disorder and rebellion. In such a context it was difficult for all but a small minority to separate the ancient teachings from the oppressive Confucian system with which they were associated.

However with the Communist victory in 1949 the situation changed. Confucianism became the target of widespread attack. A number of campaigns were organised to eradicate Confucian thinking and all old superstitions. Among other things (as discussed in an earlier chapter) these campaigns challenged the paternal and patriarchial idea of the ruler as the father of the people, the conception of the relationship between the government and the people as analogous to the wind blowing over the grass, the assumption that it is man's nature to lead and control and woman's to follow and serve, and the intellectual's right to be supported by the manual worker. As a result the influence of Confucianism as a political system which yoked the Chinese people for hundreds of years has been replaced by a new order, in which the individual and local community groups, committees, and organisations in town and countryside are expected to assume responsibility and control of their own lives in a number of ways, rather than merely obeying the dictates of destiny, the Confucian bureaucrat, and local landlord. To create space for such a new order, Confucian thinking, with its powerful respect for doing things as they have always been done, has tended to be repudiated wholesale. But this may not always be necessary. It may at some future time, be possible for the Chinese people to develop a more critical understanding and appreciation of their cultural and philosophical traditions, to separate the valuable insights of Confucianism from the oppressive system which they helped to underpin.

In medicine this has already begun. The modern Chinese have recognised the value of many parts of *The Yellow Emperor's Classic of Internal Medicine* as well as the herbal and other therapies it inspired. But a similar study and re-evaluation of other parts of China's ancient wisdom in the light of modern scientific methods and understanding has not yet occurred. The Chinese art of geomancy, *Feng shui* (literally, wind and water), is still largely ridiculed by the Chinese Communists, who see its emphasis on the interdependence of the earthly and cosmic worlds as a hindrance to their ambitions to control nature and transform China into an advanced industrial society by the end of this century. Yet *Feng Shui* offers many interesting insights into the nature of human and cosmic life.

Geomancy, which developed gradually during the early centuries of the Chinese empire, is a logical outcome of the earliest Chinese conception of the world as the manifestation of the Dao present in *The Yellow Emperor's Classic*. Since the cosmos is a unity, no part of which is finally independent from the whole, it follows that events at one level, or in one place, will have their influence at other levels and in other places. The Yin and Yang of the heavens influence the climate of the earth, the Yin and the Yang running through the crust of the earth influence the minerals, plant, animal and human life, and the Yin and Yang of humanity influence both earthly and cosmic life. The task of the human being is to understand the ways of the two principles as they express themselves in creation, so that all actions can be performed in harmony with these ways, that these ways themselves can be brought to completion by the agency of humanity. Integral to *Feng-shui* was the assumption that Heaven 'requires the aid of man to carry out its scheme of justice. Earth requires the aid of man to bring its products to perfection. Neither heaven nor earth are complete in themselves but leave the last finish of everything to man.'[14] The corollary of this was the idea that earthly or cosmic disturbances could also be attributed to the disharmony of human thoughts and actions. When Ping Ji (P'ing Chi), an important statesman under the Emperor Wu (140–87 BC.) encountered a panting ox on the road he said: 'Your Three Highest Ministers act to harmonize the yin and the yang. Just now it is spring, when the lesser yang is operative in affairs, so that there should not yet be any great heat. Nevertheless, the ox is panting because of a summer-like heat, which, I fear, means that the seasons are out of joint. There is harm in such a situation.'[15]

Geomancy claimed to teach people how to rule nature and guide their own destiny by revealing to them the ways of heaven and earth. Knowledge of *Feng-shui* was, therefore, a means of transforming people from the playthings of nature to co-creators with her; this was not only of benefit to humanity, but also to the natural world, which was seen in a sense as waiting for the helping hand of human understanding and human action for its fulfilment. This was the spirit behind Chinese landscape gardening which in the nineteenth century, was to have such a profound influence on English gardening. The gardener's task was to help bring nature to her own perfection through a knowledge of her ways. The Zen intention in gardening, described in chapter five, was not to make a realistic illusion of landscape, but simply to suggest the general atmosphere of 'mountain and water' in a small space, arranging the design of the garden in a way which suggests that it has been helped rather than governed by the hand of man. This art of landscape gardening which began in China, 'became a fine art in Japan, with aesthetic canons that have had a great influence in the occident during recent times.'[16]

The perfect conjunction of Yin and Yang, sought by the geomancer for the construction of a house or the timing of an event, was considered to be three-fifths Yang and two-fifths Yin. For instance, sharply rising ground was Yang and gently undulating terrain Yin, so in the siting of a new house it was considered auspicious to find a spot combining both kinds of land in the right proportions. If such a place could not be found, the next best place was felt to be a Yin spot on predominantly Yang ground, or the other way round. Interesting affirmation of the importance of the relation between the individual and geography is offered in Carlos Castaneda's description of one of his earliest exercises with the Yacqui Indian sorcerer Don Juan. Castaneda wanted Don Juan to trust the sincerity of his desire to become 'a man of knowledge' even though he was not an Indian. Don Juan responded by posing Castaneda the problem of finding his own 'spot', the place on the floor where he could sit without fatigue. This is Castaneda's description of what ensued:

> What he [Don Juan] had posed as a problem to be solved was certainly a riddle. I had no idea how to begin or even what he had in mind. Several times I asked for a clue, or at least a hint, as to how to proceed in locating a point where I felt happy and strong. I insisted and argued that I had no idea what he really meant because I couldn't conceive the problem. He suggested I walk around the porch until I found the spot.
>
> I got up and began to pace the floor. I felt silly and sat down in front of him. He became very annoyed with me and accused me of not

listening, saying that perhaps I did not want to learn. After a while he calmed down and explained to me that not every place was good to sit or be on, and that within the porch there was one spot that was unique, a spot where I could be at my very best. It was my task to distinguish it from all the other places. The general pattern was that I had to 'feel' all the possible spots that were accessible until I could determine without a doubt which was the right one.[17]

For some hours Castaneda rolled around the floor vainly searching for the 'spot' and as he reached the point of despair, Don Juan told him that he wasn't in the least surprised he had failed because he had not proceeded correctly. He had not been using his eyes. The sorcerer explained that it is possible to 'feel with the eyes, when the eyes are not looking right into things.' So once again Castaneda began searching. Finally at dawn he discovered a place by a rock where he fell asleep. He awoke to Don Juan saying, 'You have found the spot.' The sorcerer then explained that there are good and bad spots for each person. 'The sheer act of sitting on one's spot created superior strength; on the other hand, the enemy (the bad spot) weakened a man and could even cause his death.' He said Castaneda had replenished his energy, which he had spent lavishly the night before, by taking a nap on his spot. He explained there were many good places in the world comparable to the one Castaneda had discovered and that the best way to find them was by detecting their respective colours.[18]

In China the geomantic compass was also used to identify the correct time for building and the right direction for the house to face. The compass itself was a complicated instrument. It made use of Yin and Yang, the eight trigrams, the 64 hexagrams, the solar orbit, the lunar eliptic, the days of the year, the five planets and five elements, the 28 constellations, the 12 zodiacal signs and the 12 points of the compass. The skills of the geomancer, with the aid of his compass, were intended to reveal the patterns of the cosmos. The duty of the individual was then to perfect the natural configurations of Yin and Yang; if a hill was not high enough to harmonise with the surrounding yin ground, for example, it would be artificially raised.

Feng shui assumed that humanity was responsible for the universe, that no action could be taken without regard for its consequences on the rest of creation and that only human wisdom could reveal the patterns of Yin and Yang which needed harmonising. It implied that ignorance or denial of the microcosmic-macrocosmic relationship between human and cosmic nature and the correspondence between heaven and earth resulted in personal, public and natural disasters. In the nineteenth century, when these ideas first received wide publicity in the West, they were ridiculed by the Western imperialists who were forcing their way into China and criss-crossing the country with their inauspicious railroads. Eitel concludes his study of *Feng shui,* published in 1873, with these words:

> What is *Feng shui,* then? It is simply the blind gropings of the Chinese mind after a system of natural science, which gropings, untutored by practical observation of nature, and trusting almost exclusively in the truth of alleged tradition and in the force of abstract reasoning, naturally left the Chinese mind completely in the dark. The system of *Feng shui,* therefore, based as it is on human speculation and superstition and not on careful study of nature, is marked for decay and dissolution.[19]

The geomantic compass may well remain of little more than historical interest, but the vision of the universe it expressed as an interdependent world in which each part reflects and is reflected by the whole, and which humanity, as a miniature heaven and earth, can complete through conscious understanding, may contain some wisdom much needed by the specialised western approach to knowledge with its tendency to explore nature from within a highly specialised, fragmented framework, thereby often missing the relation between the parts. Indeed geomancy may prove to be less unscientific than it was considered by the imperialists in the nineteenth century. Modern science is already beginning to recognise what many people have been thinking and feeling for some time, that the human and natural worlds are not as separate as we have supposed.

The Yellow Emperor's *Classic* taught that the winds and seasons have marked effects on the human body, certain physical conditions being the response to terrestrial forces. It maintained that it was crucial for human beings to act in accordance with the seasons so as to avoid disharmony, for each person breathes the breath of the universe, tastes its atmosphere and reflects its rhythm.[20] Modern medicine is now beginning to investigate the effect of atmospheric and meteorological conditions on the human organism and it has been shown that the number of breaths each person draws varies according to the time of year: 'In Europe the maximum number occurs in Jan/Feb. and the minimum in July/Aug. In July the quantity of hemoglobin is highest and it is lowest in January. The iodine content of the blood decreases during the winter and rises suddenly in spring often causing a marked deterioration in the condition of patients suffering from hyperactive thyroid glands.'[21] Many animals respond to the yearly rhythms in a way which suggests an instinctive awareness of the seasons beyond such factors as heat and light. For example, experiments have been conducted with the golden-mantled ground squirrel. These animals were kept in windowless rooms with a constant temperature of 0°C and 12 hours of light. In these conditions the squirrels still hibernated during the winter and woke up in April. When the temperature was raised to 35°C the squirrels found it too warm to go to sleep, but they still gained weight in the autumn and lost it gradually through the winter, just as they would have done while hibernating.[22]

Animals and insects respond to a circadian rhythm of sunlight; human beings also manifest circadian rhythms, but theirs are less immediately apparent. Our temperature changes are now independent of light and dark, but our potassium secretion remains regulated by the movements of the sun. Each individual normally secretes three grams of this valuable mineral each day, and it has been discovered that even humans deprived for more than two years of the normal rhythms of day and night still manifest regular 24 hour cycles of potassium secretion. We also experience annual rhythms. These have been observed in regular changes of body-weight[23] as well as in seasonal hair loss.

Lunar rhythms are also known to be important for animals, fish and insects. They are of two kinds – daily and monthly. Oysters have been seen to respond to a clear tidal rhythm. In one experiment a number of oysters were moved from Long Island Sound Connecticut to Evanston, a suburb of Chicago. For two weeks they continued to respond to the Connecticut tidal rhythms, opening their shells to feed at high tide and closing them during the ebb. But on the fifteenth day their rhythm unanimously changed. After some calculations it was discovered that the oysters had begun to open at the time the tide would have flooded Evanston, had they been on the shore instead of 580 feet above sea level on the bank of Lake Michigan.[24] Many sea animals swarm with lunation. Grunions, for example, spawn on the flood tides of the full moon, and sexual activity at the full moon in the animal kingdom is the rule rather than the exception. Lunar cycles are also the sexual cycles in some of the lower animals, for instance mayflies, mosquitoes and algae.[25] The idea of the moon's rhythm influencing the earth was not foreign to the ancient Chinese; Guanzi (Kuan Tzu), the seventh century BC. political reformer, is recorded as saying that certain marine animals are subject to the lunar cycle, increasing and decreasing in size as the moon waxes and wanes.[26] The sceptical philosopher Wang Zhong (Wang Chung) (AD. 29–97) recognised the connection between the moon and the tides. He wrote 'the rise of the wave follows the waxing and waning of the moon, smaller and larger, fuller or lesser, never the same.[27] It is now known that lunar rhythms affect not only the water but the entire atmosphere of the earth. 'The moon also draws away the envelope of air that surrounds the earth and produces regular daily atmospheric tides.'[28] Its effects have even been noticed in a cup of tea. These observations we owe to modern science. The structure of water, a crystal lattice, is altered by the passing of the moon overhead. Since two thirds of the human body is composed of this crystalline pattern of water it would seem unlikely that not only some animals but humans as well are affected by the movements of the moon.[29]

The question of the moon's influence on the human body remains, however, unresolved by modern science. Nevertheless there are some interesting coincidences. The mean length of the female menstrual cycle is 29.5 days, which is also the length of the cycle from new moon to new moon (29.53 days to be precise).[30] It is also interesting that just as the word 'menstruation' comes from '*mens, mensis*' meaning 'month', and 'month' means 'moon', so the Chinese character for month and moon is the same 月 and a common word for menstruation is 月 經 (yue jing), 'an affair of the moon'. The association between the moon and menstruation is common to many cultures. German peasants call their periods 'the moon', the French term is 'le moment de la lune'. The

Sabbath which, E. Harding explains, originally meant the day of rest taken by the full moon, also meant the menstruation of the Babylonian goddesses. It was regarded as a taboo time when no work was done. The Mandingo, the Susne and the Congo tribes call menstruation 'the moon', and the Maori call it 'moon sickness'.[31]

Contemporary studies are beginning to indicate that it is not only women who experience 'lunar' cycles:

The directors of the Omi Railways Company of Japan, for instance, are pragmatic students of human behaviour and have therefore decided to accept the fact that men have lunar cycles of mood and efficiency. This company operates a private transport system of more than 700 buses and taxis in dense traffic areas of Kyoto and Osaka. Because their operations were plagued with high losses due to accidents, the Omi efficiency experts began in 1969 to make studies of each man and his lunar cycles and to adjust routes and schedules to coincide with the appropriate time of the month for each worker. They report a one-third drop in Omi's accident rate in the past two years, despite the fact that during the same period traffic increased.[32]

The affect of changes in the sun on the earth have also been noted. The influence of sunspot cycles was first noticed in 1801 by Sir John Herschel. The 11 year cycles have since been found to correlate among other things with the thickness of annual rings in trees, the level of Lake Victoria, the number of icebergs, the occurrence of drought in India and great years for Burgundy wines. If the sun and moon have these effects on the earth, then it would not be a shock to discover that other planets also exert their influence on human and natural life. The ancient Chinese were in no doubt that this was the case. The Imperial astronomer held an important post in the government throughout the empire from the Zhou to the Qing (Ch'ing) dynasty as well as long before its emergence. A passage from the *Record of the Rites of Zhou* reads:

He concerns himself with the stars in the heaven, keeping a record of the changes and movements of the planets . . . the sun and the moon, in order to examine the movements of the terrestrial world, (events on earth), with the object of distinguishing (prognosticating) good and bad fortune . . . In general he concerns himself with the five kinds of phenomena, so as to warn the Emperor to come to the aid of government, and to allow for variation in the ceremonies according to the circumstances.[33]

But astrology implies a correspondence not only between the earthly and cosmic worlds, the individual and macrocosm, but also between the physical and the spiritual. It assumes that the planets are more than different amalgamations of minerals and that there is a connection between their position in the skies and human behaviour, skills and temperaments. Modern science is still some distance from being able either to verify or refute these ideas; but the conception of two separate worlds, one physical and one spiritual, no longer tallies with the findings of modern physics or analytical psychology.

Human beings are less bound to the natural rhythms of the universe than plants and animals, since self-consciousness allows us the freedom to determine many of our own rhythms. But it is precisely this freedom which is responsible for much of the current ecological devastation; we have manipulated nature for our own ends and are now beginning to appreciate the cost. We are using our freedom to create an uninhabitable world. Before it is too late it is necessary to exchange our present exploitative attitude for one which respects and understands the ways of nature both as they live in our own psyches and in the external world. For, paradoxically, it seems we can be most free not by separating ourselves from the cosmos, but by learning to experience the interdependence of the individual and the whole. This idea becomes clearer when the relation between the individual and the cosmos is looked at with the insights of analytical psychology.

Jung was deeply attracted to ancient Chinese concepts and ideas of the Dao as the principle of creation and, therefore, immanent in creation. He was also influenced by Leibniz, who, as J. Needham suggests, may well have been indebted to the insights of the Neo-Confucian school, in particular Zhu Xi.[34] Leibniz saw the world as constituted of 'monads', each of which was a closed and separate system. In this, his philosophy contradicted both the insights of modern physics and of ancient Daoist thought, both of which regard the part as intelligible in relation to the whole. But Leibniz also believed that the monad was sensitive to the cosmos, responding to and reflecting all that happens, all that has happened and all that will happen. Moreover, he recognised that the monad was largely unconscious of its powers: 'A soul can read in itself only what is represented distinctly. It cannot all at once open up all its folds, because they extend to infinity.'[35]

This view of the monad as the mirror of the universe accords with Jung's concept of the Self. He recognised that the human psyche carries all the answers within itself, that it reflects the macrocosm. These reflections are reflections of the universe in miniature: 'They are the expressions in individual form of the processes and rhythms that move in the macrocosm of nature.'[36] In the process of unfolding Self-consciousness we learn to recognise trans-personal archetypal forms which play their part in the workings of the universe and therefore, in all its parts. In becoming aware of them we mirror the cosmos and individualise it. The spiritual world of archetypes often eludes our consciousness and, to the extent that it does, we remain unfree, influenced by principles and forces beyond our knowledge. The search for the archetypal world is the search for our Self, which Jung understood as simultaneously unique and universal; unique because only each person, alone, can realise and experience the Self, universal because that Self is, ultimately, the cosmos. Neumann wrote of the discovery of the Self as the discovery of the Dao, for 'to become and to be whole are possible only in a state of harmony with the order of the world, with what the Chinese call the Tao.'[37] We are, therefore, most individual and free only when we have realised our universal nature.

In the Self, time and space are transcended; past, present and future co-exist. Many have experienced intimations of this state of being, usually in dreams or situations of *d¡j ǘu*. At these moments we are in touch with a larger 'I', one which reaches beyond the normal limits of our experiences. Sensitivity to this larger, cosmic Self reveals the possibility of understanding the past as well as the present and the future, for inherent in every psyche is its history as well as an implicit knowledge of the direction in which it is developing. So it is possible for us all to discover the patterns of change in our lives, and to be their conscious collaborators rather than their puppets.

But most of us are far from such freedom. More often we see the world from within our protected egos where there are very clear distinctions between 'I' and the 'outside' worlds. It can be frightening even to contemplate that the true Self might not be only this 'I', but also a universal 'I'. Yet each of us have experienced a time in our own lives when we were unwittingly identified with the cosmos – the psychoid state of infancy – before the birth of the individual ego, before the differentiation of psyche and body, mother and child. But this experience precedes individual consciousness.

We acquire awareness of ourselves and the world by separating from the whole, by falling from paradise. The stage before the Fall is the Golden Age, the state of perfect serenity which exists before the birth of polarity. It is the primal chaos which knows no pain, death or suffering, but also no understanding, independence or freedom. As a stage of human development it corresponds, in individual development, to the state that some Jungians call the psychoid state:

> All future possibilities are fused together in the psychoid state, for it is a level of existence that is not yet sufficiently advanced for separation and distinctness to be necessary. The psychoid state is thus very much like the Self conceived as cosmos or as a primal chaos. It would in fact be correct to say that the psychoid level of development corresponds in the microcosm to the primal chaos in the universe.[38]

In the young child this uroboric phase is relatively brief. The world which contains the child rapidly becomes anthropomorphised. In the eyes of the child it becomes the Mother, the Mother of life and death, joy and pain, the Mother who protects and nourishes, and who regulates the rhythms of day and night. As begetter and conceiver, active and passive, She symbolises the state of consciousness in which all polarities are still contained. She is the personal and the cosmic Mother. Growing up in the embrace of this consciousness the young child re-experiences the matriarchal consciousness, which characterised human awareness before the partiarchal revolution. Biologically, of course, both the young child and humanity are sexually differentiated but, as was suggested in the first two chapters, this is not reflected in consciousness until some time after its appearance at the physical level.

The time-lag between biological and psychological development is a constant feature of the first half of life. The intrauterine state of oneness with the mother persists in consciousness after the physical separation from the mother, the matriarchal consciousness persists after the beginnings of sexual differentiation and the physical independence of the child; and it is not usually until some years after puberty, and full sexual maturity, that the individual awakens to ego-consciousness and fully experiences the sexual polarity in his or her own consciousness.

The first awakening to the masculine and feminine polarity can be traced back to the Oedipus crisis, but only much later does the individual realise this polarity and internalise it in his or her own psyche. Our frail egos succumb over and over again to the temptation to return to the secure embrace of the Great Mother consciousness in which the polarities are fused. Sometimes these regressions are cases of *il faut reculer pour mieux sauter*, but often they are primarily neurotic attempts to escape the pain of ego-development. The final development of a strong ego does not usually happen before 21, but even thereafter we are rarely immune to the attraction of the old consciousness. While our bodies appear to evolve relatively peacefully from one stage to another, some of the steps forward in masculine consciousness require Herculean efforts of will. These can be observed, for example, in the struggles of the adolescent to claim his or her identity. They can also be seen historically in the battle of the new patriarchal consciousness to slay the Great Mother. Many of the most ruthless and determined efforts to deny and oppress the feminine-maternal principle as well as the female sex identified with it, were necessary acts of self-defence on the part of the emerging masculine consciousness.

The dominance of the patriarchal consciousness has usually been associated with the repression of women. But the more we learn to recognise our potential androgyny, the less need there will be to identify either the masculine or feminine principle exclusively with either sex. It may be necessary, at the different stages in human and individual development, for one or other of the two principles to be dominant, but this need not entail the domination of the corresponding physical sex and the institutionalisation of this domination in society. Indeed, whenever one sex becomes exclusively identified with either Yin or Yang, it makes it difficult for that sex to recognise the need to allow greater initiative and direction to the polar principle.

The recognition of the need for a re-evaluation of the feminine principle and for each person to find both principles within themselves, has not come from the dominant sex under patriarchy, men, but from the oppressed female sex. Woman's relative lack of freedom has encouraged them to challenge the power of men and in this process they have begun to reject the patriarchal consciousness. But unless they wish to repeat the error of the patriarchal consciousness, women must avoid the old mistake of identifying any particular stage of consciousness with either sex. This danger is somewhat lessened if the new consciousness is recognised to be androgyny. Nevertheless the development of a feminine consciousness is a precognition of the synthesis of the two principles, and if women see this as their particular task they need to take care not to monopolise it.

But what evidence is there that humanity is at a turning point in the evolution of its consciousness and that the next stage will see a synthesis of the masculine and feminine? There are indications that sections of society are hungry for a new way of seeing and experiencing the world; the counter-culture movements of the last 20 years have not merely been attacks on the abuses of our political, social and economic systems, they have challenged the patriarchal consciousness which underpins these systems. The extraordinary popularity of such books as the Carlos Casteneda series, *Zen and the Art of Motorcycle Maintenance* and *Supernature* is but one symptom of the search for a new perspective.[39] But, in themselves, the new movements are not sufficient to suggest that there is a turning-point in the history of human consciousness. Too many of them are prompted by a nostalgia for a fictional or real past, and too many are based on a complete rejection of everything associated with the patriarchal consciousness for it to be easy to see in them a way forward. That western society is experiencing a crisis of confidence in its way of seeing, structuring and deciphering the world is clear – but the solution to this crisis is not. The clue to the next stage in consciousness needs, I think, to be discovered elsewhere, and patterns of change in individual development can provide a useful analogy.

It seems likely that certain cultures have reached their mid-life crisis: polarised between a dominant masculine consciousness and a neglected feminine one, they have reached a stalemate in which neither side can grow without listening to and absorbing the insights of the other. The second half of individual life suggests the need and the possibility of healing the divided Self, by allowing the masculine and feminine to meet in a psychological marriage in which each principle retains its separate nature and at the same time becomes more than it was through interaction with its polar opposite, so that a new androgynous Self can be born and grow. A revolution in consciousness may be beginning, comparable in significance to the patriarchal revolution millenia ago, as a result of which the search for a harmonious relationship of the masculine and the feminine will replace the rule by the masculine as the dominant human consciousness.

Obviously androgyny remains a very distant ideal; it requires the transformation of the body as well as the mind. This might entail, among other things, some form of parthogenetic reproduction, which is clearly impossible now and in the immediate future. In consciousness we have the potential for radical change. In their different ways both modern analytical psychology and ancient mysticism testify to the radical changes in the psyche which unfold through self-exploration, reflection, and meditative practices. Physically we must remain relatively one-sided. However the realisation of androgyny, is not achieved in defiance of the physical body, but, on the contrary, by the recognition that at every level of human nature, spiritual, psychological and physical, both sexual poles are present even though their relationship may be one-sided. Too little is still understood about the interaction between body and mind to know what effect changes in consciousness might, in the end, have on the body; but because of the intimacy between psyche and soma, the idea, implicit in ancient Chinese thought and explicit in Anthroposophy, that the body also has the potential for transformation may not prove as unlikely as it now sounds.

Chinese Yin-Yang theory does not, as we have observed, explore in depth the differences between physical and psychic nature and development. But it is quite clear about the fact that body and mind (psyche and spirit) evolve from the one supreme principle, the Dao, that they are different manifestations of it, not two antithetical worlds, that both express the dynamic interplay of

Yin and Yang, and that the state of any one part of the human being will be reflected in all other parts. The Chinese path towards the realisation of the Dao, towards androgyny, explored in the next chapter, involves the transformation of the body as well as the psyche.

The second chapter of this book explored some of the mythologies of the Great Goddess for what they revealed of the nature of the matriarchal consciousness. It pointed to the Virgin goddesses common to many different cultures as expressions of humanity's early sexually undifferentiated way of experiencing and understanding the world. But it may be that these myths contain more than information about consciousness; they may also tell something of humanity's biological beginnings.

That we evolved from a sexually undifferentiated biological form is stated in the writings and lectures of Rudolf Steiner. He explains that 'proto-humanity' was not originally divided into male and female but was unisexual, containing both the male and female principles in female form, and that it reproduced itself parthenogenetically. Even after sexual differentiation, neither sex lost the seed of the opposite principle in either body or soul, and because of this both sexes are free to realise their potential wholeness at each level of their being.[40]

If the Chinese and others are correct in their assertions that the true nature of the human being is a microcosmic image of the cosmos, both male and female, then it is valuable to begin to understand what it might mean to experience our androgyny as both the truest expression of our individuality and simultaneously as a way of experiencing our identity with the cosmos as a whole. As mystics, poets and philosophers have testified throughout the centuries such an experience is almost impossible to explain and communicate. It can only be understood by those who have known it for themselves. But occasionally it is possible to glimpse its meaning through the descriptions of those who have received intimations of it. One such opportunity is offered by Jung in his book *Memories, Dreams and Reflections,* in which he describes a vision which came to him during a critical illness towards the end of his life. Momentarily he experienced the bliss and freedom of identification with the cosmos. Afterwards he wrote:

> Only consciousness of our narrow confinement in the self forms the link to the limitlessness of the unconscious. In such awareness we experience ourselves concurrently as limited and eternal, as both the one and the other. In knowing ourselves to be unique in our personal combination – that is ultimately limited – we possess also the capacity for becoming conscious of the infinite. But only then.[41]

Obviously the individual 'I' is a precondition of the conscious discovery of the universal 'I'. The first is the ultimate gift of the masculine differentiating principle, the second of the feminine holistic principle. Androgyny, therefore, is not only a description of our essential nature, it is also the Way of thinking and feeling which leads to the realisation of this nature. Androgyny is an absolute state as well as a process of becoming. A similar ambiguity is implicit in the Chinese concept of the Dao and in the Christian idea of the *Logos*, the World: both signify the Truth as well as the way to the Truth. The unfolding of androgyny is a way of living as well as a goal, a path as well as a destination.

The pattern of human development suggested in these pages, although hypothetical, nevertheless, may appear depressingly fatalistic. Where is our freedom if the course of life is regulated with such tedious precision? Where is the possibility of choice if the ways of psychological growth are as have been suggested? The Chinese approach to this question of freedom may help to explain. Helmut Wilhelm summarises it in the following paragraph:

> The concept of change is not an external, normative principle that imprints itself upon phenomena; it is an inner tendency according to which development takes place naturally and spontaneously. Development is not a fate dictated from without to which one must silently submit, but rather a sign showing the direction that decisions take. Again, development is not a moral law that one is constrained to obey: it is rather the guideline from which one can read off events. To stand in the stream of this development is a datum of nature; to recognise it and follow it is responsibility and free choice.[42]

We can choose whether to live life or be lived by it and how we choose will determine the quality of our existence. In the end it is difficult not to agree with Jung's remarks that 'Life that just happens in and for itself is not real life; it is real only when it is known.'

Each person has the potential for androgyny and the freedom to choose whether or not to realise this potential. But even the recognition of this choice requires a considerable degree of self-knowledge. This is the first freedom. Its attainment depends on the willingness to explore ourselves. Two thousand years ago Dong Zhong-shu wrote:

> The nature may be compared to the eyes. In sleep the eyes are shut and there is darkness; they must await the wakening before they can see. At this time it may be said that they have the potential disposition to see, but it cannot be said that they see. Now the nature of all people has the potential disposition but it is not yet awakened; it is as though it were asleep and awaiting the wakening.[43]

CHAPTER EIGHT

The Spirit of the Valley Never Dies

The best gentleman is diligent in doing something about God, once he has been taught. The middling type reacts haphazardly, and the lowest type bursts out laughing: and we can be sure that it is God that we have taught him.

Ge Hong

Some years ago I had a dream which apart from its more personal meanings, helped to introduce me to the idea and meaning of androgyny as the potential goal of human development.

I dreamt that I was travelling to China and stopped on the way outside Canterbury Cathedral. As I stood in the grass surrounded by nature at her most perfect, luxurious, alive and green, I looked through a medieval stone arch into the interior of the Cathedral and experienced a different kind of perfection, the purity of the spirit. I was struck by the contrast between the beauty of the world of nature and the beauty of the opposite world of spirit, and the link between them, the stone arch. I began to walk through the arch into the Cathedral and was met by an exceptionally striking novitiate, 'tall, dark and handsome'! He came towards me and took my hand. It became clear that we were to be married. We walked along the aisle, and entered an inner chamber, a kind of holy of holies, and began to descend along the aisle towards the altar. On either side of us there were the people who had come to our wedding and they praised us for being the 'perfect couple'. Standing in front of the altar was an exquisite small child of about six or seven, neither male nor female, whose task it was to witness our marriage. (At this moment I did not feel as though I was either the man or the woman but both.) As the ceremony moved towards its climax the scene changed. I was no longer merely the wedding couple. My being also included an angel floating above the rafters of the Cathedral looking down on the wedding scene below.

In the beginning of the dream I am on my way to China, and, since during the period in which I had this dream, 'China' was a frequent symbol for psychological wholeness, I interpreted the story of the dream as essentially a description of the journey towards such a destination. Two of the most striking motifs in the dream are the contrast between the manifest and unmanifest worlds – nature and spirit, and the fairy tale imagery of the man and woman – the masculine and feminine principle. Both motifs are expressed as polarities: nature moving into spirit through the stone arch and the man and woman linking in marriage. My own journey in the dream embraces both polarities: it is I who walked through the arch and it is the masculine and feminine aspects of myself that are united in the wedding ceremony. Then comes a third stage of my journey which I felt to be a synthesis of the preceding ones. It begins with the symbol of the child, who is neither male nor female, but contains all in a divine undifferentiated state, and concludes with the inclusion of the angelic dimension. As an angel I attained freedom from the polarities of human life; I was neither masculine nor feminine, neither spirit nor body, but a synthesis of all. Furthermore, in glimpsing androgyny I also experienced immortality, and was thereby separated a little from the world of the congregation and the wedding. As an angel I could not communicate with them, for my language was no longer their language, nor my body theirs.

In this chapter I will explore the journey towards androgyny as it was experienced and understood by some people from a psychological and cultural context very different from that of twentieth century England – the Chinese alchemists. It is, I think, interesting to see how behind the strangeness of their language and symbols there is much in the conceptions and goals of these alchemists which corresponds to the themes in my dream.

While the Confucians promoted the Yang path of analysis, organisation and reason, and the Daoists and Zen Buddhists advocated the Yin way of receptivity, passivity and contemplation, a small and extremely esoteric group were at work through the centuries quietly, often secretly, preparing themselves to discover the androgynous and immortal centre of their own natures. These were the Chinese Alchemists. They began with the conviction that the Dao embraced both the Yin and the Yang; but they went a stage further than their contemporaries and argued that since it was this androgyny which constituted eternal creativity, all people, by discovering it for themselves, could exchange their ordinary state of ignorance, limitation and mortality for a divine state of wisdom, wholeness, freedom and immortality. Although the alchemical quest became known by many different labels (the search for the elixir of life, for the cinnabar pill or the Golden Flower, for example), these all suggested a similar idea – that only through a synthesis of the masculine and feminine principles could the adept discover the source of life, the Dao. The alchemists believed that while this unity is inherent in all things, as a spark, most are imperfect reflections of it. Human beings, however, by virtue of their minds, have the possibility of rectifying their imbalanced state, cleansing the mirrors of their mind, so that finally they can reflect the Dao in its perfection and thereby not only realise their true self, which is indefinable because illimitable, but also transform their bodies and psyches and thus free themselves from the natural separation of Yin and Yang which leads to death, and find instead eternal life.

While the full history of Chinese alchemy has yet to be written, the available studies suggest that the alchemical quest may have emerged, in embryonic form, as a natural companion to the earliest consciousness of polarity. The recognition of life and death, of male and female, provoked the longing to transcend them, by reaching back to the unity which contains both and is subject to neither. Among the many legends about the elixir of life is the famous one of Yi, the archer, who obtained the medicine of immortality from Xi Wang Mu, the Great mother of the pre-polar consciousness. His wife, Zhang E (Chang O) stole and ate the elixir and so became Lady of the Moon. The *Book of History* and the *Book of Songs* both mention the pursuit of longevity, which seems always to have been a mark of virtue in China, a sign that a person has lived in accordance with the natural laws of the cosmos and that his or her aims have reflected, rather than challenged, those of nature.[1] The *Yellow Emperor's Classic of Internal Medicine* teaches that it is possible to search beyond the natural way which leads to death, and discover the secrets of perpetual health by following the example of the ancient sages who 'never directed their will and ambition toward the protection of a purpose that was empty of meaning. Thus their allotted span of life was without limits, like Heaven and Earth.'[2] According to legend, the Yellow Emperor himself was such a man: after he had cast a bronze tripod cauldron, a celestial dragon vehicle came down from the heavens to fetch him. He stepped into it and together with more than 70 other people, ministers and palace ladies, mounted up into the sky in full view of the people.[3] His wisdom and virtue placed him beyond the confines of life and death, being and not being.

Ornamental stone beads worn by the Upper Cave Men of Zhou Kou Dian (Chou Kou-tien) dating from the very end of the Pleistocenes, were painted red, the colour of blood always associated with life, and during the Zhou period armlets of jade (a stone also associated with longevity) were placed in the mouths of the dead. A legend about the daughter of a duke in the seventh century BC. tells how she was courted by an alchemical immortal who provided her with mercurious chloride face-powder and also taught her to play the flute, after which the two of them soared into the empyrean, she on a phoenix and he on a dragon.

The first historical references to the cult of immortality do not appear until the Warring states period, 403–222 BC., in association with Zou Yan (Tsou Yen) and the School of Naturalists (350–270 BC.). The First emperor of China, Qin Shi Huandi, was an enthusiastic searcher after the elixir, and the *Han Shu* (the History of the Han Dynasty), which probably dates from the first century AD., contains an explicit reference to the alchemical process:

Sacrifice to the stove and you will be able to summon 'things' (ie spirits). Summon spirits and you will be able to change cinnabar powder into yellow gold. With this yellow gold you may be able to make vessels to eat and drink out of. You will then increase your span of life. Having increased your span of life, you will be able to see the hsien of P'eng-lai that is in the midst of the sea. Then you may perform the sacrifices of feng and shan, and escape death.[4]

Further indications of alchemical ideas were provided by Chinese archaeologists in 1972 when they unearthed near Changsha the Lady of Tai who died in 186 BC. The T-shaped banner of painted silk which covered her coffin depicts many of the symbols which appear in later alchemical texts. At the top is the heavenly world of the immortals, in the middle the earthly world, and at the bottom the underworld. On the top right of the banner are the sun and a crow, on the top left the moon, a rabbit and a toad, and beneath them the great tree with ten suns and a dragon transporting Zhang E (Chang O), with her elixir of immortality, to the Palace of the Moon. In the centre of the banner writhes Fu Xi with his serpent tail, surrounded by magical crane birds.[5]

The first great recorded alchemist was Wei Bo-yang (Wei Po-yang), a second century AD. Daoist. He was followed by Ge Hong (Ko Hung) a century later, and the period from AD. 400–800 has been called by Needham the Golden Age of Chinese alchemy. These were the centuries in which Daoism enjoyed its heyday and Buddhism flourished.

The earliest meaning of the character '*Xian*' (immortal) is a 'drunken capering'; it is in this sense that it appears in the *Book of Songs* (eighth century BC.). But by about 400 BC. the term was used in its familiar sense.[6] Thereafter the cult of immortality was a favourite topic for stories and court rituals, as well as for some of the greatest poetry. An anonymous ode of the second century BC. describes the celestial journey of an alchemist which ended in an ecstatic union with the Dao. The ode tells how the aspiring immortal asks about the union of Yin and Yang. This is the reply he received:

> The Tao can only be received, it cannot be given.
> So small that it contains nothing, so great that it has no bounds.
> Keep your hun soul from confusion, and it will come of itself (tzu-jan).
> Unify the chhi and control the spirit (shen),
> Preserve them within you at the midnight hour,

Await it in emptiness, before even Inaction.
All categories of things are brought into being by this;
This is the Door of Power.[7]

The adept sips the 'subtle potion of the Flying Springs' and holds in his bosom 'the radiant metallous jade' (both are references to alchemical elixirs). Then the transformation begins:

My corporeal parts dissolved to a soft suppleness,
And my spirit grew lissome and eager for movement.
How fine was the fiery nature of the southland!
How lovely the winter blooming of the cassia . . .

The mystical journey continues until at last,

When I looked, my startled eyes saw nothing,
When I listened, no sound met my bewildered ear.
Thus, transcending Inaction, I attained to the (Great) Clarity,
And entered the precincts of the Great Beginning.[8]

It is clear from alchemical writings that the realisation of immortality was believed to bring with it freedom from time and space as well as from life and death. It brings, also, the freedom from sexual identities, for, although the immortals are sometimes described as male or female, their identity with the Dao places them beyond the confines of either male or female and at the source of both. They have found the spirit of the valley which never dies, the wellspring of heaven and earth which use will never drain.

But the Chinese alchemists cannot be defined simply by their quest for immortality. It is their methodology and the assumptions this contains which distinguishes them. Some writers on European alchemy have restricted the use of the term 'alchemist' to those intent on creating gold, or precious metals. Others have understood the 'philosopher's stone' metaphorically, and argued that the alchemists were really talking about the transformation of their own psyches and using gold, or the 'rebis' (double being), often symbolised by the hermaphrodite, merely as an analogy. The first group tends to criticise the second for being too generous to people who were clearly out for material wealth, while the second condemns the first for its blindness. A third group, however, suggests that the alchemist works from within a cosmology which recognises the correspondence between the physical and psychic processes, so that by working with the one, he or she influences the other. Since somewhat similar disagreements dominate discussions of Chinese alchemy it is important to try and clear up this confusion by exploring the underlying principles which characterise those who adopted alchemical concepts to describe their work in China.

Whether the Chinese alchemists worked with actual minerals or plants, or whether they worked with breathing, callisthenics, meditational or sexual exercises, they shared a common assumption about the process of nature: all creation, they believed, was subject to the principle of metamorphosis, so just as metals have the possibility, in time, of becoming gold that is pure and imperishable, all humans have the potential for perfect health and wisdom, for an immortality of the body as well as the soul. They thought that since this process from imperfection to perfection is inherent in all things, and will spontaneously unfold in its own time, the alchemist could assist nature in the perfection of her progency by hastening the process of time. By learning the secrets of metamorphosis, they believed they could enter into an active collaboration with nature and so help to transform not only their own lives but the external world as well. This idea of transformation of nature is expressed in hexagram fifty of the *Yi Jing*:

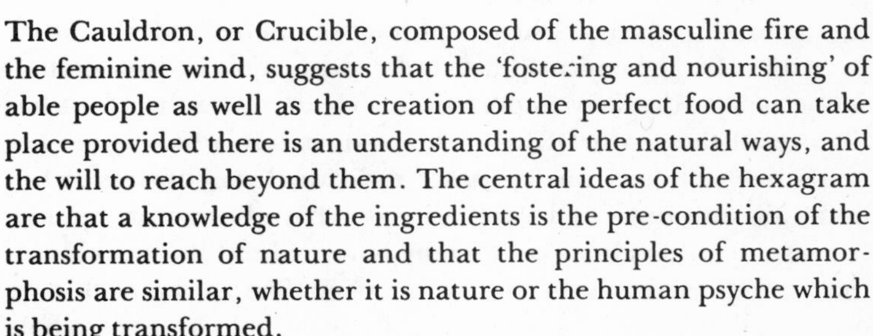

The Cauldron, or Crucible, composed of the masculine fire and the feminine wind, suggests that the 'fostering and nourishing' of able people as well as the creation of the perfect food can take place provided there is an understanding of the natural ways, and the will to reach beyond them. The central ideas of the hexagram are that a knowledge of the ingredients is the pre-condition of the transformation of nature and that the principles of metamorphosis are similar, whether it is nature or the human psyche which is being transformed.

Implicit in the idea of a conscious collaboration with nature is the conviction that each person's life depends on what she or he decides to do about it: if through understanding and action it is possible to free ourselves from the usual patterns of growth, decay and one-sidedness, then the duration and quality of the lives we lead is up to us and no one else. We are our own responsibility and the sole arbiters of our own destiny. The alchemists maintained that it was possible to transform the body and psyche so that eventually the individual, by discovering the principle of creation, the Dao, can free her or himself from the limitations of time and space as well as from the rhythms of life and death.

The relation between mortality and imperfection which underpinned the alchemists' philosophy is common, as we have seen, to much of traditional Chinese philosophy: only the Dao is perfect, being the creative source of Yin and Yang, and so only the Dao is immortal. Everything else, as an imperfect reflection of the supreme principle is, therefore, destined to perish. The only way to reverse the otherwise inevitable decline from birth to death, is by rectifying the imbalance of Yin and Yang which defines our imperfection, so that out of the harmony of these two principles the psyche can give birth to the higher Self, the androgynous individuality, which exists beyond all polarities.

The Chinese alchemists were no exception to the prevalent tendency among traditional Chinese thinkers and writers to adopt Yin-Yang imagery in a number of different ways. While they appeared to be unperturbed by the inevitable ambiguity of this practice, it undoubtedly disturbs strangers to Chinese culture. The central confusion, already mentioned in chapter three, arises from their use of the Yin-Yang concept as a symbol for all polarities, alongside its use, in the sense explored in this book, as the primal polarity whose interaction generates all other polarities. In alchemical practice the distinction is, in a certain sense, not particularly important, for clearly once the adept has discovered the centre of his or her own nature which is neither masculine nor feminine, (neither individual nor universal) but both, all subsidiary polarities will also have been transcended, because the individual will thereby have realised the macrocosm that is reflected within the microcosm. She or he will have discovered the different parts within the whole and the whole which embraces the different parts. However, for the purpose of this study it is important to remain alert to the ambivalent usages of Yin and Yang in alchemical texts and to remember that in referring to the Chinese alchemists as the seekers of androgyny, I am not using androgyny only as a metaphor but also as a description of the fundamental characteristics of the alchemical methodology and goal. The Chinese alchemists, it seems to me were in their different ways through the centuries struggling towards the realisation of the ultimate paradox, the identity of individuality and universality.

Since the alchemical task, the pursuit of the elixir of immortality, was no less a venture than the search for the realisation of God or the Dao, it is hardly surprising that it was undertaken with the greatest seriousness and shrouded in considerable secrecy. Nor is it surprising that the alchemists placed such emphasis on morality. The secrecy was not, as has sometimes been suggested, a plot designed to protect the exclusiveness of the club and to save what prizes there might be for its members, but a necessity arising out of the alchemists' recognition of the extreme dangers inherent in exploring and tampering with nature's secrets. Many of the alchemical texts were reserved exclusively for oral transmission so as to guarantee that they were not received by anyone insufficiently prepared for them. Part of this preparation entailed the development of a right attitude of mind, the right ethics. Ge Hong (Ko Hung), the famous third century alchemist, wrote: 'Those desiring fullness of life must strive to accumulate goodness, win merit, be kind and affectionate to others, practise the Golden rule, love even the creeping things, rejoice in the good fortune of others.'[9] Even this was not enough. He also wrote: 'those wishing to become earth genii must do three hundred consecutive good deeds. Those wishing to be Heavenly genii must acquire twelve hundred. If, after acquiring 1199, one commits a single bad deed, all the ones previously acquired are lost and one must begin anew.'[10]

The central purpose of the Chinese alchemists was not to increase their wealth through aurifaction (the making of real gold) or aurifiction (the making of imitation gold), nor to defy their nature by pursuing immortality, but to understand and thereby hasten the natural process of metamorphosis inherent in each person, leading to the realisation of harmony and immortality in place of disharmony and death. Unity was their goal:

> If men unity [God] could know
> Then they'd know all there below.[11]

It is clear from alchemical texts, and Daoist stories and poems that the *Xian*, the immortals, are only visible to those whose development has reached some way towards approximating their own. This is a common idea in esoteric literature. Behind it lies the assumption that people can only see what their organs of perception allow them to see. To 'see' people or beings who have reached higher stages of physical, psychological or spiritual evolution is no more possible for an undeveloped or less developed person than it is for someone who is blind to distinguish the colours of the spectrum. If we do not see the immortals it does not follow that immortals do not exist, but rather that our senses are too blunt and crude to perceive these refined beings. Only by improving our own organs of perception, learning to see more clearly, may we have the possibility of recognising an immortal. This is only one of the many assertions of esoteric literature which, understandably, invites ridicule and scepticism. There is no defence for it except through analogies like that of the blind person. We all know that the world is dark to the blind not because there is nothing to see, but because there is something wrong with their eyes. But it requires an act of trust or faith to extend this analogy to the perception of other beings or the experience of higher stages of consciousness. However, it is possible to test the validity of the assertion by beginning the process of self-development for oneself. This was the message and the path of the Chinese alchemists.

The alchemists assumed that we become what we ingest. If, for instance, we take in the purest mineral this will help our bodies, physical and psychological, in their development towards their own perfection. They also seemed to feel that the alchemical process itself had a corresponding effect upon the individual: 'The recipes we follow stimulate the gods within our bodies so that a prolongation of life may be acquired more quickly, and externally they exorcize evils so that no misfortunes interfere.'[12]

This passage suggests that following the alchemical recipes may have been considered beneficial; because of the correspondence between the inner and outer worlds, processes taking place in one would have their effect on the other. If this is so, it would help to explain why the alchemists were seemingly content to make artificial 'gold' when it was clear that what they were making was not the same as natural gold.[13]

The earliest extant text dealing specifically with aurifaction and macrobiotics, the pursuit of longevity, was written by Wei Boyang, (Wei Po-yang) in the second century AD. The book known as the *Can Tong Qi (Ts'an T'ung Ch'i), The Union of Compared Correspondence*, follows the *Yi Jing* in its assertion that *Qian* and *Kun* are the beginning of the Changes. It states that Yin and Yang are the keys to immortality and that aurifaction will yield the most valuable and effective elixir:

> If even the herb chü-sheng can make one live longer,
> Surely the elixir is worth taking into one's mouth,
> Prepared as it is by cyclical transformations?
> Gold by its nature does not rot or decay
> Therefore it is of all things the most precious.
> If the chymic artists includes it in his diet
> The duration of his life will become everlasting.[14]

The most famous alchemist, Ge Hong (Ko Hung), lived a century after Wei Boyang and, like his predecessor, he maintained that no single alchemical method should be relied upon exclusively, but that success would be much more likely if a number of different elixirs were prepared. Ge Hong's goal was to harmonise the Yin and Yang forces so that the Dao could reveal itself. Both he and Wei Boyang believed that the elixir which could help to achieve this might be created by the transformations of concrete substances as well as by the inner metamorphosis of the psyche. They worked with the parallels between the transmutation of 'inferior' minerals into gold, 'inferior' plants into 'perfect' plants, and the evolution of the 'inferior' consciousness or mind into the perfect person, the 'true' embodiment of the Dao. Their writings reflect an understanding of the continuum between all polarities: instead of working exclusively with either the psyche or the body, the inner or outer world, spirit of matter, they valued both poles and recognised that the transformations at one pole inevitably had a corresponding effect on the other. This consciousness had important consequences for the conception of eternal life in Chinese thought: it prevented the emergence of a concept of immortality of the spirit at the expense of the body, or the other way round, for it assumed that the one was, in the final analysis, inseparable from the other.

The interdependence of matter and spirit characterised Chinese psychology, which conceived of the soul as not one but two, a *hun*, active and spiritual soul, and a *po*, passive and earthly soul. It saw the human embryo as formed by the meeting of these Yang and Yin souls. The conjunction of the cosmic *Qi* was responsible for the generation of life and form. As long as they interact the individual grows and develops in some way, but because the two principles are rarely, if ever, in harmony, they gradually separate from each other until they finally part and death ensues. At this point the masculine and feminine souls immerse themselves once more in the cosmic Yin and Yang. The quest for the elixir of life is the quest to achieve a harmony of Yin and Yang, so that instead of their splitting apart they can generate a second birth, a resurrection of the Dao in the individual. And just as the Dao is both Yin and Yang, passive and active, earth and heaven, so the essential and immortal nature of the human being is both matter and spirit.

The Chinese idea of a polarity of body and mind emerging from the one supreme principle is not as foreign to some Western thinking as is often supposed. Titus Burckhardt, in his excellent study of western alchemy, writes:

> The two principles are like the two hands of God. They are related to one another as male and female, as father and mother, and cannot be separated from one another – for in whatever the earth produces Heaven is present as creative power, while the Earth, for its part, gives form and body to the heavenly law. Thus the archaic way of looking at things was 'sensible' and spiritual at one and the same time . . . In this view, matter remains an aspect or function of God. It is not something separated from spirit, but its necessary complement. In itself it is not more than the potentiality of taking form, and all perceptible objects in it bear the stamp of its active counterpart, the spirit or Word of God . . . It is only for modern man that matter has become a thing and no longer the completely passive mirror of the spirit.[15]

To discover the elixir of immortality, to realise the Dao within, is to discover the source of both matter and spirit. But it is important, as Burckhardt stresses to understand these two concepts imaginatively; matter does not refer to the tangible things of this world any more than spirit refers to the intellectual antics of the brain. Things and ideas are expressions of matter and spirit but not necessarily identical with them. The concept of immortality also requires imaginative interpretation; it obviously does not mean our *ordinary* bodies injected with some magical preservative. For our bodies as we know them are one-sided, hence incomplete. It is only through the metamorphosis of this one-sidedness into androgyny, a transformation of the body as well as the soul, that it may be possible to discover the true nature of matter and spirit and know the meaning of immortality.

Early Chinese alchemists seemed to work indiscriminately with 'inner' and 'outer' elixirs. They ingested real or artificial gold, ate and drank from gold vessels, swallowed precious elixirs and 'pills', and practised special breathing and other physical exercises, as well as developing themselves inwardly through meditation and moral training.

From the sixth century AD. onwards a significant change in the alchemical way is noticeable. More and more the elixir of life was understood in its metaphoric and symbolic rather than tangible or outer sense; instead of preparing and swallowing 'gold' and other precious metals and substances, the alchemist worked exclusively on the creation of 'inner' gold or the 'diamond body' within him or herself.

The two people associated with this development in China are Hui Si (Hui Ssu), the second patriarch of the Tian Tai (T'ien T'ai) Buddhist sect who lived from AD. 517–77, and Peng Xiao (Peng Hsiao). Peng Xiao explains that esoteric alchemy works with the 'souls' of mercury, lead and cinnabar in order to create the 'True' and perfect person. In the thirteenth century Su Dongbo (Su Tung-po) developed this idea further by associating the 'souls' of the tangible substances with parts of the body: for example, he taught that 'dragon is mercury. He is the semen and the blood. He issues from the kidneys and is stored in the liver.'[16]

By the thirteenth century alchemy had become a purely psychological process. It was no longer credible to argue that the transformation of base metals into gold, or the creation and ingestion of the perfect medicine could bring about personal immortality, for only the inner metamorphosis of consciousness was now considered capable of preparing the adept for a meeting with the Dao. These later alchemists felt such contempt for those who worked with tangible substances that some of them even repudiated the term 'elixir of immortality'. In a famous conversation between the great Daoist alchemist, Zheng Chun (Ch'ang Ch'un) and Chingiz Khan in Samarkand during the summer of 1222, Chingiz asked whether the alchemist had an elixir of immortality to bestow. Zhang Chun replied: 'I have a means of protecting life, but no elixir of immortality.'[17]

Other alchemists re-wrote alchemical history because of their conviction that the inner way was not merely the only valid path for them but had been the only way even for their predecessors. The book *The Secret of the Golden Flower*, a particularly well known Chinese alchemical text because of its illuminating introduction by Jung, can be traced back to the seventeenth century when it was first engraved on wooden tablets. It was based on an oral tradition which probably reached back as far as the Tang dynasty. This text comments that worldly people 'who do not understand the secret works of the Book of the Elixir of Life have misunderstood the yellow and white there in that they have taken it as means of making gold out of stones. Is not that foolish?'[18] Instead, as the text points out, the yellow and white refer to the jewel or Golden Flower of consciousness, the goal of the alchemist. In ancient times, it states, this was widely known and understood, but now worldly people have lost the roots and clung to the treetops.[19]

But while these later alchemists clearly experienced a more defined frontier between the inner and outer worlds, the personal and impersonal, than their predecessors, and this inhibited them from pursuing external elixirs, their goal did not change. It remained the metamorphosis of the imperfect individual into a perfect being, an expression of the Dao. According to *The Secret of the Golden Flower* the realisation of the Flower is the transcendence of body and mind, human and cosmic worlds in a final identity with the Dao.[20]

Several centuries before this, Ge Hong had written that the

secret of the alchemical way lies in willpower: 'true desire to attain calm and repose, to free oneself from covetousness, to see and hear internally, and to be entranced and freed of emotion'.[21] Only someone who has such a desire can come to terms with creation, know its ways. While 'the uninitiated may eat their fill from dawn to dusk. . . . waste their time at music in the company of courtesans . . . debauch themselves with finery. . . . or waste their days at backgammon,[22] the initiates can so transform their bodies that they become invisible and live in perfect freedom 'cherishing both sun and moon in their hearts.'[23]

The author of *The Secret of the Golden Flower* would not have disagreed with these sentiments, but he might have repudiated some of Ge Hong's recipes for initiation. The third century alchemist wrote: 'If you wish to seek divinity or geniehood, you need only acquire the quintessence, which consists in treasuring your sperm, circulating your breaths, and taking one crucial medicine.'[24] The Golden Flower taught instead that only the transformation of consciousness can reverse the gradual deterioration of mind and body, and help the adept experience a re-birth into identity with the Dao.

The Secret of the Golden Flower was the text of an esoteric group which was subject to ruthless persecution by the authorities throughout its history. In 1891, for instance, 15,000 of its members were slaughtered by Manchu hirelings.[25] The teaching of the Golden Flower draws from Daoism, Buddhism and Confucianism. According to its translator: 'It is built on the premise that the cosmos and man, in the last analysis, obey the same law, that man is a microcosm and is not separated from the macrocosm by any fixed barriers. The very same laws rule for the one as for the other, and from the one a way leads into the other.'[26] The text is designed to teach the individual the way of unfolding his or her own Golden Flower, the symbol of the highest nature. It starts from the ancient belief that human life, like the universe, begins with the conjunction of Yin and Yang. In the individual these two principles are described as the *hun* and the *po*, and the *hun* is associated with the eyes and brain and considered responsible for reason, while the *po* is associated with the solar plexus and abdomen, and regarded as the source of all desires and feelings which promote or reflect involvement with others and the outside world. The text explains that the path from conception to death is marked by the 'clockwise flowing' of these two souls until they are entirely swallowed up by the cosmic Yin and Yang from which they originated. The final engulfing is the moment of death.

The text maintains that this natural process of externalisation of energy is due to the imbalance, the lack of harmony between the two souls and that in whichever way the individual is imbalanced, whether she or he is too masculine or too feminine, the psyche will suffer. An excessive reliance on the feminine soul blinds the person to outer things, people and feelings, thereby depleting his or her inner resources, while too great a dependence on the masculine soul results in psychological aridity, isolation and meaninglessness. Either way leads, eventually, to diminishing contact between the two souls which, it claims is the only creative state, and finally to death. To avoid this decline it is essential to maintain a continual dialogue between the masculine and feminine so that they can fructify each other and, instead of dissipating their energies, lead the individual towards the discovery of the true Self that is beyond polarity.

The process bringing about the metamorphosis of the body and soul is likened to a sacred marriage in which a 'seed pearl' develops out of the communion of the Yin and the Yang. 'It is as if man and woman embraced and a conception took place.'[27] Thereafter the task of the adept is to allow the seed to mature into the Golden Flower: 'Within our six foot body we must strive for the form which existed before the laying down of heaven and earth.'[28] This must be done, the text teaches, by allowing the two souls to transform each other. The differentiating spirit of the masculine must be kept continually fed with the experiences of the receptive, embracing soul, which it is its task to distill. The teaching of *the Secret of the Golden Flower* can be summarised diagramatically, the diagram illustrating the alternatives which confront each individual; death can be the death of the body and psyche, a returning of the two souls to the cosmic Yin and Yang, or it can be a death of the old polarised consciousness and a rebirth into eternal life with consciousness of the source which embraces all polarities – the Dao.

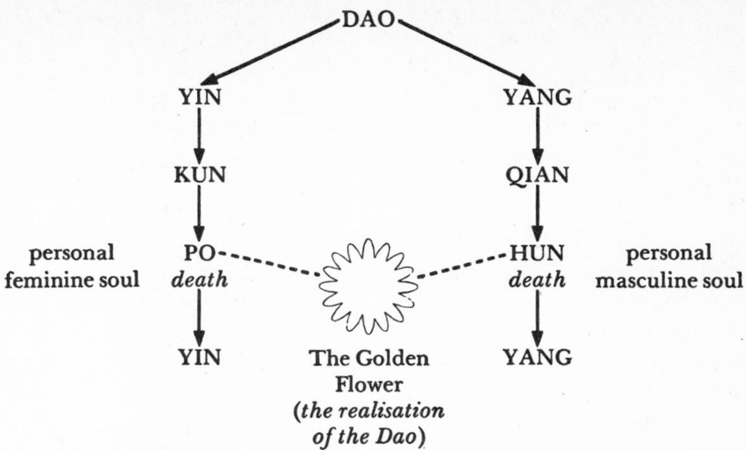

(This diagram is an adaptation of the one in the translation of the text by Cary Baynes. See bibliography under R. Wilhelm.)

The Secret of the Golden Flower guides the adept towards a discovery of the centre of his or her nature, the androgynous core which is experienced as the light that is beyond light and darkness, the life that is beyond life and death, and the love that is beyond love and hate. A 'personality develops,' according to Jung, 'that suffers only in the lower stories, so to speak, but in the upper stories is singularly detached from painful as well as joyful events.'[29] Such a personality can see and understand the world because it has discovered itself. It can perceive the androgyny of others because it has perceived its own.

Jung watched the birth of the Golden Flower in many of his patients. While he confessed to not fully understanding the mechanism of its development, he was an unwavering witness to its reality. Over and over again, in his practice, he observed the pattern of psychic development from polarity to unity, and concluded that this was a potential inherent in all people, sickness being an expression of its hindrance. When he pondered on the essential ingredient of the healing process, that thing which removed the hindrance so that the transformation of the psyche could continue, he chose the Chinese concept of *wu-wei*, action through inaction:

> The art of letting things happen, action through non-action, letting go of oneself, as taught by Meister Eckhart, became for me the key opening the door to the Way. We must be able to let things happen in the psyche. For us, this actually is an art of which few people know anything. Consciousness is forever interfering, helping, correcting, and negating, and never leaving the simple growth of the psychic processes in peace.[30]

The Golden Flower states that the natural tendency in human life is to spill the energies in the outside world. Nowhere is this more apparent than in sex. Procreation is creation at our own expense. Sex hinders the unfolding of the Golden Flower as it dissipates the energy which is needed to feed its roots. However, the text advocates transformation, not repression; it teaches that the sexual impulses can be turned inward instead of directed outward so that, rather than being the agents of decline, they can become the vehicles of re-birth. 'If in the moment of release, it [sexual energy] is not allowed to flow outward, but is led back by the energy of thought so that it penetrates the crucible of the Creative, and refreshes heart and body and nourishes them, that also is the backward-flowing method.'[31] This refers to the practice of sexual alchemy which, among some Chinese, was once a highly respected path leading to the realisation of the 'I' or Self. To understand it demands a familiarity with the Chinese concept of sex.

The Daoists as well as other schools of Chinese philosophy, believed that the world began with sex; that out of a meeting of Yin and Yang evolved the manifest world and this act of cosmic copulation continually repeats itself in nature. Human copulation is an imitation of Heaven and Earth, a way of partaking both physically and spiritually in the creative process and thereby experiencing the Dao. But since this can happen at many different levels of consciousness, a number of different schools of sexual mysticism developed. The main distinction was between those who taught that sex needed to become exclusively an internal experience and those who recognised the value of practical sex. The purpose of the second school was to teach the adepts to make love in such a way as to conserve as much as possible the seminal essence so that Yin and Yang could nourish each other. The male's fluids were associated with lead and the female's with cinnabar. The task of the adept was to so blend the two principles that a tiny, immortal foetus could form within the body.[32] This idea is similar to that of the German romantic, Franz von Baader, who wrote that sexual love should not be confused with the instinct for reproduction; its true function is 'to help man and woman to integrate internally the complete human image, that is to say the divine and original image.'[33]

Some Chinese sex books depict the act as a battle between the two sexes, each trying to extract as much of the vital principle as possible from the opposite sex, while holding on to his or her own energy. The man, for example, tries to stimulate the female to as many orgasms as she can manage while controlling his own excitement and thus preventing the emission of his seed, his Yang force. The principle behind the battle was to internalise rather than externalise the sexual forces so as to strengthen rather than debilitate the individual. Another method of conserving and transforming the seminal essence advocated by the sexual alchemists was to exert pressure on the urethra, between the scrotum and the anus, at the moment of ejaculation, thus diverting the seminal essence into the bladder. The Daoists believed that in this way the seminal essence would ascend, rejuvenate and revivify the upper parts of the brain.[34] But neither this technique nor *coitus reservatus* were, in themselves, sufficient to ensure the birth of the immortal foetus. Like the alchemists working with their crucibles, the sexual alchemists had to cultivate a calm and ethical life if they were to experience progress in their self-development. A non-grasping attitude of mind coupled with inner tranquillity was essential if the forces of Yin and Yang were to rise up the spinal cord and transform the adept from a single-sexed and mortal being into an androgyne.

One of the disadvantages of this particular practical path of development was that it promoted the adept's personal progress at the expense of his or her partner's development. Another Chinese tradition of sexual alchemy, however, allowed both partners to develop together. It taught that neither must have an orgasm but that both must concentrate, instead, on transforming their instinctive urges into higher and higher levels of excitement and communion. As one text put it: 'In order to live long without growing old a man should first play with the woman. He should drink the Jade fluid – that is he should swallow her saliva: thus the passion of both man and woman will be aroused. Then the man should press the *Pin Yi* (*P'ing-i*) point with the fingers of his left hand. [The Pin Yi point is located about one inch above the nipple of the right breast, and is also defined as 'Yin present in Yang'.] He should imagine that in his cinnabar field (ie. the lowest part of his abdomen, three inches below the navel) there is a bright red essence, yellow inside and red and white outside. Then he should think of this essence as dividing itself into a sun and a moon that move about in his abdomen and, then ascend to the *Ni-huan* spot in his brain where the two halves are united again.'[35] According to Sun Simo (Sun Szu-mo), a seventh century AD. Daoist physician, the process of making the semen return results in the union of the male and female principles, visualised as the sun and moon. In this way the semen is transformed into the elixir of life.

A Tang Daoist text stresses the importance of secrecy and moral cultivation in the pursuit of immortality through sexual mysticism.

> After they have concentrated and purified their thoughts then a man and a woman may practise together the art that leads to longevity. This method must be kept secret, it must be transmitted only to adepts. It allows a man and a woman together to activate their ch'i . . . [it is a method which] concentrates on activating *yin* and strengthening *Yang*. If this discipline is practised in the correct manner, then the *ch'i* fluid shall spread like clouds throughout the body, the seed will solidify and become harmonious, and soon all those who practise it, whether young or old, shall become (vigorous) like adolescents. The Elixir (*tan*) thus formed (in the bodies of the two participants) if nurtured for a hundred days, will become transcendental (*ling*). And if this discipline is continued over a very long period, then it will become a natural habit, the method for living long and attaining immortality.[36]

Sexual mysticism which sought the union of the masculine and feminine principles at both the physical and psychological level, could be practised with a partner but also alone. Vajrayana Buddhism, which disappeared from India in the twelfth century AD. at the time of the Moslem conquests, but lived on in Tibet, Nepal, China and other parts of South-east Asia, appears to have advocated both ways. The partnerless path is succinctly advocated in one of the Tantras: 'What need do I have of any other woman? I have an inner woman within myself.'[37]

For some centuries in China, (roughly from the second century

AD. to the seventh century), sexual mysticism was practised publicly as well as privately. The public ceremonies, which occurred on nights of the new and full moon, consisted of a ritual dance, 'the coiling of the dragon and the playing of the tiger, (male and female alchemical symbols) which ended in a public hierogamy or in successive unions of the members of the assembly in the chambers along the sides of the temple courtyard.'[38] Not surprisingly, these ceremonies offended the Confucian sense of propriety which, while acknowledging the importance of sex, regarded it as an affair strictly for the bedroom. The respect for women as the guardians of sexual wisdom, integral to certain Daoists, cannot have helped to endear sexual alchemy to the patriarchal bureaucrats and landlords. A movement designed to eradicate sexual festivals by labelling these 'immoral cults' as capital offences was already underway by AD. 415, and there were probably few such public ceremonies after the seventh century AD.[39] But private sexual alchemy continued to be practised well into the Song dynasty among Daoists attached to temples, and even in the nineteenth century certain sexual practices were approved and counselled by the medical professions. Furthermore, rebellious Daoist sects, practising sexual mysticism, continued to flare up from time to time throughout the empire. An Imperial edict of 1839 says that in one province a sect had been formed and only men and women who practised its disciplines in couples were admitted to it: 'They gather in the night many people together in one room, and without the lamps burning. Then they have sexual intercourse in the dark.'[40]

But repression may not have been the only reason for the decline of these practices during the later centuries of the Chinese empire. The sexual alchemists may have been subject to an influence similar to that which appears to have affected the gold makers when they turned their energies away from 'real' gold towards psychological gold. A subtle but important change of emphasis is apparent in the alchemical writings of the later centuries. Instead of pursuing an identity or immersion in the Dao, the later alchemists, sexual or otherwise, seem more intent on discovering the Dao within their own psyches, finding rather than losing themselves.

While, for whatever reasons, the use of practical sex as a path of initiation probably declined after the Song dynasty (AD. 960–1279), the understanding of sex which it had helped to develop left Chinese culture with an enduring respect for the potential of making love. Sex never degenerated, at least in theory, simply to a way of gratifying the senses, or of procreating children, or even to a marital duty. It was not devalued and considered base as it was in the west, particularly in Victorian England. The Chinese sexual mystics would, no doubt, have agreed with Jung when he wrote that 'sexuality is not mere instinctuality; it is an indisputably creative power that is not only the basic cause of our individual lives, but a very serious factor in our psychic life as well'.[41] The Chinese continued to believe that, alongside its other functions, sex could also be a way of getting in touch with the creative principle, the Dao, the true nature of each individual. How often the practice of sex realised or even approached this ideal is impossible to know, but the important point is that there existed in China at least one tradition which did not regard sex as a denial of the Dao, but as an expression of it. To make love was to be guided by respect for the principle of *wu-wei*, doing nothing contrary to nature and thereby partaking of the cosmic dance of Yin and Yang, giving and receiving, moving and resting, initiating and yielding. Explored in this way, making love itself becomes the only guide we need. Sex is freed from obligations or expectations about how it should be done or what ought to be attained, and becomes, instead, a way of freely experiencing higher and higher levels of excitement and sensitivity. It ceases to be the pursuit of orgasm and becomes a celebration which, while not the most direct path to an androgynous consciousness, is certainly a way of sampling the marriage between the masculine and feminine principles both as they move within the individual and as they flow between the two people making love.

Whichever alchemical path is chosen there is a certain point common to all when the adept has to accept a complete renunciation of her or his old ways of living, thinking and feeling. This is often expressed as a death in alchemical literature, the dying which is the pre-requisite of a new birth into androgyny. It is a relinquishing of single-sexedness and all the ways associated with and integral to this state. The idea of death in life as the pre-condition of growth and creativity is not exclusive to Chinese culture, but is central to most cultures. Among certain people in Melanesia and Polynesia the candidate for initiation is buried or laid in a freshly dug grave, or secluded in a dark hut beyond the village. 'His rebirth is then enacted, and frequently the neophyte must kneel between his mother's legs or appear as if spewed from the mouth of the monster.'[42] Rudolf Steiner describes the central importance of death in the old mystery centres in Greece, among the Chaldeans, Egyptians and Indians. The neophyte, he states, was 'put into a death-like sleep by the initiator or hierophant who understand the matter and there he remained for three and a half days.' He had, in a certain sense, to die before he could be reborn into spiritual understanding.[43] The idea of a psychological death as the precondition of psychic development is also central to Jungian psychology. 'If the old were not ripe for death,' wrote Jung, 'nothing new would appear; and if the old were not blocking the way for the new, it could not and need not be rooted out.'[44] Western culture contains one of the most powerful death and rebirth motifs of all – the crucifixion and resurrection of Christ. One who has not the ability and courage to die and be reborn is, as Goethe pointed out, 'like an opaque shadow on this dark earth'.

A Chinese story about Wei Boyang, the second century AD. alchemist, regards death as the portal to eternal life. One day Wei Boyang went into the mountains with three disciples to prepare the elixir. First they fed it to the dog who instantly fell down dead. Wei Boyang turned to his disciples and asked their opinion of whether he, too, should take the elixir and follow the dog. They replied by giving the question back to their master. He said: 'I abandoned worldly ways and forsook family and friends to enter into the mountains. I should be ashamed to return without having found the Tao of the Holy Immortals. To die of the elixir would be no worse than living without it. I must take it.' So he did and he fell down dead. One of the disciples followed the master's example, but the other two went back to the world. After they had gone, Wei Boyang, the disciple and the white dog revived and sent a letter to the two disciples thanking them for their kindness. When the disciples read it 'their hearts were filled with grief and regret'.[45]

The two disciples had not had the courage to undergo death, so they remained prisoners of life while their master, the white dog and the third disciple moved on to immortality. The moral of this tale is straightforward: the benefits of a new stage in consciousness cannot be experienced without the death of the old; a foot in each camp is impossible. Androgyny which brings the birth of a new self, the discovery of the Dao within, demands the death of all previous identities and ties. Just as the Shaman has to lose him or herself and undergo a death in order to find inspiration, so the seeker of androgyny has, at some point to relinquish the old 'I' to embrace a higher one. An intimation of the meaning of the new 'I' is offered by the following Zen description of enlightenment:

> One day I wiped out all the notions from my mind. I gave up all desire. I discarded all the words with which I thought and stayed in quietude. I felt a little queer – as if I were being carried into something; or as if I were touching some power unknown to me . . . and ztt! I entered. I lost the boundary of my physical body. I had my skin, of course, but I felt I was standing in the centre of the cosmos. I spoke, but my words had lost their meaning. I saw people coming towards me, but all were the same man. All were myself! I had never known this world. I had believed that I was created, but now I must change my opinion: I was never created: I was the cosmos; no individual Mr Sasaki existed.[46]

Mr Sasaki had returned to the beginning before the differentiation of subject and object, but his consciousness was, in one crucial respect, radically different from the beginning. For although he denies the reality of an individual identity, the fact that he knows he knows testifies to a sense of 'I' which does not belong to the primal undifferentiated consciousness described in the first chapter of this book. This original oneness with the world is a gift with which we are born. The enlightenment of Mr Sasaki is the reward of a long struggle which cannot be won without relinquishing the earlier gift.

The alchemists did not seek to transcend nature but to find it. As they worked to discover the 'true Person' who is neither male nor female but, in the image of the Dao, androgynous, their aim was to make themselves not less human but more human. Between them they adopted a variety of methods but common to most was the understanding that the elixir of life depends for its birth on the sacred marriage of heaven and earth, the masculine and feminine principles. But this marriage is only a prelude to a conception. To find the spirit of the valley which never dies demands that the golden foetus reach such a level of maturity that it can transform the body as well as the mind. Obviously this is not easy. Most of the alchemists died natural deaths long before even glimpsing such an advanced stage of development. In the centuries since their death little has changed to make their ideal more easily attainable, but in a modified form it has begun to receive wider attention and recognition.

In the twentieth century the Golden Flower is no longer dressed in obscure and florid alchemical language but more often appears through labels which, while still bewildering and incomprehensible to many, are generally more accessible than their precursors in European and Chinese alchemy. Some of the modern labels, like 'Self' or 'higher ego' may deceive the reader into thinking that something different is being discussed. Not really. These terms denote a more modest goal but not a different direction. While the ancient alchemists struggled for the ultimate prize of the transformation of body and mind leading to eternal life, Jungian psychology and other schools of psychological and spiritual development have chosen to concentrate on an earlier stage, the metamorphosis of the psyche through inner exploration, leading to an experience of the masculine-feminine nature of the Self. They are not directly concerned with the transformation of the body, although they implicitly acknowledge that the two – mind and body – do not, in the final analysis, belong to two different systems. They accept that the human being is psyche and soma, but maintain that the way towards greater health and self-knowledge lies through the integration into consciousness of the unconscious and the spontaneous unfolding of wholeness which results.

The search for the Self is the search for the microcosm of the universe, the image of the Dao in which all is reflected. It is not a search which demands that we become more than we are, by nature, but a search in which we learn to acknowledge that we are more than we know. Liu Jiuyuan (Liu Chiu-yuan) said in the twelfth century AD.: 'The universe has never limited and separated itself from man . . ., it is man who limits and separates himself from the universe.' The sage of Chinese philosophy and the developed person of depth psychology is one who has begun to discover this universe, and who is no longer ruled by the passions of a subjective consciousness, whether these be joy, anger or anguish. Such a personality is, as Jung suggested, 'singularly detached' from the ripples or storms which dominate most of our lives. It is not that these emotions disappear, just that they lose their power to overwhelm, or even move, the new centre of personality. This idea of a psyche that is removed from the emotions of 'everyday' life is vulnerable to misunderstanding. It has been condemned for diminishing the full-bloodedness of human life. This is an error which arises from confusing the development of the Self with repression of the personality. The true development of a higher centre of consciousness does not impoverish the feelings; on the contrary, by clearing away the luggage of likes and dislikes, irritations and resentments, obsessions and prejudices, the ephemeral passions, which clutter our lives, it enriches the feelings, making space for the experience of a deeper and more reliable joy, even bliss, which arises from the marriage of the masculine and feminine principles. The new Self is an inner guide within the psyche which helps the individual to do and see what is right in all situations, and to give to others not out of feelings of obligation but out of desire. It leads, finally, to an understanding of Nietzche's phrase 'in most loving bondage free', or St Paul's statement, 'It is not I but Christ in me,' or Confucius' saying, 'my way is that of the all pervading unity'.[47]

Androgyny is the healing of the divided soul, the soldering of the fragmented psyche. It is the realisation of a psyche which demands little from others not because its needs have been banished and repressed by puritanical or ascetic convictions and practices, but because they have been satisfied. But in the struggle towards androgyny the passions and needs are vital. They are the pointers to those aspects of the psyche which are calling for attention and understanding, those parts of ourselves whose denial will inhibit rather than promote understanding and self-development. One of the great disservices of our culture is the promotion of the 'stiff upper lip ethic'. Such behaviour destroys the individual's natural contact with the inclinations of the psyche to develop and heal itself. However, the contemporary reaction to the stiff upper lip encapsulated in the slogan 'let it all hang out', can be equally inhibiting if pursued for too long. It can deprive the individual of the possibility of experiencing a third state of being which is characterised by neither freedom nor control, but by freedom *and* control. However the preceding 'either-or' stage cannot be leap-frogged. A premature lunge at androgyny is more likely to lead to regression to the Great Mother stage of psychological containment and undifferentiation than it is to realisation of a Self that is both differentiated and united, one which is capable of complete surrender to its own nature and to the world with enhancement rather than the loss of individuality, understanding and freedom.

The Chinese were fully aware of the dangers inherent in pursuing the alchemical goal at the wrong moment. They had a saying that 'if the wrong man uses the right means, the right means work in the wrong way'. The pursuit of androgyny before an adequate differentiation of the components of the psyche can prevent rather than promote freedom and self discovery. Jung saw that 'there is no good that cannot produce evil and no evil that cannot produce good'.[48] He recognised that people are all at different stages of development. 'No doubt', he wrote, 'it is a great nuisance that mankind is not uniform but compounded of individuals whose psychic structure spreads them over a span of at least ten thousand years.' But since this is so 'there is absolutely no truth that does not spell salvation to one person and damnation to another.'[49]

But even for those whose conscious development of the masculine and feminine principles has progressed sufficiently to free them from some of the projections which influence the less developed psyche, and has prepared them for the moment when they can safely allow the feminine to guide them towards the realisation of their complete self, this step is not free from terror and pain. The discovery of androgyny is rarely the gift of a Damascene flash. More often it grows slowly, even imperceptibly, hand in hand with earlier stages of consciousness, and the first glimpses of its meaning are not always an unmitigated delight. Androgyny can confer extraordinary, unprecedented peace and confidence, but its unfolding can also bring extraordinary and unprecedented loneliness as the full depth of human aloneness reveals itself. Jung recognised this. He wrote:

> The development of personality from the germ state to full consciousness is at once a charisma and a curse, because its first fruit is the conscious and unavoidable segregation of the single individual from the undifferentiated and unconscious herd. This means isolation and there is no more comforting word for it. Neither family nor society nor position can save him from this fate, nor yet the most successful adaptation to his environment, however smoothly he fits in. The development of personality is a favour that must be paid for dearly.[50]

The first intimations of this state can make a person long for the shelter of the old dependencies, the security of blindness. But just as we cannot become children again, so we cannot escape in comfort from androgyny, however much we fear its implications. Psychological development carries us relentlessly forward, rarely allowing us to rest for long at any particular place and never allowing us to retreat for ever without incurring sickness. The way forward involves many stages, each difficult and painful but also potentially exhilarating. Our freedom does not lie in selecting the stages and determining their sequence, but in choosing whether to hasten or delay their arrival and realisation, and welcome or reject their insights.

Androgyny is the way of developing the psychological organs of perception which help us to see and understand more about ourselves and others. For those who consciously adopt it as their way, its value lies in the increase of knowledge and the more certain experience of love it brings. For those who do not recognise it, its importance as a subject lies in the questions it poses, the challenges it makes to other ways of describing human nature. We live in a culture which places a high premium on answers and a much lower one on questions and the capacity to live with uncertainty. It might be that this scale of values is upside down. It might be that we could serve ourselves and others better by learning to live with fewer answers and more questions.

Conclusion

Jesus said: 'And when you make the inner as the outer, and the outer as the inner and the upper as the lower, and when you make male and female into a single one, so that the male shall not be male and the female (shall not) be female, then shall you enter (the Kingdom).'[1]

The Christian Church offers the sacrament of marriage as the ideal relationship between the sexes. It teaches that the man's role is to look after and cherish his wife, while the woman's is to love, honour and obey her husband. When the man leads and the woman follows the two become one and together create a life-long relationship for the worship of God and the procreation of children. The marriage ceremony seals the union of the sexes with the aweful warning that what God hath joined let no man put asunder. To defy this command through divorce or adultery is to sin.

As has been pointed out many times, this idea of marriage is highly restrictive of individual liberty: it binds two people for their whole lives to a vow they made when they were probably young, inexperienced and largely ignorant both of themselves and of each other. It allows them minimal freedom to create their relationship or their personal lives as they think and feel to be appropriate, but commands instead that they live according to certain rules and conventions dictated by an external authority. As people begin to want to be their own authority as far as they can, the marriage vows become the target of vociferous attacks, repudiation and widespread defiance. Divorce and adultery flourish, fewer women are prepared to tolerate a role of subservience and service to their husbands, and fewer men are willing either to demand such behaviour from their wives or to accept that they alone should be responsible for all the providing and decision-making. So while many people may continue to marry, respect for the traditional concept and laws of marriage declines.

If, however, 'marriage' is understood not in its outer sense as a system of rules designed to organise and control relationships *between* the sexes, but in the inner psychological sense of the union of the masculine and feminine principles *within* each psyche, the realisation of androgyny suggested by the alchemists, then far from being a fetter on freedom, such a 'marriage' within each individual becomes the way to freedom through the discovery of the Self. Psychological 'marriage' of the feminine and the masculine within each person imbues its practices with new meaning and life. The injunction that the man must initiate and the woman follow, highly oppressive to many individual women and men in their relationship with each other, can be recognised as wisdom for the development of the Self. For the way of the masculine is actively to organise and initiate, while the way of the feminine is to yield, receive and harmonise, Both are valued equally. The prohibitions against 'divorce' in such a psychological 'marriage' cease to be restrictive, except in a creative sense, and become instead valuable statements about the way of androgyny which depends for its realisation on the continual interaction of the two principles. To 'divorce' one from the other is to deny our own nature, and in denying it, to sin. The idea of fulfilment of marriage through the procreation of children acquires new meaning once the word is interpreted as an inner process. Physically the union of the male and female may produce a child. Psychologically the union of the masculine and the feminine can also result in a conception, not of another human being, but of a new Self, or higher Ego. Just as the infant and young child needs the care of both a 'father' and a 'mother' to become an independent adult, so the psychological infant needs the support and insights of both the masculine and feminine principles to develop its own nature which is both male and female. The Church teaches that in marriage the male and female create one body. The inner psychological way teaches that the two principles create one androgynous Self.

Christianity as well as the ancient Chinese both point to this inner marriage as the way to the true Self, the realisation of the Dao or God within. Chinese literature and philosophy are more explicit on the subject because of the central importance of Yin-Yang theory, but it is a theme which is present, to a greater or lesser extent, in much Christian literature. In the New Testament the wholeness or oneness of Christ receives continual affirmation, particularly in St John's Gospel. Early Gnostic texts contain numerous references to androgyny as the nature of Christ and the potential of the human being. In one of these Jesus says: 'When you make the two become one, you will become the son of Man.'[2] According to the *Second Epistle of Clement*, when Jesus was asked at what moment the Kingdom would come, He replied: 'When the two shall be one, the outside like the inside, the male with the female neither male nor female'.[3]

Through the centuries of Christian tradition the idea of the androgyny of Christ as the goal of human endeavour was kept alive by different groups and emerged from time to time in different forms. For instance, it constituted a central part of European alchemy and appeared again in the writings of many of the German Romantics, who were inspired by the writings of Jacob Boehme and the Theosophists. Franz von Baader, for example, wrote: 'The aim of marriage as a sacrament is the restoration of the celestial or angelic image of man as he should be' – that is androgynous.[4] Ritter, a doctor, friend of Novalis, said that the human being of the future would be, like Christ, androgynous, and Friedrich Schlegel wrote that the goal towards which the human race should strive is a progressive re-integration of the sexes which should end in androgyny.[5] Even in the twentieth century interest in the androgyny of Christ still lingers in the writings of certain theologians. Georg Köepgen, a Catholic, wrote that Christ was androgynous and Christianity 'neither male nor female', but 'male-female in the sense that the male paired with the female in Jesus' soul'. In Him 'the tension and polaristic strife of sex are resolved in an androgynous unity'.[6]

The search for androgyny entails exchanging a partial self for a complete self through the discovery that we can see further than we have seen, know more than we have known, feel deeper than we have felt and love more than we have loved, that we are, in truth, far more than we knew. The way towards androgyny does not assume that human *nature* is inadequate or incomplete but that human *consciousness* is blinkered.

Loss initiates the journey towards androgyny. As humanity awoke millenia ago from its instinctive at-oneness with the cosmos, so each individual emerges, at some moment, from his or her pre-conscious identity with the Mother. This initial loss coincides with the birth of human consciousness. It is followed by a struggle between the desire for freedom and knowledge and the longing for wholeness and peace. The tension between these two impulses propels the restless psyche ever onwards in search of a kingdom in which freedom and unity belong together, in which understanding and peace are no longer in conflict.

Just as the union of the physical male and female is described as making love, so the union of the masculine and feminine principles within the psyche allows for an inner experience of love, which is the hallmark of the androgynous consciousness. This love, which is independent of other people for its realisation and existence, paradoxically leads the individual to a greater understanding of love and a greater ability to love others than was possible while his or her experience of love was dependent for its existence on another person. It becomes more possible to love others for what they are rather than for the unrealised aspects of oneself they provide. Such a love, Kahlil Gibran writes, 'possesses not nor would it be possessed; for love is sufficient unto love'. It 'gives naught but itself and takes naught but from itself'.[7] Jacobi describes the implications of this stage of psychological development in words which strikingly avoid glossing over what may seem, to some people, the less comfortable consequences of this kind of loving.

> Above all we have achieved a real independence and with it, to be sure, a certain isolation. In a sense we are alone, for our 'inner freedom' means that a love relation can no longer fetter us; the other sex has lost its magic power over us, for we have come to know its essential traits in the depths of our own psyche. We shall not easily

'*fall* in love', for we can no longer lose ourselves in someone else, but we shall be capable of a deeper love, a conscious devotion to the other.[8]

Such love in its freedom from possession is not free from pain. It is merely that the pain ceases to arise from personal egoism. The way of androgyny leads to a gradual expansion of the boundaries of the soul, so that while retaining a strong sense of individuality we learn that, however whole and free we may be, we are, at another level, no stronger than the weakest member of humanity, no freer than the most imprisoned; that their pain is our pain, their burdens our burdens. Source of this knowledge is love itself, or what the Chinese call 'human-heartedness'. It, alone, is the teacher.

The purpose of this book has not been to offer a hypothesis of human potential in order to underline the disparity between what we are and what we could be, nor to tantalise, depress and diminish us with visions of the unattainable, but instead to suggest that knowledge of our potential can offer not only ideals and directions for the future but, just as much, insights and strength for the present. We need to know what we can be to live with what we are. Androgyny, as the expression of the Dao in human consciousness, is the Way of the Self as well as the Way to the Self, the journey as well as the destination. Each stage along its way is an organic part of the whole, nothing can be bypassed.

The journey towards androgyny can be described and charted in considerable detail, but the meaning and experience of androgyny, the insights and feelings it brings, cannot be communicated through words, because words reflect polarity. A study of androgyny has therefore to end short of its subject so that we can contemplate the wisdom of Laozi when he said that 'those who speak do not know and those who know do not speak', and remember that the destination of one journey is no more than the beginning of the next.

Notes

Full bibliographical details for books and articles quoted in the footnotes can be found in the Select Bibliography

INTRODUCTION

1 Tai ji Quan (T'ai chi ch'uan), the traditional art of meditation in movement, sometimes called 'Chinese Yoga', teaches the individual to develop and experience a harmony of the Yin and Yang forces. In the dawn light of contemporary China, it is a common sight to see people of all ages working their way slowly and gracefully through the flowing movements of this therapy. The importance of Yin and Yang in acupuncture will be examined in chapter six

2 John Tomas Scopes was a teacher of science in Rhea High School, Dayton, USA. He violated the Tennessee State law, which prohibited the teaching in public schools of any theories denying the divine creation of humanity taught in the Bible, teaching instead that humanity descended from the lower order of animals

3 See Carol Schreier Rupprecht 'The Martial Maid and the Challenge of Androgyny', *Spring 1974*, Spring Publications, New York pp 273–4. This article explains that 'hermaphrodite'

and 'androgyne' were 'originally synonymous botanical terms, in Greek, for plants with both staminate and pistillate organs on the same flower'. 'But the former has come to be limited in denotation to an organic phenomenon, the occurrence of both female and male genitalia in the same individual. This released the compound, androgyne, from a strictly biological context, allowing its meaning to reside in qualities of character or attitude'

CHAPTER ONE THE GOLDEN AGE

1 Lin Yutang, *Tao Te Ching*, p 143

2 Trans. by Fung Yu-lan in *A Short History of Chinese Philosophy*, p 184

3 *Chuang Tzu* trans. H. A. Giles, p 215

4 A. Graham, *The Book of Lieh Tzu*, p 20

5 *ibid.* pp 18–19

6 *Tao Te Ching* trans. D. C. Lau, p 117

7 *ibid.* p 57

8 Chang Chung-yuan, *Creativity and Taoism*, p 30

9 *ibid.* p 30

10 S. Freud in *Civilization and its Discontents*, p 15

11 E. Neumann, *The Origins and History of Consciousness*, p 6

12 *ibid.* p 10

13 *Tao Te Ching* trans. D. C. Lau, p 116

14 A. Giles, *Chuang Tzu*, p 128

15 *ibid.* p 98

16 *ibid.* p 156

17 *The Bible*, Genesis 3:5

18 *Tao Te Ching* trans. D. C. Lau, p 109

19 *ibid.* p 117

20 Zhu Xi quoted in W. T. Chan, *A Source Book in Chinese Philosophy*, p 590

21 Zhu Xi quoted by W. T. Chan, *ibid.* p 628

22 D. Howard Smith, *Confucius*, p 163

23 The Five Agents, or elements, are Earth, Water, Wood, Metal and Earth. According to Chinese belief they evolved from the interaction of Yin and Yang.

24 Zhu Xi quoted by W. T. Chan in *A Source Book in Chinese Philosophy*, p 621

25 Zhu Xi quoted by W. T. Chan, *ibid.* p 625

26 M. L. von Franz, *Creation Myths*, p 97

27 *ibid.* p 93

28 Zheng He (Cheng Ho) was a Moslem eunuch from Yunnan in the fifteenth century AD. He led formidable Chinese armadas all the way across the Indian Ocean almost a century before the Portuguese reached India by sailing round Africa, and a hundred and fifty years before the Spanish Armada of 1588. But his journeys were isolated *tours de forces.* They were not followed up by further Chinese expeditions.

CHAPTER TWO THE VIRGIN BIRTH OF YIN AND YAN

1 From the Bai Hu Tong (Pai Hu T'ung) written in the Han dynasty by Pan Gu (Pan Ku) 32–92, quoted in the *I Ching* trans. Richard Wilhelm, p 329

2 James Mellaart, *Çatal Hüyük*, p 70 quoted by June Singer in *Androgyny*, p 66

3 Merlin Stone, *The Paradise Papers*

4 For a more detailed discussion of the matriarchal debate see Adrienne Rich, *Of Woman Born*

5 Robert Briffault, *The Mothers*, Vol I p 362. Nevertheless, Briffault went on to argue that Chinese society was the exception to the general pattern in that it, like many others, was originally matriarchal

6 It would seem likely that a matriarchal consciousness in a society would be reflected in certain ways in the social, political and economic structures of that society. My point is neither to assert or refute the existence of a matriarchal period in China, but merely to state that an understanding of the relationship between what I consider to be a 'matriarchal consciousness' and the social order must await more reliable evidence

7 Erich Neumann's essay 'On the Moon and Matriarchal Consciousness' in *Fathers and Mothers*, Vitale et al, pp 40–41

8 Esther Harding, *Woman's Mysteries*, pp 155–6

9 Fritjof Capra, *The Tao of Physics*, p 144

10 *Tao Te Ching* trans. D. C. Lau, Chapter LII, p 113

11 Marie Louise von Franz, *Creation Myths*, p 160

12 D. A. Mackenzie, *Myths of China and Japan*, p 185

13 See Erich Neumann, *The Great Mother*, p 243

14 Stylianos Alexion, *Minoan Civilization*, pp 72–73

15 Erich Neumann, *The Great Mother*, p 269

16 Plato, *The Symposium*

17 L. Apuleius, *The Golden Ass* trans. Robert Graves quoted in M. Stone, *The Paradise Papers*, p 39

18 Esther Harding, *op. cit.* p 182

19 *ibid.* p 94

20 *Tao Te Ching*, *op. cit.* Chapter VII, p 62

21 *ibid.* Chapter XXV, p 82

22 In *Anthology of Chinese Literature*, trans. A. Waley ed. Cyril Birch, p 36

23 Werner, *Myths and Legends of China*, p 130

24 See Marina Warner's interesting study of the myth and cult of the Virgin Mary, *Alone of All Her Sex*

25 See John Layard, *The Virgin Archetype*

26 Esther Harding, *op. cit.*, p 187

27 See *I Ching*, trans. R. Wilhelm, p 335

28 Esther Harding, *The I and Not I*, p 47

29 *Sources of Chinese Tradition*, Vol I, p 176

30 Huai Nan tzu, *Tao, The Great Luminant*, trans. E. Morgan, p 46

31 See Julia Kristeva, *About Chinese Women*, p 58–9

32 Edward H. Shaffer, *The Vermilion Bird*, p 79

33 Marcel Granet, *Festivals and Songs in Ancient China*, p 130

34 *ibid.* p 132

35 *ibid.* pp 85–6

36 *ibid.* p 173

37 *Shamanism: Archaic Techniques of Ecstasy.* Briffault also considered that the first Shamans were probably female. See also Carmen Blacker, *The Catalpa Bow*

38 Mircea Eliade, *The Two and the One*, p 116

39 J. J. M. de Groot, *The Religious System of China*, Vol VI, Book II, p 1187

40 *New Larousse Encyclopaedia of Mythology*, p 49

41 Virtue, in Daoist writings, was considered a reflection of identity with the Dao. So the gradual loss of identity with the divine principle was, according to Zhuangzi, the reason

for the progressive decline of the 'good life'. But also, it seems, the loss of this virtue, or instinctive identity with the Dao, was the precondition of human knowledge

42 *Chuang Tzu*, trans. H. A. Giles, p 157

43 The relationship between the masculine principle and differentiation will be examined in detail in chapter three

44 The nature of the feminine is explored in chapter five

45 *The Book of Poetry*, trans. J. Legge, Vol IV Part I, p 147

46 *The Book of Poetry*, trans. J. Legge, Vol IV Part II, p 306–7

47 *Festivals and Songs in Ancient China, op. cit.*, pp 233–4

48 *The Book of Poetry*, trans. J. Legge, Vol IV Part II, p 560

49 Ulanov, *The Feminine in Jungian Psychology and Christian Theology*, p 155

CHAPTER THREE THE THEORY OF YIN AND YAN

1 Chapter seven will suggest a different way of approaching the problem of gender in the light of Yin-Yang theory

2 There was a Yin-Yang school of philosophy in the fourth century BC., but none of its writings have survived. Howevei it seems unlikely, from the later references to it, that it offered much more than a slight introduction to the subject

3 The oracle bones were discovered early this century and have revolutionised understanding of early China. They were the bones on which the rulers wrote their questions to the oracle

4 See H. Wilhelm, *Eight Lectures on the I Ching*, p 26

5 Fu Xi is often depicted as a mountain out of which a leaf-crowned head emerges, suggesting that he was probably more divine than human

6 See H. Wilheim, *op. cit.*

7 R. Wilhelm *I Ching*, p 297

8 H. Wilhelm, *op. cit.*

9 Wing-tsit Chan, *A Source Book in Chinese Philosophy*, p 491

10 For a discussion of the Chinese conception of time, see J. Needham, *Time and Eastern Man*, Royal Anthropological Institute of Great Britain and Ireland, 1964

11 Zhuangzi quoted by W. T. Chan, in *A Source Book in Chinese Philosophy*, p 202

12 *ibid.*, p 204

13 R. Wilhelm, *I Ching*, p 249

14 *ibid.*, pp 249–50

15 Zhou Dunyi's diagram, Needham *Science and Civilisation in China* (S.C.C.), Vol II, pp 460–1

16 *Tao Te Ching* translated by A. Waley in *The Two Hands of God*, p 48

17 *Heraclitus*, trans. Philip Wheelwright, Princeton University Press Princeton 1959

18 Needham, Vol II, S.C.C., p 336

19 Wing-tsit Chan, *op. cit.*, p 503

20 F. Capra, *op. cit.*, pp 83–5

21 *ibid.*, p 234

22 *The Philosophy of Human Nature*, by Chu Hsi, translated by Percy Bruce p 59

23 H. Wilhelm, *op. cit.*, p 30

24 See E. Neumann, *Art and the Creative Unconscious*

25 There is another dimension in the symbolism of Yin and Yang at which there is indeed a certain correspondence between Yang and the sun, and Yin and the moon, or earth. The essential quality of Yang is its capacity to polarise and this is precisely the effect of the sun; it divides

the world into light and shadow. Whereas the essential nature of Yin is to embrace and nourish, to contain and reflect all things in her dark depths

26 R. Wilhelm, *I Ching*, p 4

27 *ibid.*, p 5

28 *ibid.*, p 4

29 *I Ching* trans. J. Blofield, p 91

30 R. Wilhelm, *op. cit.*, p 387

31 *ibid.*, p 387

32 H. Wilhelm, *op. cit.*, p 50

33 See Neumann, *The Origin and History of Consciousness* and James Hillman's articles in *Spring*, 1973 and 1974

34 C. G. Jung, *The Structure and Dynamics of the Psyche*, Collected Works (C.W.) VIII, p 133

35 C. G. Jung, *The Archetypes and the Collective Unconscious*, Part I, p 66

36 A. P. Shepherd, *A Scientist of the Invisible*, p 81. This is an excellent introduction to Steiner's thinking and insights

37 See Rudolf Steiner, *Knowledge of the Higher Worlds*

38 Rudolf Steiner, *The Gospel of St John*, Kassel lectures, p 155

39 Rudolf Steiner, *Study of Man*, Rudolf Steiner Press lectures given in 1919, p 74

CHAPTER FOUR THE MASCULINE CONSCIOUSNESS

1 See Merlin Stone, *The Paradise Papers* and Erich Neumann, *The Origin and History of Consciousness*

2 See *The First Emperor*, ed Li Yu-ning, International Arts and Sciences Press, 1975

3 See H. T. Wiens, *China's March Towards the Tropics*

4 *The First Emperor, op. cit.*, p xviv

5 *Han Fei Tzu*, trans. Burton Watson p 32

6 Confucian Classics, *The Book of Songs, The Classic of Documents, The Book of Changes, The Spring and Autumn Annals* and *The Book of Rites*

7 Carsun Chang, *The Development of Neo-Confucian Thought*, p 211

8 William MacNaughton, *The Confucian Vision*: Confucius, *The Analects*, xviii:25, p 22

9 Ch'u T'ung-tsu, *Law and Society in Traditional China*, p 104

10 *Mencius*, trans. D. C. Lau, Bk. VII part A, p 182

11 *ibid.*, Bk. II part A, pp 82–3

12 *ibid.*, Bk. VI part A, pp 167–8

13 *Mencius*, quoted in W. T. Chan, *op. cit.*, p 70

14 *Mencius*, trans. Graham, Bk. IV part A, p 119

15 *ibid.*, Bk. II part A, p 83

16 R. Wilhelm, *I Ching*, p 152

17 Confucius, *The Analects*, trans. W. T. Chan, *op. cit.*, p 40

18 *Mencius, op. cit.*, Bk. III part A, p 101

19 *ibid.*, Bk. III part A, pp 96–7

20 I am grateful to Dr Charles Curwen, lecturer in Far Eastern History at the School of Oriental and African Studies, London University, for this information

21 trans. by Andrew Boyd

22 trans. anonymous

23 trans. anonymous

24 Arthur Cooper, *Li Po and Tu Fu*, p 35

25 Jung, 'On the Nature of the Psyche' C.W.8., *The Structure and Dynamics of the Psyche*, p 226

CHAPTER FIVE THE FEMININE CONSCIOUSNESS

1 See S. Freud, *Three Essays on Sexuality*: E. Erikson, *Childhood and Society*: K. Horney, *Feminine Psychology*: M. Mead, *Male and Female*

2 See Ann Belford Ulanov, *The Feminine in Jungian Psychology and Christian Theology*

3 See Bibliography

4 See Emma Jung, *Animus and Anima*

5 Joseph Campbell, referred to in *The Wise Wound* by Penelope Shuttle and Peter Redgrove

6 Ulanov, *op. cit.*, pp 156–7

7 Alan Watts, *The Book on the Taboo against Knowing Who You Are*, Abacus 1977, pp 130–1

8 *Chuang Tzu*, trans. H. A. Giles, p 97

9 *Tao Te Ching*, LXVI, trans. D. C. Lau, p 128

10 Ulanov, *op. cit.*, p 166

11 Irene Claremont de Castillejo, *Knowing Woman*, p 16

12 *ibid.*, p 179

13 Sze-mai, *The Way of Chinese Painting*, p 119

14 Lin-chi., quoted by Alan Watts, *The Way of Zen* Penguin Books, p 171

15 Lin-chi, quoted by Alan Watts *ibid.*, p 121

16 Quoted in J. Needham, *Science and Civilization in China*, Vol II, p 61: from L. Huxley, *Life and Letters of Thomas Henry Huxley*, 3 Vols. Macmillan London 1903 Vol 1 p 316

17 Whitehead quoted in A. Watts, *Nature, Man and Woman*, p 69

18 Ulanov, *op. cit.*, pp 172–3

19 Castillejo, *Knowing Woman*, pp 14–15
For discussion of the artist and consciousness see E. Neumann's brilliant study, *Art and the Creative Unconscious*

20 Ulanov, *op. cit.*, p 160

21 *Chuang Tzu*, trans. H. A. Giles, p 185

22 *The Spirit of Chinese Philosophy*, trans. Fung Yu-lan, p 107

23 Sze-mai, *The Way of Chinese Painting*, p 118–9

24 *ibid.*, p 120

25 Chang Chung-yuan, *Creativity and Taoism*, p 204

26 Chang Chung-yuan, *op. cit.*, p 170

27 *Chuang Tzu*, trans. H. A. Giles, p 256

28 *Chuang Tzu*, trans. H. A. Giles, p 174

29 *Chuang Tzu*, trans. A. Waley in *Three Ways of Thought in Ancient China*, p 72

30 A. Watts, *The Way of Zen*, p 213

CHAPTER SIX THE YIN AND YANG OF THE INDIVIDUAL

1 *Lieh Tzu* trans. A. C. Graham, p 27

2 *Huang-ti Nei Ching Ssu Wen (The Yellow Emperor's Classic of Internal Medicine)*, trans. Ilza Veith, p 9

3 *ibid.*, p 15

4 Stephan Pálos, *The Chinese Art of Healing*, p 43

5 *The Yellow Emperor's Classic*, p 17

6 *ibid.*, p 15

7 *The Chinese Art of Healing*, p 41

8 *The Yellow Emperor's Classic*, *op. cit.*, pp 98–9

9 *ibid.*, pp 99–100

10 M. Sherfey, *The Nature and Evolution of Female Sexuality*, p 38

11 *ibid.*, p 39

12 *ibid.*, p 46

13 *ibid.*, p 43

14 June Singer, *Androgyny*, pp 260–1

15 Michael Fordham, *Jungian Views of the Body-mind Relationship, Spring 1974*, Spring Publications, Zurich, pp 172 and 173

16 Penelope Shuttle and Peter Redgrove, *The Wise Wound*, p 36 and 146

17 *ibid.*, p 31

18 Corinne Hutt, *Males and Females*, pp 54–5

19 Gail Sheehy, *Passages*, pp 455–6*

20 *The Yellow Emperor's Classic*, *op. cit.*, p 23

21 H. Maspero quoted in Needham S.C.C. Vol 11 p 153

22 *ibid.*, p 154

23 Wing-tsit Chan, *op. cit.*, p 492

24 *The Yellow Emperor's Classic*, *op. cit.*, p 17

25 *ibid.*, *op. cit.*, pp 121–2

26 *Lieh Tzu*, trans. A. C. Graham, *op. cit.*, p 23

* According to Gail Sheehy in *Passages* some of Dr. Rose's studies were reported in 'I.S. Plasma Testoserone Levels in the Male Rhesus: Influence of Sexual and Social Stimuli', *Science* (1972), by Rose, Holiday and Bernstein.

27 *Self and Society in Ming Thought*, ed. Theodore M. de Bary, New York and London 1970, p 198

28 Freud, *An Outline of Psychoanalysis*, 1940 (1938), S.E. Vol XXIII, p 188

29 Steiner, *Cosmic Memory*

30 Steiner, *Theosophy of the Rosicrucians*, lecture XII, pp 128–9. For a discussion of Steiner's view of evolution and its relation to Darwinian theory see H. Poppelbaum, *Man and Animal*

31 *ibid.*, p 130

32 Neumann, *The Child*, p 10

33 *ibid.*, p 11. See also Bruno Bettelheim, *Symbolic Wounds*, in which he refers to infants as not psychologically neuter but deuter comprising the undeveloped qualities of both sexes

34 *ibid.*, pp 24–25

35 *ibid.*, p 109

36 Neumann, *Origins and History of Consciousness*, p 112

37 Margaret Mead, *Sex and Temperament in Three Primitive Societies*

38 Steiner, *St. John Lectures*, (Cassel edition), 1909, p 187

39 *ibid.*, p 213

40 K. Millet, *Sita*, p 61

41 Jung, *Collected Works*, Vol 8, pp 398–9

42 Quoted in *The Wise Wound*, *op. cit.*, p 120

43 Neumann, *Origins*, p 416

CHAPTER SEVEN MICROCOSM AND MACROCOSM

1 *Shu Ching* trans. J. Legge.
The Shu Ching consists of remarks, announcements etc.,

alleged to have been made by Yao and Shun and edited by Confucius. Some are evidently forgeries but those ascribed to the early Zhou (Chou) are probably reliable.

2 *Li Chi* quoted by Johnson in *Alchemy*, p 15

3 *I Ching* trans. Richard Wilhelm, *op. cit.*, pp 90–1

4 *Mencius*, *op. cit.*, Bk. VII, part A, p 182

5 *ibid.*, Book VII, part A, p 182

6 D. Howard Smith, *Confucius*, p 162

7 Tung Chung-shu quoted in Wing-tsit Chan, *op. cit.*, pp 280–1

8 *ibid.*, p 282

9 *ibid.*, pp 283–4

10 Shao Yung in W. T. Chan, *op. cit.*, p 492

11 *ibid.*, p 494

12 Zhu Xi in L. T. Chan, *ibid.*, p 614

13 *The Yellow Emperor's Classic*, pp 97–8

14 J. Eitel, *Feng-Shui*, p 59

15 Fung Yu-lan, *A History of Chinese Philosophy*, Vol 11, *op. cit.*, p 10

16 Reischauer and Fairbank, *East Asia: The Great Traditions*, p 567

17 Carlos Castaneda, *The Teachings of Don Juan*, p 31

18 I am grateful to Susanne Chowdhury for reminding me of this passage

19 J. Eitel, *Feng-Shui*, *op. cit.*, p 84

20 See *The Yellow Emperor's Classic*

21 Stephen Pálos, *The Chinese Art of Healing*, p 37

22 Lyall Watson, *Supernature*, p 17

23 *ibid.*, pp 45–6

24 See Frank Brown, *The 'Clocks' timing biological Rhythms*, American Scientist, Nov.–Dec. 1972, pp 756–66

25 *The Wise Wound*, pp 150–1
See A. Solberger, *Biological Rhythms Research*, Elsevier, London and New York, 1965

26 Kuan tzu quoted in Needham S.C.C. Vol I, p 150

27 See J. Needham, S.C.C. Vol 3, p 488

28 *ibid.*, p 23

29 See *The Wise Wound*, p 164

30 See *The Wise Wound*, p 164 and 'Lunar Periodicity in Human Production: a likely unit of biological time', *American Journal of Obstetrics and Gynaecology*, Vol 77 April 1959, pp 905–15

31 *The Wise Wound*, p 136

32 E. Ramey 'Men Cycles' in *Readings Towards a Psychology of Androgyny*, A. G. Kaplan and J. P. Bean, pp 139–40

33 *Chou Li* quoted by Needham in *Science and Civilisation in China*, Vol III, p 190

34 Needham, *Science and Civilisation in China*, Vol II, p 291

35 Leibniz quoted in *Jung, Synchronicity and Human Destiny*, Ira Progoff, p 69

36 *ibid.*, p 78

37 Neumann, *The Child*, *op. cit.*, p 91

38 Ira Progoff, *op. cit.*, pp 80–1

39 See Select Bibliography

40 Rudolf Steiner, *Cosmic Memory*; *Microcosm and Macrocosm*; 'For Women Only', unpublished lecture, Berlin 1905

41 C. J. Jung, *Memories, Dreams and Reflections*, p 357

42 H. Wilhelm, *Change: Eight Lectures on the I Ching*, p 19

43 Tung Chung-shu in *Sources of Chinese Tradition*, p 167

CHAPTER EIGHT THE SPIRIT OF THE VALLEY NEVER DIES

1 See Chapter Two

2 *The Yellow Emperor's Classic*, *op. cit.*, p 122

3 . Needham, *Science and Civilization in China*, Vol V:2, p 105

4 *Han Shu*: quoted by A. Waley in *Notes on Chinese Alchemy* in the Bulletin of Oriental and African Studies, Vol VI, Part I, pp 1–24

5 See Needham, *Science and Civilization in China*, Vol V:3, p 22 for a drawing of the banner

6 Needham, *Science and Civilization in China*, Vol V:2, p 96

7 *ibid.*, p 100, quoted from Yu Ying-shih 'Life and Immortality in the Mind of Han China', *Harvard Journal of Asiatic Studies*, 1965:25:80

8 *ibid.*, pp 101–2

9 Ko Hung, *Alchemy, Medicine and Religion in China of* AD. *320*, trans. Ware

10 *ibid.*, p 66–7

11 *ibid.*, p 301

12 *ibid.*, p 113

13 Needham maintains that there is sufficient evidence to indicate that cupellation, a method of testing gold, was already known and practised in China by the third century BC. See Vol V:2, p 70

14 Needham, *Science and Civilization in China*, Vol V:3, p 72

15 Titus Burckhardt, *Alchemy*, pp 58–9

16 A. Waley, B.S.O.A.S. Vol VI, Part I, p 15

17 *ibid.*, p 17

18 R. Wilhelm, *The Secret of the Golden Flower*, p 62

19 *ibid.*, p 63

20 *ibid.*

21 Ko Hung, *op. cit.*, p 42

22 *ibid.*, p 73

23 *ibid.*, p 100

24 *ibid.*, p 138

25 *The Secret of the Golden Flower*, *op. cit.*, p 6

26 *ibid.*, p 11

27 *ibid.*, p 31 (from the text)

28 *ibid.*, p 34

29 Jung's commentary in *The Secret of the Golden Flower*, *op. cit.*, p 124

30 *ibid.*, pp 92–3

31 *ibid.*, pp 31–2

32 See John Blofeld, *The Secret and the Sublime*

33 Mircea Eliade, *The Two and the One*. For an interesting discussion of the psychological transformation of the sexual instinct see Esther Harding, *Psychic Energy*

34 Needham, *Science and Civilization in China*, Vol II, pp 149–50

35 Van Gulik, *Sexual Life in Ancient China*, p 195

36 *ibid.*, p 199

37 *ibid.*, pp 344–5

38 Needham, *Science and Civilization in China*, Vol II, pp 150–1

39 *ibid.*, p 151

40 Van Gulik, *op. cit.*, pp 89–90

41 Jung, 'On the Nature of the Psyche' C.W.8. *The Structure and Dynamics of the Psyche*, para. 107, p 57

42 Rosemary Gordon, *Dying and Creating*, p 159

43 Rudolf Steiner, *The Gospel of St. John*, p 62, lectures given in Hamburg 1908

44 Jung, C.W.6. *Psychological Types*, para. 446

45 Needham, *Science and Civilization in China*, Vol V:2, p 295

46 Alan Watts, *Zen*, p 141

47 Confucius, *The Analects*, Book IV, Ch. XV

48 Jung, C.W.12. *Psychology and Alchemy*, p 31

49 *ibid.*, p 30

50 Jung, C.W.17 *The Development of Personality*, para. 294, p 173

CONCLUSION

1 The *Gospel of Thomas* in J. Doresse, *Les Livres Secrets des Gnostiques d'Egypte*, Vol II, 1959, p 95 quoted by M. Eliade, *The Two and the One*, p 106

2 J. Doresse, *op. cit.*, Vol II, p 109 in M. Eliade, *The Two and the One*, p 106

3 J. Doresse, *op. cit.*, Vol II, p 157 in M. Eliade, *The Two and the One*, pp 106–7

4 Franz von Baader quoted by M. Eliade, *The Two and the One*, *op. cit.*, p 102

5 Friedrich Schlegel quoted by M. Eliade, *ibid.*, p 101

6 Georg Koëpgen, *Die Gnosis der Christentums*, 1939, quoted by Jung in C.W. 14 *Mysterium Conjunctionis*, pp 373–4

7 Kahlil Gibran, *The Prophet*, p 12

8 *The Psychology of C. G. Jung*, Jolande Jacobi, p 123

Glossary

BUDDHISM: arrived in China sometime during the first century AD., and was taken up by the rich and aristocratic before gradually spreading to the peasantry during the following six or seven hundred years. The greatest imperial patrons of Buddhism were the emperors of the Northern Wei dynasty (386–534 AD.) It also flourished in the courts of the sixth century AD. in south China. The epoch from the mid-fourth century to the end of the eighth century has been called the Buddhist age of Chinese history. Its decline in China reflected the anti-'barbarian' sentiments of the Song dynasty and the emergence of Neo-Confucianism as the state orthodoxy.

CHAN (Ch'an): better known by its Japanese name of Zen, Chan Buddhism was a synthesis of Daoism and Buddhism. It stressed intuitive insight or enlightenment and taught that the only true reality was the timeless Buddha nature within each person's heart. Instead of texts, the Chan teachers preferred oral instruction, often through posing seemingly nonsensical problems and questions which were designed to shock the student out of his or her reliance on ordinary logic. Although it reached its fullest development not in China, but in Japan, Chan continued to exist in China as an independent and living movement long after other forms of Buddhism had declined or merged with popular Daoism.

CONFUCIUS Kong Fuzi (K'ung Fu-tzu) 551–479 BC.: he was born in the state of Lu, probably into a lower aristocratic family. The only record of his sayings is the *Analects*, largely a collection of his answers to questions. From these it is clear that Confucius looked back to a harmonious social order which he believed existed under King Wen and the Duke of Zhou during the eleventh century BC., in which each person knew his position in the social hierarchy and behaved accordingly; a ruler was a ruler, a subject a subject, a father a father, and a son a son. He hoped to recreate such a society in his own time through his teaching that government is basically an ethical problem, the duty of the hereditary lords being to set a good example to the people. He argued that the ruler's virtue and the contentment of the people, rather than power, should be the measure of political success. Thus he is known as China's first great moralist, a sage who taught that the ideal for which all men should strive is to become a person of nobility (a junzi). Confucius described the hallmarks of the gentleman as inner integrity righteousness, altruism (or reciprocity), loyalty (or conscientiousness towards others), and above all, love, (or human heartedness).

CONFUCIANISM: became the orthodox political theory during the Former *Han* dynasty (AD. 206–8). It did not draw exclusively from the ideas of Confucius and his disciples, but, on the contrary, was a syncretic philosophy heavily influenced by Daoist and Legalist, as well as by Confucian ideas. For instance the *Record of Rituals*, one of the Five Confucian Classics, compiled during the Former Han from earlier elements, includes Legalist ideas, concepts of divination as well as more orthodox Confucian concepts. The other classics were the *Yi Jing*, the *Book of History*, the *Classic of Songs* and the *Spring and Autumn Annals*. The triumph of Confucianism in the Han occurred as scholars gradually adopted Confucius as their ideal prototype and as the advantages of a system of government supported by a carefully controlled educational system for helping to unite and control such a vast empire were appreciated. The ideological orthodoxy which emerged from the marriage of

Legalism, Confucian ideas, Daoism and various other elements of ancient and popular thought, in the name of Confucius, laid the foundations for the Chinese Bureaucratic state which ruled China for most of the following 2,000 years.

DAO (Tao): this concept acquired slightly different interpretations from the different schools of Chinese philosophy, but, essentially, it refers to the totality of the natural process, human and cosmic. It is the principle of the universe which generates all things, the One which is eternal, spontaneous, nameless and indescribable. It is the source and the way of creation. It is sometimes rendered into English as 'God'.

DAO DE JING (Tao Te Ching): although attributed to the legendary sage, Laozi of the sixth century BC., the *Dao de Jing* is more likely the composite work of several ancient Daoists. (see Daoism)

DAOISM (Taoism): this was not a unified and homogenous school of thought, but contained ideas from widely different historical and conceptual contexts. Nevertheless certain themes resound through these writings which justify the collective label Daoist. The individual is seen as integral to the larger pattern of nature, the Dao, conformity with which imbues him or her with virtue. The key to merging or harmoniously conforming to the Dao lies in knowing its ways and doing nothing contrary to them. A favourite Daoist image is water which rules through yielding. This suggests the Daoist respect for those who follow the contours of the natural world rather than attempting to impose an artificial order on them. The Daoist ideal is spontaneous simplicity, a state in which the individual is so in tune with the Dao that he or she can quite naturally and unselfconsciously reflect its ways in all actions and non actions. The most famous Daoist Classics are the *Dao De Jing*, the *Zhuangzi* (*Chuang tzu*), possibly a third century BC. text, and the *Liezi* (*Lieh Tzu*), a work of the same period. Although Daoism in part degenerated into superstition during the following centuries, its emphasis on the oneness of the human and natural worlds, its respect for passivity and quiet receptivity, remained an invaluable influence in Chinese culture throughout the history of the empire.

LEGALISM (Fa-Jia): its leading thinkers were Han Feizi (Han Fei-tzu) who died in 233 BC. and Lisi (Li Ssu), died 208 BC. Both were disciples of Xunzi (Hsun Tzu). The *Han Fei-zi* is the fullest exposition of Legalist thought, but the *Books of Lord Shang* and the *Kuan Zi*, a book of uncertain origin falsely attributed to the seventh century statesman, also contain much legalist thinking. The Legalists' ideal state was one in which an uneducated people blindly obeyed an omnipotent King. They believed that human nature is incorrigibly selfish, hence the necessity for severe laws and harsh punishments. They fostered a martial spirit and a rigidly authoritarian society founded on the wealth and might of the state. Their laws were not conceived as the expression of some higher order of Heaven or nature but purely as the ruler's fiat. The Qin (Ch'in) dynasty, 221 BC.–206 BC. was the only purely Legalist state in Chinese history, but Legalist ideas of rule through strict authority, a body of absolute laws, and rewards and punishments, constituted a fundamental part of the political orthodoxy, called Confucianism, from the Han dynasty onwards.

MENCIUS (Meng-tzu) 372–289 BC.: he considered himself as a transmitter of the ideas of Confucius, but in fact he considerably added to and amplified the sayings of his master. In his work, the *Mencius*, he states what Confucius merely implied: that human beings are, by nature, good. All people, he explains, share an innate moral sense which can develop into the Confucian virtues. However this innate goodness can easily be perverted by an adverse environment, so the right education and inner cultivation are prerequisites of becoming a junzi, or 'gentleman'. The starting point of education, states Mencius, is the gradual extension of the love which it is natural to feel for those who are near to one, to those who are more distant. The second major contribution Mencius made to Confucianism was his theory of the Mandate of Heaven. He elaborated on his master's insistence on moral virtue as the right way of the ruler by arguing that the true king acquires and maintains his power through the support of the people, and the loss of this power is evidence that he has lost the right to rule. This led to his idea that a successful rebellion against a king is evidence that the ruler has forfeited, through his inadequate virtue, the Mandate of Heaven.

MOXIBUSTION (treatment by burning): it is associated with acupuncture both in modern and traditional Chinese medical texts. Formerly the acupuncture points were burned with a smouldering herb called moxa. Nowadays they are merely warmed. According to tradition, moxibustion was mainly developed in the northern part of China. Its practice is certainly remarkably ancient; the *Yellow Emperor's Classic of Internal Medicine* (at least 2,000 years old), refers to it as a completely developed process. Whereas acupuncture is employed especially for diseases caused by an excess of Yang, the moxa method attempts to restrain an excess of Yin.

NEO-CONFUCIANISM: arose partly to counter the appeal of Buddhism and Daoism which flourished in and out of government from roughly the third century AD. to the ninth century AD. Formed from a synthesis of Buddhist and Confucian ideas, Neo-Confucianism became the orthodox intellectual and political system until the abolition of the examination system in 1905. Whereas during the Tang dynasty (AD. 618–907) only a few dozen candidates were allowed to pass the intermittent civil service examinations, during the Song, after AD. 1065, when examinations began to be held regularly every three years, they became the major path to official position and a passport to the ruling class. Proficiency, in the Neo-Confucian view of the world was a pre-requisite of access to the ruling elite. Neo-Confucianism emphasised the goodness of human nature, government by moral example, the cardinal importance of education and self development as the keys to human perfection and hence, to the ideal society. The most famous Neo-Confucianists were Han Yu AD. 768–824, Zhou Dun-yi (Chou Tun-i) AD. 1017–73, Shao Yong (Shao Yong) AD. 1011–77, Zhang Zai

(Chang Tsai) AD. 1020–77, Zhang Hao (Chang Hao) AD. 1032–85, Zheng-yi (Ch'eng I) AD. 1033–1107, and Zhu Xi (Chu Hsi) AD. 1130–1200.

RESPIRATORY THERAPY: in ancient China it was closely interwoven with philosophical and religious quests for immortality. It seeks to harmonise the active and the passive, the inner and the outer parts of the body through a method of inhalation and exhilation that requires the participation of the patient's consciousness as well as her body. It is a therapy which assumes that with correct understanding and practice the individual can be his or her own healer.

SHU JING (Shu Ching) or *Book of History*: contains semi-historical documents and speeches many dating from the early centuries of the Zhou dynasty (1127–770 BC.).

SHI JING (*Shih Ching*) or *Book of Songs*: consists of 305 songs dating from about the tenth to the seventh century BC. Their precise dates are impossible to ascertain because it is likely that many of them were gathered and written down from oral traditions.

TAI JI QUAN (T'ai chi-ch'uan): was developed, according to some sources by Zhang Sanfeng (Chang San-feng) in the tenth century AD.. He attempted to obtain complete mastery over the body by means of a combination of inner tranquillity and movement exercises carried out slowly, flexibly and harmoniously. It is a therapy of meditation in movement which seeks to balance the Yin and the Yang so that the supreme principle, the Dao, can be expressed in its entirety.

WU XING (Wu hsing) or the Five Elements: this concept probably emerged from the Naturalist school of philosophy led by Zou Yen (Tsou Yen) *circa* 300 BC. According to their theories Yin and Yang, the two primal principles, generated the Five Elements – wood, metal, fire, water and earth, which were continually involved in a process of creation and subjugation of each other. For instance metal subjugates wood and wood creates water, while wood subjugates earth and creates fire.

XUNZI (Hsun-tzu) *circa* 300–237 BC: a Confucian who disagreed with Mencius' assertion that human nature is innately good, and argued instead that it is derived from an impersonal and amoral heaven, which means that the human being's emotions and natural desires lead to conflict and are therefore bad. All men are equal in their evil natures. The remedy for this potentially explosive situation, according to Xunzi, was education. On this point he and Mencius agree. The important difference between them is that while Mencius said goodness only needed to be nurtured, Xunzi, seemed to believe it had to be taught. His ideas which easily lend themselves to authoritarian educational and political systems, were influential in the development of Legalism. His writings are contained in the *Hsün-tzu.*

YI JING (I Ching) or *Book of Changes*: a book of divination and philosophy. The 64 hexagrams of which it is composed evolved from combining the original eight trigrams, each of which is composed of Yin (--) and Yang (—) lines:

☱ ☵ ☶ ☳ ☲ ☴ ☷ ☰

For example hexagram 6, ䷅ Song/Conflict, is composed of trigrams ☰ heaven, and ☵ water. The hexagrams express archetypal situations in the process of movement. Each of the six lines is capable of change, and as it does another situation emerges, represented by another hexagram. For instance if the top line of CONFLICT changes from Yang to Yin it becomes hexagram 47 ䷮ Kun-Oppression. The hexagram expresses the situation and, in pointing to its salient characteristics, suggests an appropriate course of action. To consult the *Yi Jing* as a book of divination therefore, is to discover the present circumstances and their future inclinations. To refer to it as a book of philosophy is to discover the way or patterns of the human and natural worlds. For an interesting introduction to the *Yi Jing* as a book of divination see C. G. Jung's foreword to Richard Wilhelm's translation of the *I Ching*, Routledge and Kegan Paul London 1974.

ZHU XI (Chu Hsi) AD. 1130–1200: undoubtedly the greatest of the Neo-Confucians, Zhu Xi is famous as a synthesiser of different philosophical concepts prevalent in his time. According to his Neo-Confucian metaphysics all things are considered to have their fundamental principles of form. Together these constitute the infinite, timeless Supreme Ultimate, which, itself, is reflected in each individual thing. The task of each person is to investigate human nature so as to allow the Supreme Ultimate, the Dao, to shine forth more clearly. After his death, Zhu Xi's Neo-Confucian synthesis gradually became established as a rigid orthodoxy so that by 1313 his commentaries on the classics were recognised as the standard ones to which answers in the civil service examinations had to conform. Zhu Xi selected the Four Confucian Classics – the *Analects*, the book of *Mencius*, the *Great Learning* and the *Doctrine of the Mean*. He supplemented them with extensive commentaries.

Select Bibliography

Adler, Gerhard. *The Living Symbol.* Princeton: Princeton University Press, 1961.

Arquelles, Miriam and José. *The Feminine Is Spacious As the Sky.* Boulder: Shambala Publications, 1978.

Avalon, A. *The Serpent Power.* New York: Dover Publications, 1974.

_____. *Shakti and Shakta.* New York: Dover Publications, 1978.

Bachofen, J. J. *Myth, Religion, and Mother Right.* Translated by Ralph Mannheim. Princeton: Princeton University Press, 1967.

Balzac, Honore de. *Seraphita.* New York: Steinerbooks, 1976.

Bary, W. M. Theodore de. *Self and Society in Ming Thought.* New York: Columbia University Press, 1970.

Birch, Cyril. *Anthology of Chinese Literature.* New York: Grove Press, 1965.

Blacker, Carmen. *The Catalpa Bow.* New Jersey: Rowman & Littlefield, 1975.

Blofeld, John. *The Secret and the Sublime.* New York: E. P. Dutton, 1973.

_____. *The Tantric Mysticism of Tibet.* New York: E. P. Dutton, 1970.

_____. *The Way of Power.* London: George Allen and Unwin, 1970.

Bodde, Derk. *Festivals in Classical China.* Princeton: Princeton University Press, 1975.

Briffault, Robert. *The Mothers.* New York: Atheneum, 1973.

Bruce, J. P. *Chu Hsi and His Masters.* London: Probsthain, 1923.

Burkhardt, Titus. *Alchemy.* New York: Penguin Books, 1974.

Burton, Watcon. *Sources of Chinese Tradition,* Vol I. New York: Columbia University Press, 1967.

Campbell, Joseph. *The Masks of God* (series title): *Occidental Mythology.* New York: Viking Press, 1968. *Oriental Mythology.* New York: Viking Press, 1968. *Primitive Mythology.* New York: Viking Press, 1968.

Capra, Fritjof. *The Tao of Physics.* Boulder: Shambhala Publications, 1975.

Castaneda, Carlos. *The Teachings of Don Juan.* New York: Simon & Schuster, 1973.

_____. *Journey to Ixtlan.* New York: Simon & Schuster, 1973.

_____. *The Second Ring of Power.* New York: Simon & Schuster, 1978.

_____. *A Separate Reality.* New York: Simon & Schuster, 1971.

_____. *Tales of Power.* New York: Simon & Schuster, 1974.

Castillejo, Irene Claremont de. *Knowing Woman.* New York: Harper & Row, 1974.

Chan, Wing-tsit. *A Source Book in Chinese Philosophy.* Princeton: Princeton University Press, 1972.

Chang, Carsun. *The Development of Neo-Confucian Thought.* New York: Bookman Associates, 1957.

Chang, Jolan. *The Tao of Love and Sex.* New York: E. P. Dutton, 1977.

Chou, Yi-Liang. "Tantrism in China." *In the Harvard Journal of Asiastic Studies,* Vol. 8 pp 241. Cambridge, 1945.

Christie, Anthony. *Chinese Mythology.* London: Paul Hamlyn, 1975.

Chu Hsi: Philosophy of Human Nature. Translated by J. Percy Bruce. London: Probsthain Oriental Series, Vol. 8, 1922.

Chuang Tsu. Translated by Herbert Giles. London: George Allen and Unwin, 1961.

Creel, H. G. *The Birth of China.* New York: Frederick Ungar, 1954.

_____. *Chinese Thought from Confucius to Mao Tse-tung.* Chicago: University of Chicago Press, 1953.

_____. *Confucius: the Man and the Myth.* Westport: Greenwood Press, 1973.

_____. *What Is Taoism?* Chicago: University of Chicago Press, 1970.

Daly, Mary. "The Qualitative Leap Beyond Patriarchal Religion." In *Quest,* Vol. I, no. 4. New York, Spring 1975.

Dames, Michael. *The Silbury Treasure.* New York: Thames & Hudson, 1977.

Davis, E. Gould. *The First Sex.* New York: Penguin Books, 1973.

de Beauvoir, Simone, *The Second Sex.* New York: Alfred A. Knopf, 1953.

Duyvendak, J. J. L. *The Book of Lord Shang.* San Francisco: Chinese Materials, 1974.

Eberhard, W. *Chinese Fairy Tales & Folk Tales.* New York: E. P. Dutton, 1938.

_____. *Guilt and Sin in Traditional China.* Berkeley: University of California Press, 1967.

Eitel, E. J. *Feng-Shui.* London, 1873.

Eliade, Mircea. *The Forge and the Crucible.* New York: Harper & Row, 1971.

_____. *Shamanism.* Princeton: Bollingen Series, Princeton University Press, 1970.

_____. *The Two and the One.* New York: Harper Torchbooks, 1969.

Feuchtwang, Stephen D. R. *An Anthropological Analysis of Chinese Geomancy.* Vithagna: Vientiane Editions, 1974.

Feyerabend, Paul. *Against Method.* New York: Schoken Books, 1978.

Firestone, Shulamith. *The Dialectic of Sex.* New York: William Morrow, 1974.

Franz, M. L. von. *Creation Myths.* Zurich: Spring Publications, 1975.

_____. *An Introduction to the Interpretation of Fairytales.* Zurich: Spring Publications, 1970.

_____. *Problems of the Feminine in Fairytales.* Zurich: Spring Publications 1972.

Freud, S. *Civilization and Its Discontents.* New York: W. W. Norton, 1962.

_____. *Introductory Lectures on Psychoanalysis.* New York: Liveright, 1977.

_____. *New Introductory Lectures on Psychoanalysis.* New York: W. W. Norton, 1965.

_____. *On Sexuality.* London: Penguin Books, 1977.

Freund, Philip. *Myths of Creation.* London: W. H. Allen, 1964.

Fung, Yu-lan. *A History of Chinese Philosophy,* Vol. I and II. Translated by Derk Bodde. Princeton: Princeton University Press, 1952–1953.

———. *A Short History of Chinese Philosophy.* New York: The Free Press, 1960.

———. *The Spirit of Chinese Philosophy.* Translated by E. R. Hughes. New York: The Free Press, 1966.

Gernet, J. *Ancient China.* Berkeley: University of California Press, 1968.

Gibran, Kahlil. *The Prophet.* New York: Alfred A. Knopf, 1923.

Gooch, Stan. *Total Man.* London: Abacus, 1975.

Gordon, Rosemary. "Dying and Creating." In *The Library of Analytical Psychology,* Vol. 4. London, 1978.

Graham, A. C. *Poems of the Late T'ang.* New York: Penguin Books, 1977.

Granet, Marcel. *The Religion of the Chinese People.* Oxford: Blackwell, 1975.

———. *Festivals and Songs of Ancient China, The Broadway Oriental Library.* New York: Krishna Press, 1932.

Graves, Robert. *The White Goddess.* New York: Octagon Books, 1972.

Grinnel, Robert. *Alchemy in a Modern Woman.* Zurich: Spring Publications, 1973.

Groot, J. J. M. de. *The Religious System of China.* San Francisco: Chinese Materials, 1976.

Guenther, H. V. *The Tantric View of Life.* Berkeley: Shambala Publications, 1972.

Gulik, Rober Hans van. *Sexual Life in Ancient China.* Atlantic Highlands: Humanities, 1974.

Han Fei-tzu. Translated by Burton Watson. New York: Columbia University Press, 1964.

Harding, Esther. *The Way of All Women.* New York: Harper & Row, 1975.

———. *The I and Not I.* Princeton: Bollingen Series, Princeton University Press, 1973.

———. *Psychic Energy.* Princeton: Bollingen Series, Princeton University Press, 1973.

Heilbrun, Carolyn G. *Towards a Recognition of Androgyny.* New York: Harper & Row, 1974.

Hillman, J. "Anima." In *Spring*, 1973 and 1974. Texas: Spring Publications.

Hook, Diana Farrington. *The I Ching and Mankind*. Boston: Routledge and Kegan Paul, 1975.

Horney, Karen. *Feminine Psychology*. New York: W. W. Norton, 1973.

Hsü, Leonard Shihlien. *The Political Philosophy of Confucianism*. London: Routledge and Kegan Paul, 1975.

Humana, Charles. *The Keeper of the Bed*. London: Arlington Books, 1973.

Hutt, Corinne. *Males and Females*. London: Penguin Books, 1975.

Hume, E. H. *The Chinese Way in Medicine*. Baltimore: The Johns Hopkins Press, 1940.

Ishihara, Akira and Levy, Howard S. *The Tao of Sex*. New York: Harper & Row, 1970.

Izutsu, Toshihiko. "The Absolute and the Perfect Man in Taoism." In *Eranos Jahrbuch*, Vol. XXXVI, pp. 379–441. Aurich: 1967.

Jacobi, Jolande. *The Psychology of C. G. Jung*. Connecticut: Yale University Press, 1973.

Johnson, O. S. *A Study of Chinese Alchemy*. New York: Arno Press 1974.

Jung, C. G. *Memories, Dreams and Reflections*. New York: Random House, 1965.

Jung, C. G. *Collected Works*. Princeton: Princeton University Press: Vol. 8, The Structure and Dyanmics of the Psyche, 1970. Vol. 9, The Archetypes and the Collective Unconscious, Part I, 1970. Vol. 9, Aion, Part II, 1968. Vol. 12, Psychology and Alchemy, 1968. Vol. 14, Mysterium Coniunctionis, 1970. Vol. 17, The Development of Personality, 1954.

Jung, Emma. *Animus and Anima*. Zurich: Spring Publications, 1974.

Kaplan, Alexandra G. *Beyond Sex Role Stereotypes*. Boston: Little, Brown and Company, 1976.

Karlin, Marvin and Andrews, Lewis M. *Biofeedback*. London: Abacus, 1975.

Kerényi, Karl. *Hermes: Guide of Souls*. Texas: Spring Publications, 1974.

Ko, Hung. *Alchemy, Medicine, Religion in the China of A.D. 320.* Translated by J.R. Ware. Cambridge: MIT Press, 1966.

König, Karl. *The Human Soul.* New York: Anthroposophic Press, Inc., 1973.

Kotewall, Robert, and Smith, Norman L. *Penguin Book of Chinese Verse.* New York: Penguin Books, 1975.

Kramer, Samuel. *Mythologies of the Ancient World.* New York: Doubleday, 1961.

Kristeva, Julia. *About Chinese Women.* New York: Urizen Books, 1977.

Lao, Tzu. *Tao Te Ching.* Translated by D. C. Lau. New York: Alfred A. Knopf, 1972.

Layard, John. *The Virgin Archetype.* Texas: Spring Publications, 1973.

Le Guin, Ursula K. *The Left Hand of Darkness.* New York: Harper & Row, 1980.

Lee, Jung Young. *The I Ching and Modern Man.* New Jersey: Secaucus University Books, 1975.

Legge, James, translator. *The Book of Poetry,* Vol. IV, Parts I and II, "The Chinese Classics." New York: Krishna Press.

Li Po and Tu Fu. Translated by Arthur Cooper. London: Penguin Books, 1974.

Li Yu-Ning, editor. *The First Emperor of China.* New York: International Arts and Sciences Press, 1975.

Lieh Tzu. *The Book of Lieh tzu.* Translated by A. C. Graham. London: John Murray, 1973.

Lin Yutang. *The Wisdom of Laotse.* Connecticut: Greenwood Press, 1958.

______. *The Wisdom of China and India.* New York: Modern Library, 1955.

Lopez-Pedraza, Rafael. *Hermes and His Children.* Texas: Spring Publications, 1978.

Luk, Charles. *Taoist Yoga.* New York: Samuel Weiser, 1970.

Macciocchi, Maria Antonietta. "Daily Life in Revolutionary China." In *Monthly Review Press.* New York, 1972.

Macculloch, John Arnott D.D. *The Mythology of All Races,* Vol. VIII. Boston: Archaelogical Institute of America, 1928.

Mackenzie, Donald A. *Myths of China and Japan.* Maine: Longwood Press, 1977.

Maccoby, Eleanor Emmons and Jacklin, Carol Nagy. *The Psychology of Sex Differences.* Stanford: Stanford University Press, 1974.

Mai-Mai Sze. *The Way of Chinese Painting.* New York: Vintage Books, 1959.

Mao Tse-tung. *Selected Works of Mao Tse-tung,* Vols. I & IV. New York: Pergamon Press, 1967.

McNaughton, William. *The Confucian Vision.* Ann Arbor: University of Michigan Press, 1974.

Mead, M. *Male and Female.* London: Penguin Books, 1974.

______. *Sex and Temperament in Three Primitive Societies.* New York: Dell Publishing, 1971.

Mencius. Translated by D. C. Lau. Connecticut: Greenwood Press, 1949.

Middleton, John, editor. *Myth and Cosmos.* New York: Natural History Press. 1967.

Millet, Kate. *Sita.* New York: Farrar, Straus & Giroux, 1977.

Morgan, Evan. *Tao: The Great Luminant.* New York: Paragon Press, 1969.

Munro, D. J. *The Concept of Man in Early China.* Stanford: Stanford University Press, 1969.

Needham, Joseph. *Science and Civilization in China.* Cambridge: Cambridge University Press: Vol. 1, *Introductory Orientations,* 1954. Vol. 2, *History of Scientific Thought,* 1956. Vol. 3, *Mathematics and the Sciences of the Heavens and the Earth,* 1959. Vol. 4, *Physics and Physical Technology,* Part I physics, 1963; Part II *Mechanical Engineering,* 1965. Vol. 5, *Chemistry and Chemical Technology,* Part II Spagyrical Discovery and Invention: Magisteries of Gold and Immortality, 1974; Part III Spagyrical Discovery and Invention: Historical Survey, from Cinnabar Elixirs to Synthetic Insulin, 1976.

______. "Time and Eastern Man," *The Henry Myers Lecture 1964.* London: Royal Anthropological Institute of Great Britain and Ireland, 1965.

Needleman, Jacob. *A Sense of the Cosmos.* New York: E. P. Dutton, 1976.

Neumann, Erich. *Amor and Psyche.* Princeton: Bollingen Series, Princeton University Press, 1973.

———. *Art and the Creative Unconscious.* Princeton: Princeton University Press, 1971.

———. *The Child.* New York: Harper & Row, 1972.

———. *The Great Mother.* Princeton: Princeton University Press, 1972.

———. *Origins and History of Consciousness.* Princeton: Princeton University Press, 1970.

New Larousse Encyclopedia of Mythology. Paul Hamlyn, editor. New York: Larouse & Company, 1968.

Palos, Stephan. *The Chinese Art of Healing.* New York: Bantam Books, 1972.

Pirsig, R. M. *Zen and the Art of Motorcycle Maintenance* New York: William Morrow, 1975.

Plato. *Symposium.* New York: Penguin Books, 1951.

Poppelbaum, Hermann. *Man and Animal.* New York: The Anthroposophic Press, 1931.

Powell, Robert. *Zen and Reality.* New York: 1977.

Progoff, Ira. *Jung, Synchronicty and Human Destiny.* New York: Delta Books, 1975.

Reed, Evelyn. *Woman's Evolution.* New York and Toronto: Pathfinder Press, 1975.

Reischauer, Edwin O. and Fairbank, John K. *East Asia; Tradition and Transformation.* Boston: Houghton Mifflin, 1977.

———. *The Modern Transformation.* London: George Allen and Unwin, 1967.

Rich, Adrienne. *Of Woman Born.* New York: Bantam Books, 1977.

Roszak, Betty and Theodore, editors. *Masculine/Feminine.* New York: Harper & Row, 1969.

Rubin, Vitaly A. *Individual and State in Ancient China.* New York: Columbia University Press, 1976.

Russ, Joanna. *The Female Man.* New York: Bantam Books, 1975.

Schafer, Edward H. *The Divine Woman.* Berkeley: University of California Press, 1973.

———. *The Vermilion Bird.* Berkeley: University of California Press, 1967.

Schram, S. *The Political Thought of Mao Tse-tung.* New York: Praeger Publishers, 1969.

Sheehy, Gail. *Passages.* New York: Bantam Books, 1977.

Shepherd A. P. *A Scientist of the Invisible.* London: Hodder and Stoughton, 1961.

Sherfey, M. J. *The Nature and Evolution of Female Sexuality.* New York: Vintage Books, 1973.

Shuttle, P. and Redgrove, P. *The Wise Wound.* New York: Marek, 1978.

Singer, June. *Androgyny.* New York: Doubleday, 1976.

Sivin, Nathan. *Chinese Alchemy,* (a thesis). Cambridge: Harvard University Press, 1968.

Smith, D. Howard. *Confucius.* New York: Charles Scribner's Sons, 1973.

Stein, Robert M.D. *Incest and Human Love.* New York: Penguin Books, 1974.

Steiner, Rudolf. *Christianity As Mystical Fact.* New York: Multimedia, 1979.

_____. *Cosmic Memory.* New York: Rudolf Steiner Publications, 1971.

_____. *The Course of My Life.* New York: Anthroposophic Press, 1951.

_____. *The Evolution of Consciousness,* (lectures). London: Rudolf Steiner Press, 1966.

_____. *The Gospel of St. John,* (lectures). New York: Anthroposophic Press, 1973.

_____. *Human and Cosmic Thought,* (lectures). London: Rudolf Steiner Press, 1967.

_____. *Knowledge of the Higher Worlds.* New York: Anthroposophic Press, 1973.

_____. *Macrocosm and Microcosm,* (lectures). London: Rudolf Steiner Press, 1968.

_____. *Mystery Knowledge and Mystery Centres,* (lectures). New York: Anthroposophic Press, 1973.

_____. *Occult Science.* New York: Anthroposophic Press, 1950.

_____. *The Philosophy of Freedom.* New York: Gordon Press, 1972.

_____. *Theosophy.* New York: Anthroposophic Press, 1971.

_____. *The Theosophy of the Rosicrucians,* (lectures). London: Rudolph Steiner Press, 1907.

Stone, Merlin. *The Paradise Papers.* London: Quartet/Virago, 1976.

Stylianos, Alexion. *Minoan Civilization.* Crete: Spyros Alexion Sons, 1973.

Suzuki, D. T. *The Zen Doctrine of No Mind.* New Jersey: Humanities Press, 1969.

Ulanov, Ann Belford. *The Feminine in Jungian Psychology and Christian Thrology.* Evanston: Northwestern University Press, 1971.

Vitale, A., Stein, M., Hillmann, J., Neumann, E. and Von der Heydt, V. *Fathers and Mothers.* Texas: Spring Publications, 1973.

Waley, A. *Analects of Confucius.* New York: Vintage Books.

———. *Chinese Poems.* New Jersey: Allen Unwin Books, 1976.

———. *The Nine Songs: a Study of Shaminism in Ancient China.* Oregon: City Lights, 1973.

———. "Notes on Chinese Alchemy." In *Bulletin of School of Oriental and African Studies,* Vol. VI, Part I, pp. 1–24. London, 1930.

———. *Three Ways of Thought in Ancient China.* New York: Doubleday, 1956.

Waltham, Claë. *Shu Ching: Book of History.* Indiana: Regnery-Gateway, 1971.

Warner, Marina. *Alone of All Her Sex.* New York: Alfred A. Knopf, 1976.

Watson, Burton. *Early Chinese Literature.* New York: Columbia University Press, 1962.

Watson, Lyall. *Supernature.* New York: Coronet Books, 1974.

Watts, Alan. *Nature, Man and Woman.* New York: Random House, 1970.

———. *The Taboo Against Knowing Who You Are.* London: Sphere Books, 1973.

———. *Tao; the Watercourse Way.* New York: Pantheon Books, 1977.

———. *The Two Hands of God.* New York: Collier Books, 1975.

———. *The Way of Zen.* New York: Random House, 1974.

Weil, Simone. *Gravity and Grace.* New York: Octagon Books, 1979.

Welch, H. *Taoism: the Parting of the Way.* Boston: Beacon Press, 1966.

Werner, E.T.C. *The Chinese Idea of the Second Self.* Shaghai, 1932.

———. *A Dictionary of Chinese Mythology.* Maine: Longwood Press 1976.

_____ . *Myths and Legends of China.* New York: Arno Press, 1922.

Wiens, H. J. *China's March to the Tropics.* Hamden: The Shoe String Press, 1954.

Wilhelm, H. *Change: Eight Lectures on the I Ching.* Princeton: Princeton University Press, 1975.

_____ . *"The Interplay of Image and Concept in the Book of Changes."* In Eranos Jahrbuch, XXXVI, pp. 31–57. Zurich, 1967.

Wilhelm, R. Translation of the *I Ching* rendered into English by C. F. Baynes. Princeton: Princeton University Press, 1975.

_____ . *The Secret of the Golden Flower.* New York: Harcourt Brace Jovanovich, 1970.

Wu, L. C., and Davis, T. L. "An Ancient Chinese Treatise on Alchemy Entitled Ts'an T'ung Ch'i." In *Isis,* Vol. XVIII:2, pp. 210–290. Bruges: The Saint Catherine Press, 1932.

Index